Keepsake

True North #3

By Sarina Bowen

Keepsake

Praise for the True North Series

"Utterly fantastic. Well-written romance that runs the full gamut of emotions. Oh, and did I mention steamy? This series has it all. "
— Red Hot & Blue Reads

"I'm crazy about this series. In love with Jude and Sophie, the Shipley's, just the whole family dynamic. EVERYTHING IS WOW."
— Angie's Dreamy Reads

"A world that pulled me in and had me wishing I could read all day!"
— Shh Mom's Reading

"5-stars, Top Pick! This story will break your heart and stitch it back together again."
— Harlequin Junkie

"Another fantastic book by Sarina Bowen! I couldn't turn the pages fast enough."
— The Book Hookup

"Smart, funny and super sexy, Bittersweet is full of the kind of writing that makes Sarina Bowen one of my favorite author crushes."
—Author Sarah Mayberry

Keepsake

Part One:

Early Season

Ginger Gold

Paula Red

Zestar

Keepsake

Lark

As the crow flies, Tuxbury, Vermont wasn't all that far from Boston. But I didn't make the journey via crow, I made it in my aging Volkswagen Beetle. And in rural Vermont, the roads don't often go where you need them to go. So the trip took me two and a half hours.

The late summer sun had already set by the time I drove up the Shipley's lengthy gravel driveway. The pinging of pebbles against the undercarriage of my car was a sound that announced: *you have left the city.*

And good riddance. The past month at home with my parents in Boston had been excruciating.

I put my baby in park and killed the engine. Then I sat there for a moment, taking in the softly lit Shipley farmhouse. Laughter drifted from the screened windows. And through the lace curtains I glimpsed the bodies moving about the dining room in preparation for dinner.

The meal would be served at any moment, and I knew I should go inside. But I lingered behind the wheel another moment, putting on my game face. There was nowhere I'd rather be than here at the Shipley farm. But I'd forgotten that harvest season on a working farm would involve a cast of thousands. Okay—not thousands. But dozens. And lately, I wasn't so good in a crowd.

You'll be fine, I coached myself. *These people love you.* If I was a little off my game, they'd understand.

I got out of my car and pulled my duffel bag out of the back seat. Even before I got the car door closed, there was a squeal from the kitchen door. "She's heeeeere!"

Smiling, I braced myself for my friend's hug. I'd met May almost exactly seven years ago when Boston University assigned us to the same freshman dormitory room. So I'd been on the receiving end of May's hugs many times.

This one was a doozy. My best friend was always affectionate, even under normal circumstances. But the fact that I had lately caused her—and everyone else in my life—a steaming heap of stress, meant that she had a go at trying to crack my ribs now that I'd landed safely back on American soil.

"It's good to be here," I managed through constricted lungs. A second later, May pulled back, only to grab my hands and look at me through teary eyes. "God, it's good to see you safe. I was so worried when there wasn't any news..."

"I'm sorry," I said immediately. I'd been saying that a lot this month.

She took a deep breath. "I'm just glad you're here. But I'll get a grip now so we can have dinner, okay?"

I followed her up to the kitchen door and stepped inside. When the screen door slammed shut behind us, we left the pretty August evening behind.

I'd been hoping to make a quiet entrance, but it was not to be. The kitchen was abuzz with various members of the Shipley family trying to get a meal onto the table. And the sudden crush of humanity made my blood pressure jump.

"Lark!" cried several voices.

"You made it just in time for dinner!" Mrs. Shipley added. In her hands was a giant bowl heaped with mashed potatoes.

"I drove fast," I explained. It wasn't a clever answer, but at least I was holding it together. I'd spent the last three weeks moping around my parents' creaky old Beacon Hill mansion, ducking questions about my ordeal and just generally trying to remember what life felt like when you weren't bargaining with God to save your sorry ass.

It didn't used to be this way. *I* didn't used to be this way.

A year ago I'd had both a boyfriend and a job that I'd loved. The boyfriend had split first, unhappy with my decision to take a twelve-month assignment in Guatemala. And then the job had nearly gotten me killed. I was technically still employed by the nonprofit that sent me to Guatemala. But now I was on "mental health leave" after my misadventures south of the border.

Under the scrutiny of my parents in Boston, I'd tried (and failed) to hide how much the experience had gutted me. My parents had marched me to psychiatrists and physicians who asked too many probing questions.

Some of those questions didn't yield answers. There were a few key moments leading up to my rescue that I couldn't remember. And that made everyone edgy.

So when May had called yesterday to invite me to Vermont for the entire apple-picking season, I had put down the phone and packed a bag.

"What can I do to help with dinner?" I asked now, watching the eighteen-year-old Shipley twins—Dylan and Daphne—fly around the room with plates and serving ware.

"Find yourself a drink and a seat," Ruth Shipley answered. "We'll eat in ten minutes."

May took the duffel off my shoulder and tossed it into the TV room at the back of the house. "Come through to the dining room," she said. Then my friend paused, her hand on the dining room door. "I wish I could give you a quieter evening for your first night," she apologized. "But we have the Abrahams and the Nickels most Thursdays, unless we're at one of their places."

"It's okay." And, really, it would be. I hadn't lost my nerve so completely that I couldn't dine at a crowded table. Right?

In any case, I could get better at faking it.

She pushed open the door, and my stomach spasmed as I counted the faces on the other side. The old Lark would never have been afraid to greet a room full of people. I knew the exact date I'd stopped being fearless. It was sixty-seven days ago.

I wasn't sure I'd ever be the same again. Just hovering here on the same wide-plank floors I'd stood on a dozen times while visiting the Shipleys in college, I began to sweat.

The only thing to do was to slap on an impersonation of my usual self. Stepping into the dining room, I lowered my shoulders and lifted my chin.

Ten heads turned in my direction. No—even more. There was Grandpa Shipley, his weathered hands cupped around a coffee mug. And then May's older brother gave a familiar shout, using the nickname he'd given me seven years ago when May and I were freshmen. "Hey! It's the Wild Child!"

"Hi, Griffin," I managed. He slung his arm around his smiling girlfriend, Audrey, who had just followed us in from the kitchen.

As for the others at the table, I recognized some of them, but I needed a refresher on a few names.

"Everybody, this is Lark," May said. "She's going to be staying with us and helping out at the farmers' markets."

"Awesome," said a youngish guy seated at the table. "She can count the cash boxes. I hate dealing with money."

"And that's why you don't have any," Griffin said. He pointed at the guy. "That's my cousin Kyle. And his brother Kieran." He pointed at another guy, too.

I could see the resemblance. The Shipleys were a tall family, with dark eyes and shiny, brown hair. Kyle and Kieran were of a similar make. Kyle had a somewhat silly, lopsided smile, whereas Kieran looked more serious.

"Nice to meet you both," I said.

"And that's Jude and Sophie. They just came back from their honeymoon on Martha's Vineyard."

I'd never seen Jude before. He had longer hair and a bunch of tattoos sticking out of his shirtsleeves. He wore a sort of closed-off expression which didn't invite me to linger, but his wife gave me a cheerful wave.

"And you remember Zachariah." May indicated a blond guy in the corner.

My gaze caught on the farmhand I'd met just before I left for my trip in the spring. Who could forget him? Zachariah was a thing of beauty. He had thick blond hair, and his tanned, muscular forearms rested casually on the table in front of him. His well-worn T-shirt was stretched over broad shoulders and well-defined pecs. And even as I stared at him, he gave me a shy smile.

Yowza.

"The Abrahams sell cheese, beeswax and honey at the farmers' market," May was saying beside me.

I dragged my attention back to the introductions. There was a pause, as everyone expected me to say something. I went with: "I love beeswax candles. They smell so good."

The couple I was supposed to be meeting beamed at me from across the table.

"Isaac and Leah are right down the road," May explained. "Our two farms partner up on a lot of different things, so they're like family."

It only took one look to peg the neighbors as crunchy, young, back-to-the-land Vermonters. Leah's hair was fashioned into dreads, and Isaac wore a homemade sweater. A messy-haired toddler sat curled into Isaac's lap.

"It's nice to meet you, sweetie," Leah said.

"Likewise," I replied.

Ruth and her helpers had filled the table with food, and now May's teenaged siblings squeezed themselves into chairs on either side of the too-attractive-to-be-real Zachariah. Daphne gave him an appreciative glance before dropping her napkin onto her lap.

I had to bite back a smile at the poorly disguised teenaged yearning in her expression. Of *course* she adored Zachariah. Not only was he beautiful, but he had kind eyes.

We found seats, too. I was between Griffin's girlfriend and May. And finally Ruth Shipley took her place at the head of the table. It used to be her husband who sat there, but Auggie Shipley had passed away when we were in college.

Poor May had come home from taking her last final exam our sophomore year to hear that her father had suffered a heart attack and died before he even reached the hospital. It had been a dark time for my best friend.

At the other end of the table, Grandpa Shipley folded his hands and bowed his head. Everyone got quiet for his muttered prayer. After an "amen," he forked a piece of pot roast onto his plate and then passed the platter. Side dishes were lifted and passed, and the swell of conversation began to rise up around me. I took spoonfuls of potatoes, Brussels sprouts and scalloped potatoes, while listening to May talk about the farmers' market schedule.

"We don't do a Friday market," she said. "That's why we have our big social meal on Thursday nights. Nobody is scrambling in the morning."

There was a sudden crash, and I felt myself jerk in my chair. But it was only the sound of a serving spoon falling off one platter and onto another.

My flinch must have been distracting, because Dylan mouthed "sorry" from his side of the table.

Deep breaths, I coached myself. I'd been back from Guatemala four weeks, but my jumpiness refused to abate. I lifted another bite of food from my plate. "Who made these Brussels sprouts?" I asked. "They're fantastic. Is that...bacon?"

"Hell, yes," Audrey piped up. "I put bacon in everything."

"I knew I liked you." See? I could do this. Small talk and food. No big deal.

"Guys?" Griffin asked. "Audrey and I have some news."

"Omigod!" May squealed beside me. "You're pregnant!"

Audrey choked on a sip of water. "No!" she sputtered. "But should I burn this top?" She glanced down at her blouse.

Everyone laughed.

"What *is* the news, kids?" Grandpa asked, his fork halfway to his mouth.

"Audrey is going to France this fall," Griffin said. "For ten weeks. So you won't have bacon in your Brussels sprouts for a while."

There were noises of disagreement. "What?" "No way!" "Why?"

"I'm taking a fermentation class in Paris, where I've always wanted to study cuisine," Audrey said brightly. "My mother gave me some money, and Griff and I hatched this plan for me to take a course taught by famous vintners and brewers. So we can expand the cider business and win even more awards next year."

"Audrey, no!" Kyle argued. "You can't leave! Griff is going to be a grumpy bear for the whole harvest season. Do you even know what you're doing to us?"

There was more laughter, and, when Griff lifted his wine glass, he managed to give his cousin the finger while taking a sip.

"I know you'll miss me!" Audrey sang. "And my enchilada sauce."

Grandpa put his chin in his hand. "Let's not forget the coconut rice."

"I'm not worried about the food," Kyle said. "Aunt Ruth never lets me down."

Ruth smiled at him, but Kyle's brother Kieran murmured "ass-kisser" under his breath.

"But, seriously. If Griff gets too cranky you can expect a call from me. Can't you, like, come home on the weekends?"

"You make me sound like Caligula," Griff grumbled. "I wasn't so bad."

A silence and a half-dozen hidden smiles disagreed.

"Tell us about your classes, honey," Ruth said.

"The course on fermentation is the real draw," Audrey responded. "There's no other course like it in the world."

"My girl has a good nose for cider," Griff boasted. "We'll be unstoppable next season."

"I'm also looking forward to a short course on pastries," Audrey added. "Drinks and croissants, people! I'm perfecting all the finest things in life. I'll make pastries for you all when I get home."

While she talked, I kept eating. I'd lost more than ten pounds these past couple of months. Food had been scarce during my...ordeal. And afterwards, I just hadn't been very hungry.

But Mrs. Shipley's pot roast was excellent, and Audrey's garlic mashed potatoes were creamy and delicious. Even in a room full of people, I began to find my appetite.

This is good, I reminded myself. *These are nice people, and this is a safe place.* The safest place in the world. I'd always loved it here.

May held a wine bottle in her hand. "I'm sticking with water, but I could pour you some wine. Any interest?"

"Hell, yes."

Keepsake

Cousin Kyle laughed at someone's joke, and I smiled at him, doing my best impression of a happy, well-adjusted person. I would work on this farm and share meals with these people. I would smile and act normal for as long as it took. Until acting normal seemed normal again, and the dragons in my heart forgot to blow their fire.

Zach

Thursday dinner required a great number of pots and pans. I washed them all, one by one, hanging them from the old hooks above the sink to dry.

"Zach, honey?" Ruth came into the kitchen with the nearly empty pie plate. "You don't have to do all of these yourself, you know."

"I don't mind," I said. The Lord knew I ate enough meals in this house. And most Thursdays Ruth had the neighbors over for dinner. It was a tradition that started because of me. A couple months before I made the big move down the road from the Abrahams' to the Shipleys', Ruth had started up with Thursday Dinner as a way for me to stay connected to my adoptive family.

Ruth worked her butt off all week long, and then she threw a feast on Thursday, too. A few pots and pans were the least I could do.

"While you're here, I have some things for you," Ruth said, setting a stack of books on the countertop. "The librarian had four of the ones you requested, but she's still waiting on that C.S. Lewis title."

"Oh, awesome."

Ruth straightened the stack with the practiced hands of a mom who was used to tidying up after a big family. "Didn't we have all the Harry Potter books, though?"

"Nobody could find number six," I said, rinsing the soap off a pot.

"Ah, okay. I also brought you a book you didn't request. It's something I picked up for you at the bookstore."

My heart sank when I saw the title: *Acing the New GED Tests.* She'd been urging me to take this set of tests which would result in a certificate that was almost a high school equivalency. I wasn't looking forward to it. "Thanks," I said anyway. "You didn't have to do that."

"It's my pleasure. You're going to do well on these tests. You'll see. The last thing I have for you is the final slice of apple cranberry pie."

"Now you're talking," I said, and she laughed. "That goes down easier than a test any day of the week." I rinsed out the last saucepan and tipped it onto the rack to dry.

"I'll just find you a fork." She put the piece of pie on yet another plate that would need washing. I would have been happy to eat it right out of the pan, but that wasn't how Ruth did things. She always treated me as well as her own children, and I was grateful.

I wasn't a Shipley, though. It didn't matter how hard I tried to pretend, this wasn't my family. And the timing of the GED book's appearance felt ominous. While I'd listened to Audrey's plans to learn more about the cidermaking business, I'd realized that Griff was gaining a new business partner as well as a life partner. Audrey did part-time work for a farm-to-table program in Boston, but her real work seemed to be helping Griff grow his cidery.

And now his brother Dylan had opted to go to college only part time, using his other hours to work for the family, too. The more help Griff got from his family, the less he'd need outsiders.

No wonder they were urging me to figure out my next steps. While the Shipleys would always need seasonal help on the farm, I worried that my cushy live-in, year-round gig was drawing to a close.

Feeling blue, I took my pie into the dining room. My seat had been taken, so I leaned up against the wall and took the first bite of heaven. Nobody made an apple pie as good as Mrs. Shipley's. The buttery crust crumbled when I broke it with my fork. And her secret ingredient—sweetened cranberries—burst on my tongue when I chewed.

Before I came to Vermont, I didn't know that food could be both plentiful and wonderful. When I was a child, there was never enough. Even after four years, I still felt a little stunned every time I sat down to another generous meal with the Abrahams or the Shipleys.

Who wouldn't want to stay right here until his ass was kicked out for good?

I ate while eavesdropping on the conversations around me. Keeping tabs on everyone else was a skill I'd needed to survive my unusual upbringing. My giant, needy family had always been rife with factions and uprisings. Listening more often than I spoke was just common sense.

But the listening I did at the Shipleys' table was for entertainment value, not survival. Griffin and his cousins were arguing over where we should go out drinking tomorrow night.

"Dude, the Goat is cheap, and it's close," Griffin said. "Don't harsh on the Goat."

"Look," argued his cousin Kyle. "I'm in favor of the four-dollar beers and the short drive. But I swear they named that place after the women who drink there."

"Naa-aay!" added Kieran.

Griffin snorted. "Then why don't your chances of hooking up improve whenever we drive over to the Gin Mill?"

"How would I know? We're always at the Goat!"

I bit down on my smile. It was the same discussion every week. And invariably, we ended up at the Goat, because Griff would offer to be the designated driver, and because his ex still lived over the bar. He and Audrey liked to visit Zara and her new baby.

I turned my attention to the women's conversation, which was always more nuanced and revealing.

"We could always make up a bed for Lark in the alcove," Mrs. Shipley was saying. "Once upon a time we did all our bookkeeping on the kitchen table, anyway."

Lark shook her head. "I'll be absolutely fine in the bunkhouse. Don't worry about me."

My last bite of pie flipped over in my stomach. Lark was sleeping in the bunkhouse?

All evening I'd been rationing my glances at May's best friend. Now I helped myself to another one. And, yup. She was still just as breathtaking as I'd remembered.

Lark was named for a bird that weighed less than three ounces, but there was nothing fragile about this girl. She had giant brown eyes over high cheekbones. Her skin was olive-toned and perfectly smooth, and her dark, shiny hair was cut in a way that showed off the length of her kissable neck.

She looked *vivid*, as if God had painted her features with bolder paints than he used on the rest of the world. In addition to perfect skin, he'd softened her with lush curves and a full mouth.

Lark must have felt the weight of my gaze because her eyes tracked over to find me staring at her.

Whoops. Busted.

I felt myself flush as she studied me for a fleeting moment. Her expression was clouded by a flicker of something I couldn't quite read, and then her gaze dropped to her hands. Since I'd already been caught staring, I didn't bother looking away. I couldn't have, anyhow. Lark was the most enchanting woman I'd ever met.

She'd visited once before, back in March, during pruning season. I remembered exactly where I'd been when I'd first seen her—stacking branches outside the dairy barn after pruning all day in the orchard. The sun had been setting, which made the light gold and pink. May Shipley came walking toward the cider house door with a growler jug of cider in her hand. She was talking to somebody, but I didn't pay much attention until I heard the sound of a truly beautiful laugh. It was low and musical and knowing.

I'd looked up to see who could make such a noise. So the first view I ever had of Lark, she was smiling. Those dark eyes sparkled with mirth, and I caught myself smiling, too, even though I didn't have the first clue what the two of them were laughing over.

The girls had walked around the other side of the barn toward a hammock that stretched between two old oaks. I'd slowed down at stacking those pruned branches so that I could hear more of their laughter floating in the dusky air.

At dinnertime that night, I'd purposefully sat on the same side of the table as Lark, because I knew if I sat across from her I'd stare. She'd stayed in the farmhouse overnight and left after lunch the next day. During those twenty-four hours, I'd spent each meal feeling hyperaware of her. The sound of her voice made my chest tighten each time she spoke. Whenever her gaze touched me, even for a fraction of a second, my neck got hot.

Honest to God, I didn't know what to do with that reaction. There was nobody who'd ever made me feel that way before. My strange upbringing meant that I hadn't met many women in my life. This new, powerful tug of raw attraction was completely foreign to me.

Last spring, when May hugged Lark goodbye, she'd said, "You have to email me every day, okay? I can't believe I have to go a whole year without seeing you."

A whole year. Disappointment had settled into my gut, and I didn't know what to do with that, either.

Then Lark had driven away in her little Volkswagen, and I'd done my best to put her out of my mind. But seven or eight weeks ago, May had come crying into the dairy barn one morning. I overheard the brief story she'd told her brother: May's emails to Lark had gone unanswered for several days. So May had written to Lark's mother asking if everything was okay.

"I thought she'd tell me that Lark had lost her phone or something!" May had sobbed onto Griffin's shoulder. "But she's *missing* in Guatemala. They can't find her. They're searching..."

When I heard this, I'd walked right out of the dairy barn, my shovel still in my hands. I found myself standing on the spot where I'd been that spring day, the first time I saw Lark's smile. It was as if I didn't quite believe what May had just said.

Missing. What a bizarre, unsatisfying word.

I didn't even know the girl, but her disappearance bothered me a lot. I told myself that it was because May was so upset. Every time I came into the farmhouse for a meal, I'd check May's face, looking for good news.

There wasn't any for weeks. In fact, May had looked more distraught than I'd ever seen her, times three. It was a rough summer. But then May had come running into the orchard one afternoon last month, a big smile on her face, her eyes sparkling with unshed tears of relief. "Lark is safe!" she'd announced. "They found her, and she's okay!"

That was about four weeks ago. And I'd been so busy with picking season that I hadn't heard any more about her. Since Lark was safe, I'd put her out of my mind again.

Until today. Griffin had mentioned casually over lunch that Lark was coming to stay for the rest of the picking season, and I'd almost dropped my sandwich. I sat there at the picnic table remembering how distracted I'd been for those twenty-four hours when she'd visited in the spring. And I wondered if it was possible that one person could have such a powerful effect on me again.

The answer was yes.

Tonight I felt the very same pull. There was no part of her that didn't make my eyes want to linger—on the sheen of her hair, the warm tone of her skin. She was just as beautiful as I'd remembered. No—more. Only two things seemed to have changed about her. She looked thinner now. And there were dark circles under both eyes. Earlier, when Griffin boomed into nearly deafening laughter, she actually flinched.

I'd ached to see that.

Mrs. Shipley wasn't finished apologizing to Lark for the bunkhouse accommodations. "Your room has a door on it, so you'll have privacy. But you'll be sharing a bathroom with three men, sometimes four. They do the early milking from six to seven thirty, so that's the best time of day for a lengthy shower, I'd think."

"The bunkhouse will be absolutely fine," Lark assured her. "I always loved that funny little building. But I'm not booting anyone out of his room, am I?"

Mrs. Shipley shook her head. "Griffin used to stay there in the front bedroom, but now he's in the bungalow with Audrey. So we've kept that room for guests."

"I'll show Lark the room," May said, getting up. "Lark, you carry our drinks, and I'll get your bag."

"Deal." Lark stood, too.

I kept my eyes to myself as she left the room.

Griffin and I helped to clear the last glasses off the table. And then it was time to say goodbye to Isaac and Leah.

"Goodnight, sweet boy," Leah Abraham said, folding me into a hug.

"Goodnight."

Leah was only twenty-nine to my twenty-three. But nobody had ever been more of a parent to me than Leah and her husband. It was the Abrahams who took me in when I'd been turned out of my so-called home four years ago. And, more than that, they were the only two people who understood what I'd been through.

They knew how strange and difficult it was to make a new life after leaving the odd place where we'd been raised. Because they'd lived through the same thing, too.

I patted Leah's back awkwardly until my Thursday-night hug was finished. I knew that Leah hugged me on purpose—she was trying to prove to me that hugging was ordinary. That it wasn't a sin. When I first came to Vermont, Leah's hugs always froze me in my tracks, because holding another man's wife was just weird. Even now, whenever I received the occasional hug, I just sort of tolerated it.

Where we grew up, touching resulted in lashes from the whip. Hugging was a punishable offense, just like talking out of turn or sneaking food from the pantry. As a result, I kept to myself. I was disinclined to touch anyone or talk too much except with people I knew very well.

There were half a dozen of those.

"I'll see you at the market on Saturday," I told Isaac. "And tomorrow morning I'll do that oil change on your truck. You can pick it up any time after noon."

"Thanks, man," he said. "See you soon." He passed through the doorway in front of me with his three-year-old daughter, Maeve, passed out on his shoulder. Her sleeping face came into view. She was a lucky little girl.

Maeve would grow up to be a world-class hugger. She was the center of her parents' universe, and she had no idea that life could be otherwise. Maeve would never be lost in the shuffle of too many children competing for not quite enough food. She would never be slapped for asking a question. And that was just the beginning.

Maeve's name wasn't straight out of the old testament.

She wasn't required to call her father "sir."

She had a valid birth certificate, and she'd get better than an eighth-grade education.

She wouldn't be married off to an old man the day she turned seventeen.

Isaac opened the back door of his wife's car and gently placed his child's sleeping body into her car seat.

I'd lived with Isaac and Leah on their farm my first two years in Vermont. But eighteen months ago I made the big two-mile move down the road, because the Shipleys had a larger operation and they could afford to pay me wages.

Isaac would have kept me on if I'd needed it. He was the closest thing I had to a family. But living and working on my own felt right and good, and Isaac understood that. "You can always come back if it doesn't work out," Leah had assured me.

Standing on the front porch, I watched the Abrahams drive away, hoping I'd never have to impose upon them again.

Even after their headlights disappeared, I stood a while longer in the sweet Vermont air. The Shipley farm smelled of growing things and of ripening fruit. This time of year, the scent had a slightly vinegar undertone of apples in decay. We'd worked the cider press for six hours today, which meant that I was also thoroughly apple-scented. If I hurried, I could catch a shower before lights-out in the bunkroom.

But Griff had other plans. "Hey, Chewie. Here're your library books."

"Thanks."

His cousins came clomping onto the porch, too. "Got a second, guys?" Griff called. "I need to talk to everybody."

"Sure, Han." I had several nicknames these days. And here was an irony—Griff nicknamed me after a hairy alien from *Star Wars*, but it was meant to be flattering. And his cousin Kyle called me "choir boy," but meant it as a dig.

Strange family, this. But I loved them anyway.

Wordlessly I followed him and his cousins off the porch and across the darkening lawn. Whatever Griff had to say, he didn't want to say it on the porch.

As we crossed the grass, halfway to the orchard, the sound of crickets rose up around us. Their nighttime humming was a familiar chorus. An owl hooted nearby and was answered by another.

Walking around the Shipley property at night always made me think of Psalm 96. *Let the fields be jubilant, and everything in them; let all the trees of the forest sing for joy.* In August, the fields of Vermont were at their most jubilant.

Funny how I never really appreciated the bible until I got free of the people who'd taught it to me.

While Isaac and Leah were kind to me because they knew where I'd come from, the Shipleys were kind to me simply because they were kind people. I'd known them almost four years now, since I'd first arrived shoeless and hungry at the Abrahams' down the road. But I still felt like the new guy.

I wasn't ostracized like a freak here, but there was still some good-natured teasing. It hadn't taken Griffin Shipley long to figure out just how odd a life I'd lived as a child. "Oh my God!" he'd hollered during the first month I met him. "Zach hasn't seen *Star Wars!*"

The next week he'd corralled me into a movie marathon of the original three films. "The canon," as he referred to them. We'd both been stumbling-tired at the farmers' market the next day. But according to Griffin it was worth it, because I finally knew that Darth Vader was Luke's father.

And that was just the beginning. "I must educate you about Monty Python," came next. And a million other movies. And the rules of football. I was still a little shaky on those. There were too many positions.

The things I didn't know were an endless source of amusement to the Shipley clan. The time they fed me Pop Rocks was pretty funny. I didn't know about Halloween or Valentine's Day (both "heathen holidays" according to my former overlords). Or mistletoe. Or eggnog.

I didn't know *any* sexual innuendo. Those still got me into trouble because it seemed there were a million terms for sex, and they didn't all make sense. I'll never forget the sight of Griffin doubled over after explaining what a blowjob was.

"But nobody's blowing on anything," I'd protested while he tried to remember how to breathe.

At least they teased each other as much as me. Maybe more. This season Griffin had begun referring to Kyle as Crash-n-Burn since Kyle seemed to spend a ridiculous amount of time trying to figure out what to say to women.

Not like I'd worked that out, either.

Griffin halted in the middle of the lawn. I wasn't expecting that, and I actually walked right into him.

"Yo," he said, spinning to catch my shoulders in his hands. "My football days are over."

"Sorry."

"Why are we standing in the middle of the yard?" Kyle asked.

"Just wait for Jude and Dylan."

The other men jogged toward us. And when the five of us were assembled, he explained. "Two things. The first is about Lark."

My eyes dropped to my boots, but I hung on every word.

"She was May's roommate at BU. But this past year she's been on some job in Guatemala."

"Nice!" Kyle said.

"No, *not* nice," Griffin contradicted his cousin. "Listen to what I'm telling you. She wasn't kicking back on vacation, okay? Some bad shit went down there, and it shook her up. May isn't sure exactly what she endured." Griffin cleared his throat. "Coulda been any kind of ugliness at all."

My whole body went ice cold and I actually shivered even though it was still seventy flipping degrees outside. I took a deep, slow breath and exhaled.

"Is she okay?" Dylan asked. "She looks tired."

"Well..." Griff rubbed the back of her neck. "She's here to work, but she's also here to get away from the city and try to relax. So take it easy on her. We'll just have to see how she

24

does. I've known her a long time, and she's a strong person. And—guys, I shouldn't need to say this—the girl is *off limits.*" Griffin swung his head pointedly left and right, making sure to include both his cousins in this decree. "Got it?"

"Yes, Master," Kyle said. "I won't turn on the lady charm."

"Like she'd notice." His brother Kieran snickered.

I noticed that Griffin didn't bother to nail me with the speech or the glare. That's just the way it was. My celibacy was widely acknowledged and occasionally teased.

"The second thing is that I have a plan for while Audrey is gone to France."

"Is it a cure for sexual frustration? Because I'm all ears," Kyle said.

Griff ignored him. "I'm going to redo the kitchen in the bungalow, as well as the half bathroom."

"By yourself?" Jude asked.

Griffin chuckled. "With your help, I hope. Got any extra hours for me? The pay is the usual rate, plus all the apple pie you can eat."

"Sure, man," Jude said. "I'll give you my Mondays off. But Saturday is for Sophie. If she goes to visit her mother, I'll have even more time for you."

Griffin lifted his chin. "I really appreciate that. Thank you."

"Hang on," I said slowly. "You're going to rip out the old appliances and fixtures, re-plumb, sand and paint the cabinets..."

"And remove a wall," Griff put in. "And change out the countertops."

"And harvest twenty thousand apple trees?" I asked.

"*And* make a record number of cases of cider." Griff grinned at me in the dark. "In the next twelve weeks."

"Um... How is that all going to happen?" I wanted to know.

Griff couldn't resist a *Star Wars* quote. "Do... or do not. There is no try." He spread his arms wide, then dropped them. "I don't fucking know how it all gets done. But after Audrey leaves, I'm going to move into the bunkhouse with you guys.

That way it doesn't matter if there's no water or electricity in the bungalow."

I was already thinking through a plan of attack. "The appliances have to go first. That will give us some room to work."

Griff clapped me on the shoulder. "Yeah. And you can help me install the new ones. But mostly I have another job for you. Ready?"

"Sure?"

"I want you and Lark to handle every one of the farmers' markets this season. That's going to help me balance the farm labor and cidermaking with the renovation. I'll be ten times more efficient if I'm not driving all over Vermont four days a week. Can you do that for me?"

"Sure. Done." It took me a minute to wrap my head around this little promotion. Until now, there'd always been a Shipley at every market. Getting the right stuff on the truck and selling through the inventory was a bit of an art form. So I was happy that he trusted me with that whole revenue stream. And? Time alone with Lark.

Pinch me.

"And, Dyl?" he addressed his younger brother. "You're the dairyman whenever you're not at school. I'm paying you starting right now, since you're a part-time college man."

"Sweet." Dylan liked the sound of that. In less than two weeks he'd be driving to the University of Vermont three days a week. His twin sister was going away to Harkness College in Connecticut, full time, and would miss the harvest season.

"And nobody spill my secret to Audrey, all right? The kitchen is a surprise for her. I'm going to start the demolition the minute her plane takes off."

"Sure, man."

"That's all I had to say. G'night, guys. Sleep well because I'm gonna work your asses off."

Griff and Jude walked back toward the farmhouse, with Dylan trailing them.

Kyle and Kieran and I headed the other direction, toward the bunkhouse. "Dibs on the shower," I said.

"Damn you," Kieran muttered.

"I'll hurry," I promised as we reached the stone structure.

The Shipleys' bunkhouse was an old building that had stood for a century. It had wide pine plank floors and a big oak door. I loved this place.

The guest room was on the right as you entered, and the bathroom on the left. Straight ahead was the bunk room, where five twin beds were built into the walls. I had the one under the windows, while the others were double decker on the side walls. There was a big old closet on the final wall of the room, and we each had a trunk under the bottom bunks.

When this place was full, there was barely enough space for five guys. But it was roomy enough with just the three of us. And Griff's temporary presence wouldn't overcrowd us. I liked his company.

Dropping my books on my bed, I grabbed my towel and headed for the shower. On my way to the bathroom, I passed the door to the guest bedroom, which was half open. Lark must have brought some music with her, because a twang of guitars and a female vocalist drifted out into the hallway. I heard May giggle. Lark answered in a husky voice that seemed to resonate in my chest.

Hell.

I closed the bathroom door and turned on the shower, giving the ancient plumbing a chance to heat the water. It was time to strip, but for once I hesitated. It was a little weird getting naked if a woman could just walk right in here. I was used to the all-male environment, where I didn't have to think before taking off my clothes.

After hurriedly tossing my clothes onto the wall hook, I stepped under the warm spray. After a hard day's work, it was blissful. My muscles were tired in a satisfying way, and I enjoyed the rhythm of the water hitting my bare skin.

Like food, hot water was scarce where I grew up. I hadn't known you could indulge in a hot shower at the end of the day without feeling guilt over it.

There had been plenty that Isaac and Leah had needed to teach me after my nineteen years living at Paradise Ranch.

When I got to Vermont, I'd never touched a computer or a telephone. I'd never eaten fast food. I didn't know what Red Bull was, or a Quarter Pounder. I didn't know *Star Wars* or the Black Keys or *Game of Thrones*.

Some of my ignorance was even more embarrassing.

I'd never forget the time when Isaac had first told me the story of *his* early days in Vermont. He and Leah had run off from Paradise Ranch together, basically camping their way across the country, from dusty Wyoming to Vermont. "We liked it here, and it was August. So we picked apples all season and then stayed on." Living as frugally as two humans can, it had taken the two of them only five years to scrape together a tiny down payment on a failing farm. Even now, Isaac and Leah worked like dogs to make the place pay them a living wage.

I had listened admiringly to this story, impressed by both the pluck and luck it had taken to go from teenage cult members to landowners in the span of ten years. "It's lucky that Maeve wasn't born until after you could buy the farm," I'd said. My entire young life, I'd watched the responsibility of too many children weigh down the young mothers at Paradise Ranch.

To Isaac's credit, he never laughed at my frequent displays of ignorance. Not once. "That wasn't luck, my man. That's birth control."

"What's that?" I'd asked. I'd been almost twenty years old, and I hadn't even known there was a way to avoid getting your wife pregnant.

The next week, Isaac had given me a book about sex-ed—the kind that preteens are handed by modern parents. And just to make sure I got the message, he explained birth control to me one night after Leah and Maeve had gone to bed.

And even though we lived in the middle of nowhere and I lacked any kind of social life, Isaac had put a new box of condoms in my dresser drawer. "Just in case, right? It's different here, Zach," he'd said, which was the understatement of the century. "Nobody is going to give you a beating for having sex. But that doesn't mean you don't have to be careful."

I still had the box. It was unopened.

* * *

The reason I always tried to get the first shower was that it left time for reading. I had a clip-on book light that the Shipley twins had given me for Christmas. And even though I only had twenty pages left of *Lord of the Flies*, I opened the sixth Harry Potter book while everyone else took turns in the bathroom.

Once in a while some well-meaning person in my life would point out that after living the first nineteen years of my life on a dusty property in Wyoming, I still rarely left the farm. But they were wrong. I'd been to Middle Earth and Hogwarts and Dickensian London all in the past month or so. The difference between living on a ranch where books were banned and a farm where books were freely discussed and traded could not be underestimated.

It was almost lights-out by the time I heard May wish Lark a good night. "Sleep tight. Breakfast is at eight thirty. We do everything pretty early around here. It's not like those long brunches we used to take in Boston. Those were the days."

"I'll get up and help with breakfast. Goodnight, beautiful girl. Thank you so much for bringing me up here!"

"We're lucky to have you. Now go to bed. You look like you haven't slept in a year."

There was no soundproofing at all in the bunkhouse, so I heard the whole conversation. Then I heard Kieran come out of the bathroom and wish Lark goodnight, too. "Is it okay if I shut off the hallway light?" he asked her.

"Sure. Hey, Kieran?"

"Yeah?"

"Can I lock the front door?"

We never locked the bunkhouse. Nobody would ever trek out onto the Shipleys' property to bother three or four big guys with nothing more valuable than a couple of iPods. "Go ahead, sweetie," Kieran said after a pause. "Goodnight."

"Goodnight."

I curled the pillow under my right ear and closed my eyes. When I closed my eyes in this room, I did so without worry. The sounds of people settling in to sleep were always reassuring to me.

I didn't mind staying in the bunkhouse—not at all. The grunts and snores of my roommates were nothing new. In fact, the two years I'd spent at Isaac and Leah's place was the only time in my life I'd ever slept in a room of my own.

Living in the bunkhouse and eating free meals meant that I had virtually no living expenses. Everybody under this roof was well-fed and rooming here as a way to save money—not as a necessity.

Kieran was the first to start snoring. The Shipley cousins were just here on loan for the busy season. Their parents had a spread up in Hardwick and a business breeding highland beef cattle. They'd be gone by Thanksgiving.

That would leave only me.

I was pretty sure that most people who passed through the bunkhouse saw it as a short-term thing. For a hundred years this building had housed temporary farm labor. The place was a waystation to a bigger and better life.

The trouble was that I couldn't picture my own next chapter. And as I lay reflecting on the day's events, something began to trouble me. My promotion from apple picker to market manager was a good one, except for one big flaw. The markets were *seasonal*, ending right before Thanksgiving.

It was just dawning on me that my time on the Shipley farm might be coming to a close faster than I'd thought. I'd need a Plan B, and pretty quick.

I wasn't one to panic, but the idea was sobering. I hadn't been to high school, because the religious freaks at Paradise didn't allow it. Finding other work was a crapshoot. I could only hope that there'd be another job for someone who worked uncomplainingly and was a capable mechanic, too.

But Ruth Shipley and Leah Abraham kept mentioning school. I wondered if I could make that happen, or if it was just too late for a guy like me. When I listened to Griff's tales from his college days, I couldn't see myself on a campus somewhere, doing keg stands and writing papers about the Civil War. That was something other people did—people who'd grown up in a home where schooling was important.

I didn't have family members to guide me on this journey because I'd left them behind out West. I had a borrowed family. They were great, but they had done too much for me already. I didn't have a girlfriend, because who would want a guy with an eighth-grade education who'd been kicked to the curb by his family?

These were my thoughts as I listened to the bunkhouse settle in for the night. Whenever I stopped to think about it, I realized that the bunkhouse was a lot like me—it was annexed to the farm. It was part of it, but only in a casual way. Off to the side. Not quite independent.

I lived in the bunkhouse of life.

On that thought, and in spite of the sound of two other guys snoring, I slipped off to sleep.

Sometime later—it might have been an hour, or even two—I awoke to the sound of something going terribly wrong. My eyes flew open in the darkness, my heart pounding in response to the sound of a high-pitched, keening cry. The noise died as quickly as it had come, and for a moment I lay there wondering if I'd dreamed it.

But then it came again as a muffled scream. I felt goosebumps on my chest.

"What...is that coyotes?" someone slurred.

I listened hard. Across the room, another snore was still going strong. But the sound came a third time, and it was even louder now.

And it was coming from the guest room.

I slid out of bed, my feet clumsy on the cold floorboards. I moved into the darkened hallway without stumbling too badly. Outside Lark's door, I paused. Now I could hear her speaking, but the tumble of words was impossible to make out.

Either she was dreaming, or Lark had been visited by an unlikely intruder.

Still, I hesitated. If I was disoriented, I might not want some sleepy stranger bursting into my room. But then Lark screamed again, and the sound of it was chilling enough to inspire me to move. I pushed her door open.

The room was lit by a nightlight that someone had thoughtfully installed. Lark was curled tightly in the center of the double bed. Her face was wet and contorted in dismay.

"Lark," I said.

"No!" she moaned, twisting her face into the pillow.

"Lark," I said firmly. "Lark, you're dreaming."

But she didn't hear me. She was shaking now. "Stop!" she cried out.

I was wide awake now, but I had no idea what to do. The choices were to touch her and wake her from what looked like a violent dream. But that had the possibility of startling her half to death. Or I could walk away and do nothing.

As I hesitated, she began to cry in earnest.

Aw, hell.

I leaned over and put a hand on her shoulder. "Lark, wake up." I applied only a gentle pressure, one designed not to become part of whatever horrors she thought were actually happening. I said exactly what Leah would have said to someone suffering from a nightmare. "Wake up, sweetie." I rubbed her arm.

That did it. But now she whirled on me, sitting bolt upright.

Startled, I jumped back. "Sorry," I said quickly.

Lark stared up at me, wide-eyed. Gulping for air, she hastily wiped tears from her face. "Shit," she swore, her breathing still ragged. "Shit. I'm sorry." She drew up her knees and dropped her head between them. "Shit, shit," she continued to whisper.

Now I *really* didn't know what to do. She probably didn't want a strange guy standing in her room. But on the other hand, she was still shaking. "Lark, are you going to be okay?"

With her head in her hands, she gave a strangled laugh. "That's the big question, isn't it?" As I watched, she took a deep, slow breath and blew it out. "Go back to bed. I'll try not to yell anymore."

"Okay..." But my feet didn't move yet. I was uneasy for her. "Goodnight." I would have added *sweet dreams*, as Leah did. But I didn't want Lark to think I was making fun of her. So I simply closed her door carefully and went back to my bunk.

I got into bed, but didn't sleep yet. I listened for more sounds of distress. But all was quiet.

Lark

After Zachariah left my room, I lay down again in the darkness, eyes closed, focusing on my breathing. The shrink my parents had made me see in Boston gave me lots of exercises for relaxation, and I tried all his suggestions. Meditation. Deep-breathing exercises. Shallow-breathing exercises.

Each one worked perfectly, up until the minute I fell asleep. During the day I could hold it all together. But when darkness closed in and I let my guard down, my dragons shook their chains and began to roar.

Sometimes I dreamt of the hand that had reached out from between two shanty buildings, the hard fingers closing over my mouth, yanking me into the alley. That was how my ordeal began.

Other nights, the dream started when I was already bound and gagged in the dirty little house my kidnappers used. I would hear the rapid patter of a dialect I couldn't understand. My limited Spanish had been too textbook for that corner of Guatemala. And even though I couldn't catch all the words, I knew they were arguing over what to do with me.

My dreams took many forms, and it was hard to know exactly what happened to my body while I was sleeping. But if I had to guess, I'd bet that the crying and yelling didn't start up until my dreams were visited by a certain skinny, doomed face.

Oscar.

If not for Oscar, I think I would have done a better job of getting past the kidnapping—the days of fear and the shame of squatting over the toilet hole in front of my captors. If the story had a happy ending, I might be able to sleep through the night.

But it didn't. And a boy was dead. And even though some of the events which had led to my rescue were lost in a traumatic haze, Oscar's fate was not.

Every one of my dreams ended with a pool of his blood forming on the dirt floor and oozing closer to me.

I smoothed the quilt over my body and sighed. When May had told me that I could stay in the bunkhouse, it had seemed like a perfect solution. My parents—who had already endured three weeks of wondering if I was dead—were really at the end of their ropes now. I'd come back safely to them, only to start screaming in my sleep.

Coming to Vermont was supposed to relax me. I was counting on this place to ease my mind. And sleeping in a bunkhouse meant that I wasn't alone. There were three big, strong guys and a locked door between me and the world. *Come on, subconscious! Get with the program. We are totally safe here.*

Early results were not encouraging: Guatemala 1, Bunkhouse 0.

But maybe it would take a few days' time to settle in. Hopefully the clean Vermont air would help. *You are absolutely safe here*, I reminded myself. *Nothing ever goes wrong in Vermont.*

Now if only I could get my subconscious to believe me.

* * *

The next time I woke up, it was to the peaceful sound of three guys bumping around at daybreak. Still drowsy, I curled under the quilt and listened to their low, murmuring voices. It was heavenly to laze here knowing that if I got up now I'd only be in their way. I heard the sounds of water running and of farm boys taking turns in the bathroom.

One by one their work boots strode past my door and out of the building. The bunkhouse became perfectly quiet again, and I gave the water heater another fifteen minutes to recover. Then I got up to shower, as Ruth Shipley had suggested.

Whistling to myself, I picked out a pair of shorts and a T-shirt. I loved the idea of working outdoors with my hands. That's why I'd taken the assignment to Guatemala in the first place—the nonprofit I worked for taught modern farming technologies to people in the developing world. When they offered me the chance to leave my desk behind to go out in the field, I jumped at it.

During the first six weeks I was there, I really got to like the place. I studied soil cultures and erosion. I shared farming data and crop seeds with the locals and drank strong, sweet coffee outside their homes in the afternoon. It was everything that my inner adventure-seeker had ever wanted.

I'd been so full of optimism. Then everything went to hell—

Moving on.

When I crossed the lawn to the Shipley farmhouse a bit later, breakfast prep was in full swing. It would be a quiet affair for just ten hungry people.

Daphne and I mixed up a vat of pancake batter while Ruth fried bacon and scrambled a mountain of eggs. May made two pots of coffee, then started a third.

At eight thirty, the men clomped into the house and went straight to the washroom. They'd already milked the cows and moved the chicken tractor. Not only did Shipley Farms have a busy apple orchard and a gourmet cider operation, they raised Jersey cows and sold organic milk to the Abrahams down the road, who made it into fancy cheese.

"You can get anything within a two-mile radius," I observed as I flipped another pancake onto the waiting platter.

"Except for grains," Mrs. Shipley said. "Though some Vermont farmers are giving buckwheat a go up in Hartwick."

I was surrounded by farming nerds. And it was awesome.

My big contribution to breakfast was dropping the blueberries into the pancakes. When everyone else was served, I took my plate to the table.

There wasn't much chatter, because five hungry young men were too busy scarfing up pancakes and eggs.

"How'd you sleep?" May asked me after pouring another round of coffee.

"Great," I lied. Involuntarily, my eyes went to Zach's across the table. He regarded me for a long moment before turning all his attention to a strip of bacon on his plate.

Thank you, I telegraphed in his direction.

Ruth sat down with her own plate and lifted her fork. "Lark, your mother called the house this morning."

"Oh, crap," I said under my breath. I'd forgotten to call home last night when I'd arrived.

"I explained to her that we don't have the best cell phone reception out here," Mrs. Shipley said.

"Thank you for covering for me. I'll call her right after breakfast."

"She sounded quite worried." Ruth measured me with clear blue eyes.

"Well." I swallowed a gulp of coffee. "I've always been that kid who practiced making everyone worry. This year I turned pro."

May laughed and shook her head. "Yes you did, sweetie. I'm still not over it."

Me neither. But I was trying to keep that a secret.

After breakfast we washed up, and then it was time to face the music. My mother picked up on the first ring. "I worried about you all night."

"I'm *fine*, Mom." I said these words every day, even if they weren't true.

The phone turned her sigh into a hurricane. "After what you put us through last month, I thought you'd at least remember to call."

And there it was—the reason that I couldn't stay with my parents in Boston right now. Guilt. I had plenty of it. And I could barely steer myself through the day and night. I didn't want to be responsible for my mother's mental state, too.

So now I would grovel. "I apologize for not calling. I walked into a dinner for more than a dozen people, and the mayhem sucked me in. I'm so sorry." And I really *was* so sorry. I never wanted to put my parents through hell. But I had, and now my head was a hot mess.

"All right. Thank you. How did you sleep?"

"Well," I said, repeating the lie. But hey—I was working on it.

Whether she believed me or not, she didn't press the question. "I know you'll be fine in Vermont. I really do," she said, as if trying to convince both of us.

"It's nice here. I'm going to pick apples today."

"That does sound relaxing. You might also consider calling Gilman. He texted yesterday."

"He texted *you?*" Seriously? My ex-boyfriend was texting my mother?

"Maybe he wouldn't do that if you returned his calls."

Right. "I just don't have the headspace for Gilman right now," I admitted. "He can wait until I'm ready."

There was a silence during which I could swear I heard my mother wrestling with herself. "Be well, Lark," she said finally. "Call us if you need anything."

"I will."

We hung up, and I checked my texts. Sure enough, there was another stack of messages from my ex. *I need to see you. When is a good time?*

How does "*never*" work for you, Gilman?

Ugh. He was the only one I didn't have to feel guilty for avoiding. He dumped *me*, damn it. My guess was that he regretted it. And then when I went missing, he felt like a big old ass for behaving the way he had.

Funny how a brush with death will make old friends love you again.

But Gilman was not on the list of people I felt obligated to comfort. So I powered my phone all the way down. In the country, a phone's battery drained faster. It had something to do with the device always searching in vain for a better cellular signal.

Still, I promised myself I'd call home again tomorrow, just to put Mom's mind at ease.

I was an only child, the daughter of two university professors. My father wrote long, intellectual papers about the ins and outs of first-amendment protections. My mother spent her days studying cells in a laboratory. They liked their books and their scientific abstracts. Neither one of them had understood when I'd announced I would be roughing it in

Guatemala for a year, for very little pay. They'd hated the idea right from the beginning.

"That part of the world isn't very stable," my mother had worried.

"It isn't Honduras!" I'd argued, rejecting their concerns. But the joke was on me.

Once when I was nine, I overheard my mother talking to her sister on the phone. It was the same week I'd managed to break my arm falling off the monkey bars. "You know, when we heard we were having a baby girl, we were so relieved," she'd confided while I hid behind the dining room door. "Max isn't into sports or camping or anything dirty, and I wouldn't know what to do with a fishing rod. But God laughs at plans, doesn't he? I got the scrappiest, most adventurous girl in the world. Each new gray hair I find has her name on it."

My mother had a fine, full head of silver hair now. Each one of them my fault.

When I went to find Griff, he said we'd start the day with a quick tour of the farm. I'd been here before, but if I was going to be a contributing employee, I'd need him to clue me in on the operation.

The first stop was the dairy barn, where two dozen cows were milked twice a day. But now it was midmorning, so the stalls were empty. The Shipley cows were grass fed, so they were out munching in the meadow.

The barn was shady and cool, and it smelled of hay and manure. "Don't worry, you won't be working in here," Griffin said.

"I wouldn't mind," I said truthfully. "There are scarier things in the world than cow shit."

"That is true, Wild Child," he said gently. "But I need you for the farmers' markets. And it's not just working the table, it's the load-up, the setup, selling and breaking down. Then we make a crude inventory of how much was sold, with notes about the weather and traffic. I'll show you all of that a little later."

"Cool."

Before we left the dairy barn, Griffin pointed at a yellow box affixed to the wall. "Just in case it's ever necessary, that's where we keep the defibrillator."

"Ah." How sad. The late Mr. Shipley—Griffin's father—had died very suddenly from a massive heart attack. There was probably nothing that could have been done for him. Yet this device was a new addition to the barn. "Okay. Good to know."

"There's a fire extinguisher in every building, too." He pointed at the red canister on the wall.

"Gotcha. Good idea."

We walked out into the September sunlight again. Beyond the dairy barn lay the cider house. I followed Griffin along a well-worn path between the buildings. He stopped beside a giant pallet where apple crates were stacked. "Part of the fun of working here is learning to spot all the apple varietals at ten paces."

"Okay."

"What do you think these are?" He reached into a crate and held up an apple.

"No fucking idea."

Griffin threw his head back and laughed. "Okay, the first clue is the date. It's still August. Most of our apples aren't pickable until October. These are Paula Reds, and they ripen early." He took a bite. Then he handed it to me. "Tell me what you taste."

I took a bite and chewed. *Wow.* There was nothing like a real fall apple. The ones from the grocery store just couldn't compete. "Excellent, snappy texture," I said. It was juicy, too. "High acid. Medium sugar. Not a ton of interesting flavors."

Griffin's eyes widened. "Well done, girl. That's all true. Paulas aren't the most interesting apple, but they kick off the season for us. I can't make award-winning cider from them, though. This is a farmers' market apple."

"What do you make the good stuff with, then?"

He pulled out his phone and showed me the screensaver—a picture of some peculiar apples with mottled skin. "These here are my babies."

Only Griffin would keep a picture of fruit where other people kept a photo of the girlfriend. "Your babies are ugly, Griffin."

"I know, right? But that's the cool thing about hard cider. If you want to make the good stuff, you can't use apples that are sweet and tasty. You need bitter and complicated."

"Bitter and complicated," I repeated. "Just like me."

Griffin grinned. "If you say so. Do you have a guess why bitter apples work better for cider?"

"Tannins, maybe?"

"You are a smart girl."

"I pay attention when alcoholic beverages are discussed."

"Of course you do. Now come in here." He put his hand on the doorknob and pushed. "Witness the power of this fully operational battle station!"

Griff always made me smile. "Are you ever going to outgrow the *Star Wars* quotes?"

"Nope!" He gave me a cheerful wink, then swung the door wide.

"Wow," I said, looking up at a row of giant, gleaming metal canisters. "Impressive."

"Those are my new fermentation tanks. They're only half full right now, because it's so early in the season. That's the juicer." He pointed at a machine in the middle of the room. "We press every day. Some of it goes into the fermentation tanks, and some of it gets pasteurized to be sold at the farmers' market. That's my filtration system, and that's my blending tank. On that far wall is where I do the bottling."

"Damn, Griffin. You've been investing. This looks like a serious operation now." There had to be tens of thousands of dollars' worth of equipment in front of me. Last time I visited, Griffin had said he had plans to expand his hard cider brand. But I hadn't understood what that meant.

"Yeah. And it's going to be a pretty good harvest, so I probably won't go bankrupt. Not this year, anyway."

He smiled, but I could see the strain on his young face. Griff was only twenty-eight, but he was in charge of a big farm and the de facto head of a big family.

We all have our burdens, I reminded myself. I should probably have that reminder tattooed on my hand where it would issue me frequent reminders. "Well, put me to work." I'd come to Vermont to get over myself, basically. And that could start now.

"I will. Give me ten minutes to check my tanks, and then we'll talk about your first farmers' market tomorrow."

"Great. I'll be outside." I wanted to stand in the sunshine again and breathe some more of the clean Vermont air. I walked a little way into the center of the grassy oval that stretched between the house and all the outbuildings.

Against the wall of the tractor shed stood a rusting flatbed trailer and an ancient plastic bucket. A working farm was never pristine. There was always moldering equipment and work-in-progress lying about. And farms operated on such slim budgets that nothing was ever replaced until it broke down entirely.

But the Shipley farm sat on a hilltop, and the view in the distance was truly beautiful. The Green Mountains bumped along in a glorious ridge. You could see forever.

That was the trick to appreciating all the true beauty of a working farm, then—lift your eyes to the horizon. You had to see past the broken bits and pieces and take a long view.

My gaze wandered back to the tractor shed, where a blond head gleamed from the shadowy interior.

Zach.

I trotted across the grass toward him. He was alone and bent over the engine of an old truck. I paused in the wide doorway for a moment, wondering how best to apologize for waking him up last night. In front of me, he went on with his tinkering, unaware. A classic rock station played from a radio on the workbench, and Zach was moving his hips to the music even as he screwed a cap onto some part of the engine.

He was also *shirtless*, and I took a moment to appreciate the muscles in his back. *Damn*, he was a fine specimen. I was the kind of girl who appreciated a tattoo or ten on a guy, but there was something pure and beautiful about the golden, unadorned expanse of Zach's rippling back.

I'd thought him a little stiff at dinner last night, but alone in the garage he moved with a loose ease that made me wonder if he was a good dancer...

Crap. Now I was staring.

I cleared my throat. "Zach?"

He whirled around, almost tripping over an oil can at his feet. "Uh," he said, sidestepping it. "Hi." Not quite meeting my eyes, Zach fumbled for a rag, wiped his hands, and then lunged for the T-shirt that was slung over the truck's open window. He struggled it on over his head.

I studied my fingernails until he composed himself. "Sorry to startle you," I said gently. "I'm waiting for Griffin to give me the rest of the employee orientation. Apparently you and I are selling apples together tomorrow. What do I need to know?"

"Are we?" His face got a little red if I wasn't mistaken. Some people were sensitive to the heat, though. He must be one of them. "Let's see. There's only one important detail about the market at Norwich," Zach said, kicking a foot up onto the truck's runner.

"What's that?"

"The donut vendor in the far corner is a heck of a lot better than the one in the center."

I smiled at him. "That's it, huh?"

"That's pretty important. There's nothing like a cider donut."

"True. We should talk Griffin into making them on pick-your-own weekends."

"Because that man needs another business to run."

I laughed. "You're right. Never mind."

"My only real trick for farmers' markets is to make sure I don't leave the calculator in the truck. I hate dealing with other people's money. Griffin knows that, though. That's why he's sending you to the market with me. Because I don't mind lifting crates, but I hate making change."

"I don't mind either of those jobs, honestly. Sounds like fun."

When he smiled again, his cheeks pinked up a little. God, he was cute. I loved a man who blushed easily.

"So..." I cleared my throat. "I just wanted to apologize for waking you up last night."

"Don't apologize," he said, lowering the truck's hood. "It happens."

"Well..." I cleared my throat. "It happens to me a lot. Although I'm hoping to kick the habit. And I really don't want May to worry about me. So I appreciate that you didn't say anything at breakfast today."

Zach studied me without comment, his head tipped slightly to the side. I'd never met anyone whose looks were so...golden. He almost shimmered with health. If that's what a few years on a Vermont farm could do for a person, then sign me up.

I crossed my arms, feeling suddenly self-conscious. "If it happens again, I'll buy everyone a pack of earplugs. And a case of beer."

He chuckled, and the sound made me feel warm inside. "All right. No big deal."

I grinned at him because I just had to. All that male beauty, and it was smiling at me.

Zach stepped away from the truck, giving it an appraising glance and then a sort of slap on the flank, the way you might touch a horse. "Kept her running for another week. Isaac's truck is held together by spit and duct tape, mostly. Someday I'm going to convince him to junk it."

"It's kind of cool, though." It had a rounded, old-fashioned shape. "1950s, maybe?"

Zach's eyebrows flew up. "1954. Good eye."

"For a girl. I could hear you thinking it."

He dropped his head and laughed again. "Busted."

"I've seen a lot of farm machinery, big guy. Don't underestimate me." I followed the line of the truck around to the driver's side where I found a logo and a name painted on the old metal panel. I pointed at it. "'Apostate Farm'? That's an odd name."

Zach's smile faded. "Isaac and Leah grew up in kind of a cultish religious sect out West. They ran away together with nothing when they were both seventeen, so buying the farm was a pretty big deal for them."

Jesus. "What a story. That's why they named their place Apostate Farm? How cheeky."

"I guess," he said, shifting his weight. "But they weren't really trying to be funny. The point is that someone else might get out of that place alive. If a runaway figures out how to Google 'Isaac and Leah Abraham in Vermont' they'll get web hits for Apostate Farm. Then they'll know they've found the right place."

I felt my jaw drop. "Wow. Does anyone ever show up on their doorstep?"

Zach jammed his hands in his pockets before saying, "I did."

There was a moment of silence while I took that in. I saw his face close down, as if he were waiting for me to judge him. It had never occurred to me to shun someone for where they were born, but I could see where he might be sensitive about this. "Well, Zach," I said softly. "You must have some great hitchhiking stories. We'll have to compare notes sometime."

His pale eyes lifted to mine, and the corner of his mouth quirked up. "Yeah?"

"Yeah. Remind me to tell you about the time I rode through Kentucky with a zebra."

"A *zebra?*" He was openly smiling now.

"Yup."

"Lark!" Griffin was calling me from across the lawn. "Zach!"

"In here!" I called.

"Let's go," Zach said. "Those apples aren't going to pick themselves." He gave me one more shy smile.

As we headed toward Griffin, I realized I was in the midst of the most pleasant morning I'd had in weeks.

* * *

"This will be our first weekend for pick-your-own," Griffin said as we wandered through the orchard. "We don't let the customers pick my cider apples, obviously. Daphne and Madelyn are busy making signs that say, 'No Picking This

Section.' We put ropes up, too, but there's always some asshole tourist who ducks under. Feel free to chase anyone out of there," he said, pointing at a bunch of trees at the far end of the property.

"Gotcha," I said. "No assholes allowed. Your signage is pretty clear, though." We passed a sign with a big arrow reading: *Pick Your Own.* "Is it juvenile of me that I want to add the word 'nose' to that sign?"

Griffin chuckled. "Kyle would probably add 'ass' so I guess you're not so bad."

"Noted. Now what are we picking?"

"Paulas, of course." We turned the corner to find Kyle and Kieran standing on ladders, plucking apples off the tree and tucking them into nylon bags hanging off their chests.

"First, we get you suited up in your own sexy picking bag." Griffin plucked a blue sack off the grass. "These straps go—"

Kieran jumped in to finish Griffin's sentence. "—*criss-cross applesauce.*"

"Every time he says that I vomit a little in my mouth," Kyle muttered.

"Here," he said, setting the bag against my chest. "And see how the bottom of the bag is folded up on itself? Don't accidentally loosen this bit, or you'll drop the whole harvest out of the bag before you're ready."

"Yes, sir."

He chuckled. "You hear that boys? Lark doesn't give me any lip."

"She'll learn."

Griffin tightened the straps at my hips. "I find your lack of faith disturbing," he said over his shoulder. And then to Zach, "Which *Star Wars* is that from?"

"Episode four."

"Well done, Padawan. Now let's pick some fruit before the tourists trample the place tomorrow."

We picked and picked. After an hour I became more comfortable on the ladder. And around one, May had arrived with a picnic basket and a blanket.

"The blanket is for you," she'd said with a smile. "I usually let the guys just rough it on the grass."

"I don't mind roughing it," I said quickly. I liked this job, and it was just what I needed. I didn't want to be "The Girl" at work.

"I know you don't," she said. "That's not the point. I'm just so happy you're here that I brought a blanket. And lemonade, and also cookies."

"Cookies!" Kyle hollered. "If I say I'm happy Lark is here, can I have some?"

"If you're lucky," May said, opening the basket. "The sandwiches are ham and brie today. Dig in."

We had sandwiches, lemonade and oatmeal cookies in the orchard. Then we got up and picked another billion apples.

By four o'clock I was wonderfully tired. I'd plucked countless apples off the trees, collecting them in my sack before dumping them out carefully into the giant crate in the middle of the row. At the end of the day, Zach drove up on a tractor fitted with a forklift. He lifted the fruits of our labors off the grass, did a three-point turn and drove away.

"Now we all take a break," Griffin said, his hand landing on my shoulder. "But dinner is at six sharp, and Mom gets pissed if people walk in late."

"Gotcha," I said as I dragged my tired body across the lawn.

I would finally sleep well tonight, right? I'd have to.

Lark

An hour or so later I got it. I *finally* understood why the men sort of lounged around in the dining room while Mrs. Shipley and her daughters put dinner on the table.

My limbs were heavy and tired, and I felt *worthy* of a big farmers' meal. Like I'd truly earned it. I made a few half-assed deliveries of rolls and cloth napkins to the table before sinking into a chair and gulping down yet another glass of water.

"How was it?" May asked, plunking down in the chair beside me. I hadn't seen her since lunch, after which, she'd been sent on a bunch of errands in preparation for the first U-pick day of the season.

"I feel great. I think I needed to spend some time in the sunshine, you know? Thank you for getting me out of Boston." I wasn't just saying that, either. If there was anything that could fix me up again, it was long days in an orchard. Shipley Farm was the least stressful place on earth, and I planned to exhaust myself on a daily basis.

"You are welcome!" May said, clapping her hands. "The only problem is that I thought I'd see more of you. Tomorrow Griffin has you working Norwich while I stay here."

"But there's tonight," I argued. "We're all going to the Goat, right?"

May put a hand on my arm. "Come with me to grab some stemware, would you?"

I stood and followed her into a pantry off the kitchen.

My best friend rose up on tiptoes and reached for the glasses on the top shelf. "I'm not going to the bar tonight. I've been meaning to tell you why."

"Oh?" That was sort of an ominous introduction, and I squinted at May, trying to guess what she was about to say. She couldn't go to the bar because she was...meeting a boyfriend? God, I hoped so. But if not that, she was...working a second job? Getting a giant tattoo on her butt?

Probably not that last one.

May set the glasses on a tray and then turned to me. "On Fridays I've been going to an AA meeting in Colebury," she said. As the words knocked around in my brain, I saw her swallow roughly.

"Oh," I said slowly. "Wait...for *you?*"

She nodded, her pretty hazel eyes as serious as I'd ever seen them. "It's kind of a new thing. Last summer I took Jude to a bunch of NA meetings. So I heard a lot of what was said. And that really got me looking at my relationship to alcohol. And...I didn't like what I saw."

"Really? It can't be that bad," I blurted out. And, shit! That was *exactly* the wrong thing to say. "I mean...I'm sure you know exactly what you're doing. And let me know how I can help."

Her eyes watered. "I'd love to be someone who knows exactly what she's doing. But I do know this—I was drinking every night because I liked to feel numb. And I don't want to do that anymore."

"Oh, honey. I'm so sorry." I grabbed her into a hug, which was what I should have done in the first place. "You mean everything to me. I just had a little trouble understanding for a second there."

"It's okay," she said. "I'm sort of relieved that you didn't say, 'Oh thank God, *finally*.'"

"Well now I feel like a bigger jerk than ever," I admitted. "Not for one minute did I ever think you had a problem. But it was college..."

May stepped back and squeezed both my shoulders. Hard. "I know. College was where I learned to love the buzz, but it didn't become a problem until lately, okay? You are not allowed to feel bad about this."

"Okay," I said, studying the freckles on her nose. "Can you do that again, though? My shoulders are really stiff from picking."

"You!" May blinked away her tears and rubbed my poor shoulders.

"Do you want me to go with you to your meeting?" I offered. "I mean, I don't have to eavesdrop or anything, but I could ride with you."

"Another time. Have a night out, okay? You told me you hadn't done that in a long time."

Not since before Guatemala. "I'll give up drinking, too. In solidarity."

"No! Seriously. I'm working through some of my issues, but I'm in a good place. I mean it."

"May!" Ruth called from the kitchen. "Is the table ready?"

She gave my shoulders one final squeeze. "Go on. Sit. Eat like a farmer. We'll talk later."

Sitting back down at the table, I felt unsettled. If one of my friends was having trouble, the least I could do was notice. But I was too swamped with my own issues to do even that.

Zach gave me an appraising glance across the table. "Holding up okay?"

"Fine," I said once I realized he wasn't asking about my psyche, only about my muscles. "Nothing a little rest and a couple of aspirin can't cure."

And now I knew how Zach had such a fabulous physique and sun-kissed hair. He'd quietly picked about twice as many apples as I had today, unloading his bag again and again all afternoon long.

"And a beer, later!" Griffin said. "At the Goat."

"Not the Goat," Kyle groaned. "We haven't been to the Gin Mill in a month. Let's vote."

"Sure," Griff said. "As long as you vote for the Goat."

"He's a poet and he didn't know it," Dylan put in.

"Audrey wants to hang out with Zara tonight," Griff said.

"Actually..." Audrey put a platter of fried chicken onto the table. "I'm going over there by myself on the early side. You guys can go to the Gin Mill without me if you want. You'll all fit in the truck that way."

"Yes!" Kyle shouted.

"Et tu, Audrey?" Griff hung his head in a gesture of defeat. "I thought you loved me."

"You'll know I do when you taste this buttermilk chicken. Don't mope. And say hi to Alec for me."

* * *

Two hours later, I stood outside the bunkhouse door with Griff and the others, waiting for the last person to emerge so we could head for the Gin Mill.

"Kyle, hurry up!" Griffin called through the window. "Swear to God you take longer in front of a mirror than my sisters. Zach takes like two seconds to get ready."

"And that is why Zach is a virgin," Kyle called from the building.

What?

Before I could think better of the impulse, I glanced in Zach's direction. And then I wished I hadn't, because he was staring at his boots. It was too dark to see if his neck and cheeks were a ruddy, embarrassed red. But I'd bet they were.

The bunkhouse door flew open. "Let's go!" Kyle strode out toward Griffin's truck. "I call shotgun."

"After making us wait?" his brother Kieran complained. "You dick. We'd be in the truck if we weren't waiting on your ass."

"Not my problem."

I followed the boys to Griffin's truck and climbed into the back seat, taking the middle seat because I was the smallest. That put me beside Zach, who was staring out the window.

It was hard to say whether he was embarrassed or just lost in thought. But I guess I no longer needed to ask why Kyle called him "choir boy."

Twenty-five minutes later we pulled up outside an attractive brick building with "The Gin Mill" illuminated in neon above the door. Griffin killed the engine. "Good thing I went for the crew cab," he said, cocking the door open.

"Good thing," I agreed. Zach hopped out first, then turned around and offered me a hand when it was time to leap down.

I wasn't used to chivalrous men, and I didn't really need the help. And there had been times in my life when I would have been offended by the implication that I couldn't exit a truck without assistance from someone with a Y chromosome.

51

But that's not where my head was tonight. So I grasped his warm, callused hand in my own. And, after I jumped down onto the gravel, I released him reluctantly.

When I was clear of it, he closed the door for me. I had no idea why Zach had never had a sexual relationship. But it sure wasn't for lack of manners.

Music and laughter escaped the building when Kyle opened the door. *Damn it.* Maybe I should have pretended exhaustion and stayed home. "Is this place crowded?" My chest felt a little tight at the idea of walking into a loud, packed room.

"It's usually not bad," Zach said, his voice low and soft. "I don't like crowds, either."

We went inside and I saw that he was right. The place was pretty large, so there was plenty of room to breathe.

Griffin pointed at one of the old wooden booths that lined a wall on the right. It barely fit all five of us, but that didn't matter much because Kyle and Kieran got busy right away hitting on women at the bar. Zach and I stayed at the table while Griffin fetched us beers from the bar. He slid them onto the table in frosted mugs, and I felt a little ripple of familiarity run through my chest. Friday nights in college. Beers at a bar. The only pressing concerns were which class assignment to work on next, and whether or not we'd freeze to death at the football game tomorrow.

Those were the days.

Griffin held up his mug and I lifted mine to meet his in a toast. "Glad to have you up here, Wild Child," he said.

"Glad to be here," I answered truthfully, going for my first sip of cold beer.

See? I could do this. I could go out to a bar on a Friday like normal people. It was progress.

The owner of the bar came over to shake hands with Griffin. He was introduced to me as Alec. He had a firm handshake and two sleeves of tattoos that probably drove the girls wild.

"Where's your better half?" he asked Griffin.

"With your sister. I'm pretty sure they're plotting something."

Alec grinned. "I'll bet I can guess what it is. Care to take a tour of the outbuildings with me?"

"Sure." Griff slid out of the booth. "Back in a bit, guys."

He and Alec walked off, and then I turned to Zach. "What's up with that?"

Zach shrugged. "If I had to guess, Griff might be looking for a spot to put a few more fermentation tanks. Alec had to buy this whole property, but he's only using the main buildings so far. And Griff is trying to grow his business, but he's running out of space in his cider house."

"That's exciting," I said.

"Yeah," Zach agreed, but he frowned, which wasn't a very Zach-like reaction. But I thought all of Griff's ventures were neat. Griff had always had the kind of focus that I lacked. He was a driven football player and budding chemist when I met him. Now he was a driven business owner and dedicated boyfriend.

And what was I, exactly?

My gaze swept the bar. Since I'd returned from Guatemala my tolerance for crowds and noise was practically zero. It wasn't as if I expected to be kidnapped out of the booth. Logically I knew I was safe here. But my subconscious had learned some new tricks this year. It learned fear. And I didn't know how to make it forget that lesson.

When I turned back to Zach, I found him watching me. His blue eyes regarded me with such quiet intensity that I was a hundred percent certain he could read my fear like a book.

"So tell me about your job," I said to distract the both of us. "Where did you learn to fix farm machinery?"

"Grew up with it," he said. "My, uh, stepfather was in charge of the garage on the compound where we lived. When I was twelve I realized it was one of the better jobs there. Learned everything I could." One of his fingers traced the condensation on his beer glass. He looked lost in a memory.

"How long have you been in Vermont?"

Those blue eyes flew up to mine. "Four years. My easiest path toward finding a higher-paying job is probably by getting

53

a real mechanic's license, but for now I just work on the Shipleys' and the Abrahams' vehicles."

I relaxed while we talked about work. Our little corner of the Gin Mill began to feel cozy instead of crowded. Drinkers were two deep at the bar, but it was quieter at the tables. And in the back, two pool tables and two dart boards were in play, with plenty of elbow room.

The place had an industrial vibe that I admired. The bricks and old beams overhead gave everything a rosy hue, and votive candles shed a homey light on each table. It was very Vermont—like experiencing life with the volume turned down a couple of notches. And right now, that was exactly what I needed.

Zach's gaze followed mine around the room, and then he gave me a quick little smile. "You play pool?"

"Sure. But not well."

"I'm not good, either, but a table's free. Feel like a game?"

"I do. Let's find out which of us is the least awful." I slid out of the booth, bringing my beer along with me.

Zach got busy racking up the balls while I ogled him over the rim of my glass. I'd bet anything that Daphne Shipley sat up nights writing poetry about Zach's arms. He was all golden skin and shapely muscle, from the biceps visible at the sleeves of his T-shirt to his broad, sturdy hands. He also had an economy of motion that I admired, steering that big body calmly, with no wasted efforts.

I'd always had a thing for men who worked with their hands. It probably began as a rebellion against my ridiculously intellectual parents. But there was something really sexy about tactile abilities... My gaze lingered on Zach's thick fingers as they positioned the balls in the rack, then lifted it nimbly away.

"Want to break?" he offered, chalking a cue.

I shook my head, still under his spell. His T-shirt stretched against his pecs as he lined up his shot.

A moment later the cue ball made the familiar smacking sound into the balls, sending them in every direction. Zach sank the number two and then followed up with a successful sink of the four, before missing the next one.

When I circled the table to line up a shot, he stepped back gracefully out of my way. This was the most social Friday night I'd had in months, and all because of the easy company. I sank a stripe, and then another one. Then I missed, too.

"So let's hear about this zebra," Zach said as he lined up the next shot.

I laughed, surprised that he remembered. "Okay. I was trying to hitch a ride through Kentucky, on my way to the Carolinas. And nobody wanted to pick me up. And it started to rain..."

"And nobody wants your soggy, wet self in their car," Zach broke in, sinking his shot.

"*Exactly.* So I'm standing there, and my cardboard sign is starting to get soft, and things are looking pretty grim. Then this horse trailer pulls over on the shoulder. So I put on my happy, harmless girl face. You know the one."

He lifted his eyes from the table. "Sure. I'd like to think I've perfected my happy, harmless guy face."

"Show me. I want to see it."

"Right now?" His eyes crinkled at the corners as he smiled.

"Yep. Right now." Maybe that was flirtatious of me, but it was fun to draw Zach out of what seemed to be a natural reticence.

He laid aside his pool cue and stuck one thumb in the air. Then he smiled a smile so plastic it made me double over with laughter. "Hey," he complained gently. "I'm out of practice."

I grabbed my beer off the ledge at the side of the table, took a sip, then offered it to him. He'd already finished his.

"Thank you," he said, sipping and setting it down.

"Let's see..." I scanned the table for my next shot, but I didn't have much to go on. "Back then I had my happy face down to a science. Or so I thought. But for a long time nobody stopped on that rainy roadside. And then this truck stops, and the window opens. The most pinched, grumpy old man I've ever seen looks out. And he says, 'I don't pick up hitchhikers.'"

"Ouch."

"Right. And my happy face is starting to sag. And then he says, 'But I need a little help with my horse. She's skittish back there.'"

Zach's eyes grew wide. "Please tell me you did not ride inside the horse trailer."

"Oh, but I did. I really wanted to get to North Carolina."

"Why?"

Our conversation paused for a second so that I could try to sink the number eleven. And—goddamn it—I scratched. "Ugh." I straightened, remembering that rainy day by the side of the road, and the weight of the pack on my back. During college, there was always some adventure waiting just around the corner. And I wanted all of them. Whatever the risks, I went for it. In fact, my fearlessness was a point of pride. Back then I'd thought that bad experiences only made for good stories.

Until Guatemala, where one experience was so bad that I couldn't even remember the end of it.

"I don't actually remember where I was headed. It must have been spring break. Nashville for a concert, maybe?"

Zach shrugged.

"Well, getting there seemed important at the time. So I followed this man around to the back of his horse trailer. He says, 'You gotta stand at her head. Stay away from the back of 'er. And if she's grumpy, she wants a carrot.' Then he opens the door and there's a zebra in there."

Zach abandoned his pool cue. "Seriously? You rode with that thing?"

I hadn't told my Funniest Hitchhiking Moment in a while now, and today I wasn't finding it as amusing as it used to be. While I'd always thought this was a story about a zebra, I was just realizing that it was really the story of a nineteen-year-old idiot.

Lovely.

"I was kind of a wild thing during my teen years. And it was pouring outside by the time I climbed into the trailer. So even though I suspected this man was a little..." I made the universal sign for crazy beside my ear. "I needed a lift." Or at least I imagined I did. My trust fund would have afforded me a plane ticket any day of the week. But I'd always had this crazy idea that the adventure would be over if I didn't do everything the hard way. "So I got in and he slammed the door, and then I was eye to eye with a grumpy zebra."

Zach folded those hunky arms across his impeccable chest. "Were you in there for long?"

"For most of the night," I admitted. "I just stood there, jammed into the corner, feeding that beast a carrot every half hour when it started making noise. A couple days later, after I'd gotten to wherever I was going, I Googled zebras. Turns out they're a lot more aggressive than horses, their kicks maim people and their bite is dangerous."

He gave me a warm smile in spite of the fact that I'd just proven to both of us that I'm a moron. "Guess I'll cross 'meet a zebra' off my list of things to do."

Kyle wandered over as Zach said this. "Your list of things you need to try is pretty fucking long already," he said. "Can I play the winner?" He tipped his head back and gulped at his beer.

Shit. It killed me to hear Kyle referencing Zach's...*inexperience.* If I'd understood correctly earlier, I would bet that he took lots of flack from the other guys in the bunkhouse for being a virgin. And I expected Zach to look embarrassed.

He didn't, though. Instead, he reached over and relieved Kyle of the fresh pint in his hand and took a deep drink. "Kind of you to share," he said. "Now rack 'em up if you want in. We'll play a game of cutthroat. All of us."

Zach

My watch beeped Saturday morning at six. When I shuffled into the bathroom to get ready for the day, Lark's door was still shut.

Even though we were scheduled to work together at the Norwich market in a couple hours, I let her sleep. She'd worked hard yesterday.

I'd misjudged Lark, assuming that May's city friend wouldn't be all that helpful on a farm. But she'd picked apples like a champ all afternoon. It was *my* performance that suffered, since I kept dropping fruit whenever I'd get distracted by the stretch of her bronze arms into the tree.

Now I was scheduled to spend several hours alone with her. It was too good to be true.

After helping out with the milking, I loaded crates of apples and stacks of paper retail totes onto the back of Griffin's truck. At eight o'clock I went back to the bunkhouse to check on Lark, but she stepped outside with a smile just as I approached. "Good morning!"

My heart tripped over itself, but outwardly I kept my cool. "Hey there. You sleep okay?"

"As a matter of fact, I *did*. One in a row—the start of a streak." She jumped off the stoop, and I gave a silent prayer of gratitude for the white denim shorts she was wearing, and for the expanse of smooth, shapely legs in view.

"What do we do first?" she asked.

First, we stop staring. "First we load up the truck."

But when we reached Griff's pickup beside the cider house, Lark frowned. "Looks like you did it already."

"Well..." I hefted one last bushel crate before answering her. "There's a couple trays of late peaches over there on the table. Can you set them on the back seat?"

Since Lark was a smart girl, she first opened the truck's cab before looking for the peaches, which were stacked into sturdy cardboard flats.

When she approached the truck, I took the flat out of her hands and slid it onto the rear seat. Lark raised one puzzled eyebrow and fetched another flat, this time stepping around me so that she could slide it into the truck herself.

Whoops. I hadn't meant to make her feel incompetent, but there was something about Lark that turned me into a caveman. I was going to have to watch myself. We climbed inside without a word, and the cab smelled like peaches in the best possible way.

"Now what?" she asked.

"We're all done here," I said, putting Griffin's truck in reverse. "Now we collect the cash box and the scale and get the heck out of here. Did you eat something?"

She shook her head. "That's okay, though. You said something about donuts..."

I smiled at her, probably grinning like a fool. "You are a good listener."

"Do they have coffee, too?" she asked, and I noticed how long her eyelashes were. I don't think I'd ever sat this close to Lark before.

"Nope," I said, reversing into the gravel drive. "So I'll let you stop at the house and grab some."

"You are the best boss ever, Zachariah," she said, kicking one of her high-top sneakers onto the dash.

She was just teasing, but I liked hearing it anyway.

After she got her chance to run inside for coffee, I wound the truck down the country road toward the highway, and Lark asked if she could plug her phone into Griff's stereo. "Unless you want me to plug in yours?"

"Go ahead. I don't have a phone," I told her. "Last man in North America without one."

"Not a fan?"

"Not a fan of paying fifty dollars a month. And the cell service in Vermont is crappy, so..." I shrugged.

"Ah." She plugged hers into the jack. Audrey had upgraded Griff's stereo as a birthday present this winter. A moment later the cab hummed with strains of...I had no idea what. It was a lively guitar riff, and it sounded familiar. But a guy can only learn so much popular music in three years' time. "I like it," I said. "Who is it?"

"The Chili Peppers!" she gasped. "I know you're young, but..."

"I'm not *that* young," I said quickly. "How old are you, anyway?"

"Twenty-four. You?"

"Twenty-three. But I have the musical knowledge of a kindergartener. Music wasn't allowed where I grew up. Unless you count hymns."

"Wow." She was quiet for a second. "How did they keep it out, though? Didn't you hear music at the drugstore? Or—no TV, huh?"

I shook my head. "No TV. And I never left the property. We were out in the boonies on a big ranch in Wyoming. The nearest town was fifteen miles away. And I wasn't permitted to leave, anyway. Only married men had access to vehicles."

"So you were sort of...a prisoner," she said slowly. "Until you were nineteen?"

"That's right. Took me a long time to figure out that the way we lived wasn't normal. And even when I worked out that people off the compound didn't dress like us and didn't live like us, I still couldn't really picture it."

"Wow. That's a pretty crazy childhood you had there, Zach."

"I know. So tell me about the Chili Peppers."

"The full name is the Red Hot Chili Peppers. And nothing ever goes wrong when the Chili Peppers are playing."

She told me a little about the band—grunge with a side of funk. She rolled down the truck's window, and we left a contrail of grunge rock along the narrow Vermont highway. I'd never felt more sure that I'd left the dusty confines of my childhood behind. There's nothing more liberating than driving down a road in the summertime with the windows open, singing along to with a pretty girl by your side.

* * *

Ninety minutes later we were almost finished stocking our tables in Norwich, Vermont, where the farmers' market was already a beehive of farmers hustling to set up their stands.

"Damn," Lark said, scanning all the activity. "This market is huge."

"Yep," I agreed, hefting another crate of apples off the truck. "Griffin calls Norwich the mothership."

Lark scrambled up onto the tailgate and dragged another crate of apples toward the edge. But when she hopped down to carry it, I swept it away before she got a chance to heft it. "I can do that," she argued. "Really. I know how to lift with my legs and not with my lower back."

"I'm sure you do," I said in a low voice. "But if I'm here, you don't have to."

When I turned around, she was chewing her lip, obviously trying to decide whether or not to argue. But she didn't, and I was glad. It would cause me almost physical pain to watch a woman stagger under a bushel crate when someone nearly twice her size was available to do it instead.

Maybe she knew that, because she jumped up on the pickup again and slid the last two crates toward the edge where I could reach them.

"Thank you kindly," I said with a smile. "Can you get the peaches?" This time I wouldn't grab them out of her hands. She hadn't appreciated that. But I might have to look away and count to ten to avoid helping.

"Now what?" she asked after retrieving the peaches.

"You put on the money apron and fiddle with the signs. I'll buy the donuts."

"That's an arrangement I can agree to."

There were still ten minutes before the market would open, but I convinced the donut lady to do an illegal transaction. And when I returned to our stand, I handed the bag to Lark.

"Oh, God. They're still warm!" She peeked in at the four donuts inside. "But where's yours?" With a gleeful laugh she pulled one out and took a bite. Then her eyes rolled back in her head and she moaned.

And heck, the sound made my groin tighten. This girl made me feel like a guilty teenager again, the one who was always praying that nobody around him could read minds.

Lark handed me the bag. "These are exquisite. Have one—quick. It's almost nine." Oblivious to my suffering, she raised her arms overhead and stretched. Her top rode up a bit, exposing an inch of sleek skin over her hip. Then she bent over the Ginger Golds and straightened the sign.

It was going to be a long morning.

But then it wasn't. Market time always flew by, and with the weather so nice we were busy. Since there was only one scale, Lark was our checkout girl, while I ran my ass off restocking the merchandise and selling sweet cider by the half gallon. Norwich was a rich town, and the people who shopped here knew their food. I was continually asked about the flavor differences between varieties, and I answered as well as I could.

Lark was a natural salesperson, though. "The Zestar has more perfume than the Paulas. And Ginger Golds are the sweetest. You don't want to miss those, either." She had an easy way about her, and people always listened closely to what she had to say. And when someone asked her whether the apples were organic—this was Vermont, after all, and we got that question all the time—Lark surprised me by launching into an explanation of Integrated Pest Management that was at least as thorough as I could have given.

I wasn't the only one who noticed she was easy on the eyes, either. A bushel of lingering glances came her way from the men who stopped by our stand. And from women, too.

Lark didn't seem to notice. She weighed and sold apples and made change without hesitation. And happily, too.

There was only one moment when I thought the crowds were getting to her. I'd stepped out of the booth for a second because the Abrahams' daughter had run over to see me. Isaac and Leah's stall was just a few yards away, so Maeve always paid me a visit. I scooped her up and spun her around for a minute until she giggled. Then I returned her to Leah, chatting with her for a minute before I went back to the Shipley stall.

But even that little breadth of time was enough to stack up the customers three deep. And some grouch with a handlebar mustache was barking at Lark, asking why he couldn't buy the Cortlands his wife wanted.

"They're not ripe yet," she explained. Her voice was patient but her eyes were darting around the crowd. She looked nervous.

I ducked into the booth and stepped up beside her. "Next!" Then I gave her a little bump with my hip. "I have some bottles of water in the cooler. Can you grab 'em?"

She disappeared, and I dealt with the line. By the time she came back she looked calmer. "Thanks for the break," she said, handing me a water bottle.

"Anytime."

One o'clock arrived, and our bushels were mostly gone, and all the vendors around us were packing up their trucks. "Whew!" Lark said, pretending to sag against the table. "That was intense. But I think we did well."

"Sure did. And the crowd didn't bother you too much?"

Her eyes widened. "You noticed that about me, huh?"

"Yeah," I whispered.

"It was mostly fine." She raised her eyes to the ceiling of our little market tent. "I guess the daylight helps. And we're on this side of the table, and they stay on their own side. I don't know, honestly. Some days are just easier than others."

"Well, good." I hefted the heaviest crate onto my shoulder before she could grab it. "Can you hold on tight to that cash box? I'll have us out of here in just a few minutes."

She gave me a narrow look. "Zach, this doesn't look like a crime-ridden neighborhood. We could lock the cash in the cab and I could help you pack up."

I was so busted. "Okay, missy. That sounds like a plan."

Lark

"I can't believe you pulled that off," I said a half-hour later, after Zach managed to parallel park Griffin's truck in an inadequate space.

He cleared his throat. "Well, someone threatened to expire if she wasn't fed lunch."

I had. But when I'd made this dramatic statement I hadn't known how hard it would be to find a parking spot for the truck on the narrow streets around Dartmouth College. Hanover was right across the river from Norwich, and I was starving.

Zach locked the truck, and we walked down Main Street, past little shops selling books and Dartmouth T-shirts. "We'll be here again on Wednesday afternoon," he offered. "The Hanover market is almost as big as Norwich."

I looked around at all the college students passing us in their flip-flops, with their cups of coffee in hand. "I love college towns."

"Yeah? What do you like to eat in them? Because two quarters bought us only forty minutes on the meter."

"That's a burrito joint." I nudged his arm and pointed. "We could get take-out. How does that sound?"

"Perfect."

The place was crowded and rather loud, which I did not appreciate. Whatever good vibes had allowed me to feel cheery during market hours were starting to wear thin.

But Zach stood right behind me in line, and I could sense him there, a big wall of calm at my back. The line inched forward, and my hunger outweighed my edginess.

Working the farmers' market had actually been fun. Having a job to do had helped me focus. I'd told Zach that it was the table which kept me calm, but that wasn't really true. It was *him*. He was always there at my elbow, always ready to pitch in, always watching.

I'd never thought of myself as the damsel-in-distress type. But apparently, getting kidnapped turns you into a needy little bitch. "What's your order?" I asked, tipping my head back against Zach's chest. "It's my treat."

He made a grumpy little noise. "I got it."

I spun around and looked up into his blue-green eyes. "Zach, I want to treat. You bought donuts this morning. But more importantly—" I put a finger against his very hard chest. "—I'm not in this for the money. You're saving up for your own farm or whatever, and I'm just May's half-crazy friend who needed to get out of Boston. We're going to be working together for three months. If I buy you an overpriced burrito every once in a while, it's because I want to. And you're just going to have to get over it."

He looked down at me, his eyes softening. "I guess I can get the next one."

"Thank you." I turned back around to discover we were next in line. Zach probably thought I was a head case.

Then again, I was.

On the way home, as the Green Mountains rolled by out the driver's side window, I broke down and asked him, "So what's your story?"

He chuckled. "I told you already. Grew up with some crazy people. Got thrown out. Moved to Vermont. There isn't more to tell."

I fiddled with my playlist. I chose a Pearl Jam song and turned the volume down a bit. "So..." I pressed, because his answer hadn't been very satisfying. "Did people get thrown out often? Was it hard to play by all their rules?"

He was quiet for so long I thought he wouldn't answer. "People get thrown out all the time. Polygamy creates all this stress on a community."

"Because the numbers don't work out?" I guessed. "There aren't enough women to go around."

"That's right. And they can't increase the number of women, so they have to pare down the number of men. But then there aren't enough hands to do all the labor. So the first way they make it work is by age. Girls get married at seventeen, and men don't get to marry until their late twenties. The compound receives the benefit of their labor for those years, while the bachelors hope they'll be the next one who's allowed to marry."

"But not everyone gets a set of wives," I guessed.

"Exactly. So they need to evict some guys, and people aren't exactly volunteering. Except for Isaac and Leah. They ran away together when she was seventeen. They wanted to be together and they knew it wouldn't be allowed."

"Wow, seventeen? And now they're married with a child."

"And a farm," Zach added.

"That's a hell of a story." And really romantic.

"They're pretty great. They took me in when I got tossed out, no questions asked."

"Ouch." Maybe I shouldn't have asked him to talk about it. "Are you ever sorry you left?"

"Never," he said quickly. "Getting tossed wasn't fun. Hitchhiking eastward took me more than two weeks. I hadn't eaten for three days when I finally made it to Isaac and Leah. Even so, I wish I'd done it sooner."

"How'd you find them?"

"Started hitchhiking east. I knew I needed to get to Vermont. I was only nine when they ran away together. But Isaac was always nice to me, and I missed him when he was gone. Then, when I was seventeen, he and Leah tried to phone home. They wanted their parents to know that they were safe and settled, you know? But nobody would take the call."

"God, really?"

"Really. I'm sure their mothers would have liked to talk to them, but they were afraid to be punished."

"But you talked to them?"

"Hell no. They'd never let me near a phone. But the same extension rings in the pastor's office and in the garage. There's only one phone line to the whole compound. The next day I snuck a look at the caller ID. I didn't get the number, but I saw 'Tuxbury, Vermont.'"

"Smart boy!"

He shrugged. "I knew I needed a backup plan. Half the young men get thrown out eventually. I never thought I'd be one of them. Or maybe I knew I would. I dunno." He shook his head.

"I'm sorry."

"Don't be. These four years have been good to me. I wish they'd tossed me out sooner."

"So...what happened? You got thrown out pretty young, right? You said they usually waited until they got some more years of your labor."

He laughed. "You noticed that, huh? Yeah, I was a prodigy."

"How do people get the boot?" I asked.

"It can be for any reason. Some guys steal from the till or break a rule. And some get tossed on a trumped-up charge. It doesn't even have to be rational. They just have to drum up a little rage, and make the offense justifiable. Otherwise, the mothers of all these boys would stage an uprising. When my number came up, they threw me off a moving flatbed truck."

"Jesus. They invented your crime and dumped you by the side of the road?"

He chuckled. "In my case, I made it easy for them. I committed the crime—or I tried to. Four hours later I was hitchhiking toward Reno with nothing but twenty dollars and the clothes on my back. I'd never seen a city. Didn't know how to hitchhike. Didn't know what a homeless shelter was. I learned a lot in a hurry."

That's when I stopped asking questions. I wasn't the only one who'd come looking for salvation in Vermont.

* * *

When we made it back to the farm, the place was a madhouse. There were a dozen cars parked all along the road and families wandering around with half-bushel baskets. Audrey was selling apples, sweet cider and Griffin's hard stuff in front of the cider house. The rest of the guys were picking and moving apples around and shooing people away from the varietals that weren't ripe.

"What can I do?" I asked Zach after we offloaded the small amount of merchandise that hadn't sold.

"Take a break," he suggested. "I'm going to do the afternoon milking."

I spotted May striding toward the farmhouse. "What can I do?" I asked her.

"Have a glass of iced tea with me," she suggested. "I need a break."

"That's what Zach told me to do. But he's still working."

"That dude never sits down," May said, opening the kitchen door. "Grab us each a cookie, will you?"

We settled onto the front porch and watched tourists struggle under the weight of the apples they'd picked. And every couple of minutes Dylan Shipley would swing into view at the wheel of a tractor that was hitched to a wagon. Tourists rode the wagon out to the early-bearing trees at the far end of the orchard.

"How's the bunkhouse treating you?" May asked me suddenly. "If you're not comfortable out there I *really* hope you'll tell me."

"The bunkhouse is awesome. I have my own room. What's not to love?"

"The company, duh," May said. "It's a sausagefest out there. Kyle can be a smartass. Kieran is a little easier, though. And Zach won't give you any trouble."

"He's a really interesting guy."

"Zach? He grew up in a cult, basically. All the men had four or five wives. Everything I know about it I heard from Leah, because Zach never says a word about it. I mean—Griffin had it in his head that this place was in Texas, and for a year Zach didn't even correct him. And when Griff asked why, he just said, 'There's no point in talking about that place, no matter what state it's in.'"

"Yikes."

"Griff says he has a lot of scarring on his backside, too. They whipped him."

"Jesus."

"I know. He's a sweetie."

"The sweetest," I agreed.

"He catches hell sometimes from the other guys about his, er, inexperience. I've never seen him flirt with a woman."

"Maybe he's gay," I suggested.

"The thought had occurred to me," May said. "Growing up with a bunch of religious fanatics could do a number on you. Though I've never seen him flirt with *anyone*—man or woman."

"Maybe he's asexual."

"Maybe. But Zach plays everything close to the vest. We'll never know what's in his head if he doesn't want us to."

"Hmm." I wished I could be more like that myself, especially when it came to the screaming nightmares.

May drained her glass. "I'd better go see how Audrey is doing at the tasting counter. Save me a seat next to you at dinner?"

"Of course." I took our glasses inside and offered my services to Ruth Shipley, who had already started preparing supper. She put me to work making a giant salad.

At five o'clock, the orchard closed for business, and everybody began making their way inside.

"Why don't you arrange these on a board?" Ruth asked, handing me several wedges of cheese, a big bunch of grapes and two boxes of crackers. "We always have a short business meeting on Saturdays before dinner. And it's more fun with snacks."

"Good plan." I removed the waxed paper from the cheese and cut a small bite for myself. "Holy God. What is this? It's magnificent."

"Isaac and Leah make it from our milk. They call this one Promised Land."

I tasted another bite, just to analyze the flavors. "It's nutty—like an aged gouda."

Mrs. Shipley nodded, setting down a few apples for me to slice, too. "They would call it a raw-milk, salt-water-brined cheese aged to a firm texture."

"I call it amazing." And when I set the cheese board down on the table, all the guys lunged for it.

"Jesus." I laughed. "Almost lost a hand there."

May smacked one of her cousins on the hip. "Didn't you ever hear the phrase, *ladies first?*"

"That's only true in bed," Kyle said, reaching for another cracker.

Griffin snorted. "At least you have manners somewhere."

"Ew," Daphne complained. "Don't make me think about Kyle doing the nasty."

"But *thinking* about it is all he gets," Kieran teased.

Griffin clapped his hands. "We can talk about Kyle's sexual failures later, folks. Let's do our roundup so we can eat dinner. How'd we do today?"

May gave the totals for what the U-pick operation brought in, and Zach handed over the cash box with our final count.

Griffin opened it up and took out the bills I'd bundled together and the counting slip. "Damn. The bills are sorted and *faced*. I want all of you hooligans to see how Lark handles a cash box."

"Kiss-ass," Kieran hissed. I pretended to scratch my forehead with my middle finger, and he laughed.

"Looks like a good day to be a farmer," Ruth said, sitting down beside her son and eyeing the counting slip.

"It was," he agreed. "Today we're harvesting apples *and* cash."

"So..." His mother folded her hands. "The revenue side of our balance sheet had a good day today. Let's spend a minute talking about the expenses. I got our mobile phone bill yesterday. This is the second month in a row when we overran our data plan." She gave the side-eye to her youngest daughter.

"I can't help it!" Daphne said. "All my friends communicate on social media. It's only going to get worse next month when I'm away at the college."

"No, it's your Spotify habit," Dylan said. "Find a WiFi signal like the rest of us."

"Just because you don't have any friends..."

"Hey now!" Griff thundered, holding up a hand. "No need to make things personal. Maybe our family plan is too limited. Let's just bump it up to the next level so we can finally stop having this discussion."

70

"Now there's an idea," Daphne scoffed.

"All right," Ruth said, making a note on her legal pad. "Fine." She opened a folder, lifted out two pages and handed them to me. "Lark, honey—I need you to fill these out."

They were forms I9 and W4. Employment forms. I handed them back to her. "I don't want to get paid."

Her eyes widened. "Of course you do, honey. Everyone who works here gets paid."

"Not true!" Daphne chirped.

"You're getting paid in college tuition," Dylan growled. "Lots and lots of it."

The twins stared daggers at each other, but neither Ruth nor Griff paid them any attention.

"You have to be paid, or our workers' comp won't cover you," Griff pointed out. "We have Audrey on the payroll for this very reason."

"Well…" I tried to think. "Pay me minimum wage, and then deduct rent. Seriously—strip it down to nothing."

"Everyone else gets—" Ruth began.

I shook my head. "I'm still getting paid a salary by my nonprofit, guys. The latest check just hit my bank account yesterday. I'm really not here for the money." That's when I shut up, because I didn't want to talk about any of this. Forget my paycheck. I had a trust fund from my grandparents. Money wasn't my problem. But I wasn't about to tell them the truth. *I came to Vermont to try to feel sane again.*

Now there's a conversation stopper.

"We'll figure something out," Griff said, closing the topic for now. "Just fill out the forms, Lark."

"Last item," Ruth said, reaching for a cracker. "We still have to decide whether we're doing the Royalton market this year."

Griffin tossed a grape into his mouth. "Five markets a week feels like too many. That's a whole lot of cider production we could be doing instead. A bottle of Shipley's Best pays us fifteen bucks."

"We have Lark to help us," Ruth pointed out, and I felt a stupid little rush of pleasure hearing it. Being helpful to my friends was a balm on my soul.

"True," Griffin said, his big hands tenting together. "But it still may not make sense as an investment of our time."

"Well..." I heard myself speak up. "We could put some numbers on the issue." The work I'd done for the nonprofit in Guatemala often faced questions like this one—how to allocate scarce resources.

"Show me." Griffin tossed me his legal pad and a pen.

I clicked the pen into action. "So, each fair is three hours, right? And how much driving time do I add on for South Royalton?"

"The drive is forty minutes," Griffin said. "And loading the truck takes an hour—just to be conservative. Setup is a half-hour. And unloading is at least twenty minutes."

"So..." I scribbled numbers on the pad. "Five and a half hours, with two people working? That's eleven man hours. How much cider can you press in eleven man hours?" I looked up to find that everyone was staring at me with a peculiar intensity. "Oh, shit. Have I overstepped? I'm sorry."

May threw her head back and began to laugh. "Oh my God. We have this same discussion every week, and if you make a math problem out of it, maybe we won't have to anymore! I could kiss you."

"Amen," Griffin said. "I can press a lot of cider in eleven hours. More than two barrels, easily. So that's...after a few months and some other tweaking, four thousand dollars' worth of cider. *Eventually.*"

My pen hovered above the pad. "Even if the man hours for pressing are only *half* the true investment in the finished product, you'd still have to clear two thousand dollars from the Royalton market to break even."

Mrs. Shipley flipped a page in her notebook and bit her lip. "Last week we brought home two hundred and fourteen dollars. And that was a *good* week."

"But we have *friends* in Royalton," Daphne Shipley said quietly.

"We also have two more college tuitions to pay," her mother countered, closing the ledger book. "I'm convinced. Sorry, Royalton. We just can't fit you in." She smiled at me, her expression so gracious that I stopped worrying that I'd intruded on decisions that were none of my business.

Griffin threw his hands into the air. "Thank you, arithmetic."

"Naw," Kieran said. "Thank you, Lark's big-ass brain."

I passed the pad back to Griffin. "I think Kieran just said my ass looks big."

Everyone laughed, and I thanked the heavens for the hundredth time that I'd come to Vermont for apple season.

Lark

Nightmares don't have any respect for a person's dignity. Just when I'd decided Vermont was my salvation, I had another awful night.

Before Guatemala, I'd viewed dreaming as a passive exercise, like watching a movie in my mind. But now my worst nightmares were more like a wrestling match.

They usually began as an ordinary dream. Boring, even. This time I dreamt of the farmers' market. In the dream I left our stall and walked around, admiring the piles of vegetables and the homemade jams. I avoided a particular corner of the market, though. My sleeping brain knew I shouldn't go there.

But the place tricked me. I became turned around at a pumpkin vendor's stall. And suddenly I was in a dark, dusty place. My heart began to thump inside my chest as I spun around, looking for the exit.

A hand grabbed me and yanked my wrist, dragging me further into the darkness.

I don't want to have this dream again, I said to myself. I opened my eyes to find the walls of the Shipley guest room, right where they were supposed to be.

When I closed them again, my subconscious pounced.

I knew I was thrashing around in bed, trying to shake off the dream. But no matter which way I turned, my captors always found me again. Shouting at them to let me go didn't break the dream's grip on me, either. And through it all, I knew I was sleeping, but that didn't make things better. The scene cut to the cramped little place where I'd been held, and I couldn't escape.

And then a warm hand landed on my shoulder blade. "Shh, Lark. You're dreaming again."

I know.

The hand lingered a moment, grounding me. My breathing evened out, and I forgot to look into the shadows. But when the comforting pressure disappeared, the darkness of the shack found me again.

Then I spotted Oscar's face, watching from the doorway, looking worried. Looking doomed.

I cried out again, and the hand returned to my back. "Shh," it said. "Come on, sweetheart. It's okay."

And it was, for a little while. But that night I couldn't break free of the shadows for a long time. They tangled with me on and off for hours, until I finally pushed through the shimmering surface of my sleep state and broke free.

I heard myself let out a sweaty, startled gasp.

"Shh..." a voice slurred. Someone's hand was pressed reassuringly against my back.

I turned my head slowly. I took in a broad shoulder jutting up from the mattress. It was Zachariah again. He lay sprawled on the far edge of my bed, one arm tucked awkwardly under his dozing head, the other stretched out to soothe me. He looked a little uncomfortable. But he also looked asleep.

Guiltily, I rolled toward the wall again. But then I leaned back a few millimeters to enhance the contact between his palm and my spine. *Everything is fine*, I told herself. *Safest place in the world.* For some reason this thought made my eyes feel hot. It was almost unbearable how well I'd been treated these past few days.

Even the safest place in the world felt more elusive after you'd visited some of the ugliest ones.

I studied the quality of the darkness around the window curtains, and decided that it was still the middle of the night. It was time to shove away all my sad thoughts and get a little more sleep. If the dark crescents below my eyes grew any darker, I'd have to explain herself to May.

I closed my eyes again and concentrated on the feel of Zach's hand against my back. I emptied my mind of everything except for that simple thing—the warmth of another living person's touch. Leaning into it, I began to drift...

* * *

A few hours later, the alarm on Zach's watch woke up both of us. Embarrassed, I played possum when I heard Zach sit up fast. "Whoa," he muttered, making the sound of someone surprised to wake up on a bed not his own.

I held my breath, not moving a muscle until he was out of the room, and the door was shut on me again.

The night had been survived, but not easily. And now that morning had safely arrived, I was suddenly exhausted. I adjusted my pillow and fell back asleep for an unfortunately long time. When I next opened my eyes, the clock said ten minutes past eight.

Damn it!

I took the world's speediest shower, then hustled over to the farmhouse to help with breakfast. "Sorry," I gasped, running through the door.

The Shipley family was already furiously busy in the kitchen. Ruth stood scrambling a heap of eggs in a fourteen-inch skillet. Daphne flipped pancakes beside her, while Dylan forked bacon off a pan and onto a plate.

"I overslept. What can I do?"

Ruth looked up at me, her scrambling hand still doing its thing to the eggs. "You look tired, Lark. Is everything all right?"

You never can fool a mom, damn it. "Yep," I answered quickly. "Shall I set the table?"

"Sure," May answered, her hands full of coffee mugs. "Forks and napkins. And then carry out the bacon."

"Roger that," I agreed, diving for the silverware drawer.

It was only minutes later that the men began to tramp into the house. Griffin paused on his way to the washroom, squinting at me.

"What?" I demanded.

"Your T-shirt looks wrong, Wild Child. Thought you'd like to know."

I looked down. Sure enough, it was on inside-out. If my goal was trying to convince my friends that I had my act together, this wasn't the best display of proof.

"Can you pour the coffee, Lark? Here's the milk," Mrs. Shipley urged.

I took the pot into the dining room and began with Grandpa Shipley's cup. "Much obliged, miss!" he said with a wink. May had told me that having a house full of farmhands always made her grandfather feel like a cowboy overseer.

Daphne did a slow loop around the table, too. In front of each man, she stopped to offer pancakes. I watched with amusement as she stopped in front of Zach, forked the biggest, most beautiful pancake onto his plate and then tossed her hair in an exaggerated way.

"Thank you," Zach said, his eyes on his plate.

"Don't mention it," the girl said with a breathy voice. Then she lost her nerve and fled for the kitchen.

I caught May's eye, and my friend rolled her eyes. Biting back a smile, I couldn't help but wonder if I'd been just as horribly obvious with my crushes at eighteen. I'd probably been even worse.

"Coffee?" I offered Zach.

"Thanks." He held out his cup.

"Sorry I'm still a bad roommate," I said over his shoulder, my voice too low to be overheard.

"You dreamed about scratching on the eleven ball, didn't you?" he whispered. "Admit it."

"That was such a fluke," I argued, filling his cup to the brim. "Next time you'll get my A game."

"Bring it."

* * *

When the piles of breakfast food had been eaten, we all sat a little longer over our cups of coffee, except for Zach, who was on his fourth pancake. Daphne kept bringing them, and he kept dispensing with them. The boy could seriously eat.

Dylan and Ruth were the first to leave, heading for church in Colebury. "Anyone need anything from town?" Ruth asked.

We waved her off, and after they left, May lifted her coffee mug and studied me from over its rim. I braced myself for more inquiries into my strange attire or the bags under my eyes. But she startled me with a different announcement. "I have to tell you that Gilman called the house last night after you'd gone to bed."

I set my own cup down with a thump. "God, why? How did he know where to find me?" My ex-boyfriend was not on the very short list of people I felt like talking to these days.

The question seemed to make May guilty. "I may have mentioned on Facebook how happy I was to have you staying with me."

"Oh." I put my elbows on the table. "Facebook. It's from the devil."

Across from me, Zach put down his fork. "You know, that's one thing cults got right."

Everyone laughed, including me, and the moment of levity felt good. I'd needed that. "Well, I don't want to talk to Gilman."

"Maybe he's just being nice," May said quietly.

"I know that. It's *nice* to hear he's glad I'm not rotting in a shallow grave somewhere. But a year ago he dumped me, and that means I don't have to talk to him if I don't feel like it."

"Sounds fair to me," Griffin put in, draining his coffee.

May twirled a lock of her hair. "He sounded really worried, Lark. And so he said he might drop by next Friday."

"What?" No wonder May looked guilty. "Nobody just *drops by* Vermont from Boston."

"He's going on a corporate golf retreat at Stowe."

"I'm busy then," I said quickly.

"Well..." May said slowly. "If you really don't want to see him, you'll have to return one of his calls."

"I'm busy then, too," I muttered.

"Sweetie, if I'd known who was calling, I would have let it go to the machine. But I saw the Boston number and I thought maybe it was your parents."

I didn't want to talk to them, either. But I held my tongue. "What's on the agenda today?" I asked.

"Selling cider!" Audrey said. "You can help me pour for tourists. It's a blast. I'll train you to take over my job. Next Sunday is my last one before I go to France."

Griff pouted into his coffee cup. "Don't fall for any skinny Frenchmen."

"I would never!" She put a hand in the center of his massive chest. "I like 'em big and grumpy."

"Aw," Griff growled. Then he put down his cup and reached for her, pulling Audrey into his lap and kissing her. She wrapped her arms around him and gave as good as she got.

"There they go again," Kyle said, pushing his plate away. "You kids should probably just spend the morning in your bedroom anyway. Might as well have a cheerful boss for another ten days."

Griff flipped off his cousin without letting go of his girl.

Then we all went outside to pick apples and charm tourists into buying cider.

Zach

It usually happened like this. Every second or third night.

I was asleep in my bunk when something began to tug at my consciousness. Since sleeping was one of my favorite activities, at first I tried to ignore it. I rolled onto my side and screwed my eyes shut tightly.

But then I heard it again—a bitten-off sob coming from the other room.

Lark.

My eyes snapped open in the dark just as she made another frightened sound.

"Urf," someone else in the bunkroom said. "There she goes again."

"Got it," I whispered, stumbling out of my bunk.

Lark had woken me on several occasions. Sometimes all it took was a pat on the shoulder to comfort her. Sometimes she'd just snap out of it and apologize. But other times she didn't shake it off as easily, and I'd wake up in her bed the next morning. Those were the nights when she couldn't escape the dreams. After two or three trips to her room, I'd give up and sink down against the headboard. At dawn I'd wake up on her extra pillow.

Tonight I staggered into her room just as she uttered the name, "Oscar." And then she said, "Stop!" It was always *stop*. It made my blood run cold to imagine what it was she wanted stopped.

Lark was lying on her back and twisting around. So I sat right down and took her hand in mine, giving it a gentle squeeze. "You're just fine here, Lark. Everything is fine."

Her eyes flew open, startling me. She had a panicked stare, and I waited for her to say something. But that's not what happened. Her eyes seemed to focus on my face, and then her expression relaxed. Then her eyelids fluttered closed.

That left me holding her hand, and looking down at a beautiful, sleeping girl. She was so different from the country girls I'd grown up with. Her dark lashes pointed down toward a set of high cheekbones. It was a mystery to me how a face could be so strong and utterly feminine at the same time. The crescent of her mouth was relaxed and parted, as if she were just about to say something. I studied her lips, wondering how they'd feel against my own.

Whoops. I wasn't here to admire her. I had to stop thinking like that. Right now, preferably.

I counted to one hundred, then began to slip my fingers from her grasp. But Lark shifted on the bed, squeezing my hand.

"Shouldn't I go?" I whispered. I meant it as a rhetorical question, which was the only sort one should ask of a sleeping person. But I hoped the sound of my voice would relax her.

"No," she breathed. She turned her head away then, as if embarrassed by this request.

It was late, and I was beat. I really needed to close my eyes. Also? It was cold. The temperature had dipped into the fifties tonight, letting us know that fall was coming.

For the first time since our nighttime visits had begun, I lifted the quilts before I lay down. Two weeks ago that would have seemed crazy, but I knew Lark wouldn't want me to freeze. I put my head on her extra pillow, and straightened out my body.

I'd taken care to leave a nice spread of the mattress between us, but Lark wasn't having it. She wiggled closer to my body until her hip and leg lined up against mine. She rested our clasped hands on her thigh and let out a sigh.

The night seemed to hold its breath for me. I heard the banging of my heart against my ribs, and the soft swish of her breath evening out. Outdoors, a single, determined cricket chirped outside Lark's window.

Closing my eyes, I lay still, trying to take it all in. Lying in a girl's bed was not something I'd *ever* done before last week. Touching people didn't come easily to me. But Lark didn't have the same hang-ups. She often hugged May and Griff and Audrey. When seating was tight at the bar, she'd sit on Griffin's knee as if he were another piece of furniture. At the farmers' market, she could talk to anyone, even people she obviously didn't like very much.

Compared to me, she was socially fearless. Not that I had set the bar very high.

And she'd just ordered me to lie down in her bed. Whatever scared Lark so badly every time she closed her eyes must be horrible.

As I lay there, I became more comfortable. I loved the feeling of her slim hand in mine. Even though I was tired, sleep did not come. I listened to the settling sounds that the old building made, and the increasingly steady sound of Lark's breathing. Tomorrow's farm work would be here before I knew it, and I really ought to sleep. But there was something about this peaceful moment that held me in the present.

There were often times when I could stop to appreciate the beauty of my new life in Vermont. I might set down the rake and stare at the Green Mountains in the distance. Or I'd smell the wood smoke from the autumn's first fire, and inhale the beauty of it all. But usually it was the landscape, or a job well done that I admired. And the satisfaction of knowing that I was free to enjoy my life out from under the angry whims of those who used to rule me.

But tonight held a different kind of beauty. It was rare for me to be truly useful to anyone. Sure, I was a good worker. If you needed a half ton of apples crated, I was your man. But I wasn't close to many people, and nobody counted on me for support.

Probably the very definition of lonely.

Lying close to Lark made me want things that I usually didn't think so much about. My body was rarely touched by anyone other than me. I was a sturdy piece of equipment, like the trucks that I often repaired. My body was good for moving things from one end of the farm to another. But it didn't provide comfort to anyone, let alone love.

Until now.

As I studied the shadows on the ceiling boards, I felt Lark's fingers twitch in my hand, so I squeezed gently. She gave a troubled gasp. I picked up her hand and pressed it between both of mine, rubbing her knuckles. "Hang in there," I whispered. "The night won't last forever."

She relaxed, and I was the reason.

We both drifted off for a while. But I'd been smart to stay, because she had a rough night. She tossed and turned for a while. Then, letting out a big gasp, she thrashed her legs into mine, startling me.

Propping myself up on an elbow, I looked down at her. "Lark, sweetie. Shake it off."

Her eyes popped open. "Shit," she hissed, rolling onto her side to face me.

I found myself staring into her dark eyes, which were wide with fear. "Hey," I whispered. "You're okay."

Lark swallowed hard. "I know."

She didn't, though, and that was the problem. "I used to have bad dreams," I blurted out.

"Really?"

I nodded in the dark. "Had a lot of them after I got kicked off the ranch. Took about a year until they stopped. I'd dream about the beating I got on the day I left." Hell. That was enough sharing.

Lark sighed. "So you're saying I could have another ten months of this."

"No! Not necessarily."

She smiled, and the proximity of her mouth to mine was hard to ignore. I did it, though, by asking her a tough question. "Lark, what happened to you in Guatemala?"

Her face fell. "I got kidnapped."

"Fuck."

Lark gave me a bitter smile. "That's quite the curse word for you."

I smiled back because it was true, and because she'd noticed. I had a weird relationship with cursing. Mine was the mildest language on the farm by a country mile. When a curse was necessary, I usually opted for "dang it," or "shoot." My strongest curse was "fuck," because even after three years I couldn't bring himself to take the Lord's name in vain.

"You're changing the subject," I pointed out.

She wrinkled up her perfect nose, looking one hundred percent awake now. "I don't like to talk about Guatemala."

"I know that, and I'm not usually the kind to pry. But I am curious what keeps you up at night."

She wore her thoughtful face for a moment, and I realized that I'd already memorized all of her expressions. "I'll bet you are. And I guess you deserve to know, since you're the one who wakes up when it happens."

"Nah," I backtracked. "You don't have to tell me. Instead you could tell me why you were living in Guatemala in the first place."

"Ah." She flopped back onto her pillow. "I was working for a nonprofit that educates farmers in developing nations. I was there to teach some local farmers about seed-saving practices and multiculture. That kind of thing. I thought it was the best job ever. I was *so* brave—the kind that turns out to be stupid. People told me to be more careful, but I walked places where you're not supposed to be alone." She met my eyes. "It's not like I had a death wish. But I thought—if we all act scared of each other all the time, we'll all just huddle in our corners. And the world will stay fearful."

I gave her hand a squeeze, silently asking her to go on.

"But a few weeks into my year of living boldly, some men grabbed me off the street of this tiny town and put me into the back of a van. I was screaming, mind you. But everyone sort of vanished when it happened. I spent twenty days in a shed out in the middle of nowhere. There was a bucket to pee in and almost no food." Her voice had begun to shake. "I thought I was going to die out there."

I already regretted asking her to talk about it. And the only comfort I could offer was to rub her hand between both of mine. "Why did they take you?"

"Ransom." Her voice was flat. "Organizations that send people to work in far-flung places all have kidnapping insurance. So there are countries where grabbing stupid girls is a cash crop. But this group—turns out I was their very first target, and they hadn't figured out yet how to be kidnappers. So it took them a long time to reach the negotiator. It's almost funny, right? I couldn't even get kidnapped by the right people."

"It's not funny at all." I lay down beside her again, still holding her hand.

Her eyes got wet, but she went on. "I thought nobody was ever coming for me. So I started working on this young kid. A teenager. I was trying to convince him to just let me go."

Her voice was rough, and I wished I hadn't asked her to relive it. But we'd come this far. "What happened?"

"They found out. And they killed him. In front of me. I don't actually remember every detail. A doctor told me that the mind sometimes protects us by hiding upsetting memories."

I didn't say anything because there wasn't anything to say. So I stroked my thumb over the back of her hand.

"Aren't you glad you asked?" Her voice was bitter.

"I'm so sorry, Lark."

"Well..." Her voice faltered. "I'm sorry I scream at night. I wish I could stop." She rolled sideways to face me. We were nose to nose, staring at each other. She looked a little wild, and fierce. Like she wished she could burn her enemies to the ground. "I'm so sick of being afraid," she whispered.

"You don't have to be anymore." Her hand was still in mine, and I gave it one more squeeze. "If anyone wants to get you, they'll have to go through me."

Her eyes searched me, and I didn't have a clue what they were looking for. Her gaze landed on my mouth, and I felt myself swallow roughly. The moment pulled taut between us, like a rubber band stretched and ready to release its built-up tension.

Kiss her, my heart prodded, and I wanted to obey. But a kiss wasn't what she needed just now. So, acting on some instinct I didn't know I had, I tugged her by the hand until she landed half on my chest. Then I wrapped an arm around her back and just held her instead.

And, as they wrote in Genesis, it was good.

Lark burrowed closer to me. She tucked her nose into my neck and sighed. I had to remind myself to breathe. My heart was wailing against my ribs like a hammer, and goosebumps broke out on my skin from wanting so badly to kiss her. But it wasn't to be. And the way her body relaxed against mine was my reward—a token of my accomplishment.

A few of her demons had fled the room, and that was all that mattered.

We lay there awhile, not saying anything. The stress I'd caused by making her talk was gone now. And I loved the warmth of her curves against my body. I'd never held anyone like this. And soft brush of her breath on my cheek made me realize what I'd been missing all these years.

This.

My mind drifted, until Lark suddenly asked me a question. "What crime did you commit?"

"What?" I was too drunk on happiness to understand the question.

"When you got thrown out of your home in Wyoming? I've been wondering for a week. And you made me talk. So..."

Oh. Well, heck. The girl had a point.

"You don't have to tell me. But I just can't figure out why they'd toss you of all people."

The compliment was indirect, but it lit me up inside. "It's funny, but even after I got caught, I didn't think they'd actually toss me, until the very moment they did."

"Why not?"

"I was a really good worker, kept my head down."

"You? Nah."

I chuckled, and she giggled into my neck. Best feeling ever. I don't know why this didn't feel weird. Maybe it was the fact that it was the middle of the night, but holding her felt like the most natural thing ever. "Okay, they were pretty lucky to have me. I thought they knew that. It's just human nature—everybody thinks the bad things won't happen to them, you know?"

When she spoke, it was in a voice so low I almost couldn't hear. "I do know, as a matter of fact."

That's right, she did. I gave her back a rub, enjoying the sturdy feel of her body under my palm. "Well, so do I. And when my number came up, it had to do with a girl."

"Ah," Lark sighed. "Like Isaac and Leah? You loved her."

"Nope," I said quickly, because it was true. "We were friends, though. Her father died around the same time that mine did. Our mothers remarried to a pair of cousins. Each of these men had five wives by the time I left."

"Yikes," she hissed. "What a household that must have been."

I was used to this idea, but I'd watched enough faces to know that everyone else found the family structure on the compound incredibly weird. I closed my eyes, trying to picture my mothers' house the way it was just before I left. The memory got a little rustier all the time. "Yep. That's a story for another time. Anyway, Chastity was sixteen, and I was nineteen. She..." I'd never told this story, except to Isaac.

Lark lifted her head to look down at me. "She what?"

Good thing she couldn't see me blushing in the dark. "She liked to fool around with me. She'd come into the garage when I was working alone."

"Oh..." Lark said quietly. "Somehow I thought this story was going in a different direction."

"Nope!" I said, then laughed. "Pretty boring story about teenagers getting caught in the back seat of a car."

It had been a stupid risk to take, but I was young and horny. I didn't hear the deacon enter the garage with my father. I was too busy making out, my hand up the girl's skirt. It was the first time I'd dared to touch her. I'd wanted sex so badly that I wouldn't have heard a tornado coming. And a tornado might have been less life-changing.

The car door had suddenly flown open and the shouting began.

"An hour after they caught us, I had deep wounds on my backside from the horsewhip. And then they dumped me by the side of the road."

"Wow," Lark said. "And you said her name was..."

"Chastity," I supplied.

"Oh, Zach."

"I know. The irony," I said, enjoying her smile as much as the feel of her body against mine. "Griffin and the other guys don't know this story, by the way."

"I won't tell," she said quickly. "It really doesn't fit your reputation."

"I know, right?" I smiled into the dark. "They don't get that I have as dirty a mind as anyone else. Just haven't put it to recent use."

She was quiet for a moment. "So they just...threw you out? In spite of your talent with engines and your work ethic."

"That's how it goes. Plenty of other suckers to take my place. One less mouth to feed."

"And do you know what happened to Chastity?"

That was the big question in my life. "Nothing good. They probably married her off to an older man. That's what happens to seventeen-year-old girls there."

"Like how old a man?"

"Forty, fifty. If she was super lucky, she'd get to be somebody's first wife. But that's rare."

"Yikes," Lark said under her breath. "Do you worry about her?"

It was hard to talk about this to anyone, even Lark. "Every day," I admitted. "I feel guilty. Because I got out and she didn't."

Lark made a sleepy noise and relaxed against my body. "Maybe she did get out."

"Maybe," I agreed, just to be nice. But the odds were practically zero. The elders would have married Chastity off right away. And the old man wouldn't have waited to take her to his bed. She might have two kids by now.

I closed my eyes and pictured her face. The girl in my memory was sixteen and smiling. She sang to herself as she hung out our mothers' washing on the line. I'd see her on my way to the garage, and she'd follow me with her eyes.

It was only four years ago, but it might as well have been a different lifetime. I felt about it like I felt about the alternate universes in Griff's sci-fi movies. Nobody could ever go back and forth between those worlds. When you were a member of the compound, you stayed on the compound. And when you left, you could never go back.

Every so often I tried to imagine what it might have been like for me if I'd stayed at Paradise Ranch. At twenty-three, I'd still be toiling for other people, trying to get ahead. It would be another five years or so before they might allow me to marry.

If I was as lucky as that, my wife and I would get a crappy little house of our own—at least until the kids started coming along. I'd try to scratch out a living, always having to jockey for position among the other men.

And the moral code of that place was thorny. To keep in the elders' good graces, I'd have to look the other way whenever they tossed out the next twenty-something boy. If I'd had sons, I'd have to worry whether they'd be thrown out. If I'd had daughters, I'd have to worry that they'd be given to someone who liked to use the switch on his wives.

What a lousy, soul-grinding existence it would have been.

But here's the thing about Paradise Ranch—even if I didn't ever want to go back, it still stung that they'd thrown me away. I felt like the merchandise at the second-hand store where I sometimes bought the T-shirts I wore to work on engines. Everything was a dollar in there because nobody wanted it anymore.

Paradise Ranch was the worst place on earth, and yet I hadn't been good enough to stay.

I closed my eyes and tried to push that awful place out of my mind. I took a deep breath of Vermont air, and rubbed Lark's back again.

She did not stir. And after another long minute of listening, I decided that she'd fallen asleep, right on my chest.

I lay awake a while longer just appreciating the weight of her sleeping form on my body. Then I slept, too.

Lark

It was the first Friday afternoon in September, an hour or so before dinnertime. I'd spent the day picking Zestars in the sunshine before May asked me to come inside and make applesauce with her. We'd just canned twenty quarts, and the house smelled like cinnamon.

Even so, I was full of dread, because my ex-boyfriend was expected any minute.

"You don't have to see him," May fretted. "We could send you into town on an errand, and I could tell him you just weren't feeling up to it. I feel bad because it's my fault he's stopping here."

"No, it's fine," I said quickly. "That will just prolong the inevitable. I'm not afraid of Gilman. I just don't like drama."

"And that is why we are friends," May said, leaning against her mother's ancient butcher block prep table. "What are you going to do if he wants you to move back to Boston with him?"

Ugh. What, indeed? I tried to picture Gilman comforting me when I woke up screaming in his bed, and the image just wouldn't come. He was a good guy, but his help was the analytical variety. He'd probably whip out a spreadsheet and ask me to categorize my symptoms. Then he'd hire a team of specialists to study my sleep cycles.

"I'm not going back to Boston," I said firmly. "Not with Gilman, anyway. And not until you kick me out."

"Well, that's not happening."

"Let's bring a pitcher of cider or iced tea out to the porch," I suggested. "I'll face the ex in the fresh air."

"Great idea. I'll get the drinks ready. You go upstairs and put on one of the sundresses in my closet."

I looked down at my shorts and tank top. "Hmm. I wasn't going to dress up for Gilman. He might get the wrong idea."

"True." May plucked a pitcher off a shelf so high that I'd have needed a cherrypicker to reach it. "But I like to face trouble in a dress and lipstick. Makes me feel more confident."

"You are very wise," I said. "I'll try it." Confidence was in pretty short supply these days.

"There's a sleeveless black polo dress," she called as I headed toward the stairs. "Try that one."

Five minutes later I jogged down the stairs again, but May had left the kitchen. I went out the front door onto the porch, where she was arranging cookies on a plate.

"Oh, yum," I said, grabbing one of Audrey's gingersnaps.

"I brought out enough for everyone. Including those hooligans," she said, pointing. The guys had finished up in the orchard for the day and were playing Frisbee on the lawn. I watched them for a moment, realizing that coming outdoors was the right decision. Everything was made more bearable by watching Zach's golden form lunge for a flying disc.

The men didn't see that May and I had treats. So I picked up one of the two pitchers, put two fingers into my mouth and whistled.

My timing was unfortunate. Zach turned his head just as Griffin launched the Frisbee toward him.

"Look out!" I yelled, but Zach didn't hear me. He was staring in my direction, slack-jawed as the Frisbee clocked him right in the head.

"Ouch!" May said. "That's gonna leave a mark."

Poor Zach. He grabbed his head, and Griff ran toward him to apologize.

"Boys," May muttered.

A minute later they came ambling up to the porch for tea and cookies. "I'm so sorry," I babbled when Zach climbed up onto the porch holding his face.

"It's nothing," he said, his cheeks flaming.

Poor guy. How embarrassing to be nailed with a Frisbee.

"Let me see it, Zach," May demanded. "Only a scratch," she pronounced when he moved his hand. "But it will bruise."

"You'll look like a tough guy," Kyle said, clapping a hand on Zach's shoulder. "Chicks love that."

Zach rolled his eyes.

"Nice dress, Wild Child," Griff said. "Rawwrrr. Zach almost lost his teeth because of it."

"The dress is your sister's," I said. "I didn't pack any dresses for farm work."

"You shoulda," Kyle muttered, causing both Griff and Zach to give him grumpy looks.

"It looks great on you," May said. "Keep it, okay? It shrank in the dryer and isn't long enough on me anymore. Makes me feel like a giraffe."

"You are kind of a giraffe," her brother pointed out.

"And you're an asshole."

That's when I heard tires on the gravel and looked up to see Gilman's beemer rolling up the drive. "Shit," I swore under my breath.

"Who is it?" Kieran asked.

"My ex," I grunted.

"We can make ourselves scarce," Griffin offered, pouring himself a glass of iced tea.

"Not on my account," I said through gritted teeth. "This will be a short visit, I promise."

Griff nodded at Zach. "More Frisbee? I promise not to nail you in the noggin."

"Yeah," Zach said sheepishly. "Let's do it." He grabbed a cookie and followed Griff and the others off the porch.

As they retreated, May and I watched Gilman step out of his shiny car. It looked so out of place here in the land of rusty trucks.

And so did Gilman. I squinted at him, trying to see him with fresh eyes. He looked good, damn him. But he also looked overdressed. His khaki pants were freshly ironed, while dust from the Shipley's driveway had already accumulated on his shiny shoes.

The glint of his fancy Cartier watch was especially jarring. He was…glossier than I remembered. And it made me want to give him a shake. Who could worry about pressed trousers when the world was in such dire shape that people were killing each other on dirt floors in Guatemala? There were apples to be picked, and kidnappers to capture. And he was off to play golf with clients and order two hundred dollar bottles of red wine.

"Ugh," I whispered. "I've never been a chicken. Until lately."

May's voice was low and reassuring. "You're anything but." She jumped down the steps, that traitor, greeting Gilman on the driveway.

They hugged, and I heard his voice for the first time in months. I'd forgotten how clipped and aristocratic he sounded. A year ago, when I was about to embark on my time in Guatemala, he'd said the five words every woman dreads. "*We should see other people.*"

I'd been so angry at the time. Now I didn't give a crap.

Gilman and I had met at a BU alumni event in Boston and started dating. After three months, my lease expired and he asked me to move in. By the time I got the nod to go to Guatemala, we'd lived together for six months. He was a young lawyer for a prestigious firm. He ran half-marathons for fun. I'd been the crazy, spontaneous half of our relationship—the flighty, headstrong girlfriend who worked at an underfunded nonprofit and served oyster shooters at parties.

I thought we were pretty happy. But I'd misjudged Gilman.

He'd explained that he didn't want to wait a year while his girlfriend did an immersion program in Guatemalan poverty. He wanted someone who was available for regular bouts of socializing and sex. At the time, I'd been hurt and angry. My first few days in Guatemala were exhausting, and I spent a couple of evenings wondering whether I'd made the wrong decision.

Now I replayed our last conversation in my mind. "The thing is, I think we might end up together someday," he'd said. "But we're in our twenties, Lark."

I felt a hell of a lot older now.

I'd learned to love Guatemala—right up until the minute I hadn't anymore. And now these last couple of months had been so stressful that I hadn't thought of Gilman at all. I was over it.

So why did I have to deal with him now?

"Hey, you." Gilman's voice was tentative as he climbed the porch steps.

Taking care to school my features, I looked up slowly, as if seeing him for the first time in a year was no big deal. Although it was. His steady brown eyes regarded me in the same serious way they always had.

While we shared a bit of a stare-off, he tucked in his lips in that way he always had when he was thinking hard. The familiarity of it gave me a pang.

But I swallowed my discomfort. "Hey, yourself. How've you been?"

"All right. I'm better now that I know you're safe."

Here comes the awkward part, I thought. "Thanks," I said as mildly as I could manage. He walked over, opening his arms. I let myself be folded into a hug. His wiry runner's body was so familiar that I had to close my eyes.

He kissed my cheek for what seemed like a lengthy moment. "You had me really worried."

"I'm getting that a lot," I replied, pulling back. "Let's sit. I love this porch. Isn't it great?" Time for a change of topic. I'd begun to get a really weird vibe from Gilman. He usually wasn't an emotional guy. But he didn't want to let go of me. He had one hand closed around my forearm, as if I might slip off the porch and escape into the breeze.

Which sounded like a fine plan, actually.

I managed to get free of him by walking over to one of the rocking chairs. On the lawn, the guys were drinking their tea and talking. Except for Zach, who was watching Gilman with an unreadable expression.

My ex took the chair beside mine, and I forced myself to turn to him. My neck flushed with discomfort, hoping we could get this next bit over with soon. What a ridiculous idea it would be to get back together. There was no way to rewind my life to a time when I hadn't been to Guatemala. The old Lark was long gone. The new one couldn't recognize Lark 1.0 at fifty paces.

"There's tea, but I recommend the cider," I told Gilman. "The Shipleys press it fresh every day, and we sell it at the farmers' market. If you weren't driving, I'd ask Griffin to pour you the hard stuff."

He nodded, then took a glass in silence, and I began to feel uncomfortable under the weight of his gaze. "Is there somewhere we can talk?" he asked.

I just blinked at him. "What's wrong with right here?"

His gaze took in the guys on the lawn, and May just beyond the end of the porch, in the little herb garden. "Okay, here's good."

Of course it was.

He took a gulp of cider. "I didn't know what to think when you disappeared. It was a terrible time for me."

"Really?" I flinched. *Not as terrible as it was for me.* I looked into my glass, waiting for his apology. Even if I didn't really want to be half of a couple anymore, I wanted to hear, "I made a mistake." Though only guilt would make him say it. And a relationship based on guilt was surely a bad idea.

I wouldn't be good for him right now. Or for anyone. I was such a perfect wreck. It wouldn't be right for me to go home to Boston, dust off my old life and slip right back into Gilman's arms. Not when I was still too raw to get on with my life. With anyone.

"I'd been thinking about you a lot," Gilman went on. "And then when you disappeared, I thought I was never going to get to say it." His brow furrowed, and his eyes were pained.

Just spit it out, I thought. And then I can let you down easy.

"Lark, the truth is, we were never right for each other. I've met someone, and we're going to get married in the spring."

It took my brain a while to process that statement. Then the anger kicked in. *"What?"* It came out as a yelp. And I was vaguely aware of heads turning in my direction.

"I wanted to tell you in person, before you could see it on Facebook," Gilman went on, his words rushed.

"Facebook," I echoed stupidly.

"We were going to announce it...before," he said, stumbling on the words. "And then...and then you were missing. And I felt so terrible. Like I'd caused it somehow. I know that's stupid, but it really upset me that you were out there somewhere in trouble. And I was supposed to be deciding between the cream-colored invitations and the white ones."

I could only stare at him and wonder when the words that were falling from his mouth would start making more sense.

"So it hasn't been an easy couple of months. I'm just so happy you made it home safely."

Red hot anger rose in my veins. "Let me get this straight. You're happy I'm home, so that you can get married to someone you met in the last four months?"

His eyes shifted away from me. "I met her before then. But we, uh, didn't start dating until after you left."

"Who is it?" I heard myself ask.

"Mandy," he said, his voice cautious.

Mandy. The name was vaguely familiar. "Your...intern? The one with a different flower painted on each fingernail? The one with the pink hairbands? *That's* who you're marrying?"

"Yes. Don't shout at me." A vein pulsed in his jaw.

"Don't shout?" I squeaked. "Were you *cheating* on me?"

"NO!" he yelled. "We weren't together until after I told you we should see other people. I was faithful, except for one little slip-up."

I stood up fast.

"Well, now you can register for crystal and china without wondering whether my funeral would interfere with your engagement party." I turned my back on him. The cider, which had tasted so good a few minutes ago, was now burning a hole in the back of my throat. On autopilot, I moved towards the steps. "Have a nice life," I said over my shoulder as I ran off the porch and across the lawn toward the bunkhouse.

May stood goggle-eyed, a sprig of basil in each hand, while Griff and Zach turned to pin Gilman with twin laser beam death-stares.

Luckily, nobody tried to halt my escape.

* * *

A few hours later, the door to my room opened slowly, and someone bumped and scuffled her way inside. "Jeez, Lark. Can I turn on a light?"

I woke up quickly, sitting up to switch on the bedside lamp. "Sorry, May." I blinked furiously into the sudden light.

May carried a big wooden tray into the room, placed it on the bed and then sat at the foot of the mattress. "Did I really wake you? It's only eight."

I wiped sleep out of my eyes. "Nap attack."

"Oh boy. That's why you missed dinner. But I thought you should eat something. Audrey made her chili. I saved you a portion before the savages could finish it all."

"Thank you, sweetie." I made an effort to sit up straight. I pulled the tray closer and picked up the spoon. May had nested a salad plate over the bowl to keep the chili warm. When I uncovered it, the lovely, spicy scent began to fill the room.

"I even brought toppings," May pointed out. "That's how much I love you."

"Oh man. You're the best." I picked up the saucer of diced avocado and shredded cheese, tipping them into the bowl. I didn't feel like eating, but May had gone to all this trouble. So I spooned up a few beans and put them in my mouth. The male voices in the next room were louder than usual. "What's going on in there?" I asked, hooking a thumb toward the wall behind me.

"Griff and the boys are discussing the renovation he's doing after Audrey leaves."

"Oh." I sighed. I'd forgotten that he was moving into the bunkhouse soon. One more thing for me to worry about—waking up Griff Shipley with my night terrors.

"Do you want to talk about your shitty day?" May asked.

"Well..." I was considering what to say when Zach appeared in the doorway. *Great.* The whole world would be party to my humiliation. I knew I wasn't supposed to care about Gilman's marriage. I'd already decided another relationship with him wasn't in the cards.

For *now*, anyway. That was the sticking point. He'd slammed the door shut. He'd said he wanted to play the field, to be single. And now he was marrying someone else, and letting me know just how unlovable I really was. As if I needed one more reminder.

"He's getting married," I blurted out. There, I said it. I'd ripped that Band-Aid right off.

"What?" May yelped, leaping off the bed. "That *asshole!*"

I put a chunk of chili meat in my mouth and chewed. Audrey made a kick-ass chili, and anyway, there was really nothing more to say on the matter of Gilman.

"Should I have punched him in the kisser?" Zach offered from the doorway.

That made me smile. "It wouldn't take much effort, would it?" The idea of slender Gilman facing off against Zach was comical.

Zach shrugged, a grin tugging at his mouth. "I'm pretty sure you could drop him yourself, Lark. At least now I know it isn't *that* guy haunting your dreams."

"What do you mean?" May asked, swiveling to study me. "Someone's haunting your dreams?"

"Nah," I said quickly, avoiding Zach's suddenly guilty gaze. "But go ahead, May. You know you want to say it. Tell me you never liked him."

My best friend sat down on the bed again. "It's not nice to say 'I told you so.'"

"Today you can say whatever you like." I took another bite. This was good—both the chili and the company. Dissecting my failures with May had always been more fun than dissecting them alone.

May held her arms out, like a martyr on the cross. "Fine. He was too old for you."

"He was twenty-eight!" I laughed.

"But he *seemed* old. He was never interesting enough for you."

"Thanks, Mom."

"I mean, he's cute and everything. But I always thought he was too fastidious. If I put a cup down on your kitchen table, he'd sprint into the room and wash it. He alphabetized your books against your will."

"You're right, May," I deadpanned. "How could I have been so blind?"

But my friend just ignored the sarcasm. "I bet he alphabetized your sock drawer. I bet he got manicures. Wait— was he manscaped?"

"No comment," I said, unwilling to admit that Gilman's fastidiousness was very, very thorough.

"Was the sex good at least?" she asked.

"Oh, my virgin ears," Zach teased, bringing his hands up to cover them.

In spite of my dark mood, I giggled. "The sex was just okay." I sighed. "But he made *excellent* coffee."

Both May and Zach howled with laughter.

"But that's important!" I argued while they doubled over.

"Oh, honey," May said when she could breathe again. "He was so boring! Gilman doesn't even like Asian food, not even sushi! He had the palate of a twelve-year-old. He just didn't *fit* with you, Lark. You're more interesting, by a factor of a million."

"Mmm, Asian food." I sighed. "That's the one problem with rural Vermont. No ethnic food for a fifty-mile radius. Unless there's a new sushi joint you're not telling me about."

"I've never had sushi," Zach volunteered.

"Really?" May squeaked. "You've *never* had it?"

Zach winked at her. "When will you people stop being surprised by the things I haven't done?"

"Good point." She reached out and squeezed my hand. "I hope you'll forgive me for telling Gilman he could stop by."

"Somehow I think he would have managed to make me feel like shit even without your help. But did he *have* to say that we were never right for each other? At least he stopped short of saying that the time we spent together was a total waste of his life."

"Sweetie, you're better off without him."

I brought my knees up to her chest. "True. But I was *already* without him. Now I'm without him *and* offended."

May giggled. "Tell you what—the next time we have a free afternoon, let's drive to Burlington for Japanese food, to celebrate Gilman's stupidity." She nodded at Zach. "You can come, too. We'll order the sushi deluxe, and get you a little life experience."

"For you two? I'll do it," Zach said. "I'll eat raw fish."

I laughed again, trying to picture it. Their silliness was just what I needed. "I'm having déjà vu. The bunkhouse reminds me of college. The close quarters. The way everyone here knows everyone else's business." The lack of privacy was strangely comforting tonight.

"Yep," May confirmed.

"So there's no hiding my embarrassment. It's all just hanging out there. Like underwear on a clothesline."

"Seems that way," Zach said.

I opened my mouth wide and yelled toward the ceiling. "Okay, listen up! My boyfriend never loved me, and he's marrying someone else!"

A barely muffled male voice came from the other side of the bunkroom wall. "Bummer!"

Another one followed with, "Do I get to fuck him up?"

"I'll let you know," I called. "Also, Zach is a sushi virgin!"

"Shocker!" came Griffin's voice, and then someone else laughed.

"And May *isn't* a virgin!" I yodeled.

There came a violent thump on the wall near my head. "Better be joking!" Griffin called.

"*Now* do I get to fuck someone up?" another voice asked.

"Oh, Lark. You are such a troublemaker," May said, flinging herself onto the bed. I held up a hand, and she high-fived it. Zach just grinned at us both, and then swiveled out of the doorway to get ready to go to the Goat.

Part Two: Mid Season

Cortland

Honeycrisp

Haralson

Keepsake

Zach

The Abrahams hosted the Thursday Dinner where we all toasted Audrey's temporary departure. She and Griff sat at the head of the table, practically in each other's laps.

Nobody let Audrey cook that night, insisting that she shouldn't have to lift a finger on her last night in Vermont. Leah made grilled pork with a spicy apple chutney and a potato salad that was lavender because they'd just harvested their purple heirloom potatoes.

My job was to keep Maeve occupied so she wouldn't be underfoot in the kitchen. Even though I didn't know a thing about toddlers, Maeve and I were old friends. She was born in the Abrahams' bedroom the first year I lived in Vermont, so I was one of the first people she ever met.

"Come here," I told her for the hundredth time in an hour as she danced toward the kitchen again. "Your mama is getting the dessert ready, okay?"

"What is it?" Maeve asked, wrinkling up her little nose.

"Baked slugs with a crumb topping. And dandelion ice cream."

"Zaaaach!" she shrieked, and the pitch practically split my head in two. "Icky!"

"Fine," I said, scooping her up to sit on my knee. "You can have the apple cobbler. I'll keep the slugs all for myself."

She scrambled to stand, grabbing my shoulder with one little hand, then bracing a foot perilously close to my balls. I let her scale me like a tree because my childcare game has always been weak. She wrapped one of her stubby little arms around my head, and I peeked out beneath it to see Lark watching me with a soft expression on her face.

I smiled at her because my dignity was already compromised. And looking at Lark always made me want to smile anyway.

Maeve stayed in my lap through dessert and insisted on feeding me. Soon I had drips of ice cream on my shorts. Oh well.

I was so busy trying to wipe up after Little Miss Sticky that I almost missed what was happening at the end of the table.

"I'm gonna miss you, Princess!" Griff said to Audrey.

"Back atcha, Griff," his girlfriend said, throwing an arm around his shoulders.

"This is so you don't forget where you belong while you're yukking it up in Paris." He set something on the table, and I squinted to see what it was—a wooden fruit crate so small that it would fit in the palm of Audrey's hand.

"That's so cute!" she squealed, lifting it. "I love it. It's for…soap?" she guessed.

"Sure," Griff rumbled.

But there wasn't any soap in the little crate. Audrey lifted out a small wad of red tissue paper. She fumbled with that for a moment, finding a tiny satin bag inside.

And then she lifted a sparkling ring out of the bag.

There was a silence at the table as we all registered what Griff had done.

"Omigod," Audrey stuttered. "It's… It's beautiful."

Griff did not get down on one knee, I noticed. That was probably because Audrey was sitting on his knee. "Princess, will you be my wife?"

"Yes!" she shouted. "But you weren't supposed to spend money on a ring! Our budget is a house of cards."

He wrapped his big arms around her middle. "I think I heard a yes in there somewhere."

"You!" Audrey teared up. "Of course I want to get married. I'm just surprised." She looked around the table at all the gaping faces. "Awfully sure of yourself, aren't you, Griff?"

"Only about you," he said quietly, kissing her on the cheekbone. From the look on his face, you might guess there was nobody else in the room. Or in the world.

Audrey turned and dove into his arms, and that's when everyone woke up and cheered.

"What happen?" demanded Maeve in my lap. She'd been quietly finishing my ice cream during the grownup drama.

"Uh..." My throat was oddly tight, and I tried to think what to say. How do you explain something like that to a two-and-a-half-year-old? *Griffin just won the lottery. Someone loves him above all others.*

Leah swooped in and pulled her daughter off my lap. "Griff and Audrey decided to get married," she explained.

Maeve just yawned.

"Say goodnight to Zach," her mother said. "It's past your bedtime."

"No!" But Leah carried her toward the stairs, with Maeve protesting the whole way.

Isaac appeared in the doorway, bearing two bottles of chilled champagne.

"Awfully sure of yourself," Audrey said again, pointing at them.

"You love it," Griff argued, and then they were kissing again.

I looked away, as I always did. Everyone assumes they know why talk of sex makes me uncomfortable. They think it scares me, or I don't know what to do with it. But that's bull. I know exactly what I'd like to do with it.

With *her.*

My traitorous gaze found Lark in her chair, digging a tissue out of her handbag for Ruth, who had happy tears tracking down her face. Lark's cheeks were pink from working outside in the sun all day. Someone handed her a glass of champagne and received a glittering smile as thanks.

"God, I miss champagne," May sighed, dropping herself into Leah's empty chair beside me.

"Me too, sister," Jude agreed. "Well, I'm not really a champagne guy. But once in a while I miss the hell out of my old pal Jack Daniel's."

With champagne bubbles bursting against my tongue, I wondered whether I was a champagne guy. Probably not.

These things were likely decided by fate. That rich guy Lark had been dating probably drank it regularly.

"My brother is *engaged*," May said, testing out the concept. "Thought I'd never see the day."

"Me either," I admitted.

"Those two just kill me," May said. "It gives me hope, you know? Vermont is the forty-ninth most populace state in the union. Not exactly a generous dating pool. Last June Griff was stomping around our place looking blue, and then Audrey showed up out of nowhere."

I remembered it well. I'd put the donut on her flat tire myself.

She nudged me with her knee. "Who are we going to find for you, Zachy?"

Your best friend? "Uh, I don't know if I'm dating material."

"If my brother can find someone to love his grumpy ass, and even Eeyore here is married—" She jerked a thumb toward Jude, who grinned. "—then it's really astonishing that you and I are single."

I, for one, was not astonished. "Many are called, but few are chosen."

Jude quirked an eyebrow. "Is that a *Star Wars* quote?"

"No!" I barked out a laugh. "It's Matthew 22:14."

"No wonder I don't know it," Jude said, unconcerned. He set down his soda glass. "I'd better get home. Sophie's probably back from her coworker's birthday party. Night, guys."

I watched him congratulate the happy couple, thinking about the parable I'd just quoted. A biblical king had invited the whole countryside to his son's wedding. And when the king came in to see the guests, he saw a man who "had not on a wedding garment." The king asked for an explanation of the man's lowly attire, and none was given. So the king had his servants "bind him hand and foot, and take him away, and cast him into outer darkness; there shall be weeping and gnashing of teeth."

When I was a boy, the preacher had explained that the man's disrespect was the cause of his downfall. But I'd always sided with the poor slob who'd shown up underdressed. Even now that I had a good job and friends who were good to me, I was never going to forget that I'd been bound up like the man in the story and tossed off the premises.

Part of me was always waiting for it to happen again.

* * *

When my watch beeped the next morning I opened my eyes to find myself alone in my bunk. Disappointment settled into my chest until I realized that Lark had enjoyed a peaceful night alone in her bed.

That's a good thing, asshole, I reminded myself.

It was Friday, which meant no farmers' market with her either. I got up and headed for the dairy barn, passing Lark's door on quiet feet. I hoped she'd enjoyed many hours of blissful sleep.

This morning May had gotten up even earlier than the cows. She'd driven Audrey to Boston Logan airport for a seven a.m. flight. When Griffin walked into the dairy barn alone, Dylan handed him the shovel. "You're on shit patrol."

His brother grunted. "Should I bother asking why?"

"You're late," Dylan pointed out. "And I assume that's because you spent the night getting epically laid."

"That's not a punishable offense," Griffin muttered. But he took the shovel anyway and started cleaning out the gutters while Dylan and I finished the milking.

Afterward, I helped Griffin carry some of his belongings into the bunkhouse. "Which bed do you want?" I asked him, standing there with a plastic bin of his belongings.

Chuckling to himself, Griffin removed Kyle's made-up mattress from the lower bunk on the left. He set it on the floor for a moment while he swapped the empty mattress from the top bunk into the lower spot. Then he replaced Kyle's mattress and pillows onto the top spot.

"He's going to kick your ass." I chuckled.

"Watch 'im try."

We ate breakfast, which was a somber affair without Audrey. Everyone was used to her cheery smile and the way she flipped omelets and pancakes with the grace and precision of a circus performer.

In spite of the cooler temperature, Lark was wearing the same pair of white shorts which had driven me insane during our first market day together. I stopped sneaking looks at her when she handed me a plate heaped with scrambled eggs and bacon. It was the sort of feast I hadn't enjoyed often enough growing up.

After breakfast, I followed Griff to his house to start work on packing up the kitchen. I heard a car on the gravel drive and looked out Griff and Audrey's window to see Lark pulling up in her little car.

"I brought the bins and boxes that May left for us!" she said, coming through the door with a smile. "Where do you want 'em?"

"You're the best, Wild Child," Griff said. "Can you help pack some stuff up?"

"Of course." Lark opened the refrigerator door, a bin at her feet. "You want these leftovers?" she asked, holding up a plastic container.

"Hell yes, woman," he growled. "That's my lunch. Don't toss anything Audrey cooked. I'm heading into a dry spell, here."

Lark snorted. She moved on to the cabinets next, packing the dishes into boxes while Griff and I disconnected the old refrigerator and carefully eased it from its spot against the wall. He had to remove the front door and its hinges to get the thing outside.

"So now it's demo time?" I asked Griff after we wrestled the old fridge out onto the driveway.

"This wall goes first," he said, laying a hand on the one between the kitchen and the dining room. "I ordered a new cabinet for this spot. It will have a counter top and a couple of bar stools. To open up the place a little."

"That's going to look great," Lark said, coming to peer through the doorway at what would become the view. "It will let in more light. And someday Audrey will be able to keep an eye on the kids while she cooks whatever gourmet feast she's whipping up."

My gaze went toward the front of the house as I pictured that. And when I checked Griff's face, there was a secretive little smile on it. Like maybe he'd thought of that already. I let myself indulge in his fantasy for a second, and liked what I saw—setting up a house for my family.

My family. A small, mythical crew of people who got excited when I came in the front door from work.

Pretty hard to envision, really.

Griff shut off the gas line and we tore out the stove next. "I'll haul these away later," he said after we'd set the stove next to fridge in the driveway. "I need to do some cider pressing before lunch."

"How about I take the hardware off these cabinets?" Lark offered as we got back to the kitchen. "Got a screwdriver?"

"In the basement," Griff said.

"I'll get it for her," I offered, picturing Griff's basement. The place resembled a torture chamber. I didn't know if Lark's nightmares could be cued by basements, but it was better if we never found out.

Griff put his hand on Lark's shoulder. "Thanks for your help, Wild Child." He checked his watch. "Gonna be a long day until Audrey texts me."

"She'll be fine," Lark said. "Flying to Paris is no more dangerous than driving to Boston."

Griff scowled.

"Hey," I offered. "It's not gonna happen like in Castaway. Audrey is not going to crash-land on a desert island just because you got engaged last night."

His face only became grumpier. "Get out of my brain," he grumbled before exiting the house.

When I turned around, Lark was smiling at me. "Okay— how did you know he was thinking about a fifteen-year-old Tom Hanks movie?"

I shrugged. "We watched it a couple of months ago. And I listen to the man quote movies all day long."

"You are adorable," she said.

I liked the sound of that for a few seconds until I realized that she'd said the same thing to a puppy we met at the Hanover market the week before.

Ah, well. I went to the creepy basement to fetch Griff's toolbox, and she was singing to herself by the time I came back.

* * *

Two nights later, I came to consciousness in the dark because I heard her voice. It wasn't singing. Not this time.

"What the fuck is that?" Griffin slurred.

The next shriek woke me up fast. I lurched from the bed and beat a fast path to Lark's room.

"Stop!" she yelled as I opened her door.

"Shh, shh!" I whispered. "Hey, it's okay." I eased the door shut behind me and sat down on the edge of the bed. When I put a hand on her arm, she jerked with surprise. "You're fine," I said in a low voice. "Shh." I pushed the hair out of her face and used the same clucking sound with my tongue as I used with the dairy cows when they got spooked.

It worked, too, which never failed to amaze me. Even though Lark didn't always wake up, she calmed right down when I spoke to her in the night. As her face relaxed and her breathing evened out, I felt a surge of warmth in my chest. Even though I knew I my role was coincidental, *I* comforted her. Not someone else.

The door to her room opened slowly, and I turned my head to see Griff standing there in his sleep pants frowning at me.

For a second, a fear borne of my former life froze me in place as I pictured the scene from Griff's perspective—me hovering over a girl's bed in the dead of night.

"Everything okay here?" he whispered.

I nodded, my mouth dry. My heart hammered against my ribcage.

But Griff only stared at me a moment longer before turning to go. He closed Lark's door gently behind him.

With my pulse still racing, I sat there for a while, worrying. Lark still had trouble sleeping, and now Griff was going to know she was suffering. She hadn't wanted to worry anyone. It embarrassed her.

Lark rolled over in her sleep, muttering something unintelligible, and I reviewed my choices. I could go back to my own bed, which would look less weird to Griff. But she might start yelling again.

And she was holding my hand. I didn't want to take it away.

I pulled back her quilt and slid into the bed. The mattress depressed under my weight, jostling her slightly. She rolled immediately in my direction, one sleepy hand landing on my chest.

"Come here," I whispered.

She did, too, burrowing closer, resting on my arm. I shifted her partway onto my chest. When I turned my head, my nose grazed her sweet-smelling hair.

If there was a heaven, it would be something like this— my arms full of sleeping girl. I thought it would take me a long time to fall back to sleep, but the feel of her chest rising and falling over mine put me right under.

It was light out when I woke up again. Sunday was the only day of the week that my watch alarm did not go off. Since we were going to have so many long hours this fall, Griff had given every guy a morning to sleep in. And Sunday was my day to sleep through the milking.

I always enjoyed my late morning, but this one was the best ever. I came to consciousness slowly. *Warm* was my first reaction. And then I smelled melons. It was the soft scent of Lark's hair. And I felt the warmth of her body, pressed up against mine.

Bliss.

I was in a fine, sleepy haze. I arched my back a bit, stretching. And that's when I became aware of the fact that my erection was basically pressed against Lark's bottom.

Quickly, I pulled my hips back and executed a fast roll onto my stomach. It wasn't my smoothest move. But I lay there wondering how long I'd been holding her like that, while my body betrayed my desire for her.

Lark was silent, so maybe she hadn't noticed. It was hard to imagine how to word my apology, anyway. *Sorry, my sleeping subconscious decided to press my dick against your ass.*

I knew it was a perfectly ordinary physical reaction, but that didn't make it less mortifying. You can't grow up where I did and not feel shame. At Paradise Ranch, a boy would be beaten for asking curious questions about sex. Forget having any.

There was a quote from Deuteronomy which every boy at Paradise Ranch had been made to memorize: If one of your men is unclean because of a nocturnal emission, he is to go outside the camp and stay there.

I remember praying before bedtime not to spill my seed in my sleep, so that I wouldn't be thrown out. Four years had passed since I left that place. But its lessons were still burned in my soul.

While I lay there thinking things over, Lark eventually yawned and stretched. Her eyes opened, then blinked at me. "Hi," she said, looking startled.

"Hi. I suppose you can guess why I'm here."

She reached over to put a hand on my back, and the warmth of her touch seeped through my T-shirt. "I'm not surprised that you're here. I'm only surprised that you're *still* here. So I guess it's Sunday."

My laugh was so sudden that I snorted. *Smooth.* "You're right, it is."

She smiled at me with her eyes closed. Then she snuggled closer, her bare foot finding mine under the covers. "We have a very unusual friendship."

"That's right," I whispered. And I won't lie—the fact that she'd said we were friends made me ridiculously happy.

"What do you do on Sundays after I'm finished snuggling you?" she asked sleepily, her foot sliding against mine.

"Today I'm taking Ruth to church, because Daphne isn't here to go with her."

"Wow." Lark's eyes opened again. "That is so nice of you."

"It's nothing."

"No, it isn't."

Her hand rubbed sweetly up and down my back. I was aroused, but hiding it well. And since there was no danger of anything happening between us, I just relaxed into the sensation. Her gentle touch sent tingles up and down my spine, leaving my skin buzzing everywhere.

"I'm sure Ruth appreciates the company," she said. "And I'll bet you're not a big fan of churches. You must be pretty ticked off at Christianity."

"Nah," I said drowsily. "I don't blame religion for my troubles."

"Really? Because I'm kind of pissed off on your behalf. Anyone who uses the church to justify throwing their own people away is an asshole."

I smiled against the pillow, loving Lark's touch, and the way she sounded all fired up in my defense. "They just got it all wrong. I feel sorry for them." That was true on my better days, anyway. And today was already one of my better days.

"That's big of you. I'm not so sure about religion myself. Maybe I'm a jerk for saying that, seeing as I did some heavy-duty bargaining with God recently."

"I'm glad He listened," I said quietly.

She sighed. "There's a saying—there are no atheists in foxholes. But I've never been a good believer."

"I am," I said simply. "Especially now."

"Why now?"

Because you're so beautiful. "It's hard to explain. I never went to a real school, but they taught me to read the bible, and I know every book. They used to preach about Paradise Ranch being our very own land of milk and honey. But I was a kid, right? And a real literalist. And there was never enough milk to drink, and forget the honey."

"Aw," Lark said, her voice low.

"I heard about all the miracles, and I was bummed to have missed out on all the action. But here's the funny thing—now I live in the most miraculous place in the world. When you and I go to work later, it's to ripe apples practically falling off the trees. There'll be milk in my coffee, and someone offering me seconds and thirds at breakfast. This is the land of milk and maple syrup." I glanced down to find Lark listening to me with a soft expression on her face, and I was never more certain that God's earth was a special place. "Everywhere I look I see miracles," I finished.

She closed her eyes and stretched her arms over her head. "Zach, you're really fucking smart for someone who wasn't allowed to go to school."

"You just caught me on a good day," I said, and she laughed.

Lark

After breakfast I went out to the orchard to pick apples. I'd learned to dress in layers because the September days were still quite warm, but the temperature dropped like a stone at night. I found Griffin in a row of trees that was just for cidermaking. He was inspecting them with a level of care and precision that fascinated me. I watched him test the firmness of an apple with his thumb, and give it a soft tug to see whether it would come off in his hand.

It did.

"We want these to be ripe enough that they're starting to fall off the tree," he said as I approached. "These are ready. Where are the guys and May?"

"May is catching up on her reading," I said. She'd gone back to law school last week. "But I can grab your cousins and Zach."

"In a minute," he said, inspecting another apple. "I just want to know something."

"Mmm?" I asked, picking an apple and giving it a sniff. I loved their sunny, musky scent.

"Do you have bad dreams like that often?"

Shit. I leaned over to put the apple in the bucket, so he wouldn't see my face. "Not that often," I said carefully. Though if he were sleeping in the bunkhouse now, he was going to call me on this lie pretty quickly. Zach ended up in my bed every two or three nights. Why wouldn't the dreams just fucking stop, already?

At least I got more sleep than I had in Boston, and Zach was the reason why. Griff was going to notice that, too.

Why did I have to be so much trouble?

Griff cleared his throat. "Maybe there's a doctor who could help?"

"You think I didn't try that? *Three* shrinks, Griff. My parents called in every specialist they ever knew. But I got sick of people asking me what happened."

115

"And what did happen?" he asked gently.

"I'm not entirely sure," I whispered. "That's what freaks everyone out. The first place their minds go is..." I stopped short of saying it out loud.

"Rape," he finished for me, his big brown eyes deep pools of empathy. Then he wrapped an arm around my shoulders and hugged me.

"Right," I admitted to his chest. "But that didn't happen."

"No?"

I shook my head. "Nobody believes me, though." But I knew my own body. And when I came to after my rescue by the police, it never crossed my mind until Boston doctors began to question me. But the feeling I woke up with wasn't that I'd been raped. It was...*guilt.* Whatever happened, I knew in my bones that I was the cause of it.

"I'm sorry anything happened to you at all," Griff rumbled. "Sure wish I could make it better."

"You are, though," I said, easing back. "I just want to stay here and work and be outside with people who know me."

"All right," he said with a nod of his giant head. "I'm all for you hiding out on my farm, as long as it's not harming you."

"I already think I'm better," I said quickly. "It hasn't been that long, you know? I just need a little more time."

He chewed his lip for a long moment and then nodded at me.

"And, uh, don't mention this to May?" I begged. "Please? I don't want her to worry."

Griff gave me a skeptical look. "You don't want me to worry, but you also want me to lie?"

"Because it's not important," I argued. "And she has her own crap to deal with right now." I still felt like a heel for not saying the right thing when she told me her issues with alcoholism.

"Fine." He sighed. "Now go find those slackers I'm related to and drag 'em over here."

* * *

We all worked like plow horses that week.

Ruth had driven Daphne to college in Connecticut, and Dylan had begun his part-time coursework. May hit the law school books hard. Griff hired day workers to pick apples and help him at the presses because there were fewer hands for all the farm labor now. Meanwhile, he put in extra hours on his renovation, too.

I liked being this busy. My friends all worked so hard, and helping them felt like the best use of my time.

Zach and I did four farmers' markets a week, in four different towns, and each one had a unique flavor. Norwich and Woodstock were the fanciest. Hanover reminded me of a street fair. And Montpelier was typical crunchy Vermont.

It rained, though. For a while it seemed as if wet weather had been ordered up specifically to drench the farmers' markets. This stressed out Zach, not because he minded getting wet, but because our traffic was lower when it rained.

"You can't control the weather," I pointed out after a quiet Hanover market. He had a grim expression as we loaded half our produce back onto the truck.

"I know." He sighed. "I just hope Griff doesn't look at the receipts and wonder what I'm doing wrong."

"I think he'll look at your sopping wet self and come to the right conclusion." And, damn, Zach's torso in a wet T-shirt was a thing of beauty. His abs were cut like the antique washboard hanging in Ruth Shipley's kitchen.

The following Friday afternoon we picked Haralsons under clear skies. It was nice to be out in the sun again, except that I had to listen to Kyle and Griff debate where we'd go drinking tonight.

"The Goat," Griff said again and again.

"Gin Mill," Kyle protested. "What do you care, anyway? You're not going to hook up."

"I don't feel like driving all the way to Alec's bar. Gonna spend enough time driving over there come winter."

"Why?" Kieran asked.

"Eh, a plan I'm working on. Don't mind your pretty head over it."

117

"Let's go to the Gin Mill tonight so you can check everything out," Kyle said.

"Subtle," Griff replied with a sigh.

* * *

Last Friday night I'd begged off the bar outing in order to accompany May to her AA meeting. Afterward, we'd indulged in ice cream and a movie in the Shipley farmhouse. Since the boys had been out at the bar, we put in a chick flick that Ruth watched with us.

But this week May nudged me toward Griff's truck after dinner. "You go out. I'm going to do some homework after my meeting."

"On Friday night?" I whined.

"Yes, for one more year I am exactly this boring. Go have fun."

I was tired, though, and not exactly in the mood for the noise of a bar. But I went anyway, just to prove to myself that I could hack it.

Griffin had won the argument about where to go, so we were bound for the Goat. Once again I rode in the back of Griff's truck between Zach and Kyle. When we got to the smaller bar, I heard loud music thumping from inside, and my stomach tightened immediately. Gritting my teeth, I let myself be led inside. But there weren't any free tables, damn it.

I shouldn't have come.

As we ordered drinks, I could feel Zach giving me the side-eye. "You okay?"

"Sure." I moved a little closer to him. If I couldn't lean up against the wall and regain my composure, he was the next best thing.

Our drinks were served by a freckle-faced kid with a barbell in his eyebrow. I sipped my beer and scanned the place for a calm place to sit or stand. It didn't help that there was a shrieky pop tune on the stereo. "My ears are bleeding," I muttered.

"It's hurtin' me, too," Griff said. "Zara would never have tolerated this shit on her shift."

A broad hand landed on my shoulder, steering me toward Griff. "Wait here a sec," Zach said. Then he disappeared.

Two minutes later he returned. And a minute after that I heard the opening strains of "Snow" by the Red Hot Chili Peppers over the speakers.

"Oh, yeah," Griff said. "That's a big improvement."

I tipped my head back, and it bumped into Zach's comfortable shoulder. "Did you do this?"

He shrugged, taking a sip of his beer. "Someone once told me that nothing bad ever happens when the Chili Peppers are playing."

The corners of Griff's mouth twitched. "That's sounds like something Wild Child would say."

"Because it's true! Hey, look..." I pointed at a high table across the room where three women were getting up.

"On it," Zach said, sliding away from me again. He stood guard over the table until the women were clear of it. Each of them in turn gave him a very appreciative glance as they passed by.

Griff and I wove through the crowd, and I sat down on one of the stools beside Zach. "We need a fifth seat," I pointed out, but Griff shook his head.

"I'm going upstairs to say hello to Zara and baby Nicole. Kieran and Crash-n-burn can have the seats. I'll be back in an hour. Or less if Zara is wiped."

"Doesn't her baby sleep?" I asked.

"Sometimes," Griff said with a smile. "At her whim, you know? She's a charismatic little redhead. Keeps Zara on her toes." He left, and I settled in for some people watching as my favorite band played over the sound system.

Feeling more comfortable, I suggested a game of poker.

"You'll probably take my money," Kyle grumbled. "I'm told my poker face sucks."

"We'll play for pennies," I suggested, pulling a deck of cards out of my bag. "And we'll work on your poker face."

"I don't always remember the hierarchy of the card combinations," Zach admitted.

"That's okay," I said, shuffling. "Consider it practice."

We played our way through a pitcher of beer. Kieran won, but only on silly luck. As it happened, Zach had a hell of a poker face.

"Uh-oh, Zach," Kieran said with a chuckle. "Look who just came in."

"Great," Zach muttered, picking up his beer.

"What's the matter?" I asked, turning toward the door. All I saw was two young women—barely college age. They were heavily made up in that way that a teenager sometimes does when she's still figuring herself out. And they were both smiling a little too hard, too.

It was painful to watch.

Kieran's eyes twinkled as he took a pull of his beer. "The curly-haired one has a thing for Zach. And when she gets drunk, she tries to climb him like a ladder."

Kyle laughed. "If only. She tries to mount him like a bull on a heifer. I'd let her, if it was me."

Kieran shook his head. "Even *you* wouldn't go there. Too young, too drunk…"

"Maybe next year." Kyle chuckled. "If she doesn't have her way with Zach first. Now it's time to stand back and watch the show."

I looked up at Zach's red-faced scowl. And then I swung my gaze back to the girls, who were indeed glassy-eyed and wobbly. "Damn, did they drive here like that?" I wondered aloud.

"Nah. One of them lives a quarter mile up the road," Kieran said. "They get bombed at home and then walk here. Griffin had to escort them back home once last spring. After he peeled one off Zach."

"Now you've been spotted!" Kyle snickered. "The approach is my favorite part."

"Why me," Zach muttered into his beer.

"Because you give off that nice-guy vibe," Kyle said cheerfully. "You're approachable. Like a friendly puppy."

Zach was giving off an embarrassed vibe, if any. "You want me to scare her off?" I volunteered.

"How?"

"How?" I scoffed, stepping in front of him. "Put your arms around me."

"Plot twist!" Kyle said gleefully. "This is going to be good."

"Hurry." I took his beer out of his hand and set it on the table. Then I reached up and put my arms around Zach's neck. But he only stood there, wooden. "You are a terrible actor," I hissed, nudging his arm with my elbow. "Play along."

Slowly, his arms closed behind me, coming to rest on my waist. I stood up on tiptoe and slowly dragged my nose against his. "How am I doing?" I stage-whispered.

Kieran answered, "The heat-seeking missile is still locked on the target. ETA, five seconds. Watch your six, Lark."

That made me smile.

"Hi, Zach!" a high, wavering voice called out. "Do I get a hug, too?"

Seriously? I turned my chin in the girl's direction. "He's busy," I snapped. I heard Kyle and Kieran snort with amusement. But the girl did not walk away. This poor chickie could not take a hint.

Desperate measures were called for.

I took Zach's handsome face into both my hands, and tugged him downward until his smooth lips brushed mine. Zach's body went absolutely still.

In for a penny, in for a pound.

Hesitating only for a second, I leaned in. Tilting my head to get the angle just right, I softly joined our mouths. He made a soft, bitten-off sound, and I felt it in the center of my chest.

His arms slowly tightened around me as our lips came together. And that's when my body forgot that this kiss was supposed to be a diversion. Zach's mouth firmed to mine, and I felt my knees go a little squishy. God, he was just so freaking hot, and it had been a long time since anyone kissed me.

Seriously, I should buy the tipsy little jailbait a present for handing me this opportunity to lay a good one on Zach.

He leaned into the kiss, and the moment stretched and shimmered so unexpectedly. The urge to taste him was strong, but I wasn't going there. With great reluctance, I slid my lips to the corner of his mouth and teased him with butterfly kisses instead.

"Coast is clear!" Kyle chuckled.

At that, Zach released me, moving backward as quickly as if he'd been tagged with a Taser. I was left with cool air and unexpected disappointment. It sure was good while it lasted. Zach stood there looking startled. He put his fingertips up to his lips, and then quickly dropped them.

I turned around and scanned the bar. Zach's tipsy pursuer was in the opposite corner now, choosing a new mark. "Mission accomplished?" I asked.

"Looks like it," Kyle said, flicking me gently on the head. "You know what? I think I see someone coming to bug me, too. Can you take care of it, Lark?" He held out his hands to me.

I opened my mouth to tease Kyle, but then lost my train of thought, because Zach was giving him a death glare. Zach, who was ornery to no one, was looking at Kyle as if he'd like to kill him.

Weird.

"Well, Kyle," I said. "If a girl comes over to attack you, I'm going with a different strategy this time."

"Yeah?" He drained his beer.

"Just for variety, I'm going to hook up with *her* instead."

"*Awesome*," Kyle said. "I can watch, right?"

I had to laugh, because I should have known he'd say that.

* * *

Surprising everyone, maybe including himself, Kyle didn't ride home with us in the truck. He begged off to hook up with a college girl he met while drinking his third beer.

"How are you going to get home?" Griff asked him.

"Who fucking cares?" Kyle argued.

"Fair enough." He leaned closer to Kyle. "There's a box of condoms in the glove box of my truck."

"I'm all set," Kyle said before clapping Griff on the shoulder and heading out.

As a reflex, I checked Zach's face to see what he thought of this amusing development. But his expression was locked down tight. He looked into the dregs of his beer as if the answers to all life's questions were written at the bottom of the glass.

"Shall we head out?" Griff wondered. "Anyone object?"

At that, Zach drained his beer and set the empty glass on the table. "Let's go," he said, and then left the bar so fast I practically saw a contrail.

Uh-oh. Zach hadn't said much at all since I'd kissed him. Now it occurred to me to wonder if I'd screwed up. Sometimes I forgot that not everyone liked to misbehave. I'd hate to think my antics made him uncomfortable.

"Shotgun!" Kieran called as the rest of us headed out.

But Zach was already in the passenger's seat.

"I called it," Kieran argued.

"Too bad," Zach mumbled.

The ride home was quiet, and I worried some more. Zach had been so generous to me these past few weeks. It killed me to think that I'd screwed up our friendship.

"Hell," Griff said as we pulled up the drive. "Did Dylan leave a light on in the dairy barn? Or maybe the timer is on the fritz again."

"I'll check it," Zach murmured from the front seat.

"Thanks, man." Griff stepped on the brakes, bringing the truck to a halt. Zach hopped out and shut his door. Then Griff drove the rest of the way up the drive and parked beside the farmhouse. "I'm gonna say goodnight to Dylan and Mom. Anyone need anything from the house?"

"I'll go with you," Kieran said. "Feel like raiding the cookie jar."

That left only me. I took a few steps toward the bunkhouse. But then I reversed course, crossing the dark lawn toward the dairy barn, where the light was still on.

The moon was nearly full, which made it fairly easy to navigate across the grass. I'd gotten braver since coming to the farm last month. I could cross between the buildings at night without feeling panicky and unmoored. See? Even if progress was slow, I was behaving a little less like a head case.

"Zach?" I called when I reached the open door to the barn.

"Right here," said a gruff voice just as the overhead lights went out, leaving only dim lighting near the ceiling.

I watched the darkened figure of Zach walk toward me, patting the rump of a Jersey cow or two on his way. "Something wrong?" he asked, not quite meeting my eyes.

"Well..." I leaned against the door frame, wondering what to say. Was I overreacting? "I think I screwed up tonight. If that kiss made you uncomfortable, then I'm really sorry. I'll never do it again. It was overstepping. Maybe I offended you."

"Offended me," he echoed. When he finally lifted his chin, the heat in his expression was not what I'd expected.

"Y-yeah," I stammered.

Zach stepped into my personal space so quickly I didn't have any time to react. My backside collided with barn wood at the same moment his hand cupped my cheek. In the nanosecond before he kissed me, I took a fast breath and inhaled the scent of hay and clean flannel. Then his hungry mouth took mine.

Oh.

Oh, wow.

My senses were overwhelmed with all things Zach—his sunshine scent and the rough pad of his thumb on my cheek. And his taste, which was like beer and hunger. His kiss was impatient with me. His lips caressed mine, demanding to be tasted. My shock abated all at once, and I sagged against the wall, tilting my face toward his, looking for more.

And he provided. As his big hands encircled my waist, he touched my lip with his tongue. I opened for him faster than a hungry baby bird. The first taste of his hunger was magic, setting off an electrical charge throughout my body.

I made a funny little noise of surprise as every one of my dormant nerve endings woke up at once and saluted him. My hands found their way onto his chest, my fingers gripping his flannel shirt. His tongue slid against mine. And when he made a low sound of approval, I felt it everywhere.

"Zach?" someone called. The voice was Griff's.

We broke apart on a gasp, our gazes locking.

"Everything okay?" Griff called out from the opposite end of the darkened barn.

After a beat, Zach yelled "Fine!" in a voice too rough to sound like his own.

"Was it the timer again?"

Zach opened his mouth and then closed it again. He took a half step back from me. I would have had to be blind to miss how conflicted he was in that moment. And while there was no earthly reason why Griff needed to discuss the cows' nightlights at midnight on a Friday, I didn't want to be the reason he blew off his boss.

So I made a quick decision and removed myself from the situation. Slipping out from the space between Zach and the barn door, I headed across the moonlit lawn alone. I felt Zach's eyes on me, but I hurried on my way.

Zach

As one of the Shipleys might say, *holy shit.*

I stumbled through a conversation about barn lighting with Griff before finally making my excuses and heading back to the bunkhouse.

Lark's door was closed, with no strip of light beneath it. But that was for the best. I needed a little time for my head to clear, so I could figure out what the hell had happened tonight.

Kissing Lark was not something I'd ever meant to do. Griff had said very clearly that *the girl is off limits.* But, hey—she started it. The kiss at the bar had taken both of us by surprise. The way her hands gripped me as the kiss went on? That was not my imagination. Neither was the flush on her face afterward.

She felt it. But still—that didn't justify my audacity. I could have left it alone.

Stewing over it, I brushed my teeth on autopilot and got into bed. Griff came in, joking with Kieran. They wondered where Kyle might be staying tonight.

"I hope that girl was not a serial killer," Kieran mused.

"Wouldn't it be funny if he read the situation wrong?" Griff asked. "Maybe she only wanted to try to convert him to another religion."

"Or sell him a time-share property in Boca."

The two of them broke up laughing.

I smiled to myself as the room went dark. This was typical bunkhouse behavior, juiced up with Friday night's usual combination of beer and sexual frustration. This was my version of home. It would look strange to someone else, but it was normal to me.

As I began to get drowsy, I said a silent prayer in the hopes that Lark would stay asleep tonight. Getting into her bed right now would be a horrible idea. If she touched me, I'd probably burst into flames.

Griff began to snore first, and it wasn't long until I followed him.

* * *

On Saturday I woke up in my own bed. Shutting off my watch alarm, I hauled myself into a vertical position, got dressed and went out to the barn where Dylan and I began the milking in sleepy silence.

It was Kieran's day to sleep in, but twenty minutes into morning chores he showed up anyway. "What are you doing here?" I asked him as I hooked up a Jersey named Becky to the milking machine.

"Covering my brother," he muttered. "Lord knows when he'll turn up." Kieran even took the shovel and began to clean out the gutter.

That was big of him. Though I'd known the Shipleys for years now, I was still astonished at their generosity toward one another. No wonder I was still dragging my feet on coming up with Plan B. There wasn't anywhere I wanted to be other than here.

"Kyle really ought to be on shit patrol today," Dylan pointed out.

"You can punish him tomorrow," I suggested.

"Hey, Chewie?" Griff called to me from outside the barn. "Got a second?"

"Sure." I followed him out into the morning sunlight. Music could be heard coming from the farmhouse kitchen, and I wondered if Lark was in there yet, making breakfast with Ruth and May.

Just the thought of her made my stomach flip over. In an hour we'd be headed for the Norwich market together. The car ride could be interesting.

"I got a question for you," Griff said, startling me out of my thoughts. "What's up with Lark?"

"Uh…" The question set off alarm bells in my head. I hadn't meant to kiss Lark. I was fighting a powerful urge to lie about my feelings for her.

"Is she all right, do you think?" Griff asked while I panicked.

127

It took me a moment to realize that his query had nothing to do with a kiss in the barn. "You mean...because she has bad dreams?"

He nodded. "Looks like PTSD, doesn't it? Just like Zara's other brother—Damien. Did you know he did two tours in Afghanistan?"

I nodded. Damien turned up at the Gin Mill sometimes, and I'd seen his dog tags.

"The guy didn't sleep right for two years after he came home. Told me he still sleepwalks sometimes. He woke up once on his couch, holding a kitchen knife."

Yikes. "I can't see Lark going all *Hurt Locker* on us."

Griffin snorted. "I'm not *afraid* of her, Zach. I just don't want to be the guy who brushes aside her issues because I wasn't paying attention."

"It's not like that!"

Griff's bushy eyebrows shot upward even as the irritation in my voice echoed between us. Heck, I don't think I'd ever argued with Griff over anything before. Not even pizza toppings. "How is it like, then?" he asked quietly.

I took a deep breath and tried to be calm. If Griff made a big deal about Lark's problems, it would only piss her off. *It also might send her away*, my subconscious prodded. The truth was that I liked being the one helping her. The only one.

Was I screwing things up just so I could be the one she hugged when she was scared?

"What if we gave her just a little more time to feel better?" I suggested. "It hasn't been very long since she got back. She came to Vermont to get out of her parents' way because they were too worried to give her some space."

Griff rubbed his beard. "I hear you. And I asked her about it myself, and she said she was doing okay. But then she looked jumpy at the bar last night. Does she do okay at the market?"

"Yeah," I said quickly. "She does all right most of the time." *Unless it's really hot or crowded. Or loud.*

"What, uh..." Griff shifted his weight. "Did she tell you much about what happened in Guatemala?"

The hair stood up on the back of my neck, as it did every time I wondered the same thing. "She told me she watched somebody die."

Griff flinched. "That all?"

"Isn't that enough?" I asked, trying to keep the irritation out of my voice.

"Sure," Griff said slowly. "I just worry there's more to the story, and maybe I'm sending her off to do work that's hard on her."

"I don't think you are. If you really want to be sure, offer to send someone else to Norwich today. See what she says."

"All right. She seems to trust you." He gave my shoulder a squeeze. "But let me know if there are any problems."

"Okay," I grunted.

"Quite the kiss she gave you last night."

My gut tightened. "That was just a joke." *It was supposed to be, anyway.*

Griff chuckled. "The best jokes have a basis in the truth. Looked pretty realistic if you ask me."

I felt my neck begin to heat. "Are we gonna load the truck for Norwich or stand here yapping all morning?"

His smile only grew. "Aw, I think you like her. Make sure you let my sister Daphne down easy."

"Griff! Jesus."

My boss's grin only widened. "You took the lord's name in vain? Looks like I hit a nerve."

And now I was *done* with this confusing conversation. "Gotta load the truck," I muttered. Then I turned my back and stomped away from Griff Shipley for the first time in my life, my pulse hammering in my throat. As a hurried toward the cider house, I expected him to call out and stop me.

He didn't, though.

Lark

I was in the farmhouse kitchen when the flatbed truck pulled up outside the kitchen. In a hurry, I tucked two of Ruth's pumpkin muffins into a plastic container and slapped the lids onto two travel mugs of coffee.

"Have a good one," May said from the griddle, where she was scrambling eggs. "Looks like good weather for a change."

"Thanks, babe! Study hard so we can watch a movie tonight."

"I will."

I took the muffins and coffee outside, balancing the cups on the container as I eased the back door shut.

"Let me help you with that," Zach muttered, whisking the cups away so that I was no longer performing a risky balancing act.

"Thanks," I said, walking around the truck to get into the passenger's seat. As I climbed up and slammed the door, I wondered how things would be between us this morning. Awkward, potentially.

I'd woken up this morning remembering our moment in the barn. And at the bar. I didn't know I was so easy to impress. But two kisses had me walking around trying to keep the dreamy look off my face.

Though it wasn't clear there'd be more of those kisses in my future. And now we had five hundred pounds of apples to sell in four hours. I was fastening my seatbelt when I spotted Griff waving at us. "Hey, the boss is flagging you down," I said just as Zach let his foot off the brake.

The truck stopped again and I rolled down my window as Griff jogged up. "Hey, Lark. You feel like selling apples again today? Because if you'd rather kick around here instead, I could send Dylan for a change."

I looked into Griff's wide brown eyes and tried to figure out why he was asking me that. "Are you trying to keep me away from the cider donuts in Norwich?"

"Not at all, Wild Child."

"Good. Because I'll fight you for 'em."

Griff chuckled. Then he leaned in to ask Zach a question, too. "You got the sweet cider I put in the lower cooler?"

"Of course," Zach said stiffly.

Griff's smile slid off. "Everything okay?"

Zach's hands tightened on the steering wheel. "Yeah. I'm good."

"Okay, then." Griff took off his baseball cap and waved us on. "Go forth and sell the season's first Honeycrisps."

Checking Zach's face as we began to roll down the driveway, I saw tension there. "Everything okay?" I hazarded.

"Yep," he said, and it wasn't entirely convincing. He was stressed out about something, and I wasn't vain enough to assume it was me.

"I brought coffee and muffins."

"Awesome." His eyes didn't leave the road, and he gave his head a little shake. "I could really use the coffee this morning."

As soon as we turned onto the road, I handed him the travel cup, and he took a deep drink of it. "Thank you for this manna from heaven."

"Didn't sleep well? Because I slept great." Maybe that was laying it on a little thick, but if he had any regrets about our kiss in the barn, I wanted him to know that everything was okay on my end. I valued his friendship far too much to let things get weird.

But, hey, if he wanted to try it again, I'd probably hurl myself into his arms. It had been a long time since anyone made me feel such hunger and optimism all rolled together.

"I'm glad you slept through the night," he said softly. "I want that for you."

I waited, but he didn't say anything else. So I picked up my iPod and put on a playlist. Eddie Vedder began to sing "Black," and I relaxed against the headrest. When the Chili Peppers inevitably came on, I smiled at the ceiling of the Shipley truck. "Thank you for requesting that music last night when I was feeling a little edgy. That was really nice of you."

"No problem."

More silence.

Hmm.

I watched the Vermont countryside roll by. There was corn still standing in the fields, unharvested. And fat rolls of hay in stacks, with white plastic covering them for winter. They looked like giant balls of fresh mozzarella cheese, making me wish for a giant tomato and a wheelbarrow full of balsamic vinegar...

The radio played on, and even a tense Zach was easier company than most anyone else. I always felt relaxed with him, because he already knew I was a wreck. I didn't have to pretend. And he seemed to like me anyway.

He liked me a little more than he wished he did, I was pretty sure.

I opened the container of muffins and broke one carefully into quarters. It was still warm, filling the cab with the comfortable scent of pumpkin and nutmeg. "Open sesame," I said, reaching over toward his side of the seat with a chunk of muffin. I raised it toward his mouth.

He opened up and I fed him the bite. Then he grabbed my hand and kissed the palm. It was just a quick gesture. But somehow there was more sweetness in it than should have been possible. My skin prickled with awareness where he'd touched me. And when I dropped my hand back into my lap, I found myself inspecting it, as if the explanation for the sudden change in the air between us might be written there.

Chemistry was something I hadn't felt in a long time. It was even nicer than I remembered.

* * *

For once we were going to have stunning market weather. Not only was the sun out, but the temperature climbed to a comfortable temperature and then kept right on rising. By noon it felt more like July than September. People lingered over their purchases and chatted up their neighbors, and I had to shed my sweatshirt even though we were in the shade.

I didn't miss Zach's appreciative glance at my tank top. Luckily we were too busy to talk or even think too much about our extracurricular activities last night.

In the center of the market square a little acoustic band was playing. I didn't have a direct line of sight, but strains of a banjo and a fiddle punctuated all my transactions.

I was feeling quite relaxed for nearly the whole time until Leah popped by to ask Zach a question, "You have Maeve, right?"

Zach's hands froze on the half-gallons of cider he'd pulled from the ice bin. "I haven't seen her all morning."

"Oh," Leah whispered. She turned around fast, her eyes scanning. And Zach practically vaulted out of our booth to help her look.

"Maeve?" Leah called, her voice wavering. "Where'd you go, sweetie?"

Zach cupped his hands and called her name. Then he walked a couple of yards and did it again.

I had a customer to ring up, but my attention was shattered. I put her bag of apples on the scale and weighed it. But it took me three tries to multiply the weight by the price and charge the customer the right amount. My fingers were dumb on the calculator buttons until the customer finally just blurted out the correct amount.

"I'm so sorry," I mumbled, making change for a ten. I didn't hear the response, though, because my pulse was pounding in my ears. And my eyes kept leaving my work to search the crowd for a little girl with chubby arms in an Apostate Farm T-shirt.

"Maeve!" Zach's voice called from somewhere beyond my line of vision. It was echoed by Leah's.

I shivered, even though there was sweat running down my back now. A prickly hot wave of fear consumed me.

"Maeve!" the voices called again, and I held my breath, straining to hear a little voice answer.

But it didn't.

Another customer stepped up to the scales and set her apples down, but now I couldn't seem to focus my eyes on the readout on the scale. The edges of my vision bled yellow, and the soundtrack of the market seemed distant.

"Are you okay?" someone asked from far away. "Miss? Maybe you oughta sit down?"

That sounded like a great idea. I grabbed the edge of the table with both hands and sort of eased myself downward. My ass hit the ground, and then everything went black.

* * *

"I think she's waking up."

When I next opened my eyes, four faces peered down at me. One of them belonged to Linda, the elderly woman who sold hand-dyed yarns at the booth beside ours. She was waving an old paper fan over my face. "Give 'er some room. Awfully hot today!"

The other three faces belonged to Zach, Leah and Maeve, who were all crouching over me.

I closed my eyes and cursed.

"That a bad word!" Maeve chirped.

"Sorry," I mumbled, fumbling to sit up.

"Don't rush," Linda fussed, her surprisingly strong hand landing at my shoulder. "Or you'll just be plunking right down again. Went down like a sack of potatoes, you did."

But I didn't want to lie there on the grass with people staring at me. So I grabbed the edge of the table and prepared to haul myself up.

Zach wasn't having it. He leaned down and grabbed me off the lawn, one hand under my knees, the other at my lower back. Then I was airborne and headed out the back of our stall.

Grumpy now, I wanted to struggle, but that sounded tiring. My limbs still felt heavy, so I settled for giving Zach a stern look.

But it backfired when he gave me a sterner one. "Not a fan of you passing out like that."

"It's hot," I said in my defense.

He set me down on the back of the truck. "Stay here while I get you some water."

Water sounded good, damn it. So I did what I was told. "Who's selling apples?" I asked when he returned, twisting the top off a fresh bottle.

"Leah and Maeve. Drink this. All of it." The hottest young farmhand in Vermont wore a stony look on his perfect face, suggesting I shouldn't even try to argue.

I took a deep drink and began to feel more like myself. "Where was she, anyway?" I tried to ask the question casually, but when I looked into Zach's stormy eyes I knew I wasn't fooling him. It wasn't the heat that made me lose my shit a few minutes ago.

Today's score: Fear 1, Lark 0.

"Under the table at the flower-sellers', looking at their new kitty." He smiled for the first time since my little incident, and it changed his face back into a more recognizable landscape. "I'm like, 'Maeve, we've been looking everywhere!' And she says, 'Look, Zacky, kitty's name is Cocoa!'"

I laughed, and it made my head throb. Unconsciously, I lifted a hand to the back of my skull where a goose egg was forming. Zach's smile slipped away. "Is it bad? I didn't see you go down."

"No," I said quickly, though my answer would have been the same no matter what. "Can we keep this little incident to ourselves?"

He hesitated. "Griff is worried about you."

"And that's exactly why I asked."

"Well..." Zach rubbed the golden whiskers on his chin. "All right. If you insist. I'm not very good at saying no to you."

Two or three silly, flirty responses flew to mind, and yet I bit every one of them back. "Thank you," I said instead. "Would you go sell some apples now? I feel like a heel for causing drama."

He measured me with big, blue eyes, checking one more time for any lingering problems. "All right. There's only fifteen minutes before we close down, though."

"Still."

We stared at each other for one long beat. Then he took a step closer and I grabbed him into a hug. A tight one. He was so warm and steady against me that I inhaled like someone surfacing again after being underwater for too long. He kissed my hair and sighed. "Fifteen more minutes."

"I lean on you too much," I whispered. While leaning on him.

"Too much for what?" He gave me one more squeeze and then walked away.

* * *

For once I didn't even try to do my share while Zach loaded the truck. I counted the cash box he brought me, and then I waited with it on the passenger's seat. I drank a lot of water and tried to forget how shaky I'd felt before.

At last we were rolling toward home. I put on the Chili Peppers, of course. I needed their positive mojo to get the darkness out of my head.

"You want to tell me what happened back there?" Zach asked when we were on the highway.

"It was hot."

He gave me a pointed side-eye before returning his gaze to the road.

"I freaked out a little."

"Because we couldn't find Maeve?"

"Yeah. It was like..." I scrambled for words to define something I try never to think about. "A trigger, I guess." The shadows were always right there, waiting in the wings of my consciousness. A pair of hands coming out of nowhere. The scream I'd managed to let out. But then nobody came.

"I'm sorry," he said quietly.

"Please don't bother the Shipleys about it," I begged. I hadn't bailed on my own family only to trouble someone else's.

"I told you I wouldn't. But I sure hope it doesn't happen again."

You and me both. "You know, Griff was always the one bailing May and I out in college," I admitted. "He's the one we turned to when things went wrong."

"Yeah?" He was quiet for a second. "Did you ever date him?"

"No way!" What a crazy idea. "I'm not attracted to Griff, but I loved all the Shipleys as soon as I met them. I'm an only child, and I have always envied May her big family. And Griff was still at BU when we were freshmen. We used to call him up all the time those first two years. If we were too drunk to drive, we called Griffin instead of a cab. When we ran out of gas, or got a flat, we called him."

"Sounds like a pretty sweet deal."

"It was. I liked the way he was always there for us, but without judgment, you know?"

"He never gave you any crap for getting stranded without gas? *That* doesn't sound like Griffin."

"Oh sure! He gave us hell all the time. 'How could you need a jump right in the middle of Monday night football? Now who owes me a batch of cookies?' But there was no real guilt attached to it, there weren't any speeches about how we let him down. My parents always take my antics personally."

"That's harsh. Except at least you know they cared."

And that's when I realized what a spoiled brat I sounded like. Zach didn't have two independently wealthy parents sitting in a Boston home, praying for his continued survival. So what if my parents' overbearing nature had fed my antics as a teenager? At the end of the night, no matter how many times I'd snuck out of my bedroom window to break curfew, I'd always known they were there, hoping for my return.

"Anyway. Griff has always been good to me. But I don't want to be his problem this fall."

He reached a hand over and squeezed my forearm. "Who's problem do you want to be, then?"

Right. "I seem to be yours, I guess. I'm sorry."

His hand plucked mine off the seat and gave it a squeeze. "You can be my problem any time."

I interlaced my fingers with his, feeling a little guilty about the rush of love I felt for Zach. He was bright and shiny and flawless. And I wasn't any of those things.

"So how about this weather?" Zach said, lowering his window as far as it would go. "I just don't understand how anyone could doubt global warming is real."

"I know, right? But they'll believe soon, when more coffee plants die off in Central America. The arabica plant doesn't do as well in higher temperatures."

"No lie? Then we're doomed, Lark. The Shipley farm runs on coffee."

"I think even the most cynical politicians will come around when their access to coffee is thwarted. And hops aren't growing so well in Washington State lately. So beer could be next."

"You are just full of bad news."

Why yes, I was.

"I know something that could cheer us up. And cool us down."

"Then let's hear it. Is it ice cream?"

"No. It's a surprise. Just wait and see."

Zach

When I passed the Shipleys' long driveway and kept going, Lark gave me the side-eye. But the turnoff I needed was just a half-mile further away, past the bungalow, but on the opposite side of the road. I eased the truck into the overgrown weeds by the tree line and parked her.

"We're here," I said. "Hop out and I'll grab the towels."

"Towels? Are we going to swim?"

"Or wade. Splash around. Just cool down a little."

"Where?"

"You'll see in sixty seconds."

Lark removed her phone from her pocket before hopping out of the truck, while I searched the crate of extra supplies that I always drove around with on market days. There were two towels, one decent, one tattered.

Good enough.

"It's right through that break in the trees," I said, pointing. And we could hear the rushing water of the creek even before we saw it.

"Wow!" Lark said from ahead of me on the path. "It's like a pool."

It was. Some very big rocks turned the tributary here, creating a short waterfall of only a couple of feet, but then holding the water captive in a hole beneath it. When I reached her side, she was admiring the swimming hole and smiling. "The water is pretty fast right now," I noticed. "It's all that rain we've had. Just walk slowly, okay? The rocks can get slippery."

"I'll be careful," she promised, kicking off her shoes and socks. "I'd rather not hit my head twice in one day." She stepped carefully down the bank until the water found her toes. "Oh, this is heaven."

Heaven was watching the water lick her smooth calves.

"It's not even cold. How deep is that spot?" she asked, pointing to the central pool.

I tapped my chest. "Here, probably."

"I'm going in," she announced. Then she reached under her tank top to unhook her bra before easing it out from under the tiny shirt. The bra became airborne, landing at my feet.

White lace. Now I'd be picturing her in nothing but that with great frequency, damn it.

Off came her shorts while I tried not to swallow my tongue. Her back was to me, and I watched the little triangle of her panties come into view. "Catch," she said before flinging the shorts backward over her shoulder.

Somehow I caught them. Then I had a wrestling match with myself while I tried to decide whether it was more polite to move her discarded bra to a rock in the sun or to leave it there. In the end I scooped it up and dropped it onto the towels. By the time I looked back, Lark was chest deep in water and smiling at me. "Aren't you coming in?"

That was the question. "I hadn't planned on it. When we drive back to the Shipleys' there will be tourists everywhere."

She rolled her eyes. "So park behind the bunkhouse. We can run in for a change of clothes. Nobody will notice."

The girl made an excellent point. So I dropped the truck's key onto the towels and shed my T-shirt.

She watched with a guilty little smile on her face, too. Rolling up the hem of my shorts, I waded in very slowly, mindful of the slippery rocks. Wiping out like a loser while she watched wasn't part of my plan. The water felt great. It was cold but not punishing.

"This was the best idea ever, Zach." She kicked her feet and swam the short distance that the small pool allowed. "Thank you."

"Don't mention it," I said as she swam by again, her silky arms glistening in the water.

"Is this a public spot?" she asked. "I probably should have asked that before getting half naked."

I laughed. "It's Isaac and Leah's property."

"Oh, good."

We lasted ten minutes or so in the cold water. "Your lips are blue," she teased.

And, damn it. That made me focus on her lips. It was all too easy to remember how they tasted against mine. "Yours, too." I got out first, taking the tattered little towel and wiping myself down as best I could. I held the better one out for her and tried to avert my eyes as she emerged dripping wet, the tank molded to perfect breasts, her nipples pointing straight at me.

Lord save me, but it was hard to look away.

She wrapped the towel around her midsection, which helped. "Avert your eyes," she said after we tiptoed back to the truck on wet feet. I looked away while she stripped off her soaking tank and put on the sweatshirt she'd been wearing this morning.

"Well, that was refreshing!" she said once she'd climbed back into the truck, still wearing the towel around her waist.

"Uh-huh," I agreed.

But now I was heated up in different ways than I'd been before.

* * *

The next couple of weeks I spent a lot of time trying not to kiss Lark.

I didn't kiss her at the Montpelier market, even when she brought me a sandwich and laughed at my terrible jokes. I didn't kiss her when we were kneeling very close together, sanding the baseboards in the bungalow kitchen. Alone.

And I certainly didn't kiss her when we beat May and Dylan at cards. Twice.

I had never had more fun than sitting around the coffee table during a downpour, eating popcorn and playing euchre. It was a Sunday afternoon, and for once in my life I took a real break.

Most Sundays Griffin worked just as hard as the other six days of the week. As a paid employee, technically I had most of Sunday off. But I never took the free hours. I couldn't sit around watching a movie or reading a book if Griff was in the cider house pressing apples. It just didn't feel right.

Usually.

But the pull of Lark's company was strong. She was a card shark. Euchre was a partners' game, and there was nothing better than looking across the table at her regal face, wondering what secrets those glittering eyes held.

"Spades," she said slowly, as if weighing a grave decision. "And Zach, put your cards down. I'm going it alone."

"You don't have to!" May pointed out. "You guys only need one point to win again."

"But I'm a glory hog," Lark said. "And it's your lead."

"Oh, man," Dylan complained to his sister. "This won't go well for us."

It didn't, either. Lark's victory was swift. When she laid down her fifth winning card she let out a whoop and leapt to her feet. She leaned in to hug me over the coffee table, and I hoisted her over it and into the air.

Victory was sweet, and so was the scent of her hair.

I might have kissed her then, in front of God and everybody. I was that far gone for her. But I was saved by the distraction of a bolt of lightning which somehow shone brighter than my lust. It was followed immediately by a clap of thunder so loud that May screamed, and Lark's body spasmed in my arms.

"It's okay," I said immediately. My subconscious was always ready to soothe her. I set her down carefully.

She'd had a rough couple of weeks, if I was honest. After her incident at the farmers' market in Norwich, I'd spent quite a few nights in her bed, and not for a fun reason. She was still afraid, damn it. And the guy who soothes you when you scream should never roll over and ask for a kiss. It just wasn't right.

So even though I woke up every morning burning up with need, I never gave in to the temptation to taste her again.

"Well, it's been fun losing to you guys," Dylan said, picking up his coffee mug. "But after that drubbing I'm going to do some homework." He left the room to another clap of thunder.

May's nose was pressed against the glass, where rain was coming down in sheets. "This weather is crazy. I wonder where Griff is?" she asked.

The answer came a couple of minutes later when the kitchen door banged open and Griff yelled for his brother. "Dyl! I need another set of hands! We got a tree down."

"I'll help," I said, jogging toward the door, my leisurely Sunday forgotten. I grabbed a raincoat off a hook—a coat that had belonged to Griffin's father. There was no room for sentiment when it came to gear on a farm. A rain jacket couldn't be sacred. It wasn't a keepsake. Life went on.

"Thanks, man," Griff grunted.

"Where's the downed tree?"

"Laying across the chicken fence. Just a birch, though."

After shoving my feet into Dylan's rain boots, I ran outside with Griff. It only took us fifteen minutes or so to remove the blown-down tree and set the chickens' portable electric fence to rights.

"Thanks, again," Griff said when we were done.

"Don't mention it." He went back to the cider house alone. Before I came inside, I lifted the hinged sides of the chicken tractor and felt around for eggs, collecting a half dozen in the folds of my coat, and saving Dylan a trip out in the rain later.

When I carefully opened the door and stepped inside, mindful of the eggs cradled in one arm, Lark was alone in the kitchen.

"Oh, Jesus," she said, looking up at me with disbelief. "Looks like you went for a swim in those clothes."

"I think I did. Could you..."

She had already crossed the room to me, and when she saw what I was carrying she put down her mug and began gently moving the eggs onto the kitchen counter. "Nice haul."

"Yeah. I learned the hard way never to put them in my pockets."

"Seriously?"

"Sure. Big mistake." I unbuttoned the rain coat, and Lark pushed the wet thing off my shoulders. Her hands grazed my body, and my libido sat up and begged. Then she grabbed a dry dish towel out of the drawer and raised it to my hairline, catching the drips of water there.

We were so close together that everything went quiet inside me.

"You're always the first one to jump when Griffin needs a hand," Lark said quietly.

"I don't mind."

With one smooth thumb she brushed water off my cheekbone. The sweep of her skin against mine was at once familiar and electrifying. Whenever she touched me, I felt as if I'd loved her my whole life.

"You're *dripping*," she chided me.

I must have been staring, because now her big brown eyes were locked on mine. There were only a few inches between us, and they could have been easily vanquished. But I held my ground, unmoving even as a new rivulet of water dripped down my cheek.

It was Lark who broke our stare-down. And she did it by leaning forward, pressing her lips to my jaw, absorbing the water droplets with a soft kiss. "Hmm," she breathed, and her exhalation brought goosebumps to my neck. She raised her head a centimeter and kissed my damp skin again.

My body did its best impression of a brush pile catching fire. *Whoosh.* Giving in to the urge I'd been fighting every minute of the day and night, I reached for her beautiful face with both hands.

My heart was pounding, but I didn't attack her mouth like I'd done in the barn. This time I took her tenderly. My lips grazed hers. But even that first contact made my head spin. The softness of her skin and her feminine scent overwhelmed me. My mouth closed over hers, her hands finding my chest.

Yes, my body chanted. *More.*

I deepened the kiss, sliding a hand to the back of her neck, pulling her into my arms. Maybe I'd spent the first twenty-three years of my life without touching anyone, but Lark had changed me. I *craved* the contact. Her mouth softened under mine, and she made an achy little sound that went right to my dick.

Parting her lips with my own, I got the first heady taste of her. All logic and reason fled the building as I took sip after sip of her mouth. Her grip tightened on my wet shirt as we lost ourselves to the hunger that had simmered between us since...I didn't know when.

I didn't even know my own name. All I knew was the ache she made me feel. The need. My hunger was like a devil on my shoulder, urging my hands to coast down her back, pulling her hips against my eager ones.

More of this would kill me. Calling upon the last tattered threads of my willpower, I broke our seal, my head thumping back against the doorframe. It wasn't like me to feel so reckless. Maybe other people could afford to abandon all their self-control, but I never could.

"This keeps happening," Lark whispered, her fingertip tracing my lower lip.

Because I'm weak, I thought, just as footfalls could be heard on the back steps.

Lark took a healthy step backward just as the door opened, admitting Ruth Shipley. "Hello!" she said, sounding winded. "You look even wetter than I am."

"Sure is coming down out there," Lark said, plucking the raincoat I'd worn off the floor. We'd tossed it there during our hasty make-out session.

"Visibility was terrible! I doubt I drove above thirty miles an hour." Ruth took off her own coat. "What's everyone up to?"

Finally I found my voice. "Griff is in the cider house. Dylan and May are doing homework.

She kicked off her boots and sidestepped me. "Oh, eggs! Thank you."

It took me a moment to realize what she was talking about. I'd forgotten the darned eggs a half second after Lark smiled at me. "You're welcome," I said a beat too late.

Lark gave me a secretive smile, and then asked Ruth if she wanted any help starting dinner.

* * *

That night Jude came over after supper. He and Griff had hatched a plan to stay up late working on the bungalow's kitchen cabinetry together before the plumbers came tomorrow to install the new sinks.

I told them I'd help, of course.

There were four of us working under the night sky. The rain stopped, so we set up the cabinet doors on sawhorses. Jude and I sanded while Griff and Kyle primed by the porch light.

"Listen, Zach," Jude said as we worked together. "You helped me find my job, and I'm starting to think I can return the favor."

"But I have a job?" *For now.*

"Yeah, but this one could be pretty great. My boss has a brother who lives in the Northeast Kingdom." That was the most remote corner of Vermont, abutting Canada. "They have trouble with tractor maintenance, because there isn't enough demand in any one town. Mr. Marker wants to set up a traveling repair service. Like a van full of tools and supplies."

"But what about parts? There'd be no way to have the right stuff on hand in a van."

"Maybe not for larger repairs," Jude conceded. "But you always say that routine maintenance is key for tractors. I told Marker you'd be good at this—that you were the tractor whisperer."

I snorted.

Jude grinned. "You should call him before someone else does."

"Thanks, man."

"What's this?" Griff demanded from a few yards away, paintbrush in hand. "You're poaching my best employee?"

"And I'm chopped liver?" Kyle teased. "Don't you see me volunteering my time on a Sunday night? Where is the love?"

"The love is just inside the back door," Griff said, jerking his chin in that direction.

Kyle set down his brush and disappeared for a moment. A hoot of joy could be heard before he reappeared with a six-pack of bottled beer in each hand. "There's even some non-alcoholic stuff here for you, Jude."

"That is nice," Jude said, setting down his sanding block. "Pass me one? And Griff—you wouldn't get in Zach's way of doubling his income, would you?"

"Course not," Griff said. "Zach knows I was only teasing. He's gonna move up in the world pretty soon, anyway. And hey—if you took a mechanic's job then mom would stop trying to enroll you in the GED program. So you should probably talk to Jude's boss."

I gave a grunt of acknowledgment. I didn't know which option was worse, though. Struggling with a test or working by myself in the boonies. The Northeast Kingdom was comprised of the three least-populated counties in Vermont. Living alone in a trailer somewhere, driving around to fix strangers' tractors? Shoot me.

We took a beer break and then did a little more work. The smack talk swirled around me, but I didn't hear much of it. I was too tangled up in my own head. The best five minutes of my life kept playing on repeat in my head. Kissing Lark in the kitchen had been glorious, but it was something I probably shouldn't do again. And now there was Jude's tractor job clouding my mind, too.

"You're quiet tonight, even for you," Griff said as we walked up the path toward the bunkhouse later.

"Just tired," I mumbled.

"Yeah, I'll bet. I always take it for granted that you want the extra hours. Maybe sometimes you want to say no, but you don't."

"Nah," I said quickly. "It's not like that."

"Isn't it?" he challenged. "Even so, you might want to fix tractors for the same pay at half the hours. Marker goes to Mom's church. We could put in a good word for you."

Something twisted in my stomach. "Let's not worry about that. Too much going on right now."

We'd reached the bunkhouse door, so I didn't have to continue the conversation. Jude was spending the night with us, so I offered to find him some sheets, thereby changing the topic.

"I brought my sleeping bag, so you don't have to."

As we passed by, I saw that Lark's door was shut. But there was a strip of light underneath, and the strains of guitar music playing inside. My heart paused outside that door, wanting to knock. But I didn't do it.

In the bunkroom, Jude stood on Kieran's lower bunk in order to roll out his sleeping bag on the upper one. "Just like old times," Jude said. "Good thing you have one empty spot. Wouldn't want to see Griff sleeping on the floor," he teased.

"Griff wouldn't," Kyle said from our closet. "He's afraid of mice."

"Once a mouse ran over his foot, and he screamed," Kieran added.

"I did *not* scream."

"You screamed like a little girl," Kieran insisted.

"I was eleven," Griffin said in his own defense.

"An eleven-year-old girly man," Kieran pressed, while the rest of us laughed.

Even after everyone showered and bedded down for the night, the smack talk continued into the darkness. I closed my eyes, and their ribbing became background noise to my thoughts. I'd never minded living in the bunkhouse. And I had no idea what I'd do when the Shipleys asked me to move on.

I fell asleep to the sound of Griffin's snoring. But I didn't stay asleep.

It felt as if Lark cried out only minutes after I'd closed my eyes, but it was probably hours.

"Whazzat?" Jude murmured in his sleep.

I didn't answer him. I just hustled into Lark's room and closed the door.

"Shh...sweetie," I said. "Shh..." I knelt on her bed. I rubbed a hand on her back, circling gently. It wasn't long until her breathing evened out.

God, I loved her. What a scary thought that was, but it was entirely true. I'd never felt about anyone the way I felt about Lark. Like I'd walk through fire for her.

I pulled the covers back and slipped in beside her. The sensation of her body's warmth made mine stir immediately. But I slammed my eyes shut and prayed for sleep to take me right away. Blissfully, it did.

Too blissfully, as it would happen.

We were in a bed. It was utterly dark wherever we were, but I knew it was her. I'd know the scent of her anywhere, and the sound of her breathing. Lark's warm hands drifted down my body, teasing me. And wait—I was naked. Her soft hair dragged across my chest, and I felt every strand against my skin.

Beautiful.

With moist lips, she dropped little kisses on my stomach. As she wandered lower, I held my breath. Her lips touched the head of my dick. She opened her mouth, and then everything was hot and wet all around me. I let loose a bellowed moan. It was so good that I tensed every muscle in my body. Her mouth was both soft and insistent. Now she was sucking on me, and it was even more glorious than I would have believed. I couldn't hold still. Twisting my hips, I arched into her hot mouth. "Oh fuck."

"Zach?"

I could hear her voice, but was unable to respond. I was too far under the spell.

"Are you okay?"

Startled by the question, I opened my eyes. Lark's face was right there above mine, her perfect mouth just inches away. Trying to hold onto the dream, I lifted my head to meet her for a kiss.

Lark made a startled sound.

Startled?

Fuck!

I sat up so fast that she had to weave out of my way. "Sorry," I choked out. I looked down, and my dick stared accusingly back up at me, straining against my flannel pants. I drew my knees up quickly, then rolled over on my side, facing away from her.

"Zach?" She put a concerned hand on the back of my neck. But the contact was like gasoline on my fire. Her friendly touch was exactly what I didn't need right now. "Are you sick?" she asked.

"No... I'm... It's..." *Get a grip already*, I coached myself. *Nothing happened.*

It was only a dream. These were the same words I used night after night to comfort Lark. And now the joke was on me. My pulse was pounding just as hard now as it had been a minute ago, when I'd thought she was... "*Fuck.*"

"Shh..." Lark said, stroking a lock of hair away from my face. "What did you dream about?"

I chuffed out a strangled laugh and shook my head.

Lark made a fist and pushed it against my shoulder with a friendly nudge. I could feel that she was trying to put me at ease, but it wasn't going to work. "I tell you my secrets. But your dream is top secret?"

I exhaled on a long, hot breath. "It was R-rated," I explained at a whisper. "But not for violence."

"*Oh.*" The one word carried the weight of understanding.

Feeling my face redden, I pressed my overheated cheek into the pillow. I took a slow breath and tried to get myself under control. In my dream, I'd been seconds away from orgasm. I needed a few minutes to calm down, and then I would get up and walk back to my own bed.

"Zach," Lark whispered. The bed moved as she lay down again, too. "Is it egotistical of me to ask whether I've ever made it into one of your best dreams?"

In Leviticus, it says, *"You shall not lie to one another."* The temptation was strong. But I spoke the truth. "They're all about you."

Lark

I studied the rise and fall of Zach's muscular back with each breath. Unable to resist, I put a hand on his neck. He was so solid and warm against my touch. As my thumb stroked over his skin, the moment stretched wide between us.

The choice was mine. If I reached for him, he could be mine. Or I could do nothing. Say nothing. That would be an outright rejection, and one that I didn't want to make.

I already knew what Zach looked like splitting wood, his muscles bunching with each swing of the maul. I knew the sight of him dashing past my door with nothing but a towel wrapped around his waist. I knew how he kissed—with such thoroughness and desire that it had made my head spin.

Now I wondered how he'd look hovering above me in bed.

And who could blame me? Zach was beautiful on his worst day. But a horny Zach was the thing of fantasies. My pulse kicked up a notch, and I was filled with the urge to see every golden inch of his skin and watch his eyes darken with lust.

My rusty libido cranked to life as I focused my gaze on the place where his neck met his strong shoulder. Without conscious thought, I moved closer and kissed him right there. His skin was velvety under my lips, and the clean scent of him made me sigh.

His body stilled beneath my touch, and he let out a hot breath.

Even as I leaned into the warmth of his body, I knew on some level that I shouldn't do it. Zach wasn't just a guy I happened to be attracted to. He was special. Zach was a better person than...well, just about anybody. He ought to be handled with care.

But as I dragged my lips on a path toward his jaw, he moaned. That small sound dispensed with what little self-control I had. My inner Wild Child hadn't shown up lately. But now she announced her presence, touching the tip of her tongue to Zach's heated skin. He tasted exactly as he should—of the cool night air, the outdoors, a hint of sweat.

Zach had entirely stopped breathing, and I wondered one last time if maybe I'd overstepped. "Should I stop?"

The next two seconds were a whirl of motion, after which I found myself on my back looking up into Zach's serious face. His body was spread out on top of mine, and the weight of him was delicious.

Still, he didn't speak. The silence held between us as he dropped his head, brushing his lips against mine. It was my turn to hold my breath, as I waited to learn what he'd do next. His eyes fell shut then, and he pressed a soft kiss onto my lips. I couldn't help myself. I opened up in blatant invitation. With a needy groan, Zach accepted the challenge. His tongue glided against mine, tangling, exploring.

Desire thrummed through me in earnest. With his enthusiastic kisses, Zach stoked the embers of my libido into flames. His hands moved to cup my face, his fingertips threading into my hair. Even though he held much of his weight off my body, it was impossible not to feel the pressure of his erection against my core.

Oh, the pleasures I could share with this man. The very idea caused me to whimper out loud.

At the sound, Zach pulled back. Again he studied me with a grave expression. "I'm not freaking you out, am I?" His whisper was coarse.

"You couldn't ever," I answered. And then I put my hands under his T-shirt, finally allowing myself to solve the mystery of how all that golden chest hair would feel against my fingers. It was surprisingly silky. Everything about Zach was finer than on a normal person. And when I pressed my fingers against the flat discs of his nipples, he groaned.

Our kisses went wild, and I lost myself inside my own senses in a way that I hadn't done in a long time. For this beautiful moment, there was no fear. There were no nightmares, and no darkness hovering over my heart. There was only the slide of Zach's tongue against my own, and the friction of his callused hands on my body.

He rolled us to the side, and his fingers became more daring. He stroked up the back of my thigh, then ventured beneath my nightgown.

Oh, hell yes.

I kissed him with everything I had, pressing my aching breasts against his hard chest. His fingers splayed across my belly, their tips so deliciously close to my core that I couldn't keep still. I rolled my hips and gasped with encouragement.

Then I reached down and stroked him—just once—my hand glancing over his flannel-covered erection.

Zach broke off our kiss to flop his head back on the pillow. He let fly a whispered string of very un-Zach-like curses. "You're killing me."

"Remind me again," I whispered, "why you're a virgin?"

"Never wanted anyone enough," he panted.

"And now?" I pressed, punctuating the question by sucking gently on the skin beneath Zach's ear.

"In my dreams, we do it every night."

Hot damn. I had to clench my legs together as the idea became a craving. Zach's palm made another sweep across the waistband of my panties, and I moaned. He swallowed the sound with another of his kisses. I loved how responsive he was, and how willing. I sat up a little bit, tugging at the bottom hem of his T-shirt. Pushing the fabric up, I wordlessly urged him to shed it.

He gripped the fabric in two hands, but hesitated. "Maybe this isn't what you need right now."

"Sorry?" Getting him naked was exactly what I needed right now.

"This isn't the reason I climb into your bed at night," he whispered, his beautiful face more serious that I'd ever seen it.

"I *know* that," I hissed. "Nobody is taking advantage of me right now. And I don't need you mansplaining what I need right now."

Zach grinned at me. I loved that smile, but what I did next made it disappear. I grabbed my nightie and lifted it over my head, then flung it off the bed.

His gaze darkened to a lustful glitter, and I watched as his eyes swept my bare breasts. This time, when I gave his shirt a tug, he curled his body to let me shed it without a word.

Then he reached out with both arms and pulled me closer. Our next kiss was so hot and eager that I felt myself floating along on the pleasure of it all. We lay face to face, Zach's palms skimming reverently over my breasts. Every touch made me a little crazier. It had been so long since anyone touched me with loving hands. His kisses trailed down my neck and into the valley of my breasts. He lay there on his side, his tongue exploring first one nipple and then the other. And when he closed his lips and sucked, I felt myself absolutely flood with desire.

I wanted more. And soon. But first there was something I needed to know. "Zach?"

"Mmm?" he asked, nuzzling my breast.

"What happened in your sexy dream tonight?"

He lifted his head and moved so that we were eye to eye again. "Why?"

"I just want to know." I stroked my thumb across his beautiful lip. "Right before you woke up. What were we doing in your dream?"

His cheeks flushed red. "What if I don't want to say?"

"Your call," I whispered. "But I'd really like to know."

He swallowed roughly. "You used your mouth on me."

Well. That was a simple enough fantasy to bring to life. Giving Zach a gentle push, I got him to roll onto his back. Then I began to drop kisses onto that beautiful chest. I explored the rise of his pecs, giving special attention to the hardened tips of his nipples. He groaned when I licked into the center gully of his chest, heading for the ridges of those perfect abs. I nosed into the silky blond hairs of his happy trail, slowly heading south. His breathing became fast and shallow as I reached the elastic waistband of his sleep pants. Moving down, I dropped teasing kisses over his cotton-covered erection.

"Lark," he warned.

"Yeah?"

"You don't have to," he said quietly.

"I know that," I whispered, nuzzling him through the fabric. "Remember. No mansplaining." I hooked my thumbs in the elastic, and waited. For a moment, nothing happened. But then Zach gave a sigh and pushed his hips up off the bed, giving me free reign to jerk his clothing down. He sprang free, long and ready.

Wowza. Zachariah was beautiful everywhere. He was thick and uncut, the rosy tip of his cockhead rising above his foreskin, begging for my attention.

Pacing myself, I drew his pants all the way down and off. I tossed them on the floor. His bare body was golden and shapely, and it thrilled me to wonder if I was the first girl to ever see him this way.

Zach angled up onto his elbows, looking like Adonis in repose. "Come here," he rasped, opening an arm to me. There was such heat in his eyes that I almost obeyed him.

Almost. But I had other plans.

I ran my hands up his legs, brushing kisses onto his knees and onto the palm of the hand that reached down to collect me. I scaled his body just high enough to spend another few moments admiring his chest. Zach slipped his hands under my arms to haul me up onto his body. But I shook him off. Moving quickly, I slid down again. Wasting no time, I planted my tongue at the base of his cock and licked the length of him.

Zach's body arched off the bed in surprise. "Oh. Fuck," he bit out. "Oh..." he said as I repeated this treatment. I dropped my nose down to nuzzle his blond curls, and when I gripped his hips, he was trembling.

I put a big, wet kiss on the tip of him, earning a giant moan for my efforts. Then I took him all the way into my mouth. He was satin over steel. Sucking him in deep, I cupped his balls in one hand. Beneath me, his big body undulated with excitement. As I worked him over, he was nearly writhing. How beautiful it was to be the handmaiden to so much pleasure. I'd missed the heat and friction of skin against skin.

"Sweetheart." He reached a shaking hand down to cup my chin, trying to nudge me away. "I'm going to spill."

I caught his flailing hand in my own and sucked him deeper. "Mmm," I hummed.

Zach let out a hot gasp. I lifted my eyes in time to see him shove the heel of his free hand into his mouth. Muffling his own shout, he came with so much force that I had a little trouble keeping up with him. Every one of his powerful muscles locked as he erupted again and again, before eventually collapsing with finality on the bed.

A lovely silence settled over us. Gently, I licked him clean. Then I kissed the juncture of his powerful thighs, and moved upward to lay my head on his chest.

Zach had one perfect forearm thrown over his eyes. After his breathing evened out, he reached for me, drawing me in, folding me tightly into his arms. Beneath my ear, his heart thumped wildly. But still, he was worryingly silent.

"Are you okay?" I whispered.

He laughed, and I was glad to hear it. "I guess we won't need the defibrillator from the barn. But it might have been close." He took another deep breath. "I wasn't expecting..." He didn't finish the sentence.

"I *know* that, okay? I've never had sex with someone out of obligation."

"Me neither," he said.

It took me half a second to get the joke, but then we laughed together. I spread myself out on his body. God, he was sexy—all golden muscle in the dim glow of the night light. And arousal gave his lips and cheeks a brilliant red stain.

Still smiling, he took my mouth in a kiss which was hungry but short. "Best night of my life," he whispered.

There was something reverent in his tone that I wasn't ready to hear. "It could get even better," I countered.

At that, Zach's hips twitched beneath me, and he made a greedy little noise in the back of his throat. I wove my fingers into his sun-kissed hair and kissed him again.

Zach

Jesus Christ. Holy shit. Mother of God.

There weren't curses shocking enough for everything happening tonight.

I slid my hands down Lark's unbelievably smooth skin and took charge of the kiss. Maybe it didn't matter if I'd never really done this before. Everywhere I touched her was an education.

She nipped at my lip, and I heard a sound come from deep inside my own chest. When she opened for me, and it was the easiest thing in the world to slip inside, and to discover the heat of her mouth and the velvet slip of her tongue against mine.

Her mouth had a new, salty flavor that I realized belonged to me. At this spectacularly dirty idea, and even though it had seemed impossible a minute ago, my dick twitched to life again. I swept my tongue into her mouth and tasted her more fully. My heart galloped like a runaway horse on the range.

On the compound in Wyoming they used to speak of girls being "ruined." Right now "ruined" sounded like a pretty accurate word for how I felt. Now that I knew how beautiful it could be, there would never be another moment when I didn't crave more of Lark.

In my life there had been few moments of either love or good fortune. And both of them coming together at once...it was almost more than I could handle.

Almost.

The feel of Lark's mouth on my dick had been, hands down, the most exciting thing I'd ever experienced. But holding her nearly naked body while she kissed me was even better. Her breasts were as soft and full as I'd daydreamed they'd be.

Happiness made me bold. My hands skimmed down her smooth body until I reached the little scrap of fabric between us. When I pushed her underwear down, Lark helped by kicking them away. I needed to explore her. So I locked my arms around her and rolled. She landed beneath me with a surprised exhalation and big eyes.

"This okay?" I whispered, ducking my head to kiss her collarbone. She nodded as I tongued my way up her neck. She arched her back, increasing the contact with my mouth.

Somehow I would have to find a way to make this night last forever. "I don't exactly know what I'm doing, you know. I hope you won't mind..."

She silenced me with a finger over my lip. "Zach, you're already a good lover."

I kissed the fingers which covered my mouth, flicking them away. "Nice try. But you don't have to butter me up."

"I'm serious." Her dark eyes flashed in the dim light. "Sex is ten percent skill and ninety percent listening. Who's a better listener than you?"

I cleared my throat. "What am I listening for?"

"You'll know it when you hear it." Then, she grasped my hand and dragged it slowly, purposefully, onto her breast. "Touch me," she whispered.

Damn. The erotic sound of that two-word directive was enough to make any guy her permanent slave. I skimmed her silky breast, capturing its fullness in my palm, then brushing past her rosy nipple. I felt it harden beneath my touch. So I leaned down. With a quick peek into her heavily lidded eyes, I lowered my lips to the pretty pink nub. I flicked my tongue over her nipple and watched her expression. As my mouth worshiped her breast, she let out a happy sigh. "Yessss," she hissed.

Well, okay then.

I turned my attention to her other breast, and received the same positive reinforcement. And this time, her hips twitched on the sheets. Even as I sucked her breast deeper into my mouth, I let my hand go wandering down her body. My fingers took in the soft skin of her stomach and the perfect curve of her hip. She sighed again, her legs falling open.

Without hesitation I slipped my hand past the springy curls between her legs. What I found just beneath was the soft, wet pool of her body. I couldn't help it—I moaned onto her breast. And I was hard as a board again, my fingers stroking gently through her wetness. Lark made a small adjustment to the set of her hips, which put my fingers up a little higher. Slowly, I circled my thumb over the slip of tissue I felt there.

"So nice," Lark whispered.

I could hardly believe how beautiful she was, splayed out for me in the dim light. My fantasies hadn't been nearly this good. It was a sensory overload—the feel of her smooth skin against my own, and the salty taste of her body in my mouth. I kissed my way down her belly. Then I began dropping little kisses onto her mound. Her breathing changed then, each new inhalation more eager than the last. When I gathered the courage to drag my tongue over the hot center of her, she gave a little cry of pleasure.

The taste of her was like nothing I'd known before—a musky, honeyed goodness. I explored her with my tongue, and she moaned and panted. The sounds that fell from her lips were dappled, happy things. Now I knew the secret to making her happy. For as long as I bathed this tender place with kisses, she would remain blissed-out and unafraid.

"Mmm," I hummed against her body. My thumb swirled below, in the hot bath of desire that her body had made for me.

"Zach!" she whispered. "Wait!"

I lifted my head. "It's not good?"

"It's *so* good. That's why I need you to stop."

I smoothed my thumbs over her mound, placing one last kiss on her body. Then I crawled back up beside her.

Immediately, her hand encircled my cock, which was rock hard. "I want you to feel me come from the inside."

I stopped breathing.

"Only if you want to," she added.

"I want that so bad," I admitted, wrapping both arms around her. "But I'd need to go find a condom."

Lark shook her head. "I have a device—I can't get pregnant. And after I came back..." she cleared her throat. "I had every test there is."

A sobering thought lifted my head right off the pillow. "Lark, was that because you were...?"

She shook her head quickly. "No. Nothing like that happened. It's just that I wasn't talking much when I came back. Everybody assumed the worst."

I felt a big twinge of uneasiness. *I wasn't talking much,* she'd said. Things were even worse than she'd told me.

"Where'd you go?" she asked.

"Just worrying about you."

"Don't," she begged, a hand on his chest. "Not tonight." She kissed my shoulder. "Please?"

"Okay," I whispered, as her lips continued to torture me. Hell, I'd do anything she asked right now. Anything.

"Come here," she demanded, settling onto her back.

My stomach tightened suddenly, as nervous anticipation hit. I took a deep, steadying breath. And then I dropped my hips onto hers. The feel of her body underneath mine touched some primal part of me. No user's manual was necessary.

Spreading her knees a little further apart with my own, I rested my cockhead against her body, grazing the tip through her wetness. Lark tipped her hips a few degrees upwards, and just like that I was sliding inside. I didn't even try to hold back my groan as she surrounded me with a gripping heat. I gave a final push and seated myself to the hilt.

The pleasure was nearly overwhelming. For a moment, I had to just close my eyes and sink in.

"That's beautiful," Lark whispered.

I opened my eyes to find her looking up at me. Holding that brown-eyed gaze, I began to move. I had to. Without thought or direction, my hips began to rock. And... *Hell.* There was nothing like it. The feeling of being so perfectly joined to her was everything I'd ever wanted. She was touching me everywhere, her hands sliding down my sides, up my arms. It was my fantasy come to life. And I was not going to survive it.

Bracing myself on my forearms, I leaned over her for a kiss. She tugged me down with a moan. I hadn't thought that the sensation of making love to Lark could have been improved. But the pulse of her tongue in my mouth set off a chain reaction of pleasure throughout my body, causing me to shiver against her hot skin.

"So good. You feel so good," Lark chanted against my lips.

And I agreed, though forming words was out of the question. My body surged into hers, my senses conflating, accelerating. I needed to find a way to slow down, because I didn't want this feeling to end. Ever.

Lark arched up, changing the angle of our joining. My rhythm stuttered, and so I pulsed against her instead.

"Oh," she whimpered. It was a beautiful sound of pleasure, and I wanted to hear it again.

"You like that?" I ground my hips, meeting her body where it pressed against mine.

Her approval was unmistakable. She began to pant in shallow, hot breaths beneath me. Listening, I swung my hips again and again. With each thrust and slide, I seemed to be pushing her closer to oblivion. Her eyes went glassy, and her kisses became distracted. Lark abruptly pressed her knees against my sides and moaned. She arched, exposing the slender column of her neck to my kisses.

And then I felt it—her body shuddered inside, unleashing a series of pulses around my member. Then it was my turn to moan. I rocked into her, chasing the sensation. "Oh, sweetheart," I panted. It was coming towards me, and it was going to be overwhelming.

"Harder," she demanded.

I answered her with a thrust that I felt all the way down to my bones. Everything was heat and motion. Lark's body was locked around mine, her hips meeting me shot for shot. That loud banging I heard came either from the headboard hitting the wall, or from the pounding of my heart. One or the other.

Over and over I kissed Lark, swallowing her moans with my own. She broke our kiss to bury her face in my neck, her body spasming around mine a second time.

And then I couldn't hold myself back another moment. Every muscle in my body locked, and an ecstatic shout ripped from my lips. The orgasm was sweet and sudden. I planted myself to the root one last time. And then all was quiet, save for our ragged breathing.

Or so I thought. As I dropped my lips to Lark's damp forehead, I heard a new sound. From the other side of the wall came a piercing whistle, followed by cheering and applause.

"Oh, Jesus Christ." Lark chuckled. She wrapped her forearms over my head, as if hiding our faces from the commotion next door. "I'm so sorry."

"Why?"

"You are going to catch so much hell in a few hours."

She was right, and it was just the sort of attention that usually made me cringe. But for once I was too happy—and too sated—to care. Rolling off her, I immediately tugged her close again. She tucked her head onto my shoulder, reaching across my body to lazily rub my chest. It was delicious.

Unfortunately, the laughter and jeering from the next room had not died down. I covered Lark's exposed ear with my hand before shouting "Shut it!" in the direction of the wall.

But that only made everyone—including Lark—burst into laughter. "Just ignore them." Lark snuggled closer. "There are still two hours until your alarm goes off. You should sleep."

I closed my eyes and wondered if I could. The way her soft hair brushed my chest was something I didn't want to miss. Being this close to her made staying conscious worthwhile. But as Lark yawned and settled against me, my thoughts became slow and dreamlike.

"Nobody could have a nightmare after that," Lark murmured. "Just sayin'..."

I chuckled into her hair. "You should have said something sooner."

Minutes later, I fell asleep with a smile on my face.

Zach

As it usually did, my watch alarm went off when the sky was just a dark gray streak. Less usual was the way I woke up pancaked against Lark's naked body.

She didn't even notice my alarm, so I shut it off before staring down at her in wonder. Her dark lashes dipped towards those perfect cheekbones. The curve of her breast disappeared temptingly beneath the sheet.

And... I was hard again. With the memory of last night pumping through my bloodstream, no amount of physical labor was going to chase that away.

Another long day, coming right up.

I dipped my head to graze her neck, landing a kiss beneath her ear. "I need to go."

"I know," she mumbled.

"I sure don't want to." Truer words were never spoken. I kissed the smooth skin of her shoulder, wishing I could stay all day. "Later, we have to talk."

"If you say so." She didn't even open her eyes, and I wondered if that was a bad sign.

"Get out here, Zach," Kyle's voice came from the hallway. "You're definitely on shit patrol this morning."

"Be right there." I kissed Lark once more, this time at the hollow of her throat.

"Go, before you catch hell," she murmured.

With great reluctance, I did.

Kyle was waiting in the barn with the shovel. He and Kieran did the milking while I took the least popular job. It was just the three of us today.

Shit patrol meant seeing to all the cow poop collected overnight in the barn. It traveled on a conveyor system from the gutter behind the cows into a pile outside the building. But the cows didn't exactly aim for the gutter, and a great deal of shoveling was necessary to clean things up.

As Kyle pressed the shovel into my hands, he said, "This is for ruining all our sleep last night."

Right. There were two directions I could take this: humor or silence. "It wasn't a *lengthy* interruption," I said. Not that I'd had a lot of experience in the matter, but I was willing to bet the whole encounter had set some kind of land-speed record. Lark and I had attacked each other as if the Apocalypse was imminent.

"The hell it wasn't," Kieran grumbled from across the room, maneuvering the milking hoses into position. "Maybe *you* had pleasant dreams after four thirty. But after treating the rest of us to basically a porno sound track, it was woody city in the bunk room."

Right. Silence would have been the way to go.

"Welcome to the land of the living, man," Kyle said. "Now we can teach you the secret handshake.

I flipped him off, and Kieran laughed. "Do you feel different?" he asked in a campy voice.

"Who feels different?" a female voice asked.

"Nobody," Kyle answered quickly. "What do you need, Aunt Ruth?"

My face heated immediately, wondering how much Mrs. Shipley had heard.

"Will Jude and Griffin be coming in for breakfast this morning? Or did they already go to work at the bungalow?"

"They wouldn't miss breakfast," Kyle guessed. "I'm pretty sure they only went to let the plumbers in."

Ruth disappeared, and the others stopped ragging on me and went to work. With my head down, I began shoveling. Kieran had been kidding when he'd asked whether I felt different. But the truth was that I did. My body had a lazy easiness brought on by intense sexual satisfaction. But I also had the equally unfamiliar sensation that something good was just beginning for me.

I wanted more of Lark, and not just sex. I wanted Lark as a girlfriend. That was a word that felt unfamiliar on my tongue and sounded childish to my ear. But the vocabulary of relationships wasn't something I'd ever had to think about.

It didn't really matter what we called it. I wanted to feel Lark's heartbeat against mine when I fell asleep at night, and hear about her day just before we fell asleep. I wanted to bring her a cup of coffee in the morning, and tug her closer for a kiss.

And I had no idea if Lark wanted the same.

As soon as possible, I'd have to stumble through that conversation. I didn't want Lark to think that it had happened by accident, that I'd taken advantage of her out of lust and proximity.

Then there was Griffin to worry about. He'd warned us away from Lark.

I tipped a spade full of cow poop into the trench. Maybe shit patrol was actually kindness. The ammonia smell of concentrated cow shit was a pretty effective libido killer.

* * *

After the morning chores, it was time for breakfast. I was absolutely famished. We all headed towards the farmhouse, with me bringing up the rear. It was tempting to sprint ahead, towards the dual reward of food and Lark. But that would bring on all sorts of comments I could live without.

But Lark wasn't in the kitchen, and when I carried my plate into the dining room, she wasn't there, either.

Griffin and Jude arrived a moment later, plates in hand. When they seated themselves at the table, I risked a look at Griff, wondering whether he was going to chew me out later. *The girl is off limits*, still rang in my head.

But as his gaze settled over me, it was appraising, not angry.

It didn't matter, anyway. I regretted nothing.

"Did the plumber arrive?" someone asked.

"Yep. He's already on the job. Is there coffee?" Griff looked around. "Where's Lark?" he asked, probably because she often took charge of the coffee.

"I've got it!" Ruth called from the kitchen. Then she came trotting in with mugs for Griff and Jude. She poured a warmer for me. "You look tired this morning."

"He would." Kyle snickered from across the table.

Mrs. Shipley, thankfully, had spent years around the men and boys and their jokes. She moved off with her coffee pot without so much as a raised eyebrow.

It was one of our quieter morning meals. Dylan was already on his way to Burlington for classes. May and Ruth brought their plates into the dining room, and then only Lark was missing.

"This is why I stayed overnight," Jude said, lifting a piece of bacon. "My job is great, but there's no midmorning break for a hot meal and coffee."

"Good thing they pay twice as much as I do," Griff pointed out.

"Good thing," Jude agreed. He pointed his strip of bacon at me, and I knew what was coming next. "You going to call Marker today?"

"Maybe," I grunted. "Have to think about it."

"What's this? Is there an opportunity for Zach?" Ruth asked, lifting her mug.

"Could be," Jude said. "Marker's thinking about starting a tractor maintenance service."

"Ah!" Ruth said. "That's right up his alley."

I was saved from more of this conversation by the sound of the kitchen door flying open. A moment later, Lark's flushed face appeared in the doorway. "So sorry," she said. "I fell back to sleep after my alarm went off."

Kieran smirked and Kyle snickered. "Tired?"

My blood pressure shot up, and I turned to level Kyle with a glare.

The smile slid off his face, and he went back to his eggs.

"What?" May asked, looking from me to Kyle, and then to the other buried smiles on Jude and Kieran.

Lark's gaze found mine, and there was amusement in it. Her smile told me not to worry. That a comment from Kyle wasn't the end of the world.

I pushed my chair back. "Have a seat," I said to her, as if nobody else was in the room. "I'll get you a plate." Then I left the dining room without touching her, even though I wanted to. There were too many curious eyes. So my hug could wait.

In the kitchen I used Ruth's spatula to lift bacon and the last portion of scrambled eggs onto Lark's waiting plate.

May followed me into the kitchen. "Is everything okay?" she asked, clearly puzzled about the weird vibe in the dining room.

"Sure," I said, grabbing a fork for Lark.

May poured another mug of coffee and then tipped some milk into it, the way Lark liked. "What did I miss?"

"Well..." I gave a nervous chuckle. "Nothing bad," I said, passing her without further comment. Back in the dining room, I set the plate down in front of Lark, also without comment. But I ran a hand down the back of her head, allowing myself a single glancing contact with her silky hair.

"Thank you," she whispered.

"Anytime." Then I sat down and finished my breakfast.

Lark

I stayed to clean up after breakfast. I was still kicking myself for sleeping late. It was almost more embarrassing to let the Shipleys cook me so many meals than it was to have a screaming orgasm in earshot of the men.

Modesty had never been all that important to me. But pulling my weight really was.

While we washed dishes, May kept sneaking looks at me. But she didn't say anything because her mother was working with us.

Finally, Ruth went outside to collect eggs in the chicken coop. As soon as the door closed behind her, May tossed the dish towel onto a hook. "Okay, spill. What the heck did I miss?"

"Why?"

"What do you mean, *why?* Because I want to know! And why do the guys get to know something I don't?"

Oh, boy. "They, uh, heard it happening."

May's eyes got huge. "You fooled around with someone?"

"Yeah."

"Wait... Oh my God! It wasn't Kyle, was it? That's why you're not telling me." May shuddered. "That's just gross."

I gave her an evil grin.

"Oh my God! Nooooo!"

I laughed. "It wasn't your cousin. Jeez. But you're funny when you're freaking out."

"You bitch." May's face grew confused. "So..."

I watched the synapses fire behind her eyes as she did the math. She grabbed my wrist and squeezed. "Are you *kidding* me? You fooled around with Zach?"

I nodded.

"Oh. My. God!" May held a hand over her mouth. Then she dropped it and asked, "Did you...*deflower* him?"

Ugh. "Hello, this is 1865 calling. They want their word back. And besides—virginity is just a construct invented by men to subjugate women."

But she wasn't finished being shocked. "I had no idea you liked him that way."

"Well…" The shock on her face put me a little off kilter. "It sort of snuck up on us."

She blinked at me for a long moment. "Daphne will die of jealousy."

"Don't tell her," I yelped. "Jeez. Besides…" I shrugged. "I don't know if it was just a one-time thing."

"What does Zach think?"

"I don't know! What if you gave us a minute to process it? You told me Zach holds his cards close to his vest. It just happened, okay? I didn't know you'd freak."

My best friend looked away. "I'm not freaking. Just surprised, that's all."

A prickle of unease crawled up my neck. Was she jealous? That seemed unlikely. May never mentioned Zach. "Do you think I'm not good enough for him?"

"Don't put words in my mouth!" She finally met my gaze. "I do know this—you'll go back to Boston in a few weeks, back to your job. And he'll still be here. I just hope that's okay with him. Just treat him carefully, okay? He is really special. And he doesn't have much experience with loving anyone."

This entire conversation had given me a blood pressure spike. I *knew* Zach was special. Nobody knew it better than I did. And May made me sound aloof. Like I'd waltz back to Beacon Hill and forget this summer ever happened.

I was *never* forgetting this summer. Or this spring. Or any other damn thing, apparently.

May was watching me now, a look of concern on her face. "I really didn't mean for that to sound harsh. There's nobody better than you, Lark. But you're worldly and always on the move. And Zach isn't. I just don't want to see either of my friends get hurt."

I took a deep breath and let it out, trying to expel my anger. If May had a real glimpse at the tangled jungle of my emotions, she wouldn't describe me that way. I didn't feel worldly or daring anymore. I just felt tired. And scared out of my mind all the time.

May didn't know that, though, because I was such a shitty friend I'd never said so.

"I know Zach is special," I said quietly. "Neither of us meant to start something. But we've spent a lot of time together, and he's completely irresistible to me."

May smiled, and she seemed to recover her usual humor. "He's *so* handsome. And he doesn't know it, either. Which sort of doubles his appeal, right?"

I made a noise of agreement, just picturing him hovering over me in bed. "When he takes his clothes off, it doubles again. I probably have a sunburn from all the hotness that is Zachariah."

May grabbed a glass of water off the counter and pretended to douse herself with it.

"Oh, stop."

She grinned, putting down the water. "I would just like to point out that you have all the sex in this friendship. It's always been true."

"Not all of it. You had a smoking-hot boyfriend our junior year."

Her face seemed to close up at the mention of James, who I'd never liked. But he had been a looker. "Pretty long dry spell lately," she said with a sigh. "But I guess it's my own fault. I haven't exactly put myself out there lately. I wanted to settle a little first. Make my peace with my drinking problem."

"But that's going well, right?" I asked. I still hadn't figured out how to talk to May about it. And she didn't ever volunteer anything. Talk about holding your cards.

"Yeah," she said, closing the last of the cupboards overhead. "I have to leave now for a ten o'clock lecture. See you tonight?"

"Of course."

She gave me a quick hug, then left for school. I went outside to offer my services to Zach or whomever was working in the orchard today. I waved at Ruth in her garden, then walked toward the sound of a mower in the orchard. The Cortlands were ripe and heavy on the trees, and I wondered how many bushels we could sell at the market in Montpelier tomorrow.

I found Zach on an orange Kubota tractor, mowing the grass between a row of apple trees. When he saw me, he cut the engine. I walked toward him as it sputtered and died. "Hi there."

He gave me a big smile. "Hi yourself." He got off the tractor and approached me, taking my hands in his. "Feeling okay this morning?"

"Never better. You? Were the guys merciless?"

"Eh." He shrugged "There was some ribbing. But it had a desperate quality to it, you know? As if Kyle is all confused now because he doesn't know what to tease me about anymore."

Standing on tiptoes, I laughed. And then I kissed him.

Strong arms closed around me. His kiss was slow, his lips measuring mine as if trying to make sure he had all the details in place. I felt a happy zing of longing as he changed the angle and deepened the kiss.

Yessss. Desire was a lovely drug. I wanted more of it.

But Zach pulled back eventually. "Can we talk for a minute?"

No. "Really? This is our only moment of privacy, and you want to talk? Have I taught you nothing?"

I kissed him again, and he chuckled into my mouth. "You kill me," he whispered. "What I have to say won't take up too much time, okay?" He cupped my face in one of his hands.

"Are you going to say we shouldn't have done it?" I looked up into his serious blue eyes. "Because I have no regrets."

He shook his head slowly. "I wasn't going to say that. But I want you to know you're important to me. It wasn't just an itch I wanted to scratch."

I tried not to squirm under all that blue-eyed attention. "You're important to me, too," I admitted. He really was. I couldn't imagine getting through these past several weeks without his steady presence at my side. *Just don't fall in love with me,* I inwardly begged. *I'm a wreck and a half.*

He smiled again, and I tugged him into a kiss. He came willingly. One kiss became two, which became...we lost count.

At some point Zach turned me to the side and hoisted me onto the Kubota's seat. He stepped between my knees and kissed me again, his long fingers sweeping up my back.

It was glorious. He smelled like freshly mown grass and sunshine. I snuck a hand up under his T-shirt to skim those perfect, golden abs. I loved how silky his chest hair felt under my fingertips. He moaned softly when my fingertips retreated downward again, toward the waistband of his Carhartts.

I became aware of Griffin's voice in the distance. He was saying something about Cortlands. But I thought I could have one more kiss before he interrupted us.

But no.

"Lark?"

Unfortunately, that second voice did not belong to Griff or one of his cousins. I pulled away, giving a panting Zach a gentle nudge backward, and craned my neck to see past him. The two people standing beside Griffin were not who I was expecting. "Mom? Dad? What are you doing here?"

Zach practically leapt away from me, his head swinging toward the end of the orchard row, eyes wide as my parents walked toward us. There was no way they'd missed the fact that we'd been lip-locked a few seconds ago.

"This is a surprise," I said, my voice not entirely welcoming. They'd shown up without telling me, which made me feel like I was seven years old. My eyes traveled from my mother's tiny face, which suited her tiny frame, up a good foot and change to my father's stern expression. "Did somebody die?"

"No!" my mother said, her lips pursed. "We just wanted to see you."

"Okay," I said slowly, still feeling I was missing something. "So you *both* just drove up...on a Monday morning? A workday?"

"You told your mother that Mondays were quiet. No tourists and no markets," my father said. "So here we are. Aren't you going to introduce us?" His glance shifted to Zach.

I was still playing catch-up. "Mom, Dad, this is Zachariah," I said quickly. "Zach, these are my parents who don't call before they come to visit."

"Lark!" my mother's voice was sharp. "If I thought there was a chance you'd answer the phone, I would call more often."

"It's nice to meet you, ma'am," Zach said, extending a hand first to my mother. "Sir," he said, shaking my father's hand next.

"Well, someone has manners," my mother muttered, looking up at Zach.

Zachariah's face colored with embarrassment. I could only imagine the guilty thoughts in his head right now. It had been five or so hours ago that he'd been naked and moaning in my bed.

At last my brain caught up to the situation, and I clapped my hands. "So you both blew off work on a Monday to watch me pick apples?"

"You don't have to work," Griffin said from the end of the orchard row. "You all should take a walk. Show 'em the view."

"That's very kind of you, Griffin," my mother said, smiling up at him.

"We should have brought bikes," my father mused. Back in the day we'd all gone for bike rides on family vacations. I'd forgotten that until he said it.

"We have bikes," Griff said, brushing dirty off his hands. "Hey, Zach? You know where they are, in the back of the tractor shed?"

"Sure."

"There's four. You can go, too."

"What a lovely idea," my mother crowed.

I gave Griff the hairy eyeball. "There's really no need to blow off a workday."

He just smiled at me. "Have fun, Wild Child. Stay loose, Zach." Griff chuckled and Zach glowered.

Great. Now nobody was happy with me. Poor Zach. Meeting the parents was supposed to be carefully planned in advance. And now he'd met my parents with his tongue in my mouth, only a few hours after our big night together.

173

Ouch. I would have to make it up to him later.

Zach dutifully walked my parents through the orchard toward the tractor shed. I tried to catch his eye, but he asked my mother how her drive from Boston had gone.

Although I'd ever entertained the thought of introducing Zach to my parents, the guy was a natural parent-pleaser with those gentle eyes and perfectly deferential manners.

One by one, Zach lifted three bicycles off the wall of the shed. "Dylan keeps them oiled and in good shape," he promised. "The road is fairly flat if you go right out of the driveway. Left is a nice downhill, but Dylan says that getting back up it is a pain."

"Aren't you coming?" I asked him after he'd set us up with three bikes. My eyes begged. But Zach shook his head. "Please?" I asked. "Griff really won't mind. We can make it a short ride." *Don't leave me alone with my well-meaning but nosy parents.*

"I can't," he said quietly.

"Sure you can."

He looked up into the rafters. "No, I really can't."

"Oh." There was an awful silence while I realized what Zach was saying. It never occurred to me that he'd never had a bike. Every kid should have a bike. "We won't bike, then. We'll walk instead."

His eyes flared. "Go ahead, okay? Have some fun. See you later." Giving my forearm a gentle squeeze on his way past me, he left the tractor shed. I watched through the open doorway as he speed-walked back toward the orchard and Griffin in the distance.

After he disappeared, I turned back to my parents, who were watching me. "So," I said, clearing my throat. "That was Zach."

My mother looked down at the bicycle under her hands. "You didn't tell us you were involved with a boy."

A boy. She made me sound like a child again. "He's a nice boy," I said lightly. "Vermont has been good to me." I rolled Dylan's bike out into the sunshine. "Let's go." If I had to spend a day being observed by the parents, we might as well be in motion.

We saddled up and I led us down the Shipleys' drive and onto the dirt road which would take us past the bungalow and then toward the Abrahams' farm. "There's a swimming hole up ahead," I said as we pedaled. "It's pretty. I'll show you."

My parents rode behind me in silence, and I felt their eyes on me. But I had the breeze at my face and an open road. So I pedaled faster.

Zach

"You didn't go biking?" Griffin asked when I joined him on the way to the cider house.

"Never ridden a bike," I said, my voice gruff. "Not going to try for the first time in front of Lark's parents."

"Oh, shit."

I just shrugged. Getting left out of a bike ride didn't even make the top ten for humbling things happening today.

Griff paused outside the cider house, his hand on the doorframe. "You okay?"

"Of course."

"It's time to barrel my first fermentation."

"Then let's do it. How many barrels you need? Four?"

"Yeah."

As Griffin opened the double doors, I went around to the side of the building to fetch the empties we'd scrubbed down earlier in the season. The oak barrels that would take the cider through its second fermentation always smelled so good. The scent was a combination of wood and fruit, with an earthy muskiness that I loved.

I rolled the first barrel into place while he hooked up the siphon that would transfer the cider from the metal tank to the barrel. We worked in silence for a while. From time to time I caught Griff stealing glances at me.

"What?" I said finally, waiting for him to chew me out for starting something with Lark.

"Do you know about birth control?"

That was not what I expected him to say, and surprise made me laugh. "Yeah," I choked out. "And so does Lark."

Griff had the good sense to look embarrassed. "Well, good."

"If you're gonna lecture me, we'd best get it over with."

He rubbed the back of his neck. "I'm not going to lecture you. Just making sure you had everything you needed."

"We got it covered," I mumbled as my face heated. There was no end to the humiliations today.

"You can't blame me for checking," Griff said. "I remember a time when you asked me what fapping meant."

"'Cause that's a weird word!" I argued, and Griff laughed. "Pretty sure I discovered it at the same age as everyone else."

"Yeah?" Griff said, clamping down on his siphon now that the barrel was full. "That was probably a punishable offense where you came from."

"It was," I admitted. "You had to be stealthy. It was a middle-of-the-night kind of activity."

"I'll bet."

"They made sure to shame the hell out of whomever got caught with his hand in his shorts." I shuddered just remembering this. "One time a kid was jerking it behind the supply shed at just the wrong moment. One of the deacons made a spectacle of him that Sunday in church."

I could still remember my throat constricting as the preacher railed about it from the pulpit. Every boy in my pew looked ready to hurl. "They didn't toss that kid, though. He was only thirteen when it happened. They used him as an example instead."

"That is fucked up," Griff said quietly. "No wonder you weren't in a hurry to have sex."

That made me chuckle. "Some urges aren't so easily suppressed. As a matter of fact, the reason I got tossed from that place was for fooling around with a girl."

"Seriously?" Griff straightened up to his full height. "You never told me that."

"I know." Honestly, it was trippy having this conversation with Griff. "*That* is what made me not want to have sex. Sex made me homeless. And I can't even guess what happened to her."

"Jesus." Griff blew out a breath. "That's some kind of sex education."

"True." I checked the fit of the plug in the barrel. "Guess I prefer your version after all."

He snickered. "Last year I tried to have a little man-to-man chat with Dylan. I got out a banana and a condom and showed him how to unroll it. He was not amused, but my dad is gone, so he had to put up with my meddling..."

I had no snarky comment to make about that. Griff took good care of his family even when it got embarrassing.

"And then I realized how sexist it was to only speak to one twin. So I took the banana and the condoms and knocked on Daphne's door."

Now I laughed, trying to picture it.

"Yeah. That conversation went differently. She said, 'Let me show you this text on women's health I read when I was fourteen.' This thing was as thick as the phone book. Daphne said, 'I know chapter and verse about birth control and STDs. I don't need to discuss my vagina with my big brother, and don't forget I'm handy with the shotgun.' So I took my banana and ran away."

I doubled over.

"So thank you for not threatening my life when I tried to make my little speech."

"No problem," I said, wiping my eyes.

"There's always condoms in the glove box of the truck, by the way. I leave them there for Dylan or Kyle or whoever."

"Message received." We worked quietly for a while. "I thought you were going to give me a hard time about getting involved with Lark."

Griffin shook his head. "That's not my business. I didn't want people hitting on her when she showed up. Just out of concern for her mental health, you know? But that's not your style, and I know it's not like that."

"It really isn't like that."

Griff lifted his chin to study me.

"What?"

"Just hope you don't get your heart broken, that's all. I'm not criticizing. But I don't know if Lark's head is in the right place. I'm sure she cares for you, but I don't know her plans."

I didn't either. And it bothered me, though I wasn't about to say so.

Luckily, Griff's phone rang. "Could be Jude or the plumber with a question." He pulled out the phone. "Baby!" he said. "What's happening in Paris? Do you miss me?"

Saved by Audrey instead. I set up the next barrel while Griffin chatted with his fiancée. The sweet nothings they exchanged sounded like this: "And what kind of yeast are they using for the second fermentation? Ah, interesting."

Right before lunchtime, Jude arrived with news from the bungalow where he'd been watching the plumbers for Griffin. "Everything looks great. I brought pictures." He pulled out his phone to show Griffin shots of the new work.

"It's really coming together!" Griff hooted. "Let me buy lunch, which is probably a sandwich my mother made."

"Sounds good to me."

We all headed back to the farmhouse. Lark and her parents were already there, helping Ruth get lunch on the table.

They're probably perfectly nice people, I reminded myself. But it unnerved me that Lark's family was both rich and brainy. Lark had told me that both her parents were college professors. Her father taught at Harvard Law School. Her mother studied cells in a lab.

Lark set down the knife she was using to slice Ruth's homemade pickles. She crossed the kitchen when I appeared and gave me a pickle-scented hug. It was just a quick embrace, the same as she might give May at the end of the day. But I've never appreciated any gesture more.

She claimed me, right in front of her family and the Shipleys. And just like that, the worry train in my head ground to a halt.

Ruth had set up a make-your-own-sandwich bar on the sideboard. "Please dig in," she said. "I'm just going to run the sandwiches I made for the day crew out to the orchard."

I spotted the lunch basket near the door. "I'll do it," I said quickly, picking it up before she could argue. She had guests to attend to. "Be right back."

Fifteen minutes later—after dropping off the lunch and taking some heckling from Kyle—I went back into the dining room and made myself a plate.

Griff and Lark were talking about their college days, which made sense because that's where Lark had met the Shipleys.

"I sent a bottle of cider to that professor last fall," Griff said. "With a note telling him that organic chemistry was coming in handy in the cider house. His reply came the following week, asking where he could obtain more samples of my chemistry. For research purposes, of course."

Everyone laughed. I pulled back a chair beside Ruth and sat down.

Lark's father's gaze swung in my direction. "And were you at BU as well, Zach?"

"Uh, no. Can't say that I was." There was a small silence while Mr. Wainright waited for me to supply more information. But I didn't have any to supply.

After a pause, Lark's mother helped me out by changing the topic. "Another reason we drove up today is that you received some registered mail." She reached for her purse on the floor and then dug through it. "I believe this is from your employer, honey. Since I had to sign for it, I assume it's something important."

I watched Lark take the envelope and squint at it. She ripped the strip off the top and pulled out a single sheet of paper and read it. "Those motherfuckers."

"*Lark*," her mother whispered, mortified.

"What does it say?" her father asked.

Lark dropped the page onto the table. "Three weeks. I have three weeks to either come back to work or provide a doctor's note explaining why I can't. Or separate from the company."

"Can they do that?" Ruth asked, her eyes wide.

"Probably," Lark scoffed. "And I understand why they have to. It's a nonprofit on a shoestring budget. They can't just cut me checks indefinitely while I try to decide what to do next.

180

But it's just so cold. Their legalese makes me want to punch someone."

Griffin, who was seated beside Lark, turned in his seat and reached for her. "I'm sorry, Wild Child." He folded her into a hug that made me itch to do the same.

"It's okay," she mumbled.

"What are you going to do?" her mother asked, and my chest tightened.

Three weeks. I'd always known that Lark was only here temporarily. But three weeks would pass by in a blink.

"Well..." Lark sat back in her chair as Griff released her. "I'm not sure. I'll think it over."

"Let's find you a doctor's note!" her father suggested, and my heart leapt in agreement. "How hard could it be? That doctor at Tufts thought you should continue treatment."

"Here's an idea!" Lark yelped. "How about we don't discuss my doctor visits at the table?"

"I think it's time for cookies," Ruth said, pushing back her chair.

"I'll get them," I said, beating her to it. I jumped up and went into the kitchen alone. Once I got there, I put my hands on the counter and let out a breath. The stress I felt right now was a brand new thing. I was pissed off that Lark was upset, and I was afraid she'd leave. I was irritated at her employer for putting their little ultimatum in an envelope and mailing it to her like an emotional letter bomb.

The rage I felt was completely unfamiliar, and I didn't have any idea what to do with it.

Someone else came into the kitchen, and I straightened up, trying to remember why I was there.

"Hey, now," Griff said. He walked up behind me and put his hands on my shoulders, giving them a quick squeeze. "Where does Mom keep the cookies, anyway?"

"Cupboard over the toaster," I mumbled.

Griff wandered to that corner of the kitchen and opened the cupboard. "Score!"

I just shook my head. Griffin was famous for never helping in the kitchen. But he got away with it because he worked about sixteen hours a day on every other damn thing. Trying to snap out of my funk, I grabbed a platter and set it in front of him. He tipped the cookie jar as if to dump them out, but I took it from him. "They'll be crumbs if you do it like that." I lifted the cookies one by one onto the plate.

"Don't panic yet, okay?" Griff said quietly as I worked.

"All right," I grunted.

"Everything might work out okay. She just needs a friend."

"Just a friend."

Griff sighed. "That isn't what I meant. Just keep being there. Don't change a thing. Hey—do you know how to make coffee? I offered to do that."

"Seriously? And they let you?"

"Sure." Griff shoved a cookie in his mouth and picked up the platter. "Because they knew you'd bail me out." He offered the plate to me.

I took a cookie. And then I made the coffee.

Lark

I spent the rest of the day with my parents. I got into the back seat of their car—feeling just like a little kid—and accompanied them to the Simon Pearce glassblowing factory, where we watched a handful of guys about my age make eighty-dollar wine goblets from blobs of glass so molten they glowed orange.

"That looks like fun," I said aloud. The young men had a bevy of unusual tools at their disposal. And I hadn't realized that glassblowing was a team sport. The hipsters passed each glass back and forth on the end of a six-foot-long metal tube. I wanted to climb over the little barrier and ask for lessons. It was a familiar itch I hadn't felt in a long time—the urge to drop everything and try something new.

"Let's have a cocktail at the bar," my father said.

With a longing glance at the glassblowers, I followed him upstairs.

* * *

I didn't get back to the Shipley Farm until the hour when everyone in the bunkhouse would be getting ready for bed. Walking through the door of that stone building filled me with relief. This place was my refuge. Nobody asked me tough questions or gave me ultimatums.

Someone was in the shower, so I passed the bathroom and poked my head into the rear bunkroom. Zach was lying in bed already, reading a thick book with the help of a little book light clipped to its cover. "Hi," I whispered.

He looked up and smiled at me. "Hi yourself."

"Hi, Lark!" Kyle said from one of the upper bunks. "Did you come to give me a kiss goodnight?"

"Dream on, Shipley," I said, crossing the room to Zach. I took the book out of his hands. "Come and visit with me. I haven't seen you all day."

"Is that what we're calling it now?" Kyle asked.

I flipped him off on my way out.

The book I'd carried for Zach was the seventh and final Harry Potter novel. And he was almost finished with it. "Have you read this before?" I asked as I set it on my bed.

"Nope," he said, perching on the edge. "I know it's a kids' book. I read other things, too."

I gave him a smile as I kicked my door shut. "I know you do. And who cares?" I stripped my T-shirt over my head and then took off my bra. "Harry Potter is for everyone. Not just kids." I grabbed the oversized BU shirt I liked to sleep in and dropped it over my head. "I have the first book on my phone, and it's what I pull out when I don't have anything else to read."

"Is that right?" Zach followed my every movement with his eyes. So I gave him a peek at my thong as I stripped off my shorts. His cheeks pinked up, but he didn't say a word.

I picked up the book again and handed it to him. "Make yourself comfortable. I'm going to brush my teeth."

But he slung an arm around my waist and pulled me closer to him. "I missed you today."

I kissed the top of his head. "Back at you, cutie." Then I wiggled out of his embrace.

After I got my turn in the bathroom, I found Zach propped up against the headboard, his nose in his book. I walked around and got into bed. There was no lamp on my side, so reading beside him wasn't going to work. But I was tired and didn't care.

When I settled in next to him, he closed the book, letting it rest against his chest. "I don't want the series to end."

"Hear you." I snuggled up, putting a hand on his chest. "Nobody ever does."

"I read the first two at school when I was a kid. My fifth-grade teacher kept it on a shelf for me, because she knew I couldn't take it home."

"No?"

He shook his head. "We didn't have books, except for the bible. And there was a book about the founder of our, um, church. But the rest were forbidden. Harry Potter would never have been allowed, because witchcraft is the work of the devil."

"Yikes. Really?"

He nodded, his eyes dancing. "In fact, the Harry Potter craze was one of the things that made the elders decide to pull us all from the school district. Kids came home on the bus asking for all kinds of things they disapproved of. So after sixth grade I was homeschooled." He used air quotes around the word. "That just meant free labor for the ranch after a couple hours of bible study in the morning. So it was eight or nine years before I could pick up the series again. J.K. Rowling was kind enough to finish writing it in the meantime."

"That's a nice way to look at it."

Zach ran a hand over the book's cover. "When I was a kid I felt sorry for Harry in his cupboard under the stairs."

"Yeah. That's how she wants you to feel when you read it. She's great at establishing empathy."

"Sure. It's funny—I thought I was better off than Harry. It took me a long time to realize that Aunt Petunia and what's-his-name were at least honest about not wanting Harry. When I read the first book, I thought they were the height of evil. Took me a few years to realize how many of the boys I knew would be tossed away."

"Like you," I whispered. He shrugged, but the casual gesture didn't fool me. "They're idiots, Zach. Dumber than the Dursleys."

His eyes held mine for a long moment. Then he tossed the book off his chest, smiled, rolled, and kissed me.

* * *

Oscar has brought me something. It's in his pocket. I want it badly, but he's nervous. His eyes keep going to the door. I know I'm dreaming, and that the thing in his pocket will be our undoing. But I want it anyway. I want to know what it is, and I want to know what happens next. I'm tired of the fear and of the not knowing.

"Por favor," I say.

Please.

His dark eyes measure me. I can see he's conflicted. I'm scared, as always. But I'm angry, too. I'm burning up with anger. The dream won't let me go until we reach the end.

He reaches into his pocket, but the shouting starts immediately. Someone's banging on the door...

I awoke on a gasp in the dark. My eyes flew open and my heart was racing. Behind me, Zach shifted in his sleep, pressing closer to me. By now he'd basically programmed his subconscious to comfort me in the night. Half the time when I finally wrestled free of my dreams and woke, he was rubbing my back in his sleep.

I took a slow breath and tried to calm down, but it wasn't easy.

Lately there were two different Larks. One of them was lying in perfect safety beside Zach. That was the Lark who picked apples and wanted to learn glassblowing. The other one was still inexplicably trapped in Guatemala, and freaking out.

By day I pretended that Lark didn't exist. But she did.

I lay awake now, my thoughts sifting through the awkward day I'd spent trying to convince my parents that I was fine. I'd put on a good show. They'd driven back to Boston after hugging me goodbye, and they didn't look too worried about me.

Except they'd brought me that fucking letter.

I tried to imagine myself walking into the office two weeks from now, a latte from Starbucks in one hand, my laptop in the other. I'd given my whole self to that job. I'd took their transfer assignment with good cheer and upended my life for them. Now they wanted me to come back and pretend like it never went badly.

Or quit.

Shit.

Closing my eyes, I concentrated on the feel of Zach's firm hand against my back. What did I want, anyway? Did I want that job? I liked working for a nonprofit. I liked trying to make a difference. They did some good work in the world, too. They helped Brazilian sugarcane producers become more efficient and offer their employees a better life. They helped Guatemalan coffee growers cut down fewer rainforest trees.

And working for them had almost gotten me killed.

The truth was that I didn't need that job. If I wasn't ready to go back to work, I didn't have to. Money wasn't a problem for me or my family. I had several paychecks from the Shipleys in my purse. Uncashed.

But, damn it! I'd won that job after college. I'd interviewed and impressed them. And now they were tossing me out like a used-up, environmentally sensitive, unbleached tissue.

I could get a doctor's note and prolong the decision. I could go back to the psychiatrist in Boston and tell him exactly how bad things were when I tried to sleep.

The problem with that would be admitting the problem to my parents. I didn't want therapy. I didn't want to talk about my feelings or—worse—be hypnotized to try to tease out my scary memories.

It was not a problem that would be decided tonight. But I lay awake for hours anyway, worrying about it.

I must have drifted off again, eventually. Because I was sleeping when I heard Zach's alarm go off. He turned, and I reached back to touch his sleepy body, my hand finding his chest, which I caressed.

"You sleep okay?" he asked with a yawn.

"Yes," I lied. "You?"

"Perfectly."

A strong arm wrapped around my waist and soft lips traced the back of my neck. His kisses were slow and sleep-warmed. They trailed down into the collar of my T-shirt, while one of his work-roughened hands slid under the fabric to caress my waist. He ventured lower, his fingertips brushing the tiny scrap of fabric between my legs.

"Mmh," I sighed. "You're torturing both of us."

"I know," he said between kisses. "Wish it was Sunday."

"How many days away is that?" I mumbled.

He counted them out with kisses. "Five."

"Fuck."

He chuckled. "See you at breakfast?"

"Yeah. Go before I grab you and don't let go."

"I like the sound of that."

But he got up anyway.

Zach

Tuesday we did the Montpelier market together. Lark rode beside me in the truck with her hand on my knee. It made me crazy. I wanted to pull over on the side of the road and have my way with her. Instead, I settled for a few stolen kisses and sleeping in her bed again that night.

Something had shifted. The rules had changed, and now I could touch her whenever I wanted to. I didn't know how that had happened, but I wasn't arguing. When I passed behind her in our market stall, I put a palm to her lower back. And when we got back into the truck for the drive home, I kissed her before starting the engine.

Winning the lottery wouldn't have been half as exciting to me.

The one thing I didn't do, though, was try again to have any kind of Big Talk. I'd wanted to tell Lark how much I cared. But now there was a stopwatch ticking over us. Three weeks until she had to figure out whether to go back to work in Boston or make another plan for the future.

So I didn't weigh in. I didn't want my selfish desires to get in the way of her plans. And worse—if my feelings on the matter weren't going to count as a factor in her decision-making, I didn't want to know.

Griff had told me just to be there, not to panic. And that sounded like good advice. If I only got three weeks, I was going to make them count.

Wednesday was our day to do the Hanover market. But as I was loading up, Griffin loaded ten cases of hard cider onto the truck, too.

"Who're those for?"

"It's a delivery to Woodstock. Lark has the details. Have fun." Griffin walked away before I could ask any more questions.

"Griff wants us to drive to Woodstock after the market?" I asked Lark when she got into the truck. "We won't get home until late." The Hanover market was three to six p.m. And Woodstock was a half hour southwest of there. Maybe more.

"We'll have dinner in Woodstock together," Lark said. "I told Ruth not to expect us." She gave me a funny little smile.

"Okay." She had something up her sleeve, but I decided just to roll with it.

"Do me a favor?" she said. "Run into the bunkhouse and get long pants and a button-down."

I hesitated. "Really?"

"Yeah. Go." She made a shooing motion.

So I went.

The Hanover market went well, and we sold nearly everything.

"This is perfect," Lark said, surveying our empty apple crates. "Not much inventory to worry about. Let's go to Woodstock."

"Should I change now?" I asked. "I should have thought of that while we were loading up."

She shook her head. "No need." She got in the truck.

At the Woodstock Inn, I parked in back, by the loading dock. It was a fairly large hotel for this area. We offloaded our ten cases. But then Lark asked the kitchen guy an odd question. "Where can we park her overnight?"

He looked around. "That corner should be fine," he said, pointing.

"Why did you ask that?" I wondered when he disappeared.

She gave me a catlike smile. "I reserved a room. And I warned Griff that you won't be available for the milking in the morning."

"Really?"

"Really. He said you never took a day off in two years. So why not now?"

My gaze went to the truck. Could I really just leave it here for a night and fritter off with Lark? I supposed I could bring the cashbox inside with us. Was that safe enough?

Once in a while Griff and Audrey blew everything off for a day or two and got away together. And the earth didn't stop turning.

"Okay," I said slowly.

She laughed. "You sound like I've suggested an evening of dental work."

"Just give me a minute to get used to the idea." I tossed the keys in my hand. "I'll park the truck. Then we'll go inside and change for dinner. Was that your plan?"

Lark nodded, bouncing on her heels. "It's the world's shortest vacation. But I really need one."

I gave her a quick kiss, still marveling at the fact that I was allowed to do that. "Give me three minutes."

* * *

The hotel lobby was fancier than I'd expected. I felt out of place in my work boots and Shipley Farms sweatshirt. And I cringed when Lark handed over her credit card. "Let me pay you back," I said when the clerk turned her back.

"Nope," Lark said cheerfully, making me wonder how much this was costing. "But you can pay for dinner if you really want to."

When Lark had secured our key, we walked through the rather fancy lobby and past a giant stone fireplace. A few other guests milled about, looking like they'd just stepped off the golf course. It wasn't really my scene.

But the advantages to this outing became clearer as soon as Lark swiped the keycard through the reader outside our room. She pushed the door open to reveal a king-sized bed and a fireplace, where a fire already crackled.

Now that was more like it.

Lark set her backpack down against the wall. "This is nice." She wandered past the fireplace and disappeared through another door into what looked like a huge bathroom.

"Sure is." I set my bag down, too.

"I could use a shower," she called.

"Go for it." I went to the window and peered out at the well-kept grounds. It was already dark outside.

190

"Oh, wow," Lark said from the bathroom. "This is giving me ideas." The next sound I heard was running water.

I unlaced my dusty work boots and kicked them off. They looked all wrong on the ornate carpet. The room was beautiful, with a sloped ceiling and shining wood moldings. I wasn't used to luxury of any kind. Standing there between two upholstered chairs made me feel like an imposter.

That four-poster bed covered in white bedding, though? I saw the potential.

A few minutes later the taps stopped flowing in the bathroom. "Zach," Lark called. "Come here, please."

I walked into the bathroom to find her chest deep in a claw-foot bathtub. The sight of water lapping over her breasts sent my blood rushing southward. "Wow."

Her smile was sweet. "Well, don't just stand there. Get in."

Maybe I'd been too quick to judge this hotel.

I shucked off my sweatshirt and then the flannel shirt beneath it. Lark's eyes followed my every movement, and it made me a little self-conscious. I toed off my socks, then popped the button on my shorts. She licked her lips.

My increasingly dirty ideas about how this might play out were made obvious by the bulge in my boxer briefs. I'd certainly never stripped for a woman before, so pushing those underwear down was a unique experience. My cock popped straight up, and there was no disguising my desire.

I'd never been so naked before now.

"God, you're beautiful," she said on a gusty exhale. "It's not even fair."

Her words hit me like a warm breeze, tightening my balls, bringing goosebumps to my flesh. Every inch of me felt alive with yearning.

"Turn around," she whispered. "I want to see all of you."

But I hesitated. "There are scars. It's not the best-looking part of me."

Her head tipped to the side, and her gaze was soft. "I know, cutie. I felt them. But there is no ugly part of you."

Feeling a little self-conscious, I did what she asked, rotating slowly. I tried never to let anyone see the results of the beating I got on my last day at Paradise Ranch. But I showed her now, because she was going to see anyway.

I heard the sound of water sloshing, and then a wet hand skimmed over my ass cheek. "This is very 'Outlander,' you know. You're almost fashionable."

My laugh was a snort. The next thing I felt was the brush of her lips back there. She kissed my scars—actually kissed them.

You can bet nobody ever did that before.

"Now get in here," she said.

When I'd turned around, she bent her knees to make room for me. I stepped in, then sank down slowly, the hot water embracing me. When my ass found the porcelain, I took Lark's ankles in my hands and stretched her legs out, sinking mine below the surface. She wiggled, making room for me to unfurl, lengthening her limbs over mine.

"I have scars," she said quietly. "Mine don't show."

"I know," I whispered, stroking her foot. "I hope they heal up so you can't feel them anymore. Mine don't hurt now. I never think about them."

Her beautiful face became thoughtful. "Do you ever wish you'd gone to the police? Beating you was illegal. Assault and battery."

"Nobody ever went to the police. The boys who walk away from that place are too ashamed. They're convinced they did something wrong." No matter that my ass bled for days. I got a new pair of pants at a homeless shelter in Omaha, but I didn't admit that the blood on the old ones belonged to me. "I'm so happy to be gone from there now, I just try not to think about it."

"I'll bet."

"Isaac and Leah have a friend—Maggie—she lives in Massachusetts now. She ran away, too. She took Isaac and Leah's advice and gave her farm a name that'll help people find her. Isaac and Leah say that helping others is the best kind of revenge."

The look Lark gave me then was so heavy with love that it stopped me from breathing. "What?" I finally asked when she'd been studying me for long enough to heat my cheeks.

"I really want to crawl over there and kiss you."

My cock pulsed underwater. "What's stopping you?"

The next thing I knew I had a lap full of Lark. I pulled her wet, seal-like body onto mine and our mouths fused immediately. Each pull of her tongue made me moan. Each slide of her sleek skin against my cock made me crazier than the last.

My hands wandered her body unbidden. I cupped her heavy breasts in my palms and slid my fingers everywhere. When I dipped between her legs to stroke her, she moaned into my mouth.

"Need you so bad," I panted between kisses.

"Tell me what you want," she whispered.

"Everything."

"No, be specific. I want to hear how your dirty mind works." My face burned immediately, and she smiled again. "Just tell me one hot little detail."

"All right. But then I get to hear one of yours."

Lark laughed, and the sound broke up some of the tension in my chest. "Okay. Fair's fair. You first."

It wasn't easy, though. "Never talked like this with anyone," I admitted.

"I know." She kissed me on the nose. "But lust isn't shameful, no matter what they used to tell you. Now's your chance to stick it to 'em. Name a desire. It doesn't even have to be realistic."

I want you for my very own.

Yikes. That would be honest, but that wasn't what she'd meant.

Slowly, I leaned forward until my lips were just millimeters from her ear. "I want to make you come with my tongue."

"Unnng," Lark said, her forehead landing on my shoulder. "I'm not going to argue with that idea."

"Now you."

She lifted her smile and then put it beside my ear. "I want to sit you up in that big bed and ride you until you burst."

Mother of God. My head went thunking backward, hitting the wooden wainscoting on the wall. "I'm available, then."

She giggled. "Good. Your turn."

"All right." My dirty mind was on board this little train. "I want to take you with all the lights on, so I don't miss a thing."

Her big eyes widened. "But of course. Now let's see…" She chewed her lip for a second. "I want you to spread me out on the bed and fuck me from behind. Hard and fast."

A wave of pure, heated lust washed through me, and, instinctively, I tightened up every muscle in my lower body.

"That's a good enough start on our to-do list," she said, eyeing my tortured grimace. She put her hands on the edge of the tub and leaned down to kiss me slowly.

I opened for her, drawing her in, making love to her mouth. I was so ridiculously turned on, and she threw fuel on the flames by rubbing her soft sex all over me. It was entirely possible that I was about to become the first man to ever burst into flames in a bathtub.

Lark's flailing hand reached up to find a lever on the wall. She flicked it and I heard the drain engage, and the sound of water running out of the tub. We kissed, and the contact with her slick, soft breasts tortured my chest as the water level fell.

But she hit the lever again before the tub emptied. She lifted her hips off mine and I looked down to see that while my ass was still sitting in four or five inches of water, my aching dick was no longer submerged.

We dove in for another kiss, because any other action was impossible. I'd never felt so overpowered by need. My arms locked around her back. I swear, the building could have crumbled around us and I wouldn't have noticed.

As we kissed, she levered herself higher on my body until she was right there, teasing the tip of my dick with her slickness. "Do it," I begged.

On a sigh she lowered her tight heat over me. I was sheathed in bliss, and my moan was matched only by hers. Our desperate sounds bounced off the nearby walls as she began to rock her hips against mine.

Luckily it was close quarters, and she didn't have a lot of room to maneuver. That's what kept me from erupting on the first slide of her precious body over mine. I took sip after sip of her mouth and gave myself over to the moment, my hips rolling to meet hers. We were so close together that the sound of every tiny breath was magnified. The water droplets echoed. The click of our teeth was audible as we kissed.

Her brown eyes stared into mine as her body welcomed me inside again and again. When I looked into her big-eyed gaze I saw my own desperation reflected back at me. The need we had for each other was bottomless. I gripped her against me as if more of this glorious friction could drive away the vulnerability I felt whenever I pictured her leaving me.

She picked up the pace, and her breathing accelerated. Those beautiful eyes fell shut, and she pushed her face into my neck. "I need...to come," she gasped.

"Show me," I panted. "Come all over me." I put both hands to her breasts, stroking my thumbs across the nipples. I'd never get enough of the way her body tightened wherever I touched it.

She bucked and mewled against me, her rhythm stuttering. I grasped her chin and lifted it, finding her mouth with mine, sucking on her tongue. She gave a muffled cry, and squeezed my cock with her body, gripping me like a fist.

My own climax roared through me then, sending me into freefall, blotting out everything but pleasure and release. My head fell back against the wall and I let out a bellow of satisfaction as her body milked me in sweet pulses.

A few moments later it was quiet again. The only sounds were the dripping faucet and our panting breaths. Lark was collapsed on my chest, and my clumsy fingers were woven into her hair.

"You cold?" she asked eventually.

"No," I laughed. What was cold? I couldn't even remember feeling anything unpleasant. "Are you?"

"Not yet. But we should probably rinse off and get out. Our fingers are probably pruny."

"Totally worth it," I mumbled.

She smiled at me as she peeled herself off my body. She turned on the warm water and rinsed that beautiful body off while I watched. Then she carefully got out of the tub and wrapped herself in a big white towel.

Reluctantly I stirred, too. "Can I take you to dinner now, before it's too late?" I asked.

Her eyes darted to the clock. It was eight-thirty. "Let's go before I tuck myself into that bed with you instead."

As if I'd argue.

Lark

I put on a pair of dark-wash jeans, along with a cashmere sweater. They were the nicest clothes I'd brought to Vermont. I'd considered asking to borrow something from May, but then I chickened out. We hadn't discussed Zach again, and her disapproval had really bothered me.

When we were both ready, Zach took my hand and led me to the tavern room for dinner. It was a gorgeous room—low and long, the ceiling and walls clad in dark wood. Candlelight flickered on every table.

"Sit anywhere," a waiter in a crisp white shirt invited us.

Zach chose a small table by the fireplace and pulled out my chair. Then he sat down opposite me. There were two red stains on his cheeks, and his lips were still flushed red from our lovemaking.

"You clean up nice," I teased, admiring the V of honeyed skin showing in the open collar of the shirt he'd chosen. "Who'd guess we spent the day selling apples off a truck?"

"As do you." His blue eyes smiled at me.

"Not bad for a redneck."

He leaned back in his chair, looking relaxed and happy. "The growing season in Vermont is really too short to make me a redneck. Pink, maybe."

A waiter hurried up with two menus. "Good evening. Here is our wine list. There is also a selection of local craft beers, and I'm told we just received a new shipment of local ciders by Shipley…"

Zach and I burst out laughing, startling the waiter.

"Sorry!" I said. "We delivered the cider."

"Oh." He gave us a polite smile. "I guess I don't need to describe it, then."

"Not to us," I said. "We'll probably choose a bottle of wine. Cider is our day job."

He left us with the menu, and I realized I was starving. "Ooh, oysters! Are you a fan?"

Slowly, Zach shook his head. "I've learned to eat a ton of new foods since I came to Vermont. But those don't do it for me."

"They're supposed to be an aphrodisiac," I teased.

He beckoned to me, and I leaned across the table. "Just smile at me. That's all it takes."

My heart contracted with happiness. Zach was a beautiful person inside and out. And for some reason he chose me. I didn't know why. I couldn't understand why, and my confidence was shot to hell. But whenever he calmly put a hand on my back, I felt less alone. And when he held my hand he reminded me that I hadn't always felt this way.

That it might get easier.

I ordered the red snapper with Israeli couscous and he ordered the saddle of rabbit with porcini risotto. "Red wine okay?" I asked.

"Of course."

I chose a bottle of chianti.

When our food came, it was rich and satisfying. This restaurant was fancier than the word "tavern" suggested, without being fussy.

Zach examined the crystal goblet in his hand. "I like this place, but it makes me feel like an impostor."

"What do you mean?"

"Every other guy in here is probably named Ethan and drives a Mercedes."

"Well, maybe." I glanced around. It was a weeknight, which tended to bring out the retired couples. And Woodstock was one of the most moneyed towns in Vermont. "But the point of staying in hotels isn't to worry about whether you fit in. Nobody does. We're all just borrowing a little corner of someone else's world."

"Hmm." He sipped his wine and smiled at me again. "So I'm an Ethan for the night?"

"Exactly. And I'm..." What would Ethan's girlfriend be named? I took a sip of wine and tried to decide. Jessica? Emily?

"Beverly," he suggested.

"Beverly?" I tried not to aspirate my wine. "Ugh. That's not sexy."

He shrugged. "If I'm Ethan, you're Beverly."

"Fine," I gave in. "You're my insurance salesman, and I'm your interior designer. We fell in love over an annuity contract." I found his feet under the table and tucked mine against them.

"Later I'll show you my policies." He lifted his eyebrows at me, and I giggled.

* * *

After dinner we made a half-assed attempt at pretending we weren't in Woodstock for the sole purpose of having lots of sex. We walked up and down the town's adorable Main Street, window shopping, since all the stores were closed for the night.

Zach was always more talkative when it was just the two of us. He held my hand and told me a funny story about Audrey's first time picking apples this season.

"She said, 'Griff, there's something wrong with this one tree.' And he said, 'That's okay, baby, you won't find apples on it because that's a plum tree.'"

"Aw! When does Griff get Audrey back?"

"Three weeks? Something like that."

The words *three weeks* just sort of hung in the air for a moment, making us both glum.

We headed back up the Inn's long walkway, toward the elegant porch. "Where did the fall go already?"

Zach didn't say anything, so I checked his face, which was downcast.

Shit. "Hey. Thank you for being the only person who hasn't quizzed me about what I'm going to do about that letter." I squeezed his hand.

He sighed. "It's not that I don't care, but I assume you'll let me know when you figure it out."

"I'm frustrated with them, but also myself," I admitted. "I've never been a drama queen. I'm not fearful. I don't hide from *anything*."

Zach squeezed my hand as we walked through the double doors and the lobby toward our room. And he listened. Like he always did.

"But I don't feel like I can walk in there and sit down at my old desk and handle their bullshit anymore."

"So don't," he said. "Maybe a different job would feel better. You could work for someone who doesn't make you angry."

"Except I don't know who I'm angry at," I admitted, pulling out the room key and swiping it past the reader. I pushed the door open. "It's not their fault that I didn't listen to instructions. They're not the ones who grabbed me off the street. God, I'm so sick of being inside my own head. I'm so sick of me." I flung myself down, stretched across the giant bed.

Zach lay down beside me, his chin on his arms. "I'm not sick of you." He slid a hand down my hair. "And I won't ever be sick of you."

I tipped my head to the side, and the sight of his kind face calmed me down. He stroked my head in a way that was more comforting than sexual. "I'd do anything for you, you know that, right?"

My eyes burned at the idea. I *did* know that. It scared me, too. And I didn't know why.

* * *

"Lark. I'm here. You're fine. Wake up for me," Zach's voice urged from somewhere in the distance. "Please," he begged.

But the comforting sound came from too far away.

I'm back in the dusty shack. It's been weeks since I felt safe, but Oscar is here and he has something for me. A candy bar! The wrapper is the same design I've known my whole life. I marvel at it, because nothing else here is connected to the world I know.

Oscar has snuck this in for me, and my mouth has begun to water just seeing the package. He can't untie my wrists. Instead he unwraps the chocolate carefully so as not to make noise and holds it up for me. I eat it in three greedy bites, I'm so hungry.

Then he uncaps a bottle of water and brings it up to my lips. "I'd do anything for you," he says in Zach's voice.

NO, I want to shout, but I can't because I'm drinking cool, clean water from the bottle he holds.

The door slams open and Oscar jumps. The water spills on my face, but I barely notice because The One In Charge is shouting. The words are fast and furious, and I know right away that this is bad. He unsheathes his knife, and I start to tremble.

Oscar looks terrified. And then the man orders him to do something so frightening that I feel like throwing up the chocolate bar.

And all I can do is watch it play out. I know I'm dreaming, but I'm dreaming what really happened, and my limbs are frozen in place. I want to look away as I always have before, but tonight I can't.

Oscar doesn't argue with his tormentor. He just stands there beside me and holds his ground. Even when The One in Charge trades his knife for a gun and shoves Oscar until he falls over my body.

Even when The One In Charge tells Oscar to do something that takes my breath away.

The shouting draws the other two men from outside. The words are still flying and I can't understand many of them. But one word in particular is all too clear. And when the other men appear, there is amusement on their faces. They've come to watch the spectacle of Oscar and a challenge.

They are all staring at me now, but I can only look at Oscar. He watches me instead of the gun.

The One In Charge repeats his command. I feel my body shaking. I'm afraid that Oscar will do as he asks. I'm also afraid that he won't.

I was just afraid. More afraid then I'd ever known I could be.

Oscar's eyes are as round as saucers. I'd do anything for you, they say.

The One In Charge screams at Oscar and shoves him onto me. But Oscar rolls away, finally barking something back at the man with the gun.

A refusal.

The gunshot comes out of nowhere, deafening me.

I let out a bloodcurdling scream that finally woke me.

Zach scooped me up out of the bed and pulled me to his chest, the way you'd comfort a toddler. "Shh, sweetie," he said, his voice shaking. "Shh. Shh."

When I was finally able to focus on his face, his eyes were wet. That's how I knew I'd been inconsolable for a while. "Oh, fuck. I'm sorry."

He shook his head and held me closer.

Tears began to drip down my face. Because even as I slept beside Zachariah in a luxurious king-sized bed on one-million-thread-count sheets, the dream came for me.

And now I knew how Oscar had died. Defending me from something awful. Sobs wracked me.

"You're okay now," Zach whispered. "You're fine."

But I wasn't. Not at all.

Part Three: Late Season

Ashmead's Kernel

Keepsake

Baldwin

Zach

Lark had told me that our night in Woodstock was a vacation that she'd needed. But afterwards, she seemed sadder than ever.

Nobody noticed except for me. May was busy with midterms and with writing a beast of a paper for one of her classes. The fall days ticked by, and Griff was eager for Audrey's return. His kitchen renovation was almost done, too. He was still waiting on the countertops he'd picked out. He wouldn't have plumbing until they were installed and the water was hooked up again. But it was close.

The harvest was in full swing, and Griff and I were pressing cider every night after dinner. A few times he asked me how Lark was doing, and I said she was fine.

I would later realize how big a lie this was.

In my defense, I was fooled by the fact that her bad dreams subsided. She was still prone to talking in her sleep, and reaching for me in the dark. But the screaming and thrashing had quieted. So I was able to convince myself that things were better.

Though her face told a different story. Whenever she thought nobody was looking, Lark wore a troubled expression. By now she was really good at faking it. She never walked into the farmhouse with anything but a smile. For the Shipleys, she put a brave mask on it.

Alone, though, she was broody. She'd lapse into silence while we drove to the market, staring out the window as the meadows rolled by.

I didn't worry as much as I should have, because I didn't want to see it. At night she kissed me like she was drowning and I was her oxygen. Sex was her escape, I think. We learned to do it almost silently, waiting until the chorus of snores started up in the bunkroom, then making love slowly, swallowing each other's moans.

204

Part of the reason I didn't pay enough attention was—and this always happens—I got sick. One Friday I woke up exhausted. Moving my body around the farm felt like wading through hip-deep snow. At lunchtime I actually fell asleep in my chair while Griff and Lark went over the market receipts.

"You okay?" Griff asked me after my head grew heavy enough to do that bobbing thing that's so disconcerting. Even after being away from the Paradise compound for a few years, I startled awake, expecting the switch to land across my hands as it used to if I fell asleep in church.

"I'm fine," I said, shaking myself awake. "Maybe I just need another cup of coffee."

That afternoon Lark and I helped with the picking. May was there, too, since her usual class had been canceled. Even though I felt ill, it was relaxing to listen to the female chatter as we picked. And when I lifted my eyes to the mountain ridge in the distance, I saw the most beautiful color of red-orange.

Fall in Vermont was spectacular. That's why people came in droves to pick apples and buy pumpkins on the weekend. It kept the hotels full and the tips high at the bars my friends owned. The air was crisp and scented with leaves.

But there was a stopwatch ticking over me all the time. Lark would leave Vermont, and Audrey would return. And at some point—probably after all the season's cider was pressed—Griff would give me the bad news. That I'd have to move on, too.

Usually I wasn't such a pessimist. The headache creeping across my forehead wasn't helping.

"These are funny-looking apples," Lark said, picking another Keepsake off the tree. "Are they for cider?"

"Nope," Griff's voice said from another row nearby. "The Keepsake is an heirloom apple. The grocery wholesalers don't want 'em because they're small and irregularly shaped."

"Just like Kieran!" Kyle volunteered.

"Fuck off," his brother grumbled.

Griff continued as if they'd never spoken. "I like 'em, though. They have a nice acidity, and they keep forever. It's not like a Macintosh that gets squishy in a week. These babies have staying power."

"Huh," Lark said. "Good to know."

By evening my nose began to run, and my head was full-on pounding.

"Oh dear," Ruth said over dinner. "Here comes Zach's fall flu."

"Maybe I'm just fighting something off," I said quickly.

"I'll get the Motrin and heat you a cup of cider," she suggested.

"Thank you," I said with a sigh. I hated being the one who was always leveled by the flu. It really put a dent in my goal to be the MVP of farm work.

That night I stood in Lark's doorway and told her I was going to sleep in my old bunk so she didn't catch anything from me.

"Come here," she demanded from the bed. "I never get sick. It's my special skill. And you look like you could use a little TLC." She raised her arms, her pretty face lifting toward me with expectation.

And I went. Never could resist her.

She had me sit in front of her in bed, then she rubbed my neck and shoulders, and finally my scalp, with slow, loving strokes.

I let out a loud moan, and she laughed. "They're going to tell us to keep it down in here," she joked.

"Don't care," I mumbled. "I thought sex was good. But that's before you ever rubbed my head."

I felt her smile, even though I couldn't see it. "It's nice to be the one who comforts you for a change. Do you get sick a lot?"

"A couple times a year. The Shipley's family doctor said it's because I was never exposed to a lot of the common germs as a kid."

"Ah. That makes sense." After a few minutes of heavenly attention, I repositioned myself on my side of the bed. But she wasn't done with me yet. She curled her body close to mine and rubbed my chest. "I'm sorry you don't feel well."

"I'll be fine. It's no big deal." A man didn't bitch about his aches and pains.

I don't know how convincing I was, though, since I fell asleep in the middle of our conversation.

The next morning, I woke up to see sunlight streaming into the windows. I was alone in the bed. I lifted my wrist in a hurry to check my watch, but it was missing.

Either a watch thief had relieved me of it in the night, or it was Lark's doing. The clock on the bedside table said nine thirty.

Shit!

I got up fast, stumbled into my clothes and headed for the farmhouse. Through the kitchen window I spied Lark alone, her face downcast. Her expression gave me pause. But when I opened the back door and stepped inside, she lifted her chin and made her expression cheerful again. "Hi. Did you sleep?"

"Yeah," I said, my voice hoarse from disuse. "We're supposed to be in Norwich."

"Kyle and Kieran went," she said, sponging down the countertops. "They were pretty giddy about it, honestly. They said they hadn't gotten one of those cider donuts all year."

"Oh." I was still uneasy. "So who's selling apples to the tourists?"

"Griff, May and Dylan. Grandpa is pouring the cider samples. Don't *worry*, okay?" She gave me a smile that was more genuine than any I'd seen on her face in a week. "Everything is *fine*. And I saved you some breakfast. It's a weird morning anyway, because Ruth had to drive out this morning to pick up D—"

She didn't get to finish that sentence, because I'd pulled her into a hug. Giving her my mouth wasn't a great idea, given that I felt even sicker than yesterday. But I dropped my lips to her neck and gave her a soft kiss. And then another.

"You're hot," she said, her hand cupping my cheek and then my forehead.

"So are you, baby," I joked, even though I knew she meant that I felt feverish.

Lark's concern for my health pulled my heartstrings in unfamiliar directions. Other people had helped me before when I was sick. The Shipleys had always brought me soup and took me to doctors when necessary. Also—they never docked my pay. I don't know why, but my paychecks were the same amount even when I was flat on my back for a few days during cider season.

But Lark's care felt different to me. It was tender in a way I'd never experienced. It was *personal*. Just for me.

"Let's get you some more aspirin," she suggested, rubbing my arm.

But I wasn't done loving her. I pushed her up against the refrigerator and kissed the sensitive skin under her ear. Soft hands crept beneath my T-shirt in a soothing way, and I sighed as I kissed her again.

That's when I heard a gasp.

Now, Lark and I usually didn't indulge in PDA. But it wasn't a very risqué moment, even by my standards. I lifted my head in surprise, wondering who found this behavior shocking.

Daphne, that's who.

"Hi there," I said, straightening up, trying to be polite. "You're home for the weekend?" I hadn't seen her since Labor Day.

She didn't answer the question. She just looked between Lark and me, and then back again. I took a half step backward and waited for Daphne to say something. Instead, her eyes got wet. Then she spun around and ran away.

"Shit," Lark whispered beside me.

I just stood there staring after the younger Shipley daughter, addled by both confusion and a fever. "What the hell did I say?"

"It's not that." Lark put a hand to my back. "Have a seat in the dining room, okay? Can you eat?"

"Not really hungry."

"You? That's it. I'm calling the paramedics. Did I mention there's bacon?"

"Oh. Well, I suppose I could eat." No flu was terrible enough to put me off a few strips of bacon.

She laughed. "Go sit. Coffee?"

"Always."

I sank into a dining chair, feeling miserable. Lark brought me a plate a minute later. She'd saved me a slice of quiche and several strips of bacon. There was coffee and a big glass of ice water, and two Advil tablets.

I picked up my fork and did my best. "What do you think that was all about in there?" I asked Lark, thinking of Daphne's quick exit.

She gave me a sad smile. "Wow. Thank you for demonstrating that even you can be clueless."

"Even me? Especially me."

She shook her head. "You are anything but clueless, except when it comes to teenage girls who are in love with you. She's got it bad."

I set down my fork, feeling ill all of a sudden. "No. That's just Griff's joke."

"Not so much."

"But Daphne's just a kid."

"She isn't. Not anymore. And even kids can fall hard. I thought I'd die when my tenth-grade biology teacher got engaged."

My head swam as I tried to make sense of what she was telling me. "I don't know what to say." *Or think.* Daphne was a great girl. But she was Griff's little sister. I never looked at either of the Shipley girls that way. That would just be weird.

Lark pushed the medicine closer to me. "Take this before you give up on breakfast. And don't feel bad. You're pretty irresistible. Ask anyone."

I rolled my eyes at her, because that was just ridiculous. But I took the medicine like she told me to.

Lark

After breakfast, Zach went out to find Griffin and offer his services. But the moment the back door closed, I texted Griffin. *Don't let Z do anything strenuous. He has a fever.*

His reply: *Got it Wild Child. Don't worry.*

I probably would, though.

The Shipleys had known Zach longer than I had, and they obviously cared about him. But I saw the way he always jumped out of his chair the minute there was any work that needed doing. He always put everyone else's needs before his own. And while I had no doubt that it was mostly due to his lovely character, there was something more at stake.

I worried that he was *compelled* to give so much because he was still afraid. Of abandonment. And that was no way to live.

May entered the kitchen just as I was washing lettuce for a lunchtime salad. I'd offered to do some prep work for Ruth. "How are sales?" I asked my friend.

"Fine. Have you seen Daphne? She was supposed to relieve Dylan and drive the tourist cart." On weekends, a couple of the Abrahams' Percheron horses drove tourists up into the orchard to pick apples.

"Well, I think she might be in her room."

"No way. That's just mean." May darted out of the room in a huff, heading for the stairs.

"Wait." I jogged after her, catching up to her on the stairs. She turned around, surprised. "She might be upset," I said in a low voice.

May's eyebrows flew up. "Because of you and Zach?"

"He and I were having a moment in the kitchen. Nothing too interesting." My cheeks were heating, which made me feel like Zach. "But that's when she walked in, and…" I cleared my throat. "Seemed like a big surprise."

May's face fell. "Ouch."

"Yeah."

One of the bedroom doors flew open, and Daphne appeared on the landing, her eyes red. "What are *you* doing up here?" she spat at me.

"Hey," May warned. "Don't cop an attitude with Lark. She didn't do anything to you."

"The hell she didn't!" Daphne said, her voice shrill. She faced me. "Go home to your fancy house in Boston already. We all know you're just slumming it here for the season. First you freak out May so bad she goes on a bender and loses her scholarship. Then you waltz in here and—"

"*What?*" I gasped, my mind stuck on that last bit.

When I turned to May, her eyes were bugging out. "Enough!" she shrieked at her sister. "You are *way* out of line."

"Me?" Daphne squeaked. "All I ever did was hold your hair when you puked. And tell the truth, which you'll never do."

"*Daphne*," May said, her voice weirdly shaky.

"You don't want Lark to know you've been in love with her forever? Whoops, sorry! And now she's with *him*..." That last word came out sounding like pure pain. She whirled on me. "That must be fun for May to watch. I hope you take better care of him than you do of the rest of your friends. Because—" A sob heaved from her chest. "—he's the best there is."

The slam of Daphne's bedroom door was like the exclamation point on the end of a very long, very confusing sentence. May and I were left there on the stairs together while my brain quietly imploded. "What was she...?" I didn't know how to finish the sentence.

"Don't listen to her," May whispered.

"But..." I studied my friend with fresh eyes. "What did she mean about your scholarship?" And then there was that other really troubling implication I didn't know how to address.

May cleared her throat. "This spring I didn't show up to take an exam. It was a pretty big deal, and it complicated my life. But that's not anyone's fault but mine."

The pressure in my chest argued otherwise. "Was that, uh, while I was missing?"

"Yeah. I didn't handle that too well." May hung her head.

211

"Why?" I pressed as the pieces of the puzzle began to slide into place. "What did Daphne mean when she said—"

"No." May raised a hand in the air. "We aren't going to talk anymore about my freak out."

"But, um." I swallowed the growing lump in my throat. "Once again I'm missing something important here. Aren't I? Why won't you just level with me? I'm sorry I'm so slow."

May pinched the bridge of her nose, and then wiped tears from both eyes. "You're not slow. There's just no point to discussing it further."

My eyes began to sting, too. "Isn't there always a point? I care about you, and I want to hear what's in your heart."

"But maybe it embarrasses me to tell you," she said quietly.

"Well, I'm sorry to hear that." A tear ran down my cheek. "Because I love you and I don't ever want to cause you pain."

"Sometimes we cause each other pain without meaning to." May sniffed. "Excuse me."

My best friend turned around, marched up to her room and shut the door.

Numb, I walked slowly back down to the kitchen. The prep work I'd promised Ruth was still there on the counter. In a daze, I washed the lettuce and shredded it into a bowl. But my mind was a million miles away, trying to make sense of what I'd just heard.

Daphne said May was in love with...me? Did that just happen?

I stood there, staring at my work without seeing it, trying to sift through my memory for clues. May had once hooked up with a girl who lived on our floor of the dorm. I knew it, and May knew I knew it. It wasn't a secret, but it wasn't something she talked about afterward. Just like we didn't discuss the time I had a threesome with a lacrosse player and his girlfriend in the basement of a fraternity.

It was college, right? We tried some things and had some fun. To my knowledge, May had dated only men. All the crushes she confessed to me were on men. There were lots of those.

Too many, maybe? Was she telling the truth about those?

My worried train of thought was interrupted by Ruth, who came in the kitchen door. "Hi, honey," she said with a smile. "Everything okay?"

No, not at all. "I washed the lettuce," I said stupidly.

She gave me a patient smile. "Thank you. And how is Zach?"

"Feverish."

"I'm not surprised. A cold that might bounce off the rest of us always cuts him down. Shall we heat a bowl of soup for him at lunchtime? I have some in the freezer."

"Good idea," I said, my heart heavy. "Excuse me for a moment." Dumbly, I walked outside, my feet pointed in the direction of the bunkhouse. Maybe it would have been better if I hadn't come to Vermont this fall at all.

* * *

The next two evenings were unbearable. May didn't look me in the eye at all. She always disappeared right after dinner, claiming she had to study. And poor Zach was sick. Both nights he fell asleep on his bunk right after dinner and slept for twelve hours.

I spent those nights tossing and turning in my bed, alone for the first time in a while. It wasn't bad dreams that kept me up, either. But guilt. And yet it seemed egotistical to imagine that my best friend had been harboring a secret crush on me.

If that were true, wouldn't I have noticed it before? I loved May, and I'd always considered myself a good, loyal friend. Yet Daphne had accused me of callous disregard for everyone's feelings. Lately I'd become a big believer in my own cluelessness, which made Daphne's theories easier to swallow.

On Tuesday, Griff sent me to the Montpelier market with Zach, who was mostly recovered. Or at least he said he was. Zach looked awfully pale, and he was terribly quiet. I wasn't great company, either.

"Did May get her paper written?" Zach asked me in between customers.

"Not sure," I mumbled. Zach hadn't noticed that May was avoiding me. He'd probably noticed Daphne staring daggers at me the whole time she was home. And now May wasn't speaking to Daphne, either. And Daphne wasn't speaking to Zach.

Griff had driven his youngest sister back to college last night. But the damage was already done. I'd come to Boston to relax, and give my parents a break from their worry. And in doing so, I'd come between several members of the Shipley family, and broken Daphne's heart. And maybe May's.

"You okay?" Zach asked as we finally got into the truck to go back to the farm.

How many times had he asked me that question this fall? A million? Shit. I was sick to death of being needy.

I was sick to death of *me*.

"I don't need you to ask me that anymore," I said quietly.

"Okayyy," he drawled.

Since I'd made conversation nearly impossible, the ride back to Tuxbury was long and quiet.

When we got back home, Griff met the truck and helped us unload. I tried to slip away to my room, taking my bad humor someplace private. But Zach followed me. "Hey," he said, appearing in my doorway just after I'd sat down on the bed. "Why are you mad at me?"

I looked up into his kind blue eyes, and my heart tightened in my chest. "I'm not mad at you. And I never would be."

"Then who are you mad at?"

Me. As if I had any right to be angry with anyone else. "I'm not mad. But I'm in a tough spot. I have to go back to Boston." The words just fell out of my mouth, but as I said them, I knew it was true. "My job..." That part was a lie, but it made for a convenient excuse. I couldn't stay here.

"So that's it?" he asked quietly. "You made up your mind?"

"Yes," I lied.

"I am in love with you."

My eyes filled instantly. I didn't think he'd go there, and it hurt me to hear it. "Well, don't be," I said, my voice a scrape. "I'm a mess, Zach."

"I'm not scared of messes."

"I can't be anybody's girlfriend."

He stiffened. "You can't, or you won't?"

I really couldn't. I'd known that from the start, too. But then I went ahead and got involved with him anyway. Once again, I'd taken when I thought I was giving.

"Can we start this conversation over?" Zach asked, rubbing the back of his neck. "That didn't come out the way I meant. And this isn't how I wanted this to go."

"This is the only way it can go."

"Why?" His voice cracked a little on the word.

Damn it. You had to give him points for honesty. Another man might try to protect himself—to back away from the sentiment. But not Zach. He was the best kind of person in the world, as Daphne had said.

And I was the worst. He didn't get it. But it was high time that he did. "It's not about love, Zach."

"It is for me."

"You knew I was only here for the picking season. What did you think would happen?"

His eyes reddened, and he turned the question right around on me. "What did *you* think would happen?"

This. May had warned me. And Daphne called it.

The dragons in my heart blew their noxious breath. Again. And now I was too tired to hold them back. I needed to leave Vermont before I caused this beautiful man any further pain.

"It was just sex," I lied, unable to meet his eye. "That's all. It was good, but it's over now."

The first second after I inflicted this wound was all shock—mine as well as his. His face turned an angry red. Then, after another two beats of my heart, Zach finally turned his face away from me and walked off. A second later I heard the bunkhouse door slam.

Steady, I coached myself. It's better this way.

On shaky knees, I got up and closed the bedroom door. Then I opened the desk drawer and pulled out the Boston letter demanding my presence next week. I also took out every paycheck the Shipleys had written me, and I tore them in half and dropped them into the wastepaper basket.

Then I sat very still on the bed and tried hard not to cry.

Zach

Manual labor. That was the only thing I was good for right now.

Luckily, another silver birch had managed to fall in the night, angling its papery trunk from the forested windbreak on the north border of the farm across the cow pasture. Luckily, it had taken out a section of the old split-rail fence.

I stood there swinging the ax with more force than was strictly necessary, happy when a satisfying chuck of wood went flying away from the cut. I wound up and swung again.

"Whoa, killer," Kyle cautioned. "Lemme go get the chainsaw. We'll make quick work of that."

"I got this one," I muttered, waiting for Kyle to clear out of the way so I could swing again.

"What's eating you?"

I shrugged, not wanting to talk about it.

Kieran had to pipe up then. "Lark giving you heartburn? Now that I think about it, you're smarter than all of us. You went twenty-three years without girl trouble."

My chest tightened, and I was seconds away from dropping the ax and walking away.

"What does she want from you?" Kyle pressed.

"Nothing. That's the problem."

"Hey, Griffin!" Kyle yodeled. "C'mere. Zach has woman troubles!" Of me, he asked, "Was she just looking for a quick round of fun? That happens sometimes."

Lord, that was all I could take. Dropping the ax, I said, "It's not like that." It wasn't, either. In my gut I knew Lark wouldn't just toy with me. Something was wrong, and she wouldn't tell me what.

Oblivious to my discomfort, Kyle followed me. "Then how is it like?"

Ugh. Spilling my guts to him wasn't on the agenda. "I thought we could be together. But she thought differently."

"So she fucked you and then abandoned you? That's cold."

"You know," Kieran put in, "women have been getting that treatment since sex was invented. You're the rare dude who's getting a taste of that medicine."

My answer came through gritted teeth. "I knew I was special."

"That's a tough break, man," Kieran said with real sympathy. "You want to get drunk later?"

"Now that you've had your first breakup, you might as well drink," Kyle suggested. "Comes with the territory."

"Shoo, morons." Griffin waved his cousins away and picked up the ax. "Don't listen to those two," he said, lining up his own whack at the tree. "On the subject of women, they're as useless as tits on a boar hog."

Griff swung, and I watched the ax bite into the pale yellow wood. "I don't know what's troubling her, and it's killing me."

Griffin swung the ax again, dislodging another chuck of wood. Then he knocked the wood chips out of the cut with a kick of his boot. "I told you already. Lark is too raw right now to make good decisions."

My heart sank. "She's pushing me away, so I can't even help."

"Give it time, Chewie." He clapped me on the back. "That's something you can give her, right?"

"She's going back to Boston."

"Boston's not that far away."

"That's not the song you were singing last summer."

Griff's face fell. "I know you're having a rough time. But so is she. If you really care about her, you gotta hang in there."

"I'll try."

"I know you will, because you feel it deep. Here." Griff patted his own chest. "Trust me when I say it's never the wrong thing to put yourself out there. I know you don't trust people very easily."

"Sure I do," I sputtered.

Griff raised a bushy eyebrow at me. "Uh-huh. That's why none of us can get a straight answer out of you when we try to talk to you about the GED program or the job for Maker. You want Lark to open up to you, right? But something scared her so bad she can't do it. You of all people should understand."

I just sort of stood there, choking on this idea, glaring at him. "I'm not afraid of anything."

"Yeah? Then why do you look like you want to puke every time someone asks you what you want to do with your life? Nobody is going to give you the boot, Zachariah. I like seeing your face every day, and you have this job as long as you want it. You can stay in my bunkhouse until you're Grandpa's age if you want, and then my kids will probably make you move into the farmhouse."

Griff handed me the ax, and I took it, dumbstruck.

"But don't tell me you're not afraid of being alone. We all are. It's fucking terrifying. I hope you don't lose Lark for good, man. That would blow. But you'll still have the rest of us to kick around, no matter what."

And then his cell phone rang. He gave me one more piercing Griffin stare, then pulled it out and answered. "Hey, Isaac. What's up?" I heard him laugh. "Yeah, one more week until my princess comes back."

He walked away, leaving me standing there with an ax, a fallen tree, and my jaw hanging open in surprise.

Lark

Night fell while I made my plans to leave Vermont. I called my parents and told them I was coming home, possibly tomorrow. They made all the right noises, then asked me what I was going to do about my job.

I told them I didn't know.

Next, I cleaned the room where I'd stayed all fall. Then I cleaned the bathroom I'd shared with several men. I threw away the little sign inside the plastic bag in the shower stall. *Warning: these are girlie-scented products. Use them and you'll never hook up again.* I packed away my pink razor.

When I was done, the room was a man's domain again, with nothing but their giant bottle of bargain shampoo and the straight razor Kyle used for shaving, because he thought it was macho.

My preparations were done, except for one important thing. I still needed to talk to May, but I could do that tomorrow morning.

Griff interrupted my preparations by knocking on my door. "Wild Child."

"Yeah?" I called, sounding guilty to my own ears.

"Turns out I need you at the Hanover market tomorrow."

"Um..." I opened the door. "I was going to head back to Boston."

"Go on Friday," he insisted. "Something's come up at Isaac's so we're down a man again. It's always something around here."

"All right," I said slowly. "But—"

He cut me off with a wave of one of his big hands. "Do me this favor?"

"Okay. Sure." It gave me more chances to talk to May, anyway. I didn't want to leave here without apologizing to her.

I tried to do that after dinner when we were both putting away the washed and dried dishes. But May waved me off. "I wasn't kidding before. We're never having that conversation."

"But you're avoiding me," I pointed out in a whisper. "We've never avoided each other before."

Her eyes closed for a second and then opened again. "Maybe I just need some space."

Ouch. "I'm going back to Boston in a couple of days."

Her hands paused on the silverware in the rack. "Okay. Thank you for telling me."

Her calm response was worse than if she'd just yell at me and tell me I was a shitty friend. I wanted her to tell me the things that best friends confided in each other. I needed to know what had happened in the spring, and if Daphne spoke the truth.

Did I even have a right to ask? I'd been the same kind of shitty friend since I'd stepped onto the property two months ago. I didn't tell her the scary things in my heart, either.

Claiming homework, May went upstairs as usual. Kyle and Kieran wanted to watch one of the Bourne films, and Zach had disappeared. So I watched half of an action movie with Kyle and Kieran, then slipped out to head for bed alone.

I still didn't love walking through the moonless night to the bunkhouse by myself, but I did it. The place was quiet when I ducked inside. I stood there a moment, staring at the closed door to the men's bunkroom, wishing I could see Zach's face.

Please be okay, I begged from the hallway outside my room. But I'd already forfeited the right to ask if he was.

Tiptoeing about, I got ready for bed. Sleep would not come easily, not with Zach just ten paces away. I closed my eyes and imagined his warm body curled beside mine. If I'd met him at a different time in my life, he might be lying beside me right now.

If only.

I studied the ceiling boards, each one outlined with a shadow cast by my nightlight. Before this fall, I hadn't needed a nightlight since I was six years old. I was so, so sick of being afraid of everything. So I pushed off the covers and tiptoed over to switch it off.

Lying down again, I stared into the dark. The glowing numbers on the digital clock were sufficient to outline the room. I wasn't afraid. I was, however, lonelier than I'd been in a long while. My eyelids began to feel monstrously heavy. I was just so tired. *But that's good*, I told myself. Tired people sleep better. With one more sigh, I rolled over and gave in.

* * *

Six hours later, I woke to the familiar sound of Zach's watch alarm going off. My sleep-coated mind offered up no memory of when he'd arrived in my room, or what bad dream I'd failed to fight off.

But I did remember with painful clarity the last conversation we'd had, and how awful I'd been. And even so, one of his hands was pressed sleepily against my spine, the way it always was when I'd been dreaming. I squeezed my eyes shut, horrified to have woken him in the night. *Again.* And even after the horrible thing I'd said to him, he'd come to my rescue anyway.

Hot prickles began to form behind my eyelids. Why did he have to be so fucking nice?

I held perfectly still like the coward that I was. I felt a tear slide from each eye, but luckily my back was to Zach.

There was a grunt, and the sound of Zach fumbling for the button on his watch. I held my breath, waiting for him to roll off the bed and leave. But that's not what happened. Instead, he rolled over to curve his body around mine. He swept the hair off my neck and nuzzled me softly under the ear. "Take care of yourself today," he said. Then he kissed me very gently on the neck.

Oh, hell.

I clenched my fists against the desire to roll over and dive into his arms. My next breath came as a sob. *Great.* I couldn't even stonewall someone the right way.

But Zach didn't call me on it. He just wrapped his arm around my waist and held on tightly while I swallowed my tears and evened out my breathing. *Calm*, I ordered myself. *Right now.*

Later today we were scheduled to do the Hanover market together. I didn't know if I could stand it.

Behind me, Zach sighed. He stroked my wrist with the pads of his fingers. "I'll see you later, sweetheart," he whispered. "It'll be okay," he added, just to prove he could read minds.

He got up then, dropping one more kiss onto my hair. And the air felt doubly cool against my back when he was gone.

Zach

When it was time to go to the Hanover market, I was surprised to see Griffin appear to load up the truck with me.

"It's the two of us?" I asked.

He shook his head. "Lark is coming, too."

That put me in a foul mood. Did Griffin not trust me to sell apples with Lark without a babysitter? Like I might lose my ever-loving mind between now and six p.m.?

I didn't say a word about it, though. That wasn't my way. And when it was time to leave, Lark appeared and climbed into the back seat, leaving Griff and I up front together.

It was a long drive.

Griffin parked the truck at the edge of the Dartmouth green in Hanover, where tents had already begun to sprout in one corner of the big grassy square in front of the old library. Hanover was usually my favorite market. The bustle of college students made the people-watching fun here.

Usually. But today things were just plain uncomfortable.

Lark hopped out of the truck first. Before Griff could follow her, I asked him a question. "If you were coming to the market today, why the heck am I here?"

"Isaac asked me to lend him your services this afternoon. Leah has to leave the market after setup."

"Oh," I said stupidly. "Okay."

"Is that all that's on your mind?" he asked. "Seems like you're carrying a heavy weight today. Lay it on me." If I wasn't mistaken, he almost looked amused.

I had the unusual urge to punch him. But of course I didn't. "Look..." I cleared my throat. "There are only a couple more weeks until the markets shut down. So I've been meaning to ask you about your winter work plans. Specifically—how is it that they, uh, include me?"

"Work doesn't stop when the markets finish," he said. "You know that."

"Sure. But if Audrey's coming back to help you run the cider business, what will you need me for?"

Griff chuckled. "Oh, Chewie. Yeah, Audrey is going to help me experiment with some new fermentation techniques. That'll be a hoot, but it doesn't change the workload at all. Especially because Audrey and Zara are going to open a bakery and coffee shop in one of the outbuildings next to the Gin Mill."

"Oh," I said slowly. "Another new business?"

"Yup, and I'm sure you think we're insane. But Zara needs to manage a business that operates in the daytime hours. She's figured out that you can't run a bar with a kid, unless you have live-in help, which she does not. Audrey's going to bake the pastries. That's part of what she's getting out of her Paris studies. And since Zara's brothers live on the property, they can pitch in if Zara's overwhelmed."

"I see. So you're going to help them get that running over the winter."

"Of course. And that will be happening while we do the usual pruning and make twenty percent more cider than last winter with the apples I'm buying from an orchard in the Champlain Valley."

"Damn, Griff."

"Yeah. You're gonna want to sign up for that GED class just so you can sit down a few hours a week. The job is yours as long as you want it. Now let's go sell some fucking apples."

We got out and began to set up the stall, while I made sidelong glances at the source of my heartbreak.

It wasn't easy to set up three tables and fifteen crates of fruit and cider without looking anyone in the eye, but Lark gave it her best shot. It was just a few minutes to three, and the customers were already milling around, getting ready to pounce. Lark taped the correct signs to each crate of apples that I brought over, while Griffin balanced the scale.

Look at me, I inwardly begged her. But she didn't.

"Hello! Lovely girl!" I looked up to see Linda, the aging hippie woman who sold hand-dyed skeins of yarn. She was our neighbor at both the Hanover and the Norwich markets. I had never been sure if "lovely girl" was a nickname just for Lark, or if Linda called everyone that. "Could you help me for a moment?"

"Sure," Lark said, ready to help. "Are we setting up your table?"

Linda leaned slowly down to tilt the folded table off the ground. Lark extended the legs, banging the locks. Together they raised the table into place. "Is something the matter with sunshine boy?" Linda asked. "He's not right today." She turned to gaze at me.

Crap. I must be wearing the face of a storm cloud.

"I guess so," Lark said to her shoes.

Linda shook her head. "You know, if I were twenty years younger..." She gave me a saucy wink.

That made me smile. If Linda were twenty years younger, she'd still be old enough to be my grandmother.

I stole yet another look at Lark, and got caught this time. Her guilty eyes met mine before skittering away.

I was still so angry at her for pushing me away. This was my first broken heart, and I didn't know how to mend it.

A child rang the bell to start off the market, and customers swarmed.

Leaning out of our stall, I looked down the row. In the space where the Apostate Farm booth should be, there was only green grass. "Isaac isn't here yet," I pointed out to Griffin. "That's kind of weird. What did you say they had going on today?"

"I didn't get all the details, but it wasn't any kind of disaster. Don't worry. There they are, anyway." Griff pointed at the Apostate truck, which was meandering past the rows of cars, in search of a place to park. "I'll go say hello. Stay here with Lark for a few more minutes?"

Lark gave him a stiff nod, so we ended up working side by side.

She sold bag after bag of apples, and quite a few half-gallons of sweet cider. I restocked them just as quickly as she sold them, my hands growing cold from handling the chilled fruit and the cider jugs. Fall was here, and a stiff wind blew past as we worked.

Lark's fingers must have grown numb, too. As I watched, the handle of a cider jug began to slip off her thumb. Lunging, I caught it before it hit the ground.

"Thanks. Sorry," she stammered as I set it to rights on the table.

"You need gloves?" I asked her quietly. "Might be a pair in Griff's truck." My subconscious slipped up then, forgetting that we were over. I put a hand on the small of her back, and the contact—even through several layers of clothing—felt right and necessary.

She turned vulnerable eyes in my direction and sighed. "I don't think I'd be able to make change with gloves on. But thank you."

"No problem," I mumbled, forcing myself to let go.

The apples were selling fast, and I stacked more of the five-pound totes on our table, giving myself over to physical labor, which had never steered me wrong.

"Excuse me, sir," said a female voice. "Do you have any bananas?" I looked up to see a pretty girl standing across the table from us, a hand up to shield her eyes from the afternoon glare.

"Bananas?" I asked. Now there was a ridiculous request. I was trying to decide how to politely explain that bananas don't grow in Vermont when she dropped the hand that was shielding her face.

And my heart seized at the sight of a familiar face, and that too-long hair all the girls were required to have at The Compound.

Chastity.

Speechless, I took in her pale skin and clear blue eyes. Her face had filled out some, becoming more womanly than it had been at sixteen.

Holy...

"Zachariah." She laughed. "You should see the look on your face! I'm sorry to take you by surprise. It was all my idea."

"God." I stumbled around the end of the table towards her, trying to find words. "What happened? How did you get here?"

"Same way you did, I think." She held up a thumb, making the universal sign for a hitchhiker.

"No you did not," I said, unable to take my eyes off her. "That's dangerous."

Chastity rolled her eyes. "I took a bus first. But when I ran out of money, I did some hitchhiking. I Googled your name before I left and found Isaac and Leah. Your name must be in the website's metadata."

"I...I don't even know what that means," I stammered.

Her eyes widened, and she laughed again.

"God," I said again. A nineteen-year-old girl who'd never left the Compound couldn't possibly hitchhike across the country. She would never have even *met* an outsider before she stepped off the property. The idea of her all alone like that made me feel lightheaded. I curled my hand around one of the tent posts as a way of grounding myself. It was as if my brain and body couldn't keep up with everything I was seeing and hearing. I didn't know whether to shout or cry. I'd worried about her so many times. And now here she stood.

"Zach, you just took the Lord's name in vain. Twice."

"Sorry," I said quickly.

"I'm *joking*. I didn't want to live with their rules anymore. That's why I left. It's a long story but..." She gave me another huge smile. "You look *great*, Zach. Seriously. I can't stop staring at you."

"You...look amazing. I'm amazed to see you here." I tried to smile. My heart was splintering in the strangest way.

She grabbed my free hand. "I'll tell you all about it later. But right now Isaac is waving you down. Look."

I turned to see Isaac beckoning from his place down the long row of stalls.

When I glanced at Lark, she was staring at Chastity the way someone looks at a ghost. But then she seemed to snap out of it. "Go," she said without meeting my gaze. "Here comes Griff, anyway."

So I let Chastity lead me by the hand over to where Isaac and Leah were setting up their stall as fast as possible. "Zach, come grab these crates with me?" Isaac called.

"Sure." I dropped Chastity's hand and followed him. My head was still spinning.

But when we got to the truck, Isaac only leaned against the tailgate and handed me a bottle of water. "Drink that. You look like you're about to pass out." I tipped the bottle into my very dry mouth with a shaky hand. "Steady, kid," Isaac said. "This changes her life, but it doesn't have to change yours."

I looked down at him in surprise. "What are you saying?"

"I'm saying that I know you. And right now you're tearing up your life plan, trying to figure out how to help the girl you think you once harmed." Isaac hoisted a crate filled with honey jars off the truck and handed it to me.

"She's nineteen and she hitchhiked here," I whispered.

"Yep. And she did a fine job of it." Isaac grabbed another crate for himself. "I need you to take a deep breath. We're all going to take care of Chastity and figure out what she needs. But don't freak out, okay?" He hitched the crate up against his chest and trotted towards the booth.

I followed him, still in shock. I'd always wondered who Chastity had been forced to marry and how bad it had been.

It must have been pretty damn bad for her to run away.

* * *

Two hours later, Isaac and I were alone in the booth, except for Maeve, who was playing at our feet. Leah had taken Chastity off to a doctor's appointment, maybe the first one in her life.

"Why does she need a doctor?" I'd worried.

"She got frostbite in Iowa," he said calmly. "No coat. And Leah just wants to make sure there isn't anything special she should do to treat it."

Already, Isaac had sold all the cheeses he'd brought and a bin of late-season potatoes. He sold some honey and a few candles. And he played with Maeve, who had designated the area under the tables as her fort.

I'd done almost nothing except stare into space. "Sorry," I said, moving out of Isaac's way for what was probably the tenth time.

"I didn't actually need your help today," he admitted, sitting down on an overturned crate. "You're really here to talk to me."

"What is there to talk about?"

"Don't be thick. I just wanted to tell you that even though Chastity says she came to Vermont looking for you, Leah and I are going to take care of her. You have a lot going on in your life right now. And we're set up to help. We named our farm to help people like her find us. And now she has."

"I still want to help."

"And you shall. But there's more we need to talk about. What happened with Lark? Griff said you were walking around like a zombie. Gotta agree with him about that."

I groaned. "There's nothing to tell. And now it's time to pack up. The market's over."

Isaac let me get away with that dodge, and I helped him load his truck.

"Come on, Maeve," Isaac called his daughter when we were through. "The market's over."

"Aren't we waiting for Leah and Chastity?" I asked.

Isaac shook his head. "We brought two cars."

I spotted Griffin waving at me from his truck, beckoning me. But I pointed at Isaac's, then opened the passenger door and climbed in.

"What are you doing?"

"Riding back with you."

Isaac shook his head. "You don't have to come back home with me. Give your hero complex a day to get used to Chastity showing up, okay?" He lifted Maeve into her car seat in back and buckled her in.

"It's not about that." I sighed, suddenly exhausted. "Just give me a ride home, would you? You can drop me at the end of the Shipleys' drive."

My friend studied me for a moment. "All right."

I looked out the window to get out from under Isaac's stare. I was still chafing under that comment about my hero complex.

Isaac pulled the truck slowly out onto College Street. Then he had to brake again as two college guys, in their green Dartmouth sweatshirts, stepped practically in front of the truck. One time the same thing had happened, and it had set Lark off on a mini rant. *"This is one of the most selective colleges in the country, and the students aren't smart enough to look both ways before crossing the street!"*

Every time I thought of Lark, my heart gave a painful kick. I looked out the window and tried to think of something else.

"Are you going to tell me why it's so hard for you to sit in a truck with Griff and Lark?" Isaac asked as we crossed the bridge into Vermont.

Lark called it the Bridge of Big Balls, a moniker that described the concrete ornaments decorating it. I'd never cross this bridge again without cracking a smile because of her.

"Earth to Zach," Isaac prodded.

"Can we just drop it? There's not much to tell. I love her. She isn't on the same page. It's not a very original story." Every song on the radio was about the same thing, pretty much.

Isaac was quiet for a moment. "Nobody has a bigger heart than you, Zach. Just don't give it away, hasty-like."

"Too late." I swiveled my head around, wondering why Maeve hadn't bailed me out of this conversation with one of her rambling interruptions. But the little girl's head was tipped onto the padding of her car seat. She was already asleep. So I turned back to watch the road go by and sank a little further into my own discomfort.

"How do you know she won't come to love you?" Isaac asked in a quiet voice. "You've only known her a little while. Maybe things don't have to go fast."

I snorted. "They went plenty fast. And then there was a sudden squeal of brakes."

"Ouch." There was a pause, and then Isaac said, "So... While we're on the topic, is there anything you're unclear about, sexually? If you have any questions..."

I let out a frustrated grunt. "Nope. No problems there." I couldn't even think about sex with Lark without feeling sad. I hadn't known that holding her in my arms was a privilege I'd soon have to give up.

"Okay." Isaac sighed. "I just wonder…"

"You wonder what?"

"She just came back from some terrible trip, right?"

"Yeah."

"Tell me this—if you'd met the perfect girl just a month or two after you got shot out of Paradise Ranch, do you think you would have been ready for her?"

"I dunno," I said, hoping to get off the topic.

"Think about it. Maybe she just needs time."

That sounded like the kind of thing you say to someone who's all out of hope.

We drove on in silence for a minute, and I thought the conversation was over. But then Issac said, "Sometimes you have to take a step back before you can move forward. A month from now, she might realize her error and come back to you."

I wanted to believe him. But I just couldn't summon the optimism. "Not everybody gets what you have. Not everyone finds their Leah."

"You're too young to call off the search, man. Trust me."

I didn't answer. I stared down the double yellow line of the little two-lane highway and tried to think of nothing at all.

* * *

The next night was Thursday Dinner, this one at Isaac's place. Hemmed in between Kyle and Dylan at Leah's dining table, I drank more wine than usual. But it didn't bring on the sort of pleasant fuzziness I'd been hoping for. Instead, it only made my sad thoughts more muddled.

Lark hadn't come to dinner at all. In fact, she'd made herself so scarce these past twenty-four hours that I had barely glimpsed her. Griff sent her to the market today with Kieran, keeping me on the farm to press cider.

Tonight on my way out, I'd wanted to knock on her bedroom door. But what would I even say if she opened the door? Griff had told me she was leaving tomorrow, and I'd already told her I loved her. There were no more confusions to clear up; there were no new questions to ask.

Except for "please?" and "why?" Those two questions were burned on my heart. I'd told her I loved her, and that hadn't been enough.

She hadn't even needed me to chase off her dreams last night.

So here I sat, drowning in my wine glass. Since I wasn't known as a talker, my silence wouldn't be noticed. Chastity sat down at the other end of the table, happily planted in a chair with Maeve on her lap.

Hell. Even Maeve had abandoned me.

"I've never been further from home than Casper. So when I saw the lights of Omaha, I thought, wow! The big city! But then came Chicago." She laughed.

Funny. I'd had that exact same experience four years ago.

Sitting there surrounded by the people I knew best in the world, I got a strange chill. Chastity's storytelling brought me back to those early days, and not in a good way. I was beaten and alone. Didn't have any money for a bus ticket like Chastity did. All I had was the name of a town in Vermont, and I was going to walk there if nobody would stop for me. On the worst days I froze alone in the rain. Some nights I lay awake on park benches, too afraid to fall asleep.

One time I watched a group of teenage boys eat McDonald's hamburgers in the park. They saw me watching. Eventually one of them held up half a burger. "You want this?" he asked.

My stomach was so empty and I nodded.

Then the boy threw the burger to his dog, and all his friends laughed.

It had been a really long time since I'd thought about those days. The wine made a left turn in my stomach just remembering this.

After dinner, I washed the dishes as an excuse not to socialize. But when everyone began to depart, I told Griffin that I didn't want a lift back to the bunkhouse yet.

"You want us to leave you here?" Griff asked, keys in hand. "It's a long walk in the dark."

"Leah will drop me. Or I'll just crash on the couch," I suggested. "I want to catch up with Chastity."

"Okay, man. See you in the morning."

Maeve wrapped herself around my knees and I picked her up and carried her into the Abrahams' TV room. "Chassity!" the little girl said when we found my old…friend? Hookup?

"Hi, baby girl," Chastity said. She patted the sofa beside her. "God, Zach. I can't believe you're right here."

I cleared my throat. "I'd say the same about you."

"I'm so happy I found you guys. Took me long enough."

"So…" There was no more containing the question that had long been on my mind. "I just have one question. How much trouble did I get you in four years ago?"

"Lots!" she said with a smile that made no sense. "I got a beating like you read about. Still have the scars."

There wasn't enough air suddenly. "Sorry."

"Hey! Wait until you hear the rest of the story, okay? It gets better. Everyone assumed that I'd been compromised." She winked, and I wanted to die. "Nobody believed me. My mother didn't speak to me for months. And nobody wanted to marry me when I turned seventeen."

I set Maeve down on the floor and put my head in my hands.

"Zach." Chastity prodded me with her toe. "I told you— this story isn't over yet. Listen to me."

I lifted my head and tried to cooperate.

"Nobody wanted to marry me, so I was a pariah for a while. My sisters were awful, and my mother wanted me out of the house. But my father was still in charge of provisions. Remember that?"

I nodded. Her father made many of the trips into Casper for fuel and cattle feed.

"So I asked him if there was a job I could get. And he set me up as a cashier at Walgreens."

"The pharmacy?" I asked. I'd never heard of a girl on the compound having a job.

"That's the place. He wanted the cash, you know? My whole paycheck went to him. I wasn't allowed to keep the money."

"Oh. Of course not."

She smiled, and the look of it was so familiar it broke my heart a little. "I loved that job anyway. It was fun to watch the customers. And the manager was an interesting lady. She saw the position I was in, and she didn't like it. So when I got a raise for seniority, she started to pay me the extra in Visa gift cards. And I hid those."

"Really? And you didn't get caught?" Hiding money from the elders would take balls. Chastity was braver than I'd ever known. A trespass like that would have earned her another beating for sure.

"I never got caught. That became my savings plan. I knew I wanted to leave. Working behind that counter taught me a lot about the larger world. And I wanted in."

"Wow." I pictured Chastity standing behind the cash register in her long yellow dress and braids, watching girls her age come and go as they pleased. "You would have met a lot of people."

"Sure! And I read newspapers and magazines. The other people who worked there let me borrow their phones sometimes. Of course I never admitted any of that to my family. But I started to plan my escape. I looked up the cost of bus tickets and worked as many hours as I could to save up. But then my dad started making noises about trying to find me a husband. He thought that the scandal had probably blown over, and that he could get one of the Levite brothers to have me. And I didn't want that. So I knew it was time to go."

Just thinking of Chastity married off to an old man made the cold feeling return.

"So I started planning, and that's when I searched your name on someone's phone and found Isaac's farm. I knew you must have landed here, and it made me so happy. Because—Zach, I felt like I *killed* you." Her eyes were glassy now.

"Naw, don't go there." I reached over and patted her hand. I found it easier to touch people now than I had just a month or two ago. "Getting kicked out was the best thing that ever happened to me."

"You don't know how relieved I am." She moved over and threw herself in my arms.

I hugged her back, but she felt entirely unfamiliar to me. My brain couldn't help but do a comparison with Lark. She wasn't the right size, and she didn't smell like Lark.

Luckily, Maeve got jealous. "Me too," she said, forcing herself between our legs, wrapping herself around my knees again.

I broke off the hug to pick her up, and the little girl wrapped her arms around my neck.

"Aw," Chastity said. "That's the cutest thing I've ever seen."

I felt the familiar sensation of my face flushing. "I lived here when she was born," I explained. "I showed up a few months before."

"Good timing. They probably needed your help then."

"You have no idea," Leah said, entering the room and the conversation at the same time. "After Maeve was born, Isaac and I didn't sleep for five months straight. But Zach got up every single morning at dawn to milk our cows. He made coffee. He fed the chickens and collected eggs. He held this place together, and I'll never be able to thank him enough."

My cheeks burned brighter at the praise. I'd forgotten those days. In fact, my own memory of that time was different. Sure, I'd done all the farm work that Leah mentioned. But manual labor was easy. The hard part of those months had been my confusion. I'd spent my first year feeling about as valuable as a clod of cow shit on the bottom of someone's boot.

Being thrown away will do that to a guy.

"The only thing he *didn't* do was hold the newborn baby." Leah laughed. "It wasn't until Maeve began to crawl that he'd pick her up."

That was also true. "She seemed really breakable," I said in my own defense.

"Is that why?" Leah teased. "I assumed it was because she screamed her head off for the first few months of her life. And what nineteen-year-old guy wants anything to do with a screaming baby?" Leah held out her arms for Maeve, but the little girl shook her head and clung to me. She knew that Leah wanted to put her to bed.

"I don't scream," Maeve said then, sliding to the floor and resting her chin on my knee.

"You're right," I agreed, and she gave me a silly smile. "What a crazy idea." I reached down to wiggle a finger in the soft place just below Maeve's ribs, which was a tickle spot. And she let out a shriek that could wake the dead.

Leah seized the moment, grabbing a cackling Maeve from me and hurrying out of the room with her.

In the silence, I turned to Chastity and found her smiling at me. "It makes me happy to see you doing well."

"Thanks," I said, wishing she were right. A week ago I'd been doing great. Tonight? Not so much. But that wasn't her fault. "Tell me how I can help you."

She shrugged. "I'm sure there will be some way or another. But Isaac and Leah have been great. They're going to help me find a job somewhere. My old manager will give me a reference."

I wondered if it could really be as easy as that. "There must be something. I want to help. It's my fault that you got in trouble. I've always felt bad about it."

She cocked her head. "Haven't you been listening? You did me a favor. If you hadn't ruined my virtue, I'd be married to a sixty-year-old man right now, and I'd have two kids and a third one on the way."

Isaac walked in then with a glass of water. "If Zach's not listening, it might be all that wine he guzzled at dinner. Drink this." He offered me the glass.

And here I'd thought nobody had noticed. I took the water and drank it down.

"Good boy." Isaac ruffled my hair like I was a kid. Then he sat down on the footstool. "I noticed that your girl didn't come for dinner tonight."

"She's not my girl," I said, with a shake of my head.

Isaac and Chastity made almost identical woebegone faces.

"I can't fix that right now," I said slowly. But in spite of the wine, tonight's weird reminiscing had got me thinking. Yesterday Isaac had asked me that question—would I have been ready to meet Lark right after I left Wyoming? I'd brushed the question off. But I'd been a bigger mess back then than I cared to admit.

Poor Lark. She was right back where I'd been, still too close to the park bench and the lonely highway to relax.

"Give it time," Isaac said again.

"I'm going to," I decided. "She's leaving tomorrow, and I can't change that. The only thing to do is regroup for a second assault on her defenses."

"That's my boy. And you sound like Griff's movies." Isaac chuckled.

It was true, and it gave me an idea. "Maybe it's time to introduce Chastity to *Star Wars*. Why wait, you know?"

Chastity sat up straighter. "A whole movie? That's something I've never done."

Isaac grabbed the remote off the TV table. "All right," he said. "Chastity, welcome to the free world, where we are allowed to rot our brains any way we see fit."

"You have no idea how happy that makes me," she said.

"What else is on your bucket list?" I asked her.

She ticked a few things off on her fingers. "Beer. Dancing. Television. Chocolate. Coke."

"All the finer things in life," Isaac said with a grin. "We can have soda right now, too."

"I'll get it," I said, standing up.

Isaac shook his head. "Nope. Just take a load off for once and let someone else run the errands." He handed me the clicker. "Find the movie. I'll get the sodas."

I made myself comfortable on the couch and tried to relax.

Lark

I'm there again. Same shack. Same dust motes hanging in the only beam of light in the room where they're holding me.

Oscar is angry tonight. That's new. We're standing toe to toe, which is unusual. He's speaking rapid-fire Spanish, but in my dream I can understand him perfectly. He's upset at me for being mean to Zach. "That's just like you," he says. "You're doing it again."

"Which way is it?" I demand. "Are you angry that I had Zach? Or are you angry that I don't anymore! How do I satisfy you so you'll go away? Just tell me and I'll do it!"

As I shout at him, his eyes go dim. And then I feel something wet at my feet.

I look down. His blood is pooling around my bare toes. He's bleeding out on the floor. I look up again in horror, but now his eyes are lifeless.

While I stood there arguing with him, he bled to death. And it's all my fault.

I scream, and I scramble backward, away from the blood. But it runs toward me. And the other men are coming. They grab my shoulders, and they push me down in the dirt.

"That's not what happened!" I yell. But they don't listen. A hand clamps down on each of my shoulders and I scream with everything I've got.

A strong hand squeezed mine. "Shh, baby. You're dreaming."

But the touch didn't comfort me the way it was supposed to. Something was still wrong—the voice. It was all wrong. Still panicking, I struggled against this unfamiliar hand. I screamed again. "Let go!"

He released me immediately. "Calm down, Wild Child. You're okay." The big hand pushed hair out of my face.

I sat up with a sudden violence, and the darkened Vermont bedroom came into focus. I whipped my head around to find Griffin sitting on the bed beside me. But the look on his face scared me even more. He watched me with the caution you'd reserve for unexploded ordnance. And behind him, Kyle and Kieran stood framed in the bedroom doorway, their mouths hanging open.

I needed to get a grip. I needed... Shit. "Where's Zach?" I whispered.

Griffin looked, if possible, even more uneasy. "At Isaac and Leah's, I guess. He didn't come home tonight."

My brain caught up for a second, and I remembered. I'd sent him away.

And that was the moment when all hope died. I was all alone with my awful memories, and I would be for the rest of my life.

Unshed tears collected at the back of my throat while three sleepy men stared back at me. I'd come to Vermont to get better, and failed. This pain would never go away. While I tried to sleep, I was always going to see that room—and Oscar's face—for the rest of my life.

A big sob shuddered my chest as the certainty descended on me like a cold mist, bringing goosebumps to my arms and the back of my neck. Another sob followed the first one. And then another, like swells in the ocean.

"Lark," Griff growled. "Calm down, honey."

"I...can't," I gasped, my teeth chattering together. "Griff, I t-tried. But I can't do it anymore. I'm so t-tired."

"Shh. I got you."

Things went fuzzy then, like a camera's lens knocked out of focus. I felt my body begin to shake, and I heard a rushing sound in my ears. The walls tilted unpredictably.

Strong arms caught me. "Get my phone and my keys," a gruff voice ordered. "Put on some shoes, then go outside and pull my truck around."

I didn't want to hear any of it. Everything was mayhem, and I'd had all I could take. So I squeezed my eyes shut, closing myself off to the voices, and I pushed my consciousness into a tiny place, even smaller than a shack in the desert. I pinched my whole self tightly together, folding my soul like a flimsy scarf, until there was barely anything left.

My last conscious thought was of Oscar's stricken face.

And then nothing.

Zach

I dozed, my body tipped forward against the hospital bed, my head propped in the crook of one arm. My free hand held Lark's. I'd tried to doze and listen for her at the same time. But I'd been here and mostly awake since three a.m., so the sleeping won out.

That's why it took me a minute to discover when Lark awoke. Her hand jerked from mine, and valuable seconds were lost as I struggled to pull myself from the depths of sleep.

"No," she whispered, and the sound brought me fully awake. But Lark wasn't dreaming. She was looking around the hospital room in dismay. And then her face crumpled.

I was on my feet and leaning over the bed the next second. I pulled her in, kissing her forehead. "It's okay," I said. "You're okay."

"I've really fucked up now," she whispered. Her shoulders began to shake. "Griffin... And you... My parents are going to kill me."

"They got here an hour ago," I said as calmly as I could.

"This isn't supposed to be me," Lark rasped. "I'm not really like this."

"I know, sweetie."

She surprised me then, by putting one hand in the center of my chest and giving a sharp push. "You should get as far away from me as you can. Just fucking *run*—" A sob cut off the sentence. "Look where we are right now! Why are you even here with me?"

I pulled her into my lap, my arms caging her in. She relaxed immediately, resting her forehead against my collarbone. "Zach, I'm so sorry."

"I know."

"When I said... Before... That was mean. And not true."

"Shh. It's not the time to worry about that." I cradled her head, which lolled against my shoulder. The doctor had told me the sedatives they'd given her were pretty strong.

"It's just that I couldn't be what you want me to be."

I took a deep breath in through my nose. "I get that now. It's okay. I still have you as a friend, right? I don't have too many of those." I tried, but it was hard to keep my voice from sounding raw. The very person I needed to be strong for was the one who could make me fall to pieces.

"I'm a wreck."

"I noticed." I rocked her against my chest. "I've been a wreck, too. It doesn't last forever." I held on tight. It was hard to shake the notion that if I just held her indefinitely, everything would be okay. It was naive, though. I was ready to admit that she needed more help.

Though everything seemed steadier whenever I could feel her heartbeat. And I knew I was good for her, because I felt her body relax against mine.

I *was* good for her. I was. But my love wasn't enough to cure the problem, no matter how much I wished it was.

The door opened, and her parents walked in.

"You said you'd call us if she woke up!" Lark's mother's voice was shrill enough to make me wince.

"Jill," her father warned, putting a hand on her shoulder. "Stand down." The only reason her parents had been willing to leave the room at all was to hunt down and interrogate the psychiatrist on duty.

And now the doctor entered the room wearing a crisp white coat and a studiously mild expression. "Lark, I'm Dr. Richards. I'm a psychiatrist."

"Wonderful," Lark grumbled into my shirt. At that, the doctor smiled. That was a shred of good news—at least the man had a sense of humor. Lark would need that.

There were five people in the little room now, and Lark was clinging to me for dear life.

"Sweetheart," her mother said in a teary voice. "We're so worried. You could have told us that things weren't getting better."

"But I hoped they *were*." She lifted her teary face and took a deep breath. I watched her forcibly put the calm back on her face. I'd seen her do this many times before, too. But I'd never understood how much it cost her.

"It's all right, Lark," her father said. "We're not mad at you. But we need to make sure you get the help you need. You picked a hell of a way to get that doctor's note."

Lark groaned. "Send me somewhere as an outpatient," she said quickly. "I'm not going anywhere with locks on the doors. I wasn't going to harm myself."

I watched her parents and the doctor exchange glances. "Sweetheart," her mother tried again. "It's important to get better. And you scared Griffin pretty bad last night..."

My stomach rolled. I'd heard the story of her breakdown. The fear and the screaming. The doctor was concerned about a host of PTSD-related complications, like anxiety, depression, and suicide risk.

I couldn't even think those two words without wanting to be sick.

"It's hard to be your daughter sometimes," Lark said, her voice flat. "You always warned me away from risk. But I thought I knew what I was doing—" Her voice broke. "—until very recently."

"Oh, honey," her mother said, tears running down her face. "You don't have to feel that way. I'll listen. We'll work something out."

The doctor cleared his throat. "Your treatment plan won't be a hasty decision, I promise. But I'll need to interview Lark, when she's ready. It will help us figure out the right choice for her treatment."

Still sitting in my lap, she straightened her spine. "Okay. Let's get it over with."

The doctor smiled. "Why don't you have a little something to eat, and steady yourself? I'll come back in half an hour and we'll talk then."

"Okay," Lark whispered.

Lark's father disappeared to the hospital cafeteria to buy his daughter a pastry. Her mother and I waited while Lark freshened up in the bathroom.

"You can go home," her mother said when it was just the two of us. "We'll take it from here."

"No way," I said immediately. It was probably the least polite response I'd ever given to a lady. But I had the terrible feeling that if I walked out that door right now, I'd never see Lark again. "I would never leave without saying goodbye."

Mrs. Wainright didn't even attempt to conceal her frown of displeasure.

It's not that I couldn't see her side of things. Here sat a big farm boy in her daughter's hospital room, taking up space. But that was just too bad. If Lark told me to go, I'd listen. But I wouldn't take orders from anyone else.

Lark ate half the croissant her father brought and drank half a cup of coffee. Then she pushed the tray away. "I don't really have an appetite."

"Eat, Lark," her mother said. "You need your strength."

Her daughter's eyes narrowed. "Really, Mom? If I come back to Boston, is it going to be like that?"

"Everything is easier with a little something in your stomach. It's just a fact."

Her father sighed. "Easy, Jill. Sedatives can make your stomach wonky."

"It's just a little bread..." her mother argued, and I thought I might actually throw something at her. Instead, I reached across and grabbed the last piece of croissant and popped it into my mouth.

Lark laughed for the first time in twenty-four hours. "*You're* probably starved, but nobody here gives a damn."

I shrugged. "I'm fine."

"Drink this," she said, passing me the coffee. "It's hitting me like battery acid."

"Now there's a recommendation." She smiled, and I held her eyes. For that split second, everything was easier. I took a sip of the coffee.

"Your friend is free to get something to eat while you speak to the doctor," her mother said just as Dr. Richards entered the room.

"Zach is staying," Lark argued.

"The doctor wants to see you alone," her father said.

She just shook her head. "I'm only telling this story once. And since Zach has basically been holding me together with prayer and duct tape for the past two months, he gets to hear it, too."

There was an uncomfortable silence while Lark's family stared at one another in turn, and then everyone's gaze landed on the doctor.

"She's in charge," the doctor said easily.

Lark's mother gave me another glare, and then she turned and left the room.

With an apologetic smile, her father did the same.

The doctor shut the door, and parked his hip against the window sill. He pointed at the plastic visitor's chair. To me, he said, "Please have a seat. You're welcome to stay as long as Lark wishes it. And so long as you can listen quietly."

I sat down and nodded, hoping to prove my competence at staying silent.

The doctor folded his hands. "If we're going to get this right, Lark, we need to go over a few things. I spent the early hours of this morning with your file."

She nodded. "Sorry about that."

The doctor shook his head. "That's what they pay me for. But I'm going to tell you what I think I saw there, so we can figure out what to do, okay?"

"Okay." To my surprise, she slid off the bed and sat right down in my lap. She leaned back against me, and the nearness of her felt so good that I had to close my eyes. Later, when they whisked Lark off to some fancy hospital in Boston, I was going to have to find a way to let go.

"The notes in your file seem to indicate that you're experiencing post-traumatic stress disorder, brought on by your recent troubles in Guatemala. Does that sound right?"

She nodded, and I kissed the back of her head.

"And things are the worst during the night?"

"Nightmares," she confirmed. "Three or four nights a week. I didn't remember some of the details when I first came home. But a week or so ago I dreamt very clearly about the night it all ended."

He gave her a slow nod. "Lark, people have every sort of reaction to trauma. There's no right way to react, and no wrong way. Your file describes a kidnapping, a very frightening time as a hostage, and witnessing the shooting death of one of your captors. Is that accurate?"

Again, she nodded, but her hands began to squeeze mine.

The doctor closed the folder. "Whichever psychiatrist you see is going to ask you if there was anything else that happened. Not that your fear needs a better explanation. But they'll want to be sure they're dealing with the source of the trouble."

Lark's body went completely still.

"Was there something else, Lark?" the doctor asked carefully.

"Yes and no," she whispered.

The doctor dropped his voice, too. "Can you please elaborate?"

"The boy who died... I killed him," she said.

To his credit, the doctor didn't even blink. "Did you pull the trigger?"

Lark shook her head. "No, but I might as well have."

Dr. Richards held her gaze. "Tell me what happened."

At that, Lark slid off of my lap and walked over to the bed. I must have telegraphed my desire to follow her, because the doctor held up a hand in my direction that seemed to say, "Stay where you are."

Lark tucked her knees up to her chest and curled into a protective ball. "I tried to get him to help me."

"How did you do that?" the doctor asked.

"I..." She swallowed. "I talked to him alone. His name was Oscar. He was just a young kid. And he..." Lark's eyes filled. "He liked me."

"He liked you in what way?" the doctor pressed.

Lark looked at the ceiling with a world-weary expression. "He liked me. He was attracted to me." She dropped her eyes. "I led him on. I encouraged him."

"How did you do that?" The doctor's voice was soft.

246

"I told him I thought he was handsome." A single tear dripped from her eye. "I told him that if they let me go, that we could spend more time together." She swatted at the tear on her cheek. "I implied that we could have a sexual relationship." Her eyes were on the doctor. Her throat bobbed as though she were trying to swallow bits of glass.

"How did you imply it?" the doctor asked, his voice soft.

"It's really not that difficult," she said in a hard voice. "You toss your hair. You touch his arm. You stare at his lips." Two tears tracked down her face. "I told him he was handsome. *Usted es un hombre muy guapo.*" She scrubbed the tears away. "I said these things so that he would take risks for me. He did favors for me. He brought me a bottle of water, and sometimes food when no one else was looking..." She trailed off. "I wanted him to figure out how to just let me go free."

"And why was Oscar killed?"

Lark was sniffing now, trying to hold back the tears. "I'm not sure exactly how they figured out he was planning something. My guess is that he confided in someone, or was overheard. It's possible they just got mad because he snuck me a..." She swallowed roughly. "A candy bar. But then everything happened so fast. They were shouting at him, and then all of a sudden they shoved him against me."

She was quivering with stress, but she didn't look at me. Not once. I gripped the arms of the ugly plastic hospital chair and worked hard at not reaching for her.

"I was down on the floor." Her voice was shaking, and the tears were running freely now. "And they ordered Oscar to rape me."

My throat closed up completely, and I gagged on nothing. I turned my chin to watch the doctor's calm face and tried not to come unglued.

I had to hand it to the doctor—he hadn't changed his listening face at all. "What happened next, Lark?"

"He...he...*wouldn't do it*," she sobbed. "They threatened him, and he didn't hurt me like they wanted." She was actually choking on her tears. I couldn't take it anymore. I pushed out of the chair.

"Sit," the doctor commanded with a single word.

I sat.

The doctor handed the tissue box to Lark, who took it with shaking hands. "Did they kill him then?"

"*Yes,*" she gasped. "The man in charge put the gun right in front of his chest and pulled the trigger. There was so much blood. And he was *staring at me after he died.*"

My own face was wet too, now.

"Did anyone rape you, Lark?" the doctor asked.

"NO!" she screamed. "People keep asking me that, and I keep telling the truth. But I'm not the victim. I'm *guilty.* This is on *me...*" She broke off, sobbing into her knees.

"Okay," the doctor said, his voice reassuring. "I hear you."

I'd had enough. I lunged for the bed, scooping her up into my arms. Sitting back down on the mattress again, I folded Lark into my lap. "I'm so sorry," I whispered. "I'm so sorry."

"He's *dead,*" she sobbed. "And I'm alive, waiting to find out which Ritz Carlton psych ward they're sending me to. Where a staff of thousands will tend to my every need."

"I'm so glad you're alive," I said.

"But I let him die! I'm not a good person!" she howled. And her shoulders shook as if they would never stop.

"Bullshit," I choked out. I knew I was right. She was proving it this very minute. "Only good people care so much. Every time..." I had to stop to wipe my own eyes. "Every time I look at you, I see a good person." At least she was clinging to me now, instead of pushing me away. "You had shitty choices, Lark. And that poor boy had only shitty choices, too. In fact, it sounds like he'd have had them whether he ever met you or not."

She was listening to me. That was something.

I wanted to fix it. I'd take all her pain myself if I could. "I know I can't just talk you into my way of seeing things. You need time. But I won't ever stop believing in you." All I could do was to cup her head to my shoulder and hold her while she struggled with herself.

"You shouldn't love me," she whispered.

I rocked her in my arms. "Too late." I just held on tight. It's all I'd wanted from these past few days, anyway.

"I've been horrible to you," Lark sobbed. "I said shitty things."

"I don't listen too good," I said. At that, Lark coughed out something that was supposed to be a laugh, but it changed back to sobbing right away. I just pulled her a little closer, and let her tears soak through my shirt.

The doctor was standing near the door, watching us. "I'll give you a few minutes," he said. "And we'll go over our options." Then he winked at me and walked out.

Lark relaxed against me bit by bit. "Didn't want to end up here," she said on a sigh.

"I know. I watched you fight it."

"Never meant to take you down with me."

"You didn't," I promised. "I know I'm going to have to let you go now, so that you can get well. It's okay, sweetheart. Listen to me. Eyes *right* here."

Her frightened eyes found mine and focused. And the amount of pain I saw there nearly broke me in two. "*Everyone* has a time when they need a lot more than they can give. It doesn't matter how much you hate it. It's just true." I squeezed her hands tightly, not knowing any other way to make the truth sink in.

"But—"

"Four years ago," I cut her off. "I hitchhiked two thousand miles from Wyoming to Vermont with strangers. I *begged* for food, Lark. I knocked on strangers' doors, and I asked if they had anything I could eat. And then I showed up at Isaac's door with nothing. Not even shoes. I hated doing that. It made me feel like useless garbage. But sometimes there's no choice."

As I watched, her brown eyes began to fill again. But her gaze didn't waver.

"When you're ready to give back, we'll be ready to receive it. Whenever it is. But for now you just have to dig in, sweetheart." I pulled her arms forward until her head came to rest on my shoulder. I felt the first tears begin to soak into my flannel shirt. "I can handle it, Lark. Just lean on me. I'll be your Apostate Farm."

Tears spilled out of her eyes. So many tears. But I just hung on. It's what I do.

* * *

Later, after Lark's parents came back into the room, and another long conversation commenced about where Lark might get a month of intense therapy, I excused myself to go find the men's room, where I did my best to freshen up. On my way back, the doctor buttonholed me in the corridor.

"Son, can I have a word?"

I nodded blearily. My stomach was empty and my eyes were heavy, but I tried to give the man my attention.

"Look, I've never seen a guy so young handle this kind of situation so well. Usually I have to cut the boyfriend out of the situation. You impress me. But you're still going to have to step back from this process."

I'm not the boyfriend, I reminded myself. It stung, but it was the whole truth. "I know," I said, my voice hoarse. "She needs more than I can give." Griff had warned me, and I hadn't listened.

"I'm sure you've been a great help, but she's going to have to do this alone. If you want her to come out strong on the other side, there's no other way."

I swallowed, my throat rough. The doctor was kind, but the message was clear. We never had a chance as a couple. Lark's parents were going to take her away, and by the time she was herself again, I'd be just a memory. Hell, I'd be a *bad* memory. Who would want to go back to someone who knew you only when you'd hit bottom?

"Hang in there," the doctor said, putting a hand on my shoulder. "She's going to be okay. You know that, right? She's a strong one."

I only nodded. It had taken me until now to realize that I'd never been given a speaking role in this drama. I was merely a walk-on, and there was nothing at all I could do about it.

An hour later she was gone.

Lark's mom drove her back to Boston. But Lark's dad had to drive the Volkswagen, which I'd driven to the hospital in the dead of night. Mr. Wainright dropped me off at the Shipleys'.

"Thanks for all your help, son," he said.

I barely heard him. "She has clothes in the bunkhouse," I pointed out.

"Ah. I'll grab those."

"First bedroom on the right," I said, my throat closing up. "Pretty sure she was all packed to go home."

"Thanks."

It would have been polite to walk him in there and help, but I couldn't do it.

He walked away, and I just stood there in the driveway, trying to get my bearings. It was Friday, so not a market day. It was eleven o'clock or so. My empty belly could wait two hours until lunch.

I was still in yesterday's clothes, but I wandered over to the cider house, where I found Griff and his cousins sorting apples and washing them for the press. May was sitting on a cider barrel, chewing her thumbnail.

"Hey," I said. "Where do you want me?"

Every head turned in my direction, and everyone stared.

"Sorry I'm late," I added. "You can give me shit patrol, or whatever."

Griff was the first to speak. "Hey."

"Hey," I echoed.

"Her parents took her home?"

I just nodded, trying not to think of our very last hug, or the warm scent of her hair as I tucked her into the passenger's seat and kissed her on the top of the head.

"You okay?" Kieran asked.

Stupid question. "Yeah. What needs doing?"

But nobody answered me. Instead, May hopped off the barrel. She walked up beside me and put her arms around my waist. She put her head on my shoulder and held me tightly.

Then Griff did the same damn thing on the other side.

"Don't," I said as the first tear slid down my face.

They didn't listen, though. Four arms braced me as I fell apart, right there on the grass beside the cider house. The first sob sort of broke a dam inside me I hadn't known I had. I'd never cried before. Not that I could remember, anyway.

Even when I had my pants around my ankles, taking the pastor's whip on my bare ass, I hadn't cried. Didn't feel the urge. I would have rather smashed someone in the mouth. Where I come from, crying was just a good way to bring on another beating.

But saying goodbye to Lark hurt me in an entirely new way. Like I was bleeding and didn't know if I could stop. Didn't know if I even wanted to.

So I just bled my tears out onto the Shipleys' soil, while they tried to say all the right things. It took me a few minutes to get the worst of it out. Kyle and Kieran wandered off to give me time. Then Griff gave my shoulder a squeeze and told me I should just have a nap before lunch. We could make cider later. "There's always later," he said.

May went into the farmhouse for some tissues and a bottle of water. I used my time alone to calm all the way down, sitting on the grass, my back against the side of the building, studying the mostly blue sky overhead. There's a line in Job that reads: *Look at the heavens and see; And behold the clouds—they are higher than you.*

Many things were just plain bigger than my desires. I'd always been good at accepting it. Today it was just a little harder than usual.

I reached into the bin of apples beside me and plucked one out to have as a snack. It was smallish and lopsided, but firm and juicy when I bit into it.

Lark

Until you've had two hours of gut-wrenching therapy a day, you haven't lived.

I'd feared being locked in some kind of mental institution, but the reality of my next few weeks was much less dramatic. My doctors had found a daytime mental health center just outside of Boston. Every morning I woke up in my parents' house and got ready. Then my dad dropped me off at this place, the same way he used to drive me to my private school.

"Have a nice day," he'd say. "Play nice with the other kids."

"See you at six," I'd say, because it just wasn't funny. Though he meant well.

The place was like a country club for rich people who weren't doing so well. Or a day camp with expensive medication.

After checking in, I went to a yoga class. Then I saw a doctor who gave me an antidepressant. Then I was sent to another activity, where I tried weaving or decoupage. Or I meditated. (Or tried, anyway. My mind kept wandering to more interesting subjects.)

I did everything they asked of me. Almost.

My doctor—a nice lady with a white streak through her dark hair, whom I was to call Dr. Becky—needed me to stop feeling guilty about Oscar's death. But it wasn't so easy.

"The goal," she said, "if you want to make this burden manageable, is to forgive yourself. Accept that not everything is your fault. And to let the people who love you carry some of it for you."

"I tried that," I pointed out, thinking of Zach fighting valiantly to ease my pain. "But I was the only one who got Oscar into trouble."

"Really? Did you force him to be part of your kidnapping?"

"Of course not."

We went around and around like this a lot.

"Lark, nobody can carry one hundred percent of her own burdens. Humans aren't cut that way. A baby sea turtle never meets its mother, and most of them die before they reach the waterline. Humans are interdependent by choice. You have a burden of guilt, and it's brave of you to want to carry it yourself. But it's foolish not to let others help you. Give some of it away to your parents and your friends. And when they need your help, you'll be strong enough to support them, too."

I swallowed thickly every time she said this. The logic of it had already made inroads into my mind. The hard part was letting it into my heart.

Zach had said something similar at the hospital in Vermont. I couldn't remember that morning very clearly. Foggy from the sedative and dizzy with remorse, much of what happened that morning was a blur. But I remembered the softness of Zach's shirt against my cheek, and the strength of his arms around my body. He'd told me a little piece of his own story—torn-up shoes, and begging for food. What were his words? *I'll be your Apostate Farm.*

God, how I missed him.

"I tried letting Zach carry my burden," I told Dr. Becky. "But that didn't seem fair."

"That's because you were cheating," she said. "Zach didn't know you like your family or May. He was a stranger, so it didn't feel like much of a risk to show him all the scary things in your heart."

"So it wasn't fair to him," I finished.

She smiled at me. "Maybe not at first. But Zach needed you, too. He needed to know how it felt to love someone he didn't owe. He had his own burdens to unload."

Dr. Becky was a huge fan of Zach's, even though she'd never met him. Figured. Zach was pretty irresistible.

"I wish Zach could have known the stronger me. The healthier one," I told her.

"But he can," she said gently. "Every time you confront the things that scare you, it's a step back to feeling like yourself again. Right now it feels like you spend all day talking about your sorrow. But it won't always feel like that. Every time we stare it in the face, it becomes a little more banal. Pretty soon you'll bump into your sorrow on the street, and just give it a little wave. It will still be familiar, but not so startling."

"I'm going to kick it in the shins."

"Have at it," Dr. Becky said with a smile.

The antidepressants turned me into a slug. I fell into bed before ten and could barely drag myself out of bed in the morning. My expensive team of experts took their time tinkering with the medication and dosage.

"You won't always need the meds," Dr. Becky promised.

I hoped she was right, because they made me feel even more like an invalid.

To be fair, my parents were lovely during these difficult days. Somehow my mother was a model of restraint. She didn't nag or hover. And the toughest question she asked me during the first week was which comedy I wanted to watch with her on TV.

One time I woke up screaming, and she just sat down on the edge of my bed and held my hand. She didn't look terrified anymore. I think I'd managed to burn through all our mutual terror already. We'd moved on to a place where the worst had already happened, and all there was to do now was pick up the pieces.

Every night I went to bed alone in my old childhood bedroom. It was bigger than the room I'd had in the bunkhouse. And quieter.

I missed Zach terribly. I wanted to call him just to hear his kind voice in my ear. I wanted to get into my car and drive up to the Shipleys', just to get one more of his hugs.

But I didn't do it. I wasn't ready. If I saw Zach again, I needed it to be at a moment when I didn't need him for a crutch.

On my hardest days, the ones where I couldn't stop crying, I worried that day would never come.

Letters

Dear Lark,

According to these instructions from your doctor that Ruth pried out of your mom, we can only reach you by writing letters on paper, and we're supposed to stick to happy, casual topics.

That's easy for me because you're my happy thought.

Don't feel obligated to write back. I really mean that. I'd rather you just concentrate on feeling better. But I think of you whenever I walk into the Shipleys' kitchen, or pass the door to your room in the bunkhouse. So I thought you might want an update on what's happening here.

Audrey is back! Griffin is so smiley it's like his face is broken. Kyle teased the crap out of him the first few days, but of course Griff doesn't care. By the way—Audrey loves the kitchen in the bungalow. She cried when we showed it to her. That shade of ivory paint you chose for the woodwork looks great, by the way.

We're picking the last of the late season apples this week and next. Then Kyle and Kieran will go back to their parents' place, and Griff and I will spend all day pressing cider. The first barrels of the season are almost ready for bottling.

It's cold in the mornings now. When I let the cows into the dairy barn, you can see the puffs of their breath from those big velvet noses. And Griff sent the male calves off to freezer camp, so we'll be eating (humanely raised) veal soon.

The calves were really cute, though. Griff always looks a little extra grumpy on the day he sends them off to the butcher. And Dylan found two or three different reasons he couldn't be around when we loaded them onto the truck.

I'm going to sign off now because Audrey is in the kitchen making her famous braised pork enchiladas and Dylan wants to set the table where I'm writing.

By the way, May is at the other end of the table, also trying to write you a letter. She keeps tearing off sheets of paper and crumpling them up into balls, though. So I'm thinking you might be waiting another week to get hers.

All my best,
Zach

* * *

Dear Lark,

At Thursday dinner Maeve asked me to read her a story. Ruth has this basket of children's books she keeps for Maeve. So I read that one about the red hen who asks all the other animals to help bake the bread, but they won't say yes until it's time to eat it.

Maeve pointed at the chicken and told me she was a "red sex-linked, maybe a Golden Comet, except the feet are wrong." I laughed my ass off because I'll bet most toddlers can't name the species of their storybook chickens.

Then on Sunday I took Ruth to church, and Father Peters read from Thessalonians. "For even when we were with you, we gave you this rule: The one who is unwilling to work shall not eat."

Funny, right? I don't know what message God is trying to send me, though. I picked about a million apples this week. Maybe He wants two million.

We had a dusting of snow last night. It's melted already, but Dylan got excited and waxed his snowboard. Every year he asks me if I want to learn. Maybe this year I'll say yes.

Audrey has been testing pastries for the coffee shop that she's opening with Zara. There's an apple turnover so good it made me want to cry. But my favorite thing so far is a pumpkin whoopie pie with cream cheese frosting.

Now I'm hungry again, darn it.

In other news, Chastity already got a seasonal job working at the pharmacy in Colebury. Isaac has to drive her there for now, until she can take driving lessons and save up for a car. I told her I'd help her find a junker, and that Jude and I would help fix it up.

I hardly recognize Chastity. They took her to the salon for a trim, and she got a buzz cut instead. Leah is amused. She says that Chastity's M.O. is to spend each day showing Paradise Ranch her middle finger.

Getting sleepy now. I'm writing this from my bunk, and Kyle started snoring already. A week from now I'll be alone in here. I've fired up the masonry heater so it's nice and warm. I've started studying for the GED, so the quiet will help with that.

Be well, Lark. Look kindly at yourself. That's all I ask of you.

Best,
Zach

* * *

Dear Lark,

I started this letter a hundred times, because I want to show you some love in a way that's not a burden. My quandary: I don't want to ask your forgiveness at a time when you're already going through a lot.

But I <u>am</u> sorry. You were offended that I kept a secret from you. It didn't feel good, trust me. So I'm just going to try to explain why.

Having you as my friend and roommate in college was the best thing ever. From the minute we met I loved you as a friend. You made college more fun every single day. And no matter what shenanigans we got up to, I knew you had my back.

That's just priceless. I love you so hard for it.

So when I started to realize I was attracted to you, it scared me. I wasn't expecting that to happen, and I had no idea what to think. Honestly I just hoped it would go away. I dated boys. And of course I fooled around with that girl down the hall.

That incident didn't help, either. I did it because I was trying to have an "aha!" moment about sex with girls. I thought I'd love it or hate it, and then I'd learn something important about myself. But it was just meh, because I wasn't very attracted to her. So I became more confused, not less.

Whenever you and I were together, though, I never worried. We were friends and that was more important than anything. I always knew you loved me. I also knew you'd never love me <u>that</u> way.

The year that dad died you were AMAZING. Seriously. I was so blindsided and afraid and mad and sad. It was an awful, awful time. But you were just <u>there</u>. You hugged me and steered me through the funeral. Afterward, you collected notes from all the classes I'd missed. I wouldn't have made it through that semester without you. Not kidding, here. I would have dropped out and set myself back a semester.

I'm so, so grateful. Pass the tissues. :(

But I only loved you more after that. I didn't tell you how I felt because I didn't want to scare you off. If our friendship had dimmed even 1% from my confession, that would have been unacceptable to me. So I just sat on this big secret. I swallowed all these feelings knowing that it was a big lie of omission but I didn't feel like I had a choice.

Believe me, I never doubted your worth as a friend. Not for two seconds did I worry that you'd reject me or anyone else for being queer. I know you better than that. If the object of my attraction would have conveniently been <u>anyone</u> else, ours would have been an easy conversation.

I just didn't want to make it weird between us. So I ended up making it weird between us. Ugh. I'm so sorry.

Part of the work I've been doing in AA is talking about my bisexuality. Some of my drinking had to do with not wanting to face that. The more people I talk to, the more I hear that crushing on your best friend is a queer rite of passage. So thanks for making me a cliché, babe. :) Thanks a ton.

Keepsake

I know you're going through a lot, so I don't feel like I should ask anything of you. But all I want is this: when you're ready, please let me know that we can get past this? I'm sorry I didn't tell you what was in my heart. Please forgive me.

Love always,
May

* * *

Dear May,

I'm not feeling very eloquent yet, but I had to respond to your letter. I love you so much, and I'm sorry to have ever inadvertently caused you any pain. I don't blame you even a little bit for keeping your secret. There's no Best Friend Clause which requires you spill your guts when you're not ready.

I probably would have done the exact same thing.

If one of us owes an apology, it's me. I came to Vermont with a heavy burden. There probably is a Best Friend Clause which demands that if you show up at your best friend's front door feeling like a grenade with the pin pulled, you should probably warn a girl.

So the moment when Daphne spilled your secret was a moment when I just couldn't handle one more emotion. I felt like the most toxic human alive. Like I'd spent the last two months just inflicting all my issues on your family. And Zach. :(To hear that I'd also hurt you made me feel terrible.

But reading your letter has reminded me of something important. I forgot about that time after your father died, and how much you needed me. I've spent the last couple of months hating my own neediness and feeling terrible for it. But of course I didn't judge your moment of need at all. I was happy to be there for you.

The circumstances weren't the same, of course. But my doctor has been trying to convince me to cut myself a break. To stop feeling so much guilt.

Your letter just made that a little easier. So thank you.

Again, I apologize for trying not to let you know how bad things were with me. I thought I could shove it under the mat and pick apples and forget.

You mean so much to me. That will never ever change.

Love,
Lark

P.S. Please tell Zach that his letters are perfect. They lift me up completely. I'm not quite ready to write him yet, because I haven't sorted my emotions well enough to make any damn sense. But every letter makes me want to give him a big squeeze. —L

* * *

Dear Lark,

It's almost Christmas. Daphne is home on break, and she's decided she's speaking to me again. It may have something to do with whomever she's texting all day long. She smiles at her phone like she just won the lottery.

The Shipleys got a big tree and set it up in the corner of the dining room. It smells fantastic.

Did I ever tell you that my first Christmas was just four years ago? We didn't have Christmas at the ranch, because there's no mention of celebrating Christmas in the bible. (Did I also mention that the people who raised me didn't know how to have fun?)

I'm taking the social studies GED test right after New Year's. It's not that hard, although this is the first time I've had homework since I was a kid. I'd avoided this because I thought it would make me feel like a dunce. But it hasn't. Instead, I'm thinking—heck, I can do this. Why did I think I couldn't do this?

Next task: Christmas shopping. For the Shipleys I always get something tasty that they wouldn't buy for themselves. Last year I bought imported chocolates and champagne for Christmas. But now May doesn't drink and Audrey brought a bunch of chocolate home from France.

So I need a new idea. Like, yesterday.

I know I told you not to write to me. But if you are suddenly struck with a great idea for what to buy them, please

261

feel free to shout it out. I feel like Harry Potter trying to pick out a gift for all the Weasleys.

Love,
Zach

Lark

Sometimes the end of a stage in your life doesn't announce itself with trumpets or fireworks. Sometimes it just seeps in, like the smell of snow on the air as fall gives way to winter.

When I began to feel like myself again, it was a gradual thing. My mind began to become preoccupied with ideas that didn't have anything to do with Guatemala. And in therapy I stopped arguing with my doctor.

I didn't notice the change until I began to get *bored*. I started choosing movies without any fear that they'd trigger me. (Although they sometimes did.) I began to surf the web, looking for jobs and ideas. My dragons took long naps on their chains and forgot to frighten me with their fiery roar.

Then one day I picked up my phone and impulsively touched May's number.

Maybe if she hadn't answered, another month would have gone by before we spoke. But that's not what happened. The moment after I touched the button, she said hello right in my ear.

"Hi," I said, startled at my own nerve. "It's Lark."

"Hi sweetie," she said, sounding every bit as warm and familiar as I would have hoped. "How are things with you?"

"They're better," I admitted. "I know it's true, because I'm more bored than scared."

She laughed. "Okay? That could be a good sign, right?"

"Trust me, it is. What have you been up to?" The question sounded frustratingly stilted to my own ear. I really did understand why she'd been worried about things getting weird between us, because that would be an unparalleled disaster.

"Studying for finals. AA meetings. It's a laugh a minute with me. But we've also been planning Griff and Audrey's wedding."

"Yeah? What are they going to do?"

"An outdoor farm shindig in June."

"Nice. In the orchard? What's the rain contingency?"

"They'll rent a tent, but there's no indoor option."

"Risky!"

"I know, right? Griff will just command the heavens not to rain, and they'll probably obey, because he's such a grump."

I smiled into the phone, because May sounded like May, not a stranger. There was hope for us yet. "Has Audrey gone dress shopping? Where do you get a wedding dress in Vermont, anyway?"

"You don't. We'll have to come to Boston."

"You can visit me," I offered immediately.

"Of course."

Still grinning like a fool, I confessed my curiosity about something. "Can I ask you a really needy question?"

"Yeah. Shoot."

"Is there any reason why Zach didn't write me a letter this week? He's been like clockwork. Every Tuesday I get one..."

"Oh man. Maybe it's a tactic to make you wonder."

"You think?"

She giggled. "No. Zach got another flu, the poor guy. He slept for three days straight."

"Oh!"

"He's okay, though," she said quickly. "He's much better today."

"Are you sure?" My heart thumped against my ribcage at the thought of him sick again.

"I'm positive. And the doctor said he'd eventually stop getting so sick every year."

"Good."

"Why don't you visit him, if you're so worried?"

"Well..." I cleared my throat. "I want to see him. And *you* of course."

"Lark, you don't have to be careful with me like that. We're still tight, whether you have a boyfriend or not. That was always true, you know? You were *never* that kind of friend who ditched me whenever the boyfriends came along."

She was right. "You're too important to ditch."

"I *know*, okay? Jeez. What if you came up here next week? A couple days after Christmas?"

"All right," I said quickly. "If you're sure it's okay."

"Do it. Let's not be weird. Except in a fun way."

"Deal." I laughed. "Maybe I should send a note to Zach first, just to make sure he's okay with me visiting. He's been sweet to me with his letters. But sometimes when someone leaves you, it's better when they stay gone."

"Do you want to stay out of his life?" May asked.

"Hell no. I miss him like crazy."

"Trust me when I tell you that he wants to see you, too."

"Yeah?" Hearing that made me so happy. Dr. Becky would probably have me examining that reaction later.

"Oh yeah. He's not mad, honey. He's trying to move on, but he still loves you. I think he always will."

I closed my eyes right there on the phone, picturing Zach's smile. If I could see that smile aimed at me one more time, I knew I would do my best not to fuck it up. "Okay," I said softly. "I'll visit. Let me talk to my parents and then we'll iron out the details."

"I can't wait!" May said.

"Me neither.

Dear Zach,

I'd like to visit you and May right after Christmas. But I wanted to make sure it was okay with you. Being with me this fall couldn't have been easy, so I just wanted to check that you're ready to see me. If you'd rather I reschedule for another time, just let May know, and I promise I'll understand.

Love,
Lark

Lark

Zach wasn't the only one who had trouble with his Christmas shopping.

Now that I'd made a plan to visit the Shipleys, I hit the stores, looking for gifts. I got May some of our favorite overpriced lip glosses from a crowded shop on Newbury Street.

It was another sign I was feeling better—my zeal to shop outweighed my new dislike of crowds.

Choosing a gift for Zach should have been easy, since he didn't own much. But I struggled anyway, not wanting to choose something so personal that it seemed laden with expectation.

I eventually made my choices, then went home to wrap gifts. It was the evening of the twenty-third. There were still three days until I'd visit Vermont, but I was in a holiday mood, damn it. If I'd learned nothing else this year, it was that levity was fragile and should be enjoyed.

On the radio I found a Christmassy a cappella concert. I spread out my wrapping paper and purchases on the dining table, since my parents were headed out to a party for the evening.

"Are you sure you won't come with us?" my mother asked, hovering.

"I'm sure! This is fun." I didn't feel like making small talk with their friends from the law school.

"What will you eat?" she worried.

"I'll order something from the ramen place."

My mother—God bless her—brought me the menu and the phone. So I ordered while she waited, just to make her happy. Finally, they left.

I'd bought two things for Zach. One was a real gift, and one was…a gesture of sorts. Only Zach's main present would be wrapped.

He'd told me that he hadn't had Christmas as a child, and so I put a lot of effort into making the package beautiful. The gift went into a green box with red tissue. I wrapped it in candy-cane paper and tied a white bow around it.

The doorbell rang just as I wrote his name on a sparkly gift tag in the shape of a polar bear. Take that, Martha Stewart.

Humming along with the radio, I went to the door to retrieve my food order. When the delivery man handed over the bag, I tipped him fifty percent, because this was the holidays. He thanked me with a nice smile, which I easily returned. *Look at me getting into the holiday spirit. Go me!*

As I stepped back to close the door, my gaze snagged on a tall figure pacing slowly down the street, a scrap of paper in hand, studying the house numbers. The streetlights glinted off the most golden strands of his hair and illuminated a familiar set of broad shoulders swinging as he walked.

Still, I didn't trust my eyes until he was only one house away. Even then, it felt premature to call out his name. I must be mistaken. "Zach?"

He stopped, his chin lifting quickly in my direction. Then he smiled.

We just stared at each other, until I finally snapped out of it. "Omigod!" I squealed. Even though I wasn't wearing shoes, I set my dinner down in the open doorway and ran down the four steps, onto the short brick walkway that connected our row house with the sidewalk.

He opened his arms just before impact. I launched myself onto him, grabbing him into a tight hug. Then I found myself leaving the ground. "You have bare feet," he laughed into my hair. "Come on." He carried me toward the house and up the stairs. Over his shoulder I saw a passerby giving me a frown. Just jealous, probably.

"How did you get here?" I asked, but then didn't wait for an answer. "You feel amazing." His hair tickled my cheek, and the strength of his broad body against mine did fizzy things to my stomach.

He set me down in the entrance to my home. "I just couldn't wait," he said quietly. When I stepped back, I found serious blue eyes regarding me. "I tried to imagine you coming for dinner—getting out of your car and being dragged into the dining room with a dozen other people. I'd have to sit there for two hours before I had a moment alone with you." His big hands landed on my shoulders. "So I borrowed May's car and drove down here, hoping you were free to go out for a cup of coffee with me or something. It wasn't good planning, but I just couldn't wait."

I tugged him further inside, nudged my dinner out of the way and shut the door. "My social calendar is remarkably free at the moment," I teased. Then I put a hand on his muscular arm, because he was so close to me and I couldn't resist touching him. "But I always have time for you, Zach. No joke."

His face softened. "Didn't know if you'd want to stay friends. This hasn't been your happiest year."

"But you're the happiest thing in it." I scooped up the noodle bag and took his hand. "Come with me to the kitchen. Want to split some ramen noodles with me?"

"You eat. I already had supper."

"Okay. Christmas cookies, then?"

"Well, sure." But our progress was halted in the narrow hallway to my parents' kitchen, because Zach stopped to look at a bunch of framed pictures on the wall. "This you?" he asked.

Funny, I walked by these photos every day without seeing them. "Oh yeah. It's the Only Child shrine."

"Wow." He was studying a shot of me at age four. I was wearing a tutu and ballet slippers. "Cutest thing I've ever seen."

"Good thing they got that picture. I was interested in ballet for about seven seconds. Then never again. I wanted skydiving lessons, and I wanted to go with the scouting troop to explore caves in Kentucky. My parents didn't get the girly girl they were hoping for."

He put a hand to my hair and smoothed it down. "You're perfect, Wild Child. Just like seeing what you looked like before I met you. That's all."

In our kitchen, Zach looked around and then whistled.

"I know," I said. "My mom is really house proud." Her kitchen spared no expense. There was the trophy range—an

Aga—and the SubZero. There was a marble baking counter for rolling out dough and a backsplash made of imported tile that gleamed like jewels under the expensive lighting.

"Pretty impressive."

"Yeah. At least she cooks. Some of her friends have the same gear and order in every night. Like I just did. Are you sure you won't have some of this?"

He shook his head, just smiling at me.

"Then sit."

I took his jacket. Then I made him a little plate of my mother's Christmas cookies and brewed him an espresso in Dad's Illy machine.

While I ate my soup, we perched on stools and had the requisite preliminary conversation. He said I was looking healthier, and I agreed. I told him I'd heard about his flu, and he said it was all gone now. Neither of us was really focused on the conversation, though. We were too busy staring into each other's eyes.

I couldn't quite get over his presence in my kitchen. His flannel shirt brightened up the house. The curve of his smile was more lively and fascinating than anything I'd seen for weeks.

Everything was better when Zach was in the same room.

At one point I realized a full minute had gone by with nobody saying anything. We were all about the hot gazes and shy grins.

"Can I tell you I'm sorry now?" I blurted out. "Really, really sorry."

His smile faded. "Don't be sorry. I'm a big boy. I regret nothing."

"I regret a few things," I admitted. "I didn't walk into your life so much as I sort of splattered into it—a hot mess, ready to blow. You deserved better, even if I was doing the best I could at the time." That last bit would make my therapist proud.

He shook his head slowly. "You have nothing to apologize for. Like I told you last time I saw you—sometimes we can't control that stuff."

"I know. But I still wanted to tell you how much I appreciate all you did for me." His blue-eyed gaze fell to the crumbs on the plate, and I realized how my use of the past tense might sound to him. Like a dismissal. "If you wouldn't be opposed, I'd like to make it up to you."

He swallowed hard, lifting his chin. "You don't owe me anything."

I slid off my stool and moved closer, putting my chin on his shoulder. He smelled woodsy, like Vermont, and so familiar it made my eyes sting. "Everything that happened to me almost seems worth it when you're sitting in my kitchen. Because I love you, Zach."

He went completely still in my arms.

"You're so much more than part of a bad memory. I love you, and even if my life is kind of a mess right now, I still want you in it."

When he inhaled, I felt its shakiness. And when his arms came around me, they wrapped tightly. "Say it again," he whispered.

I turned my head to kiss his cheekbone. "I want you in my life."

"No, the other part."

"I love you?"

He nodded against my cheek, his stubble rough against my chin. "You're the first one to ever say those words to me."

Now it was my turn to freeze in astonishment. "Really?"

"Oh yeah."

I thought it through and realized it was possible. He hadn't told me much of his childhood, except that it was crowded and impersonal. "Then I'm honored," I whispered. "Except I'm sure there are more people who love you." The Abrahams and the Shipleys, for instance. "Maybe they just haven't said so out loud." They probably didn't realize what it would mean to him to hear it.

"Maybe," he said lightly. "Sure like hearing it from you, though." He took another deep breath and let it out slowly while hugging me to his body. I kissed his throat and he made a low, happy sound.

271

"Thank you for driving to Boston tonight. I missed the heck out of you."

He chuckled. "It was hard to wait. Every day I thought, *'Not today. She'll tell you when she's ready.'* And then I got your note saying you wanted to see me, and suddenly I couldn't wait another minute. I asked to borrow May's car, and she didn't even ask why."

I pressed my lips to the underside of his jaw, and he smelled so good. So familiar. So *Zach.* I kissed his cheek. Then his ear. I dropped little kisses into his hairline. They said, *Thank you for coming, my love.* I rubbed his neck with my palm, and it said, *You're so special to me.*

Zach lifted his gaze to mine. The kiss he gave me was slow, the way you'd play a carol slowly the first time through, because it's been a while since you'd heard the melody.

But this was a song I knew well. I made a hungry little noise of approval and softened my lips beneath his. With a groan, he cupped the back of my head and deepened our rapidly escalating kiss.

It said, Show me to your bedroom.

We made out like teenagers. His tongue stroked mine, and I panted into his mouth. He tasted like espresso and hunger.

It was completely intoxicating. The weeks I'd spent away from Zach had made me forget how much natural chemistry we shared—how well the heartbeat rhythm of our kisses were in synch, and how much heat we threw off together.

We were just like a bundle of fireplace starters I'd contemplated in a shop in Back Bay. *Guaranteed For a Fast Blaze.*

"Unngh," I moaned into his mouth, and he laughed.

I'd forgotten how easy this was between us—how right. I could stop fretting now that I'd seduced Zach as a means of forgetting my pain. The reason I'd ripped off his clothes was that we wanted each other. Like, yesterday. I skimmed my fingertips over his shirt and downward, until they traced the waistband of his jeans.

He caught my questing hand and broke our kiss. "Time out," he said with a smile. "I need to cool down."

That was the opposite of what I wanted. "Or," I suggested, "you could come upstairs with me."

"Well..." He chuckled. "Are you home alone?"

"Yes, thankfully." I tugged his hand until he got up off the stool. "Follow me." I led him to the foot of the stairs. "Climb up to the third floor. My room is straight ahead at the top of the second set of stairs. I'll be there in two seconds. I have to grab something."

He lifted a questioning eyebrow.

"It's a little surprise. Just trust me."

Zach kissed me on the nose, then climbed the stairs.

Zach

Lark had not made a secret of the fact that her parents had money. But I wasn't really prepared for the extravagance of her family home. When I'd walked down her street, I'd realized I was completely out of my element. The houses weren't enormous—they were packed too closely together for that. But each one was more ornate and historical than the last, and each appeared to have been primed and polished to a high sheen.

The inside was utterly glamorous. Lark's parents had kept the antique plasterwork and the fine wooden details. The staircase I climbed had a gleaming dark wood banister, and I saw art on every wall. The first landing branched off toward a couple of darkened bedrooms and a dimly lit library—the kind with books to the ceiling and a rolling ladder attached to the wall.

Wow.

I kept climbing. The third floor had sloping ceilings. Straight ahead I found Lark's room. The bed was another antique, an iron-framed number with a white cloud of a comforter on top. There was a big-screen computer on the desk, and more floor-to-ceiling bookshelves. I didn't know what I was supposed to do, so I headed over to inspect their titles. She had all the Harry Potters prominently displayed, along with novels of every style and color, and two shelves of travel books. Most of these were dog-eared. I ran my hand along the spines, marveling at all the places she'd been. Spain, Italy, France, England. Mexico. Japan. Australia.

We were not an obvious match, Lark and I.

But I forgot to worry about that a minute later when she arrived in the doorway looking a little breathless. "Sorry. There was something I had to do."

"Okay?"

Lark switched off the overhead light, leaving a low, beaded lamp by her bed to cast a rippled glow on the slanting wall. "Come here," she said, patting the bed. "Every night when I go to sleep, I wish you were here with me."

Hearing that just lit me up. "I may have thought the same thing once or twice," I said with a smile. "Or, you know, every single night." I sat down beside her.

She turned and scrambled onto my lap, straddling me. "Take off my sweater," she demanded.

"If you insist." I kissed her, smiling. Then I put my hands under the soft sweater she wore. My fingers found her velvety skin, and I had to kiss her again. As our mouths melted together I had a rather unfamiliar thought. *I'm so lucky.*

Slowly I pushed her sweater higher, my fingertips skimming her soft curves. She dipped her chin and I lifted the sweater over her head. Then my breath caught in my throat, because she was wearing a shimmering red satin bra in a sexy design. It cupped her in a mouthwatering way, lifting her breasts as if they were on offer to me.

I groaned, my palms cupping her, my thumbs stroking over the swells. Leaning down, I had to kiss the valley between her breasts, and the skin was even softer than I remembered.

Lark slid off my knees, standing up. She unbuttoned her jeans and dropped them to the floor.

I almost swallowed my tongue when a matching pair of tiny red panties appeared, clinging to her perfect hips. "Damn," I swore. "You're killing me."

She kicked her jeans away and stepped toward me, going to work on the buttons of my shirt. "It's a little surprise I had planned. Didn't think I'd need it until I visited in Vermont. I just did a hasty change in my dining room." She laughed.

I put my hands on her waist, because I had to touch her. "You don't have to wear anything special for me. I think you're perfect in anything."

She kissed the patch of skin she'd exposed on my chest, then finished removing my shirt. "I know it's not important. But it's something I did to show you I was thinking about you. And that when I push you down on the bed—" She gave me a little shove, and I fell back, grinning. "—that it's with *intention*. It's not because I had a bad dream, or you had a good one. Or because I need the escape. This—" She indicated the lingerie. "—was a little gift to let me say that."

"Then I accept."

She put a hand on my fly, and all the blood left my brain. "You still have too many clothes on."

"That's your fault, I think."

Her eyes widened at my boldness. "I think you're right. I'd better fix that."

If she said any more after that, I didn't hear it. I was too busy watching the only woman I'd ever really wanted remove the rest of my clothing. When she was finished, I was naked on the bed, and she was wearing only the red lingerie. "Come here," I rasped, my fingers itching to touch her.

When she fell into my arms, I rolled, lying her out on the bed. Then I began to methodically kiss her everywhere, starting at the tender place underneath her ear, and wandering slowly down her sleek form. Every time we'd been together, it was always a fantasy come to life. I worshipped every inch of her skin, humming my pleasure.

Every brush of my mouth against her skin made me more ready to combust. With both thumbs, I traced the outline of red lace which barely concealed her breasts. Then I traced the same line with my tongue.

"Yesss..." Lark hissed, and I smiled on my way down to kiss her soft belly, the curve of her hip. I took my time, teasing my way across the line of her panties, then down even further, placing wet kisses into the junctures of her thighs. "More," Lark demanded, reaching a hand down to push away the scrap of red fabric.

I caught her hand and pinned it to the bed. "Patience." I chuckled. I needed time to appreciate her body. I'd been waiting for this moment for too long. Lark squirmed suggestively, and so I pinned her thighs in place with my elbows. With painstaking deliberation, I continued my slow journey into the V of her legs, kissing my way across the satin, and taking a moment to inhale the sweet, musky scent of her desire.

"You're killing me," she panted.

"Nah," I said, trailing my tongue back up, crossing her abdomen until her muscles quivered. "You're tough. You can take it." Parting her thighs with my palms, I put my lips over the satin center of her and exhaled slowly. In my arms, Lark began to tremble. She let out a whimper. "Take them off," she begged.

"Nope." I kissed her pussy over the silky panties. "It's my present. I'll open it when I like. Now roll over."

She shivered at the command, and then she rolled onto her stomach, resting her cheek against the bedding. If I'd been worried about whether she was enjoying this torture, her smile would have given her away.

I took a moment to appreciate the perfect globes of her ass, palming them one at a time. Then I let my fingers dip between her legs, and she gasped in pleasure. "You ready?" I whispered.

She nodded, her eyes closed.

Taking one thigh in each hand, I tugged her down on the bed until her hips were right at the edge. That allowed me to ease the panties off her hips without snapping the delicate things in half. She looked so beautiful all spread out on the bed for me. It gave me big ideas. Taking myself in hand, I teased her between the legs.

"Fuck, yes," she said, digging her toes into the rug underfoot. "Please."

Enough with the teasing. I grasped one of her hips in my hand and thrust forward. Her body yielded, welcoming me with a liquid grip that had me groaning out loud. The sight below me was almost too much—Lark splayed out, her dark hair fanning on the comforter, which she gripped in her fingers as I began to move.

Holding her hips in my hands, I tried to go slowly. But the sight of our joining was the sexiest thing I'd ever seen in my life. The visual was so stimulating that I had to take a deep breath and close my eyes.

Easing Lark's hips onto the bed, I leaned down, my forearms beside her head, my stomach covering her back. "You are the sexiest woman alive," I whispered in her ear, while my hips moved with the rhythm of my heart.

She turned her chin another degree and I leaned down to kiss her. She moaned into my mouth, and it sounded like encouragement. Kissing her deeply, I worked my eager body against hers, as she drank in my moans and kisses with her own.

It was so, so good.

"Turn over," I panted, wanting even more of her. I pulled out and the two of us worked to hastily roll her to her back. I joined us again, and she dug her heels into my hips, and now I could hold her in my arms as we fucked.

"Yesss," she panted as I picked up the pace, her breasts bouncing, her cheeks flushed. I wouldn't last much longer. And I realized Lark had made a good point about our union. I wasn't so afraid for her anymore. The sex was fast and sweaty and just the kind of enthusiastic romp that two people can share when they're not trying to hold one another's psyches together.

"Oh!" She arched her back and gasped, her fingernails digging into my back.

That was it for me. As soon as the bliss settled across her face, I burst like a firework. Burying my shouts in the comforter beside her head, I shuddered and pulsed until finally I was still.

"God," she whispered into the silence. "I think we really needed that."

I wasn't even sure I could move, I was so spent. Gingerly I pulled out and then prowled up the bed beside her. "Come. Here," I muttered.

Her flushed face appeared beside mine. We kissed lazily, and caught our breath. "I waited at *least* twenty minutes after you stepped into the house to jump you," she said.

"You don't hear me complaining," I mumbled.

"Stay with me tonight?"

"All you have to do is ask."

"Mmm. Do you think we could get under the covers? Still not sure I can move my limbs."

"We'll give it a whirl. In a minute."

She kissed me again.

* * *

Eventually I sat up, and Lark showed me to the luxury bathroom in the hallway. When we got in bed again, I held her in my arms, and it was at least as good as the sex. "I can't stop touching you," I whispered as my fingers drifted over her breast and down to her hip once again. There were soft caresses and lazy kisses.

Neither of us was in a hurry to sleep. "How're the nights treating you?" I thought to ask.

"Not bad. The dreams still show up sometimes, but they don't feel as raw. It's like watching a storm blow out again after the worst is over."

"Mmm. All right."

"It is all right. I don't know how to explain it. I'm not as upset as I was before, so it's getting easier to roll over and go back to sleep."

We drifted off for a little while. But at some point Lark rolled over and shut off the light. The friction of her skin against mine felt so good that I opened my eyes again. And then we were kissing, and touches soon followed...

Until someone knocked on her bedroom door.

"Lark?" It was her mother's voice. "Are you all right? Can I come in?"

I froze like a deer on a country road at night.

"Uh, give me a second," Lark said, sounding unfazed.

She slipped out of the bed and pulled a bathrobe over her naked body. Then she left the room, shutting the door behind her. I heard whispered voices, which then moved away from the door.

It was five minutes or so until she came back. "Sorry," she said, tossing the robe aside and slipping into bed. "I'd left all the lights on downstairs. And..." She began to laugh.

"What?"

"I left my regular underwear on the dining room floor when I changed into the bombshell lingerie. Not my smoothest move."

"Um..." I clapped a hand over my eyes. "So your parents assume we had sex in their dining room?"

"I'm twenty-four years old, Zach. Even if we did have sex in the dining room, it wouldn't be a big deal."

"I could drive home," I suggested.

"No! It's almost one in the morning. Tomorrow we're going to wake up slowly and go out for breakfast together."

That sounded pretty nice. And even though I wasn't looking forward to greeting her parents in the morning, I cuddled her and fell asleep.

* * *

Waking up slowly was just as great as it had sounded. When I opened my eyes in the blueish morning light, there were snowflakes floating past Lark's window. My girl was sleeping with her head on my chest, her sleek arms wrapped around my body.

I just lay there, drinking her in, feeling lucky.

Eventually she stretched and yawned. I rubbed her back, and she began dropping kisses on my chest. My dick stood up to say hello, and Lark took me in hand.

"We shouldn't," I argued while she stroked me.

"Shh," she said, climbing on top of me. "I'll be absolutely silent. Besides, I can hear my father's radio playing. He never goes without his NPR while he showers and shaves."

So I lay back on her mattress while she seated herself on me. And while the news of a cease-fire in Syria played faintly in the background, she rode me toward a leisurely orgasm. It was the slowest we'd ever made love. I took deep, shaky breaths, staring into her heavy-lidded eyes as she smiled down at me. Each thrust ratcheted me a little closer to the brink. My hands wandered her magnificent body, cupping her swaying breasts. When I stroked her nipples with my thumbs she closed her eyes and bit her cherry-colored lip.

I loved watching her pleasure play out in slow motion. "You're so beautiful," I whispered. "Thought so the first moment I ever saw you." I slid my fingertips down between our bodies, finding that soft, luscious nub where her arousal bloomed.

She dropped her head and sucked in a breath. And then I felt her pulse around me. The shimmy and the sudden slickness tipped me right over the edge. I clamped my jaws shut to avoid moaning as she milked the seed right out of me.

I saw snowflakes in front of my closed eyes just before she collapsed onto my chest. "Wow," she said in a gust. "Feel free to drop by whenever."

Smiling, I pulled her closer. "That was hot."

"It's always hot." She sighed. "Hot was never our problem." We snuggled quietly for a while longer. "We should shower and go downstairs," she said eventually.

"I don't want to go downstairs," I admitted, and she laughed.

"There's coffee down there."

"That helps."

She kissed my neck. "But first a shower."

After I'd scrubbed myself clean and combed my wet hair, Lark found me a travel toothbrush. I shook the wrinkles out of my shirt and put myself together as well as I could.

Even so, my face burned as we descended the stairs.

Lark was unflappable, though. Taking my hand, she led me through to the kitchen, where her father was reading a newspaper at the table, and her mother sipped from a coffee mug beside him. "Good morning to both of you," her mother said calmly enough.

"Good morning," I said quietly as her eyes studied me. "Happy Christmas Eve."

"Is there coffee?" Lark asked breezily. "Or shall I start another pot?"

"I made plenty," Jill Wainright said. "But I haven't started breakfast yet, because I didn't know your plans."

"I thought Zach and I would go out for breakfast," Lark said. "Seeing as I have the morning off from psycho day camp." She turned to me. "Since it's Christmas Eve, they only want to see me for the afternoon session. And, hang on..." She pulled her phone out of her pocket and came to stand beside me. "Smile."

I smiled. Sort of. And whether I was ready or not, Lark took a selfie of us. "What's that for?"

"Dr. Becky is a fan of yours," she said, tucking the phone away. "I think she's got a major crush, so I thought I'd show her your handsome face."

I laughed, in spite of all the tension I felt. "That's... flattering."

Reaching into a cupboard for mugs, she patted my chest. "You should be flattered. She thinks very highly of you."

"Why?"

Lark pulled a stainless steel carafe from its berth in a high-tech coffee machine. "Because you took such good care of me, and you never show any fear. Grab the milk?"

"Fear of what?" The smell of the brew was comforting. I could almost handle the parents if it meant I got some of that. I looked around for the refrigerator, not finding it anywhere.

"Most young men would run screaming from a girl with a raging case of PTSD. The fridge is right there." She pointed at one of the paneled wooden cabinets, and I realized that her refrigerator had been camouflaged to look like a fine piece of furniture. Rich people were weird.

I located the milk and turned around to find her father watching me over the edge of his newspaper. Yikes. I felt my neck start to heat, because whatever he was imagining I might have done with his daughter was all true and then some. Under his roof.

He looked a little too tame to whip out a shotgun, though, so at least I had that going for me.

"So," her father said.

Lark handed me a milky mug of coffee and I took a gulp. For fortitude.

"If you go out for breakfast, who's going to help me put this thing together for Jimmy?"

Lark frowned. "Is it really all that tricky?"

"There's about a million parts." He looked at his wife. "Next year I'll choose the presents and you can put 'em together."

"I have an idea." Lark put a hand on my arm. "Is there any way you'd take a look at this toy we bought my cousin's son? And afterward I can take you out for waffles."

"Sure?" If it got me out from under her parents' gazes, I was all for it.

Her father came with us to the living room, though. There was a big, beautiful Christmas tree in there I hadn't glimpsed last night. I'd only had eyes for Lark. And on the rug beside the tree were the parts for a shiny metal convertible. It was going to be a big car—like three feet long. I saw a seat and a pedal apparatus for a child to sit inside and drive.

"Wow," I said. "That's so cool."

"I thought so, too," her father admitted. "Until I saw the parts spread out everywhere. The instructions are only pictures, no words. I spent a half an hour and got three pieces attached. The fourth part won't go on like I thought it should."

He handed me the schematic, and I took a quick glance at it. The chassis was to be built first, and then the body could just be pieced onto it. Then I looked at Mr. Wainright's work, and saw that the axles were reversed. "All right. I assume there's an allen wrench for this?"

He handed it over, but then he groaned when I took his work apart and reversed the pieces. "Was that the problem? Shit."

Laughing, Lark sat down beside me and held my coffee mug. "Sorry, Daddy. Remember my potter's wheel that never quite worked?"

"That wasn't my fault," he grumbled, and she laughed.

It took me about fifteen minutes to assemble the chassis, with Lark's assistance. Next I added the wheels, the pedals and the steering column. "These pieces are really nicely tooled," I said, running a hand over a body panel. "Like a German car."

Lark flipped over the schematic and squinted at it. "Huh. This company is in Munich. Good guess." To her father she said, "Zach works on tractors for the Shipleys, as well as on cars."

"So you're a mechanic?" Lark's dad asked.

"Not officially," I muttered, taking care not to scratch the paint job on the world's smallest functioning convertible.

Lark's mom stuck her head into the room. "Ten minutes until waffles. Can you take a break?"

"You didn't have to cook, Mom," Lark said.

"I know." Her mother disappeared.

Lark squeezed my knee. "Sorry. Can we stay in for breakfast?"

"Of course," I said even though I wanted her all to myself. But it was Christmas Eve, and she had a family who loved her.

I finished building the car even before her mother called us to the table. When it was done, I tested the steering wheel, feeling the wheels rotate smoothly underneath. This toy was so exceptional I could hardly believe it. As a child, I would have died of joy for just five minutes with something so shiny and sleek.

We ate breakfast around the kitchen table, which was a little crowded. But I guessed that was preferable to sitting in a dining room where her parents would have spent the meal wondering if we'd done it on the table.

Gah.

Lark parked her leg up against mine and squeezed my knee under the table.

Her mother put a plate in front of me with a big waffle in the shape of a Christmas tree. Beside it lay three strips of bacon and a pile of fluffy scrambled eggs. "Wow," I said, looking down at it. "Thanks."

"Eat up," Lark's dad said. "You just saved me three hours of cursing."

When everyone was seated, I waited for someone to say grace, but nobody did. Lark's father reached for a slice of bacon and bit off the end.

Thank you Lord for these gifts, I mentally rattled off. *Especially the beautiful one sitting beside me.* Then I dug my fork into the eggs and had a bite. The waffle was calling my name, but it was almost too artistic to eat. "You know, I never saw a waffle until I came to Vermont," I said because I knew it would amuse Lark.

"Really?"

"Sure. We went to a diner in Montpelier right after I got there, and I thought, that's a funny thing to do to a pancake. But I love them now."

Mrs. Wainright studied me. "Where did you grow up where there were no waffles?"

"On a...ranch," I said, choosing that word instead of *cult.* "Not the nicest place in the world."

"No—a perfectly dreadful place," Lark argued. "They also didn't have coffee. Or Harry Potter."

"Really?" Lark's father asked.

"Really." I sighed.

"Why?" he asked, and it was a perfectly good question.

"They had a lot of strange ideas. It's a long story." I drained my coffee cup, hoping for a change of topic.

"Let me pour you some more," Lark's mother said. "And you take milk?"

"I sure do. Thank you."

"How was the party?" Lark asked as we all ate.

"Lovely, as usual. The Whites are always fun." Her mother took a sip of coffee. "But Gilman was there with his little..." She made a noise of disgust. "I swear the girl was practically directing traffic in order to wave that ring on her finger around."

Lark laughed out loud.

"And he looked like the cat who swallowed the canary. But I'm sure she's a gold digger. I hope he got a prenup."

"Mom!" Lark gasped.

Suddenly my plate became very interesting to me. If Lark's parents thought I was hanging around their mansion for a shot at their fortune, I really didn't want to know. I cut the pretty waffle and lifted a corner to my mouth.

"Now hang on," Lark argued. "I actually doubt that very much. My theory—since you brought it up—is that Gilman needs to marry someone seven years his junior because she's too young to see that his success is a thin veneer which hides a whole lot of boring." Lark put a hand on my arm. "And, I swear to God, my mother is not a snob."

I risked a glance at her warm eyes, and they put me at ease.

"She's just loyal. The moment Gilman admitted to cheating on me with his intern, the girl became the devil incarnate. She's just protecting me."

Across the table, Lark's mom sighed. "I'm sorry. That was a crass thing to say. You're right, honey. I don't know anything about that girl. And I still want to choke her."

Mr. Wainright laughed. "Choke Gilman instead, dear. But don't get caught. He works for some great litigators."

"Who needs more syrup?" Lark's mom asked. "It's the real thing. From Vermont. I bought it that day we visited the farm."

I drizzled some onto my waffle. It was delicious.

But an hour later I had to say goodbye.

"Goodbye for now," Lark corrected me as we stood on the sidewalk together. "It's only a couple more days until I come to Vermont."

"Okay," I said, leaning in for one more kiss. There would never be enough of those. "I have to go now."

"I know," she said, still hugging me. We kissed again. And again.

Until finally I pulled myself together and left.

Zach

As it happened, Lark's trip was postponed for a reason I never saw coming. Over Christmas, the Shipleys got sick. First it was Griff and Audrey and Dylan. And the next day, Daphne and May and Ruth. They all got a stomach virus, except for Grandpa.

For the first time ever, I was unscathed.

May texted Lark, telling her to stay away. *We don't want to give you the plague.*

For a few days it was just Grandpa and I doing the milkings and feeding the livestock. We delivered cups of tea and slices of toast to whomever could eat. In the kitchen alone, I made sandwiches for Grandpa and I, and reheated soups from Ruth's freezer.

"You're a lifesaver," the Shipleys would say as I brought them another dose of aspirin or a glass of ice water.

But really, it was nothing. I didn't mind taking care of the people who take care of me.

Christmas was basically postponed. I didn't give anyone the gift I'd bought, because a puking family doesn't care about gifts. I just rode out the storm, wondering when the virus was going to hit me next.

It never did.

On the morning of the twenty-seventh, everyone finally felt human again. I helped Ruth make some pancakes, and she announced we should all open gifts.

They opened mine first. It was a solar-powered bird feeder with special powers. "When a squirrel lands on it, the motor spins the bar around, flinging the squirrel right off."

"Omigod, I've seen a video of this!" Daphne said with a squeal. "They try to hang on and it's hysterical."

"That's fun, Chewie," Griff said with a chuckle. "We'll hang it from the crabapple outside the kitchen window."

From his mother, Dylan got video games, and Daphne clothes. Griff got lined work gloves, and Audrey got a gorgeous cookbook from the French school where she'd just spent two months. May got several books she'd been wanting to read.

It was a flurry of wrapping paper in the living room. "Who's got Zach's present?" Daphne asked.

"Right here," May called, producing a small box. "Open it, Zach. It's from all of us."

I took the box. It was wrapped in shimmering green paper. I never unwrapped a gift before I came to Vermont, and it always made me a little self-conscious. This one was smaller than a cigar box, but not heavy enough to be a book. It kept me guessing 'til I got every scrap of paper off. Even when I saw the box, I wasn't sure it was real, because sometimes boxes were repurposed.

But not this one. When I lifted the close-fitting lid, there was a shiny smartphone inside. "Wow," I said. "Fancy."

"You need this!" May crowed. "To text with Lark."

"And Skype," Griffin added under his breath.

I lifted the sleek thing from its package. "Geez. Thanks. I'll activate it soon," I said slowly. But phone plans were pricey.

"Nope!" Daphne said. "It's already activated. On our plan."

"You shouldn't," I said immediately.

"It's not even expensive," Ruth said. "We put you on our family plan, because you're family."

I pressed the power button and the phone blazed to life in my hand. "Thank you. Seriously. This is so cool."

May sat down beside me and put an arm around my shoulders. "You're welcome. Time for your first selfie. Come on. It will be the two of us." She poked the icon for the camera. "I know just who we can send it to."

I lifted the phone and took our smiling picture.

* * *

Lark: You got a phone??? I love the selfie.

Zach: I did. I've joined the 21st century.

Lark: Does this mean you'll send me a dick pic later?

Zach: Let's not get carried away.

Lark: 😊

288

<u>Zach</u>: How do you make that smiley face?

<u>Lark</u>: Oh honey. I'll show you in person. When can I visit?

<u>Zach</u>: Soon. May doesn't want you to get the pukey flu. Everyone is waiting for Grandpa and I to start hurling.

<u>Lark</u>: You feel sick?

<u>Zach</u>: Nope. And I just at six pancakes. How about New Year's Eve? I've never kissed anyone on New Year's.

<u>Lark</u>: Okay. It's a date. I should tell you about a New Year's Eve tradition I adopted one year in Spain. You're supposed to wear red underwear for luck.

<u>Zach</u>: Shut the front door.

<u>Lark</u>: I'm not making this up. Guess who's all prepared to visit you in four days?

<u>Zach</u>: This just became my favorite holiday.

<u>Lark</u>: I ❤ you.

<u>Zach</u>: I

<u>Zach</u>: How do you make the heart?

<u>Lark</u>: ☺

<u>Zach</u>: I hope four days goes fast. Love you.

<u>Lark</u>: ❤ ❤ ❤

* * *

"What do you think, Zach?"

I looked up quickly to find Chastity's questioning face across the big dinner table. As I tried to rewind my brain to come up with the topic of a conversation I was supposedly following, Chastity grinned. "Aw. The poor guy can't concentrate."

"Quick, someone deal a hand of poker!" Griff cried. "I can earn back the money I lost to him last night."

May set a salad down in the center of the table, and then patted Zach's shoulder. "Hang in there. She can't be long now."

I touched the button on my brand new phone and checked the time. Again.

It was one minute later than the last time I'd checked.

Another glacial minute ticked by while I tried to listen for tires outside over the hum of the family gathering.

Down the table, Chastity was taking some flak about her new hairdo. She'd shown up tonight with her hair dyed pink.

"That's very Strawberry Shortcake," Kyle said.

"Dude," Kieran argued. "What do you know from Strawberry Shortcake?"

His brother socked him in the arm. The cousins had come over for dinner tonight and to talk Griff into going to the Gin Mill later. Or the Goat. They'd probably go another seventeen rounds before it was settled.

There was a lull in the conversation, and that's when I finally heard it—the sound of gravel pinging the undercarriage of a Volkswagen Beetle. My stomach got tight with anticipation. I'd get one night with Lark before she went back to Boston again. Our time together was precious.

I stood up and headed for the door.

"There he goes!" Kyle yelled. "Go get her, man."

"Is she here?" Audrey asked as I passed through the kitchen. "Just in time for dinner."

Without a word, I strode past her and out the back door. The motion sensor lights came on, illuminating Lark's face as she stepped out of the car. My heart stuttered.

Then she smiled, and it was the most beautiful thing I'd ever seen. "Hi there, handsome," she said. "I sure did miss you."

I made it over to her in three long strides. And when I got there, Lark threw her arms around me and planted her nose in the center of my chest. "Happy New Year. Almost. It's going to be a good one. I just know it."

We just stood there holding each other in the cold nighttime air, and I'd never been happier.

"Dinner is just about ready," I said finally. She kissed the underside of my chin. And who knew there was a direct line from my neck to my dick? So instead of heading for the door, I gave her a kiss.

"Mmm," she said against my lips. "Dinner first. But I want to get you alone later."

"Deal."

Inside, Lark made the rounds, greeting her friends. "Wild Child!" Griff said, giving her a squeeze. "You look great."

"Thanks," she said, her expression bashful. "I'm doing a lot better."

Everyone wanted to hug her. "Where's May?" Lark had to ask.

"Primping," Daphne said. "She's going to a party later. There are clothes all over every surface of her room."

"Then I'll save her a seat," Lark said. "Move over, Kyle."

Ruth carried the platter of ham into the dining room, and then Audrey hurried in to set down a covered crock. Griff opened up a growler of cider and began to pour it for whoever was drinking. "Pace yourselves, fellas. New Year's is still five hours away."

"Can't wait to celebrate it *at the Gin Mill*," Kyle said.

Griff just shook his head.

"Sorry!" May called from the other room as her footsteps hurried toward the dining room. She skated into view a second later.

"Wow!" Lark said. "Vavoom!"

May spread a hand across her cleavage. "Do you think it's too much?"

"I'm not known for my superior judgement in these matters," I pointed out. "So I'd say go for it. You should have told me this was a dressy occasion. Where are we going?"

"Well. *I'm* going to a party," May said, sitting down.

Grandpa interrupted this line of discussion by starting to say grace. I watched my girlfriend and May close their eyes respectfully until he said amen. Then both their eyes popped open and they continued where they left off.

"But you're not coming, and neither is Zach," May said. "I'm going to hang out with you guys for an hour or so and then I have a date."

"Go you!" Lark interjected.

"With a woman."

"Finally," Daphne muttered, spearing a slab of ham off the platter.

Wait. What? That didn't compute. Unless I'd misunderstood May? I glanced at the faces around the table, but nobody else had seemed to notice what she'd said.

"May, honey. Could you start the black-eyed peas?" Ruth asked. "They're right in front of you."

Frowning, May took the lid off the crock. She plunged the serving spoon inside, but then looked up, her eyes scanning the table. "I just said I had a date tonight with a woman. A date. I'm wearing a dress and everything."

"Lookin' good, too," Kieran said. "Do the peas have bacon in them?"

"Have you met me?" Audrey asked. "Of course there's bacon."

May scooped some peas onto her plate. Finished, she lifted the crock, but then hesitated. "Isn't anyone surprised? Am I not speaking English? I'm dating a woman. Well, not dating. Not yet. But maybe. Anyone?"

I raised my hand. "I didn't see that coming."

"*Thank* you! Jeez. I thought my queerness would at least be newsworthy."

Kyle took the crock of black-eyed peas from May. "If your date had, like, four tits, that would be newsworthy. Does she?"

"No!" she howled. "She's a very beautiful law student."

"And you look very beautiful tonight too, dear," Ruth said.

"Thanks, Mom," May said tightly.

"Does anyone else have anything they want to share?" Dylan asked in a campy voice which made his sister's scowl deepen.

"Actually..." I said, and everyone turned expectant faces to me. "I bought a truck today. Jude found it for me. It's a 1997 Ford F-150."

All the men's faces lit up. "No way!" "Whoa!" "What's the mileage?" "Does it need a lot of work?"

"Seriously?" May hissed.

"They're men." Lark soothed her with a pat on the hand. "Just tell yourself you made the right choice for the evening."

"Obviously."

"Where did Jude find it?" Griff asked. "Tell me it's not a junker like that Avenger of his."

"It's bad, but it's not *that* bad," I said. "I started looking at all the used cars for sale, just to get a feel for the prices, because

Chastity will need a car eventually. And then I realized I needed one, too." I stole a glance at Lark, and she smiled at me. "I can't borrow a vehicle every time I want to go to Boston, right? So I just bought it."

"Did you take out a loan?" Griff asked.

"No. Cash."

"Good man. Though an old Ford will be a gas guzzler. Gonna cost you to drive it to Boston every weekend."

"Maybe he won't have to drive that far," Lark said quietly. "*Maybe.*"

"Why?" I asked, slipping my hand into hers under the table.

"I had two interviews this week," she said. "One was in Boston. But the other was across the river in Hanover."

"At Dartmouth?" May asked, her face brightening. "I love this idea."

Lark nodded. "I had a long talk with the dean of the geography program. There are a couple of professors in the department who work on food security and environmentalism. I asked myself, 'What does a spoiled rich girl do after her life blows up?' And the answer is—go to grad school. I'm thinking of applying to the PhD program."

I smoothed my thumb over her hand. "You're not the least bit spoiled, Lark. But that sounds interesting."

"I really like the idea," she admitted. "But of course I might not get in."

"Do your parents know anyone at Dartmouth?" Griffin asked. "Might be time to call in a favor or two."

"I'm sure they do," Lark said slowly. "But I don't want to be that kid who relies on her parents' connections. We'll just see what happens, I guess. My other interview was a little more practical. There's a non-profit in Boston that sources sustainable ingredients for luxury food companies. You know— shade-grown coffee and fair-trade chocolate. They might have a new position opening up."

I squeezed Lark's hand. "Is there travel?"

"That's *some*. But you know what? They'd heard about me."

"Who had?"

"The people at this company had heard about my troubles in Guatemala. I guess nonprofits are a small world. And—this really surprised me—they said, 'We never would have sent you to that region. And we sure wouldn't have sent you there alone.'" Her eyes darted up to mine. "I really needed to hear that."

"I bet," Griff said.

"Yeah. I just spent a month trying to forgive myself for what happened. And today, this guy who interviewed me was better than my overpaid psychiatrists."

"Why?" I asked softly.

"Because it wasn't his job to try to make me feel better. He was just stating his opinion. And his opinion was that the timing and location of my trip to Guatemala was a terrible idea."

"Amen!" May said. "We're glad you're here. Eat some black-eyed peas just for insurance. They're good luck on New Year's."

"Do we know how that tradition got started?" Kyle asked. "Not that I need a reason to eat Audrey's cooking."

"They're humble," Ruth said. "So we'll start the New Year with humility."

"I'm already humble," Kyle said, stabbing another slice of ham off the platter. "It's hard to walk around all day and not boast about all this perfection."

A chorus of groans ensued, but I wasn't paying attention. I was holding hands with Lark under the table, and trying not to get too excited about her potentially moving to Hanover.

Lark

After dinner, I made a point to hang out with May for a while. It's something I would have done anyway, even if it weren't for her recent confession of love I couldn't return. I'd always made time for her, and that wasn't about to change.

So I dragged her into the TV room while Zach was washing dishes, just so I could give her my Christmas present—the luxury lip glosses in their sleek little silver case.

"I love these!" she said when she opened my gift. "You shouldn't have."

I shrugged. "This brand always makes me think of you. It was our college splurge."

"Haven't had much reason to wear makeup in a while," May said, dabbing the perfect little brush into one of the glosses and pursing her lips in the pocket-sized mirror.

"Me neither. But once in a while it's fun. And I have a question."

"Mmm?" she asked, rubbing her lips together.

"When two women make out, is it a problem if your lipstick clashes? What if one of you is wearing a cool shade of pinkish purple, and the other has an orangey red? Like, omigod. That's a fashion no-no."

"You crack yourself up," May said, tucking the brush back into the compact and closing the lid. "That was the most blatant fishing expedition for details that I've ever heard."

"Fine. I'll just ask outright. Has there been any nakedness yet? And was it awesome?"

May shook her head. "She just asked me out last week for the first time. Took me completely by surprise."

"A secret admirer! What's her name?"

"Daniella." She grinned. "Yeah, it was a nice ego boost. But of course I didn't realize she was into girls. So we had this stumbling conversation where I had to ask a few clarifying questions about whether this was a date or a hangout. That part is just easier with men."

"No kidding. If a guy asks you to go anywhere with him, you can just assume he wants sex."

"Right?"

"Hey, Lark?" Zach's head popped into the TV room where we were sitting. "Can you come outside with me?"

May and I promptly burst out laughing.

"What did I say?" Zach asked.

"Nothing!" I protested. "We were just talking about things men want."

He came in and sat down on the sofa next to me. "I just want to show you my truck."

"Aw," May said, reaching across me to pat his knee. "Don't ever change, Zach. You're the best kind of guy." She stood up. "I'm going to peek at my hair one more time and then go. You two kids be good."

"Do me a favor?" I asked May. "Don't be good tonight. Be naughty."

"We'll see," May said coyly. "Don't leave tomorrow until I get a chance to say goodbye."

"Wouldn't dream of it."

After she left, Zach waited at least a whole minute before he asked me to come outside and see his truck. "I've never bought anything expensive before. It caused me almost physical pain to write that check."

"Sure. Let's go outside."

On the way to the tractor shed where he'd parked it, I stopped at my car and grabbed the box from inside.

"What's that?" Zach asked.

"Your present."

"Aren't you wearing my present?"

"You'll have to verify that later. But this is something that's really for you."

He patted his coat pocket. "Okay. I have yours right here, too. But first..."

The truck was black and looked to me like every other truck on the road. Even so, I made all the right sounds of admiration. Zach had taken this risk because he wanted to be able to see me, and that was the sexiest thing in the world.

I opened the passenger-side door and climbed in, putting my box up on the dash. "Do you have to do a lot of work on it?" I asked after Zach climbed into the driver's seat.

"Some. I got a great deal because it failed its emissions test, and the elderly man who drove it just didn't want to bother with fixing it up. But if I do the repairs myself, it won't be very expensive. I just can't drive it until I can fix the hoses and tune up the engine. Are you cold?" he asked, rubbing his hands together. "It's freezing in here."

"A little." I moved closer to him on the seat. "Let's snuggle."

"Twist my arm." He pulled me closer to his body. "I love the idea of you being in Hanover. That's about…thirty miles?"

"At least. But I could live in Norwich or somewhere on the Vermont side of the river. Lots of people commute into Hanover."

Zach put a tender kiss on my temple. "Doesn't matter. I'd drive all night to see you."

Those words sent a happy little shimmy through me. "If we're lucky, it won't come to that. I'm going to write a really good application to this program. And the dean said they had a couple of part-time jobs opening up—organizing research data—stuff like that. I told him I'd love to consider that job even before they made their application decisions. I was an eager little beaver. Now open my present. I want to see if you like it."

"Of course I'll like it." He took the box I handed him and loosened the ribbon. After unwrapping it, I watched him smile when he lifted the lid. "This is nice." His fingers stroked the fabric of the shirt I'd bought him—it was flannel, but insulated with fleece. "And warm."

"That was the point. Every morning when I wake up, I think of you out in the dairy barn in the cold. And I wonder if you are wearing the right clothes."

Zach lifted the box and the shirt back onto the dash, then hugged me, burying his face in my hair. "Thank you."

"I hope it fits."

"It will," he whispered, kissing my neck. "Thank you for thinking of me when you wake up in the morning."

"Of course I'm thinking about you! I'm wishing you were there so I could rip off your clothes."

He chuckled, his lips teasing my ear. "It's more than that. I'm not used to anyone looking after me. I like it."

I drew back and forced him to look me in the eye. "*So* many people look after you. You have a big fan club, Zachariah Holtz. And I'm the president."

"Sometimes I forget, though," he mumbled. "People treat you like garbage for nineteen years, it takes a while to get past it."

"I think you're almost there."

He kissed me. "Now open my present." He fished something out of his coat pocket—a small box. "I went with Daphne and Ruth to a craft fair in Hanover, and I found something there that made me think of you."

The little box was made of wood, with a single gold ribbon around it. I tugged the ribbon off gleefully. When it fell away, I lifted the lid.

Inside, a silver pendant and chain lay on a felted cushion. The pendant was an artist's representation of an apple. In pure silver, the jeweler had captured the unmistakable curve of the fruit's shape. But the form wasn't symmetrical. Like a real apple—and God knows we'd both handled thousands of those—it was uneven, its stem bowed. Yet the metal had been burnished to a beautiful bright texture, and it glowed with an uncanny likeness to the real thing.

"An apple," I whispered. "It's perfect."

"It *isn't* perfect," Zach argued. "But I like that. The first day you were here, Griffin gave you his long speech about how the most bitter apples make the best cider. When I saw this, it reminded me of falling in love with you. A lot of bitter things happened to you this year, but without them we wouldn't be sitting right here."

I swallowed hard. "I get that now. Will you put it on me?"

He took the delicate chain from her fingers, but then hesitated. "There's one more thing. I was chatting with the woman who made this, and she told me an interesting fact."

"I'll bet she did. That's probably because you were the most interesting thing she saw all day."

Zach teased open the tiny silver clasp. "Unfortunately, much of the world's silver comes from Central and South America."

"Ah," I said, tilting my head to make his job easier. "I'll always be dragging a big piece of Guatemala around with me, so what's one more ounce?" When he was done fastening the chain, I lifted my head and kissed him. A real kiss—right on the mouth.

"Mmm," he said with a growl. "Guess we can't wait for midnight."

"Nope," I agreed, throwing a leg over his and leaning in. Even though it was cold out here in the truck, Zach and I had enough chemistry to heat the eastern seaboard. Tasting him slowly and thoroughly, I forgot about Christmas presents and New Year's wishes. Kissing was suddenly all I cared to do.

Okay, not *all*.

I slid a hand down to Zach's zipper, cupping the erection inside his jeans. Then I opened the button. "We need to break in your truck," I whispered. He groaned as I slid off his lap and bent down to unzip him. I tugged the denim away and reached into the handy fly on his boxers. I untucked his cock, his length in my hand. Leaning in, I began to drop light kisses up and down his shaft. I nuzzled the curly blond hairs at the base of his dick, and won an aroused groan for my troubles.

But when I began to lick him, he caught my chin. "None of that," he chided, "or I won't last."

"We have all night," I argued, getting in one last good lick.

Zach put a hand on my head. "I know. And I want to spend it inside you."

It was a simple statement, spoken in Zach's understated cadence. But the effect on me was the sort of heat that nearly required one of Griffin's fire extinguishers. And when Zach's fingers curled around my hair and tugged me upward, I was ready and willing to go inside the bunkhouse with him.

"Hey," I whispered as he tugged himself back together in the dark. "Are those boxers...red?"

"Of course! I didn't want to mess up the tradition."

I laughed all the way to the bunkhouse. When we entered the guest room, there was something sitting in front of the bed—an ice bucket. A bottle of champagne sat inside it, and there were two champagne glasses on the nightstand. Lastly, a card sat propped up on the pillow. *Lark*, it read on the outside.

"Wow. Did you do this?" I asked.

"Uh, no."

I opened the card.

Lark—

This is my present to you! I stoked up the fire and chilled the wine. Have a nice night with your man. I'm ecstatic for you both. And it's great to see you looking so happy.
Love you always,
May

"Aw."

"That was nice of her," Zach said, reading over my shoulder.

"It really was."

"Want some champagne? It's not midnight yet, though."

I sat down on the bed and reached for the bottle. "Let's not wait. It took us a long time to get here."

Zach sat down on the bed and then moved to kneel behind me. He kissed me on the back of the neck. "You're worth the wait." He dropped another soft, open-mouthed kiss on the back of my neck.

It felt so good that my hands fumbled on the twist of wire holding the champagne cork. "Don't stop."

"I never will."

Seven Months Later

Zach

It was late on a Tuesday afternoon in July. Also? It was my birthday.

Nothing had gone exactly as planned today, though. Griff and I had meant to spend the day fixing split-rail fencing. Instead, we'd ended up at The Busy Bean, the coffee shop Zara and Audrey owned. Their power had gone out around noon, and Zara had called Griff in a panic. They were worried about losing the stock in their fridge and freezer and needed help with a generator.

Griff had said to me, "You can hook up a generator, right?"

"Sure," I'd said. But what I should have said was, "Sure, if you have all the right parts."

Two hours later I had the thing going, but I spent another couple of hours calling HVAC companies to try to get someone to look at the air conditioner behind the building, because I was pretty sure a faulty capacitor had caused the problem in the first place.

After fetching a lot of ice for Audrey and Zara, Griff had left me at the coffee shop. "You're doing important work here, man," he'd said. "If it gets late in the day, I'll just see you tomorrow, okay?

"Yep! Later."

I liked tinkering with systems, and I loved fixing things for my friends. When we'd arrived, Zara had been pacing the cafe, her copper-haired one-year-old in her arms, a worried look on her face.

Even after Zara's mother had arrived to take little Nicole off her hands, her mood didn't improve until I got the refrigerators humming.

"You are a prince among men," Zara gushed then. But I had to break it to her that her troubles might not be over unless the AC unit was fixed.

"We'll be fine," Audrey had insisted. "And we really appreciate all you did for us today. And on your birthday! Let me give you a treat."

"After I make these calls," I'd insisted. Tomorrow was supposed to be a scorcher and I didn't want them turning the AC back on until I found somebody look at it.

By four thirty I'd found a repairman who'd help them first thing tomorrow. After I'd washed most of the grease out from under my fingernails, Audrey sat me down at a cafe table with a plate of cookies. And Zara made me one of her famous lattes. It was served in a bowl, with a swirl of cinnamon on top.

Heaven on earth, I swear.

I texted Griff to let him know what I'd accomplished, and he replied with an offer of dinner. *I'll see you tomorrow*, I told him. *Lark has something planned for tonight.*

I'll bet she does, was Griff's snarky comment. It came with a wink emoji. *Go home to your girl.*

Okay, I'm heading home soon. See you tomorrow. The old me would have rushed back to the farm for an hour of fence repair instead of enjoying a moment here in the cafe. I still loved working for Griff, but I didn't need to work the longest hours or stay the latest to prove that I cared.

He already knew.

I was so busy with these thoughts that I almost missed an interesting customer in the coffee shop.

Audrey was tidying up while Zara served the day's last few caffeine junkies. A man I didn't recognize walked in and began to glance around the place. People did that, because the interior of The Busy Bean was quirky. The posts and beams had been painted with a chalkboard surface onto which Audrey and Zara had written some of their favorite quotes. The furniture was homey but mismatched and upholstered in bright colors.

I didn't form an opinion of the unfamiliar customer until I glimpsed Zara's expression. She and the newcomer were face to face, but she'd gone white as a sheet.

"Hey, no way!" the guy said, his back to me. "I'm back in town, and I looked for you at the Mountain Goat. Didn't know you worked here now. We should exchange numbers."

Zara stared at him for a long beat. Her mouth had fallen open. "Do you...have a b-business card?" she'd finally asked.

Zara's freaked-out expression was so unlike her that I took a closer look at the man. He was a big, muscular guy in jeans and a faded T-shirt. On his feet he wore hiking boots. That was pretty much all I could tell about him from the back. Except for one detail that really set him apart from the other men I knew around here.

His hair was a very distinctive shade of coppery red.

I wasn't the only one who noticed, either. Audrey stood a few feet away from Zara, a sponge in one hand and a startled look on her face.

The red-haired man dug a wallet out of his back pocket and fished out a card, which he handed to Zara. She took it, then mumbled an excuse of some kind.

Then she fled the room.

Audrey recovered. "What can I get you?" she asked the stranger.

But the man had turned to watch the door where Zara had just disappeared, a frown settling over his features. "Um, a coffee. Black. Thanks," he said.

Two minutes later he was gone.

Audrey came around the counter and plunked herself into the chair in front of me. "That was..."

"Really odd," I said, finishing her sentence. Then we both laughed.

"I'm not going to jump to any conclusions," Audrey said, a thoughtful look on her face.

"Me neither."

But then our eyes met, and we both cracked up. "Okay, I'm going to jump to all kinds of conclusions," Audrey admitted. "But privately."

I mimed turning a key in front of my mouth and tossing it away. "I'm a vault."

"I know." She jumped out of her seat and came close, grabbing me into a hug. "Happy birthday! I love you!"

"Love you, too," I said easily, giving her a big squeeze right back. Lark had changed me into someone who could do that. I was a world-class hugger these days.

"Now go home," she said, slapping me on the back. "Kiss Lark for me. And I'll see you both tomorrow night, right? For the concert on the Hanover green?"

"Absolutely."

"You're bringing wine and dessert," she said, pushing in her chair. "I'm bringing a picnic feast."

"I can't wait," I said, and it was the truth. Then I thanked her again for the killer cookies and made my way outside.

Humming, I got into my old truck and started the engine, letting it warm up, and listening for problems. Over the six months I'd owned it, this vehicle had kept me busy with repairs. I'd had a string of bad luck, first with the exhaust and then the transmission.

Today everything sounded fine. Fineish. So I pulled out my phone and tapped Lark's number.

"Hi!" she said cheerily. "I'm walking home from work. Are you on your way?"

"Leaving now. Give me forty minutes." My commute wasn't the greatest, but I loved the people on either end of it, so I wasn't complaining.

"You hungry yet?" she asked.

"Not for food," I said slowly.

Lark cackled. "Come home, birthday boy. Let the celebration begin."

We hung up and I hit the road, getting on highway 89 southbound. After Lark secured a job with the professor at Dartmouth, we'd started looking around for somewhere for her to live. Chasing down leads, I'd met an elderly couple—Lionel and Millicent Bern—in Norwich who wanted to rent out the cottage behind their farmhouse to someone who could help take care of the property.

And on their property? An old apple orchard. It was only five hundred trees, but the Berns couldn't care for it themselves anymore.

So I got that job with no trouble. Griff was my reference, of course. But they were all too happy to meet a young guy who would look after their apple trees. "They're like our children," Mr. Bern explained. "These last couple years we couldn't harvest much. We let a group of school children come to pick apples, but so many just fell to the ground and rotted. It killed me."

That was how Lark and I came to live together barely six months after we met. And every day we had together was a blessing.

We paid very low rent plus utilities for a little cottage behind the farmhouse. It had a creaky little kitchen and an office nook, as well as our bedroom and a living room with a woodstove against a pretty brick chimney.

"It'll probably be drafty as hell in the winter," I'd pointed out, wary of the single-paned leaded windows everywhere.

"I don't care," Lark had said, putting her foot down. "It's adorable. And it's on the Vermont side of the river, but just a few miles from Hanover. And it's cheap as hell, Zach! If it's cold in here, we'll just snuggle."

That plan worked for me. Lots of snuggling happened in our little house, even in warm weather.

So now I had a few different jobs. I worked for Griff, but not quite so many hours. I did maintenance on the Bern's property—landscaping and orchard work. Griff actually drove down once every two or three weeks or so to help me with that. He always knew what to do for the problem trees.

It was going to be a decent harvest, and the Berns had already told me that I could sell off the crop this fall. "I want two bushels of the best ones," Millicent had said. "The rest you two can use to build up your rainy day fund."

My third occupation was a new one for me—student. This fall I'd be taking classes at one of the many branches of the Community College of Vermont. I hadn't decided what degree to pursue—a B.A. or something more technical. Everyone told me not to worry, that I could figure it out later.

"You don't know what kind of student you are until you get back into the classroom," Lark pointed out. "We have enough money to live like this for a while. Your job, my job, my trust fund. I'll get fellowship money for the PhD program. You don't have to figure everything out at once."

As the book of Ecclesiastes puts it: In the morning sow your seed, and at evening withhold not your hand, for you do not know which will prosper, this or that, or whether both alike will be good.

And what was one more year of not quite knowing which direction to go?

One part of my life was all figured out—the most important part. Every night when I drove home, I pulled up my aging truck behind Lark's VW and then went inside. And there she always was, waiting for me. It gave me a thrill every single night. No lie.

Even though we were very busy, we were happy. Lark smiled more easily now. She slept easier, too. These days, when she rolled over in bed to seek my body in the sheets, it was for love.

And pleasure. We had plenty. *Take that, Paradise Ranch.*

Every night it was an effort not to speed toward home, just to be close to her. But now I drove very carefully through the well-kept center of Norwich, where the cops had nothing better to do than ticket people who drove over twenty-five miles-per-hour on Main Street.

As I rolled up Turnpike Road toward our little lane, my phone rang. After checking the rearview mirror to make sure no cops were behind me (Vermont had a very strict no-cell-phone law) I answered it.

"Honey, my parents are here," Lark said in a low voice.

"What?" That wasn't part of our birthday plan.

"They brought you a gift. It's so nice that I didn't even give them a hard time about showing up unannounced. Just wanted to warn you before you get here."

"Okay... I'm three minutes away."

"Love you, Zach."

I never got sick of that. "Love you, too."

Dropping the phone into the cupholder, I tried to rearrange my expectations. Now we'd be dining with the Wainrights. They were really nice to me—nicer than I'd ever expect a couple of Boston intellectuals to be toward the farm boy who was shacking up with their only daughter.

I'd really wanted Lark to myself tonight. Ah, well. There was always tomorrow night. And the one after that.

Sure enough, there were a couple of extra vehicles on the part of the gravel drive that doglegged over to our cottage. I recognized the Wainrights' Volvo, but there was a late model Highlander there as well—a hybrid. I didn't know anyone who drove a vehicle as new and sporty as that one.

Did we have more guests?

Outside our door, I took a minute to brush as much of the farm dirt off my boots as I could. Then I plastered on my meet-the-parents face and went inside.

"Happy birthday!" Jill Wainright called as I stepped into the door. She was holding a glass of lemonade and wearing a dress. So we were probably headed out to dinner somewhere. Maybe I could at least get a quick shower first.

"Thank you!" I said, giving her a smile. "The big two-four. I feel ancient."

Lark's father rolled his eyes beside her. "You shouldn't, since you're dating an older woman."

"Good point." Lark was eight months older than I.

"We're taking you two out to Carpenter & Main," he said.

"Thank you," I said, trying to smile. The restaurant was one of two in Norwich, but Lark and I favored the casual, college town fare across the bridge in Hanover. Carpenter & Main always made worry that I was using the wrong fork. The food was really good, though. So at least I had that. "Let me just clean up real quick."

"You go ahead," Jill said, still giving me a strangely bright smile. "Then we'll give you your birthday present."

"But you're taking us out to dinner," I pointed out. "I don't need a gift."

She gave me that grin again. "Oh I really think you do!"

Huh. "Back in five," I promised.

Literally the second I stepped out of the shower, Lark handed me a beer. I was still naked and dripping on the mat when she put it in my hand. "Split this with me?"

"Sure?" I took a swig.

"Try not to freak out about my parents' gift, okay?"

I gave her a kiss—my first of the evening. "I won't freak out. But, why? Is it not my style, or something?"

She chewed her lip. "No, it is. You'll see."

"You could give me a clue." I rubbed the towel through my hair.

She shook her head. "Nope. I'm not spoiling it." She took a sip of our shared beer and then handed it back to me, readying herself to walk back out of the bathroom.

Then I had an alarming idea. "Where are your parents staying tonight?" Our little house wouldn't really accommodate guests. Our couch didn't even pull out.

"At the Norwich Inn."

I smiled, because at least one of my birthday plans was still intact. "Okay. I'll throw on some clothes."

After I'd donned a newer pair of jeans and a button-down shirt, I found everyone in our small living room. "Thanks for waiting. I'm ready to go whenever you are."

"First the present!" Mr. Wainright announced, while his wife and daughter both grinned like crazy women.

"Uh, okay. Thanks for thinking of me."

"Thinking of you!" Lark's father boomed. "We've been worrying about you! That's why we bought this." He walked over to the front door and opened it.

I followed him, but everything outside was the same as it had been before. "I don't get what you mean?"

He laughed. "The car, son. We brought you the car. Your truck just isn't reliable enough, and you drive so many miles every day just to live here for Lark."

What? My gaze landed on the Volvo. Lark had once said they were thinking of upgrading, and might want to sell. "You traded up from the Volvo?"

"No, we had a better idea." Mr. Wainright held up a keyring with a bow tied on it. "Happy Birthday." He handed it to me.

The key said Toyota. And when I pushed the button to unlock it, the shiny Highlander blinked to life. "That car looks so new," I said stupidly.

"It's one year old. Has nine thousand miles on it. Four-wheel drive, because you need it in the snow on those dirt roads. And it's a hybrid." He put a hand on my shoulder. "Won't cost a mint to fill it up."

"You brought us a car," I said, still not quite believing it.

"I knew he'd freak," Lark said. "They brought *you* a car. Mine does just fine for my three-mile commute."

"You can't gift me a car, though." I was still staring at the SUV. It didn't look like something I'd ever own. Too new. Too upscale.

"Sure we can. Look." Lark's dad waited until I tore my eyes off the shiny toy parked in my driveway and met his gaze. "You need this. We can give it to you, so we did. You don't have to spend any more time on repairs, because it's warrantied under their pre-owned program for a while. And you take such good care of Lark's Bug that it gets better mileage now than it did before."

"More than that," Jill broke in, "you take such great care of *Lark*. You moved out of your friends' home to be with her. You work harder than any other twenty-four-year-old we've ever met. Take this. Drive it. Enjoy it. And we promise to bring you just a sweater or a case of beer on your next birthday."

Finally I laughed out loud. "Thank you. I don't know what to say. Nobody ever gave me a car before."

"Nobody ever gave you *anything* before," Lark said. "And yet we still have everything we need."

That was startlingly true.

"Drive it down the hill for dinner," Mr. Wainright said. "Let's eat." He pulled his own keys out of his pocket and moved off toward the Volvo.

"I'll ride with Zach," Lark said, darting ahead to open the passenger door. "Ooh! Leather seats!"

"No way." I followed her over to the driver's side and opened the door. "Jesus."

"You just took the Lord's name in vain!" she yelped, because I never did that. But the car's interior was beautiful. It had all the latest gadgetry—a Bluetooth stereo, a GPS system. Satellite radio.

When I sat down and put the key in, it hummed alive with a sound that was absolutely nothing like the old Ford. "Wow."

"That is the sound of you not lying under your truck, trying to fix everything again."

I drove down toward Main Street feeling like a car thief. "This is so much nicer than anything I would have bought myself. This is an Ethan car."

Lark grinned. "But so what? You might drive it for the next ten years. Why not be comfortable? There are even heated seats. If we want to break it in on New Year's Eve, our butts will be warm."

"Oh, Beverly," I teased. "Let's not wait until New Year's. It's my birthday." I swung into the parking lot behind the restaurant and found a spot.

"Happy Birthday, honey," Lark said with a little smile. "Ethan is about to enjoy a nice meal with my parents. I know it's not the evening we planned, but..."

"It's perfect," I finished. Then I leaned over and kissed her. "And there's always later tonight. We can cross off a few more items on our to-do list."

"I'm in," Lark said.

And she was.

❤

The End

Also by Sarina Bowen

THE IVY YEARS
The Year We Fell Down #1
The Year We Hid Away #2
Blonde Date #2.5
The Understatement of the Year #3
The Shameless Hour #4
The Fifteenth Minute #5

THE BROOKLYN BRUISERS
Rookie Move
Hard Hitter
Pipe Dreams

GRAVITY
Coming In From the Cold #1
Falling From the Sky #2
Shooting for the Stars #3

AND
HIM by Sarina Bowen and Elle Kennedy
US by Sarina Bowen and Elle Kennedy

TRUE NORTH
Bittersweet (True North #1)
Steadfast (True North #2)

86169036R00172

Made in the USA
Columbia, SC
30 December 2017